PIRATE IN MY ARMS

"Sam?"

No answer.

"Sam? If you won't come here, can I come over there? I'm cold."

Another sigh. "Aye."

He groaned inwardly as she settled down beside him and snuggled her sweet young breasts up against his damp chest.

"Maria, must you lie there? So . . . close?"

"I just wanted to be next to you." Slowly Maria pushed the shirt over his strong, hard shoulders. Her hand came up, her fingers trailed through the soft hair that roughed the smoothness of his chest. She heard him catch his breath.

"Jesus, woman, just *how* close?"

"Close enough to hear your heartbeat. Close enough to feel your blood rushing through your veins. *This* close." And then she lowered her golden head, pressing her lips against the warmth of his chest . . .

PIRATE IN MY ARMS

DANELLE HARMON

AVON BOOKS ◆ NEW YORK

PIRATE IN MY ARMS is an original publication of Avon Books. This work has never before appeared in book form. This is a work of fiction, and while some portions of this novel deal with actual events and real people, it should in no way be construed as being factual.

AVON BOOKS
A division of
The Hearst Corporation
1350 Avenue of the Americas
New York, New York 10019

Copyright © 1992 by Danelle F. Harmon
Inside cover author photograph by Thomas F. Keegan
Published by arrangement with the author
ISBN: 0-380-76675-2

First Avon Books Printing: January 1992

AVON TRADEMARK REG. U.S. PAT. OFF. AND IN OTHER COUNTRIES, MARCA REGISTRADA, HECHO EN U.S.A.

Printed in the U.S.A.

RA 10 9 8 7 6 5 4 3 2 1

This book is for my husband, Bruce, who never stopped believing in me.

I would like to extend a very heartfelt thanks
to all who helped make this book possible:
My agent, Pesha Rubinstein; Ellen Edwards and
Marjorie Braman at Avon Books;
Rochelle Alers, Donna Foote, and Jennifer Hossack;
Sandra Anderson, Elaine Berglund, Trena Haroutunian,
Karen Hayes, Leone Laferriere, and Barbara Moriarty;
Reverend Ed and "Dr." Bob G.;
Dennis Laurie, Joanne Chaison, and Marie Lamoureux
at the American Antiquarian Society
in Worcester, Massachusetts;
and,
Dad, Mom, and Jody for their love and support;
and *especially,*
Barry Clifford, Ken Kinkor, Gareth McNair-Lewis, and
the entire "crew"
(from this century as well as the other)
at Maritime Explorations, Inc./the Whydah Joint Venture
Lab,
who were always eager to answer my questions,
tease me about my own *Whydah* project,
and hunt up an artifact that "might've belonged to Sam"
for me to draw when my work
for them took me to the lab instead of the library.

Thanks, guys.

The natural medicines referred to in this book are included to enhance the authenticity of the story. Readers are advised not to use them without securing the prior consent of a medical doctor.

PIRATE IN MY ARMS

Chapter 1

Was he devil or man?
He was devil for aught they knew.

TENNYSON

There wasn't a lot of activity in Eastham's Billingsgate Harbor that spring of 1716: a few scarred-up fishing vessels, a leaky dory tied at the quay, and exactly fourteen bored sea gulls that were too lazy to chase the incoming boats for scraps of cod. When a threatening storm forced a battered old sloop flying the colors of England at her masthead into that little harbor, naturally, tongues were wagging.

"A tight little ship," mused Joseph Doane, the Justice of the Peace, as he stood on the wharf with his sea-grizzled neighbors and watched the sun sink down through thickening cloud-bars and into the gold, then crimson, waters of Massachusetts Bay. The vessel's sails turned to fire before darkening in silhouette against the painted sky. Through the smoke that crawled about his craggy features Doane stared hard at them, then pulled his pipe from his mouth with methodical slowness. "Who'd ye say her master is? Some chap named Bellamy?"

William Smith, just arriving after a long—but bountiful—day of net-casting in the shoal waters, tossed a mooring line up to one of Doane's cronies, hauled himself out of his fishy-smelling boat, and clambered up to join them. "Aye, Bellamy," he grunted, deftly wrapping the rope around one of the tired old poles that supported the dock. "From Devon, or so John Knowles tells me."

"A West Countryman, eh? Can't be all bad, then. Wonder what he's doing in these parts. . . ."

1

"Heard he's come to try to stir up interest in some treasure hunting scheme of his."

"Sakes alive! *Treasure* hunting? Be serious, man!"

"Aye, 'tis true. That's what Knowles told me."

"Knowles? What's he know, anyhow? Always starting rumors and getting folk all riled up about nothing." Doane shoved the pipe back between his teeth. "I'd no sooner believe him than I would those two scatterbrained daughters of his!"

But such puzzled speculations were not shared by the pious, white-haired Reverend Treat, who had his own firm beliefs as to why such a bold, adventurous sort as Samuel Bellamy had chosen to drop anchor in Billingsgate Harbor. "The devil's own!" he expostulated to his faithful flock that Sunday morning. "Come to stir up trouble, no doubt!"

And judging by the way some of the twittering, mob-capped female members of his congregation were ignoring his sermon and whispering about the Devonian sea captain instead, it would seem his prediction was beginning to ring true. The devil was already at work.

"I don't see why you're getting your hopes up, Jane. 'Tis said he's only staying here 'til the weather clears," whispered young Thankful Knowles, pretending to be engrossed in her hymnbook.

"Hopes? You watch, sis. I'll catch his eye before week's end, I promise you. And I don't care a whit about the weather. If that's what's keeping him here then Lord, I hope it rains all summer!"

Heads were turning. Old matrons glared disapprovingly, and the younger ones wondered what the loud whispering and hushed giggles were all about. A deacon scowled at them from beneath beetled brows, and the pastor shot them a warning glance.

The whispers lowered. "But Jane, the Reverend Treat says he has the devil in him."

"I know, ninny. 'Tis what makes him so . . . appealing. Think I'd waste my time if he was as *tame* as everyone else around here?"

"Really, Jane, you go too far! After all, you *are* promised to another!"

But the glance that Jane tossed her sister was arched and dismissing.

"Maybe he brings news from England," speculated Maria Hallett in the pew directly behind them. "You can't say he has the devil in him just because he didn't come to the service. He probably has good reasons for not attending."

"Maria, hold your tongue! You heard the reverend!" snapped the dour-faced woman who sat stiffly beside her. She shot a withering glance at the Knowles sisters before glaring at her niece's bent, golden head. "He brings naught but trouble, and if you girls had brains in your heads you'd stay away from him!" She lowered her voice for Maria's ears alone. "Shameless hussies! Such talk, and on the Lord's day besides!"

But her words, meant to dissuade her niece from setting her innocent young eye on the reputedly handsome English captain, were not necessary. Maria Hallett, sitting quietly with her gaze on her hymnbook—and her thoughts on Jonathan Dratham, her hoped-for suitor—had not the slightest bit of interest in either the bold adventurer from the West Country or Reverend Treat's lengthy sermon. And given the fact that the town *had* such a handsome visitor, it was purely coincidental, of course, that today's sermon warned of the just rewards of those who partook of the sins of the flesh. . . .

But Maria didn't know what the sins of the flesh were, had not made the Englishman's acquaintance, and if truth be told, had no desire to. And even if she did, the sharp scrutiny of her aunt's eagle-eyed countenance would quickly smother any romantic notions on her part such as those the Knowles sisters were entertaining.

It certainly wasn't that she hadn't reached marriageable age. Maria was fifteen years old; a young fifteen in that her aunt allowed her to lead nothing but the most sheltered, protected life: an old fifteen in that her winsome, head-turning beauty—piles of thick, gilded hair now pinned up off a graceful neck, eyes of a startling shade of turquoise, and a face so delicate, so perfectly formed, that its flawlessly creamy skin only emphasized the faint hollows beneath her high cheekbones and the soft shades of rosy apricot that were apt to bloom there whenever Maria was thinking, as she was now, about Jonathan Dratham—gave her two or three extra years that she really hadn't earned. But if one looked closely there were indications, despite the high, budding breasts, the blossoming curves, that marked Maria Hallett as the young girl she actually was.

Namely, the innocence in her sea-green eyes.

For if Maria Hallet was not paying attention to the reverend's ardent sermon, it was because she was too innocent to understand it.

So instead, she sat in the hard pew, the unforgiving wooden seat beginning to make her squirm and earning her another sharp glare from her aunt. It was still pouring outside; she could hear the Cape Cod wind tossing handfuls of rain against the windows, could hear it whistling around the walls and tickling the eaves. The room smelled like wet wool and leather, and although it was a futile attempt, candles tried desperately to inject some cheer into the gloominess that the gray day spawned.

And it seemed that the sermon was determined to last forever—or for at least another hour. Sighing, Maria glanced down at the leather book in her lap and her heavy skirts, spread damply across her knees. The Knowles sisters were whispering quite loudly now, and beside her, Auntie's hawkish face was tight with disapproval. If the girls weren't careful, they were going to earn the chastisement of a deacon—or worse, Reverend Treat, something about as welcome as frost in August. Dutifully, Maria lowered her gaze once more, trying her best to understand the sermon, indeed, trying just to hear it.

"Seriously, Jane, how long do you think he'll be here?" Thankful was asking.

"I told you, ninny, 'til the storm blows out to sea!"

"Well, can you find out for certain? After all, your friend Prudence does work at the tavern. That's where he's staying, isn't it?"

"Uh-huh."

"I wonder why he didn't come to the service—"

Reverend Treat looked up sharply. "Girls!"

Surprised, the Knowles sisters hushed in mid-whisper.

"Thank you," he said with affronted dignity. Raising his old white head, he cleared his throat and continued in a voice that seemed far too loud for his small stature. "Yes, my good children, the torments of Satan's Hell await those who succumb to the wicked call of the flesh! Eternal damnation is reserved for those who partake of and savor the devil's own pleasures! Repent, my faithful flock! For impenitent sinners will writhe in Hell, with a thousand devils rending and tearing and ripping them throughout all Eternity!''

Caught up in his sermon once more, the reverend's voice rose in passionate conviction, drowning out any doubts his congregation might've had regarding the truth of his words, the sound of the rain beating against the windows' thick glass panes, and the whisperings of the Knowles sisters, which had resumed once more.

Outside the meeting house Thankful and Maria stood waiting in the drizzle, for after the service it was Aunt Helen's habit to speak with the reverend and Mrs. Knowles's to gossip with her neighbors. The fact that it was still raining seemed to make no difference; if anything, the two were dallying longer than usual. Now even Jilly, Aunt Helen's mare, who was no less ornery than her owner, was growing restless, and steam had begun to rise in fine little wisps from her sorrel neck as she tossed her head and stamped her feet in impatience.

"Really, Thankful, for your own sake I wish you'd be more careful," Maria said, taking a firm grip on the mare's wet bridle. "Did you see the looks you were getting from Reverend Treat? Next time he'll make a spectacle out of you in front of everyone, mark my words!"

"Good heavens, Maria! You're starting to sound just like your aunt. Next you'll be telling me the wrath of God will be 'pon my head for not listening to the sermon."

"Well?"

"Well, what?"

"Well, Sunday service is hardly the place to be discussing men."

Thankful rolled her eyes. "Oh, for goodness sake! Where else are we to discuss them? Doesn't God want us to choose good, Christian men as our husbands?"

"This Sam Bellamy does *not* sound like a good Christian man to me," Maria declared importantly. "After all, he wasn't at the service today, was he? And he doesn't sound like he'd make a good husband, either.''

"Oh what do you know. You haven't even met the man!"

"The way everyone's talking about him, I don't think I want to!"

Thankful raised her chin, but it was impossible to look down her nose at Maria, who stood taller than she—and every other woman in Eastham—did. So instead she shrugged, huddled deeper into her woolen cloak, and watched Maria's brown-and-white pointing dog leap into the cart, where he tracked muddy pawprints all over the already wet seat. "And I suppose Miss High and Mighty Hallett has her own ideas of what constitutes a good husband?"

"As a matter of fact, yes, I do!"

"And?"

Maria stroked the side of Jilly's warm, wet nose, first slowly, then with agitated, nervous movements. The peachy blush was ripe beneath her cheekbones. "Well, for one thing, he'd never miss Sunday service. Second, he'd have to be someone who's *not* a seaman. Auntie says they're the worst of sorts. And third, he'd have to be a man whose name wasn't on the tongue of every woman in the parish."

"But aren't you even *curious* about Bellamy?"

"No. Should I be?"

Again, Thankful rolled her eyes. "Heavens, Maria, you have *such* a lot to learn."

"Well, there are men right here in Eastham who'd make far better husbands than some foreigner who doesn't even go to Sunday service."

The blush, now the color of fall apples, spread all the way up Maria's curved, high brow to the bottom of her golden hairline. Seeing it, Thankful grinned and gave her a poke in the ribs with a lace-draped elbow. "Still got your cap set for Jonathan, Maria?"

Maria's blond head shot up. Panic darkened her exotic eyes. "Yes, and don't you dare go breathing a word of it to anyone!"

"Oh, don't be a goose. Of course I won't. But why you don't want anyone to know is simply beyond me. Are you going to keep it a secret when the two of you marry?"

"Marry!" Maria gave a short, dismissing laugh. And then

she sighed, and her shoulders drooped hopelessly. "He's not going to marry me, Thankful. He doesn't even know I exist."

"Oh, come now—"

" 'Tis true!" she cried, a note of despair in her clear, melodious voice. "He says hello to me, but aside from that he treats me as though I'm a child, beneath his notice and nothing but a bothersome nuisance. I wear my prettiest gowns when I come to town, I weave blankets and give them to his mother—she has so many little ones to worry about, you know—and still he doesn't pay me one bit of attention. I've even tried praying, but even *that* doesn't work!"

Thankful assumed a look of surprise, for Maria's beauty was, after all, the envy of every woman in Eastham. She should have no trouble netting Jonathan Dratham. "Oh, I'm *sure* he cares about you," she said convincingly. "He probably just doesn't know it."

"That's the most ridiculous thing I've ever heard."

"Oh Maria, you're so . . . *young!* Some men are blind to what's in their hearts, others are not. Both can be eternally frustrating, the first if you happen to have your cap set for him, the second"—she laughed—"if you do not. But I tell you, making blankets and praying are *not* going to be the things to make Jonathan notice you." She took Maria's slight shoulders and looked into the beautiful eyes that she'd always been so jealous of. "Now listen to me. You're a woman. The good Lord gave you beauty—more than he did the rest of us, that's for certain—but he also gave you something else to go with it. Something he gives *every* woman. They're called feminine wiles. Use them to get what you want!"

"I *have* no feminine wiles. And if I did, I wouldn't have the faintest idea what to do with them. In fact, I don't even know what they are."

"Oh, you have them all right," Thankful declared with all the importance of one who *knows*. Confusion flickered across Maria's lovely face, and she nervously dug her moccasin into the wet grass. "Listen. You want to catch Jonathan's eye, right? Well then, what you must do is give him some . . . competition. Some very *proficient* competition."

"There is no one more 'proficient' than Jonathan."

"Don't be a dolt, Maria. Sure there is."

Maria looked up, hopelessly. "Who?"

"Why, the Englishman, for one. Samuel Bellamy."

"Honestly, Thankful, now you're *really* being ridiculous!"

"Shh! Keep your voice down, someone will hear you!" She lowered her own to a conspiring whisper that, coupled with the brightening gleam in her eyes, made Maria even more apprehensive. After all, Thankful had a jealous streak that often culminated in practical jokes—jokes that could be downright mean at times. Wishing she was anywhere but here, Maria dropped her gaze and watched the rain plunking into a nearby puddle. But Thankful was not about to let up.

"Now, hear me out. I have a plan and once you hear it you won't think it's so ridiculous. Besides, we haven't much time. Mother will be out any minute. Maria, are you listening to me?"

Maria sighed helplessly and looked up. "Yes."

"Good. Now pay attention, it's really all quite simple. All you have to do is make Jonathan jealous. And who better to use for that end than the handsomest man in town—"

Maria turned away. "Jonathan *is* the handsomest."

"Hah! *You*, my friend, have not seen Sam Bellamy. Now listen. This is the plan—"

"Thankful, I can see right now that I'm not going to like this. The last time you came up with one of your 'plans' I was the laughingstock of Eastham! Play your jokes on someone else! I've no wish to be the butt of them again!"

"But you won't be the laughingstock, you'll be the *envy.*"

Uneasiness stirred somewhere in the nether regions between Maria's heart and stomach. But there was nothing to be lost by just *listening* to Thankful's idea . . . was there? "And just how does this Sam Bellamy figure into anything?" she asked warily, not at all sure she wanted to hear the answer.

"Why, he figures into all of it. All we have to do, Maria, is get him to fall in love with you. And *that*, given your looks, shouldn't be very difficult." She hurried on as Maria's mouth fell open in horror. "I know, 'tis *Jonathan* you want, not Sam Bellamy. But think about it, Maria! Once Jonathan learns you've caught another man's eye, he'll come around—I promise you!"

Maria stared at her numbly, heedless of the rain pattering

upon her brow and trickling down her cheeks. What could Thankful be thinking of? Had she gone positively daft? She shook her head and held up one finely boned hand. "No, Thankful. I've heard too much about this Sam Bellamy. I told you, I don't even want to *meet* him, let alone get him to fall in love with me!"

Thankful shrugged, tightened the hood of her cloak, and turned away, "All right then. Be that way. But don't come crying to me when Jonathan marries someone else. Someone like Sarah Freeman, or plain little Amanda Nickerson . . ."

Sarah Freeman? Amanda Nickerson?

Maria wrung her hands and chewed fervently on her lower lip. Jonathan . . . Strong, handsome Jonathan. *Would* he go for Sarah, or even Amanda? It was too dreadful to even consider! And then something stirred in her young, romantic heart, something that occasionally prompted her to defy her aunt and cause that same venerable woman to pronounce her too brazen for her own good. Courage. There wasn't much of it, but it was there. And now it yawned, stretched, and came awake.

"Thankful . . . wait."

Hiding her smile, Thankful turned. Innocent, naive Maria had taken the bait. Oh, what a grand joke *this* would be! Why, she could even get Prudence down at the tavern to help play it. And maybe afterward all the young men wouldn't be quite so taken by Maria's beauty and innocence, an innocence that surely wouldn't be intact after *this* idea bore fruit! Perhaps they'd even seek out her, Thankful, instead!

"Yes?" she purred.

Nervously, Maria glanced about, afraid that someone—the good Lord included—might hear her. "What do I have to do, then . . . to make this man fall in love with me?"

Thankful grinned. "Kiss him," she announced.

"What?" Maria cried, and her voice was no longer a whisper.

"Really, Maria, you make it sound like a fate worse than death! But oh, maybe it is. . . ." Dreamy-eyed, she gazed up at the piles of dark clouds scudding toward the sea. "If Sam Bellamy were to kiss *me*, I'd think I'd died and gone to Heaven."

Maria rolled her eyes.

"Well, do you have any better ideas?" Thankful snapped.

Maria shook her head, swallowing the lump of apprehension that clogged her throat. Her hands were moist, and it was not from the rain. Sam Bellamy! They said he carried the look of Satan himself in his coal-black eyes, said he'd fought as a privateer in England's long-standing war with France over the Spanish succession. They said he'd been places they'd never even heard of, drank more than old Peter Cotter, and could swear vehemently enough to make your hair curl.

And he hadn't been to church this morning.

"Think of Jonathan, Maria," Thankful advised.

"But I don't *want* Sam Bellamy to love me! You heard what they said about him!"

"I didn't say you had to love him back. For God's sake, Maria, 'tis just a kiss! That's all you'll need to make him fall in love with you." She held up her hand, pressing her thumb and forefinger so close together that a piece of paper could not have slipped between them. "Just one little kiss. Trust me. Men have hearts like candle wax. Heat them up and they'll bend any way you want. Get them to love you and then, when you tire of them . . ." She snapped her fingers and shrugged her shoulders in a casual gesture of indifference. "Simply leave them and find someone you like better."

It was a callous plan, but what difference did it make? She'd never be able to carry it off, anyway. "You make it sound simple," Maria said glumly, her trepidation finally lodging itself in the pit of her stomach and making her feel sick. But she knew as well as Thankful did that she'd go along with it. Jonathan was, after all, worth a simple, harmless kiss from Sam Bellamy.

"Now, stop looking so frightened." Thankful shot another glance toward the meeting house door. "You'll never catch Bellamy's eye looking like you just walked into the boneyard at the stroke of midnight. You have to learn to look . . . well, seductive."

"Seductive? What does that mean?"

"Never mind," Thankful said, shaking her head at the extent of Maria's artlessness. "It doesn't matter, anyway. Besides, you're too naive, too innocent to play the seductress.

Bellamy would surely see through that! So instead, you'll have to pretend to be . . . a seductress playing the innocent!''

Maria fought rising panic, blissfully unaware that becoming a laughingstock would soon be the very least of her troubles. ''And when, Thankful, do you plan on putting this . . . plan . . . into effect?''

The girl's smile was sly, secretive. ''Tonight.''

Samuel Charles Bellamy was a godless rogue, and he knew it.

He was also a freethinking recalcitrant, and he knew that too.

And the good Reverend Treat knew it, which was why he expounded upon the sins—and just rewards—of those who didn't go to church.

And the womenfolk also knew it, which was why the young maidens (and some who weren't so young) went to bed each night with very *unmaidenly* dreams of the handsome Englishman beckoning them to sleep.

And the people of Eastham must've known it too, which was why Sam was having such a damnable time convincing them to back his latest, most brilliant scheme, a scheme which could only increase their investment tenfold.

''Goddamned Puritans,'' he muttered into his ale.

But Sam, as the youngest child in a motherless family of one brother, three sisters, and a father—all of whom had resented him from the moment he'd bawled his way into this miserable world and his mother had bled her way out of it— had grown quite adept over his twenty-seven years at manipulating people to do his bidding, and he was confident that he could bring these stingy villagers to do just that. And while he most certainly did not consider himself a God-fearing, estimable man, he was damned good at portraying one, and if he allowed a flicker of his true self—one that was not quite so good, so tame—to show through from time to time, well then, that only fanned people's interest in him all the more.

But these damned Cape Codders, they were a different story.

He'd thought to play them like a prize fish, but he'd underestimated their grit, their shrewdness, and their total lack of a sense of adventure. They sure as hell weren't risk takers. To them, with so many shipwrecks off their own coast that even the elders had lost count of them, putting up the money to salvage a Spanish treasure fleet claimed by a hurricane a year past and a thousand miles distant was not an idea that was even worth considering, especially if the salvor happened to be an adventurer, and a foreigner at that. Never mind that the wrecks were just offshore, where the waters were so shallow one could practically wade out and pick the treasure up. To them and their Puritanical ways, what they didn't know about him—and it wasn't much, mind you—was not cause for intrigue, but suspicion.

Nevertheless, Sam Bellamy liked attention, and he was getting more than his fair share of it tonight as he sat in Eastham's Higgins Tavern nursing the ale that foamed clear up to the top of his dew-flecked pewter tankard.

They might be canny, they might be suspicious, but these Cape Codders could sure brew damned good tipple.

"Another mug, Captain?" purred the tavern wench, a brazen little tart named Prudence who was anything but. She, like a good many of these sweets-loving Colonials, boasted a mouthful of bad teeth and a figure that was far too plump for his liking.

He tossed down his ale and smacked the foam from his lips. "Aye, and another round for the lads here," he said amiably, handing her his empty mug and digging into his pocket for coin.

She was back a moment later, eyeing him with undisguised invitation, her eyes roving in places that good Puritan maid's should never have gone. Giving her a devilish, charming smile, he took the ale, plopped the coin into her fat little hand, and surveyed the group of fishermen and farmers clustered around his scarred-up table. Some leaned against the rough-hewn walls, others sat in creaking old chairs and fixed him with sea-bleary eyes. Above their heads a thick haze of pipe smoke capped the room and hung suspended from the rafters, but through it he could see that even those in the far corners had their eyes—and their attention—focused on him.

Not interested in his treasure hunting scheme, but in-

trigued by him all the same. Ah, the injustices of this bloody
world.

With just the right amount of indifference, Sam leaned
back in his chair and savored his ale, his dark eyes gleaming
and belying his casual pose. Thick waves of glossy black hair
framed a clean-shaven face that was all hard angles and
planes. It was a handsome face, with a strong, lean jaw, high
cheekbones, and commanding eyes that danced with roguery,
and the tavern maids who fought each other in their eagerness
to refill his mug gave it as much attention and interest as the
men did his words.

And Sam was aware of that too, although to all outward
appearances he remained indifferent to just about everything
that was going on about him. But his perspicacious, intelligent black eyes missed nothing. He knew what the tavern
wenches thought of him. He knew what the people thought
of him. And he knew that just as soon as this cursed storm
turned tail and headed back out to sea, he'd be following in
its wake, for getting financial backing in Eastham was like
pulling hairs off a bald man.

But what the hell. Tonight, he had nothing better to do
than sit here in this tavern that reeked of grease, ale, sweat,
and pipe smoke; talk about treasure 'til their eyes lit up; and
drink away the hours until closing time. Maybe by then he
might work up some interest for Prudence, who'd brazenly
invited him to meet her at midnight in some godforsaken
place called the Apple Tree Hollow. . . . Not that Prudence
was anything to look forward to, mind you, but he enjoyed
rolling a wench on her beam ends as much as the next normal, red-blooded seaman did. Besides, she'd be far better
company than this stingy pack of tight-fists—even if she *was*
a bit on the plump side.

"Tell us again about those ships, Captain," said one of
them, taking a seat on the bench across from him.

Idly, Sam slid his thumb up and down the side of his tankard, smudging the condensation there until tiny drops trickled down to leave wet rings on the tabletop. "I've told you
all there is to tell, lad. What more would ye have me say?
Spanish treasure ships, they were. Eleven of them, caught in
the hurricane last summer and driven onto the reefs just off
of Florida, so close to shore that their gold and silver is just

lying on the bottom waiting to be picked up by anyone willing to expend the effort"—he lifted the tankard to his lips, savoring the cool, slightly bitter taste of the ale—"and the money."

"But I *have* no money to invest in such a venture," the farmer lamented. He gazed down at his hands, where the honest soil that was his lifeblood stained his fingers and lined the undersides of his nails. He looked up hopefully. "But I'm a hard worker, and I learn quickly. Perhaps you could use an extra hand aboard your *Lilith?*"

"Aye, perhaps," Sam said vaguely, but his attention had gone to the door, which had opened to admit a gust of wind laced with rain and the scent of wet pine—and yet another patron. His keen eyes narrowed thoughtfully. The man was tall and fashionably dressed, his green velvet coat, silk hose, and embroidered gold waistcoat setting him apart from the Cape men in their worn, nondescript homespuns and broadcloths like a peacock in a barnyard. He raised a dark brow. Here might be the financial backing he so desperately needed.

Removing his hat, the newcomer stamped the sand from his silver-buckled shoes and let the door creak shut behind him. His warm brown eyes perused the patrons as he raised his hand to them in greeting. It was obvious he was a frequent patron.

With the patience of one who sees a good thing and is content to wait for it, Sam propped his long, booted legs atop the table and reached for his ale once more. And he didn't have long to wait, for out of the corner of his eye, he saw the newcomer's gaze go directly to him.

Forty-year-old Paul Williams, just in from Rhode Island, where his father had once been attorney general, reached out and grasped Prudence's arm as she bustled past in a swoosh of rustling skirts. "Who's the stranger?" he asked, inclining his head toward Sam.

"Why, Paul!" she exclaimed, whirling about. Her features looked harassed and her hair fell in wisps about her face, but she had a smile for him, as she always did. " 'Tis good to see you again, you old scoundrel!" Remembering his question, she glanced at the Englishman, who sat like a king while his subjects paid court. "He's from Devon. Sam Bellamy's his name." Her smile grew sly. "Handsome rascal ain't he?"

Grinning, Paul relieved her of one of the mugs in her hand. "Always the roving eye, eh, Pru?"

"Roving! Hah! Speaking of roving, *you're* the one who has a wife and brats waiting for you back in Rhode Island. You and your adventuring! Why don't you go home to them and settle down?"

He gave her a lopsided grin that made no promises whatsoever. "I will, Pru, I will. All in good time, of course." His curious stare went again to the Englishman. "So, what's he doing in town, anyway? Starting trouble?"

"Oh, you might say that," Prudence said, wishing for the hundreth time she hadn't let those stupid Knowles sisters talk her into this foolish plan. She'd give anything to be the *real* person meeting Sam Bellamy in the Apple Tree Hollow tonight—but as Thankful had pointed out, young Maria Hallett was arousing just too much interest these days. And as long as that shrewish aunt of hers forbade her to see any of those suitors and kept dangling her just out of their reach, that interest would continue. "At least, that's what Reverend Treat thinks. But you know him. Suspicious of anyone he doesn't know, and not afraid to say so. Of course, the people believe whatever he says. Lord, if he told them pigs grow wings at night they'd probably believe that, too." She rolled her eyes and bent to wipe a puddle of spilled ale from a nearby table.

"So what's he doing here?" Paul persisted.

"Going after sunken treasure galleons off of Florida, and trying to stir up some interest and money to back him."

"Oh?"

"Don't tell me this wild idea has caught your fancy, too!"

But Paul was already elbowing his way through the crowd.

Out of the corner of his eye Sam saw him coming. Ah, just as he'd predicted; the fancy gentleman was interested. Casually picking up his ale, he took a draught of the brew and hid his smile with practiced ease. He mustn't seem too eager. Yet the newcomer had the look of one who had aspired to and achieved much, but whose ale had grown flat; a man who probably wouldn't be afraid to spit in the wind, to toss a coin and hope his side came up. . . . Bored with life, perhaps, and ready to try something new. Sam allowed his gaze to flicker over him, noting the tasteful clothes, the expensive, full-bottomed wig, the bearing that hinted of good birth and affluence; but to Paul, that one fleeting perusal left him feeling as if the Englishman knew his life story in the space of several seconds.

It was a casual, almost dismissing glance and it fanned Paul's curiosity—as Sam intended it to—all the more. "What's this about treasure?" he asked, and this time, when the Englishman swung his astute black gaze upon him once more, it was far from dismissing.

"Pull up a chair, lad, and I shall tell you." His words bore the cadences of a West Countryman, his voice a clipped, pleasant baritone that was easy to listen to. As he raised a hand to beckon the tavern maid, Paul noted that his skin was dark and deeply tanned, a striking contrast to the white lace at his wrist and throat. "Prudence, dear, be a good girl and get my friend here something to drink," he said, as though he was accustomed to giving orders. But the manner in which he did it was not pompous, and it was said in the way one might speak to an old friend.

"Honestly, there's no need—" Paul began.

"Nonsense. What'll it be, lad? Ale, rum? How about some cider? They make the best here, I'm told!"

Paul grinned, warming to the Englishman's generosity. "An ale then, Pru," he said after little deliberation.

"Make that two," Sam said. "My cup's gone dry again." He shot a speculative glance at Paul. "And you?" he asked, one dark, aristocratic brow raised in question. "You seem an enterprising sort. What's your name, lad?"

Paul extended his hand. "Williams." He cleared his throat, and said, rather self-consciously, "Palsgrave Williams."

"Palsgrave . . ." Sam chuckled, and a twinkle lit his dark eyes. "I hope you don't mind if I call you Paul."

"Not at all. In fact, all of my friends do."

"Do they, now? Good. 'Tis a damned sight easier to say than 'Palsgrave'!" His laughter faded and his eyes became serious once more. "Glad to make your acquaintance, Paul." He extended his own hand, and Paul found his grasp sure, firm, and strong. "I'm Sam Bellamy."

And now it was the Cape Codder's turn to be dismissed by those obsidian eyes, for Sam had finally found someone who was genuinely interested in his plan. He told Paul about the sunken Spanish treasure galleons, the silver, the gold, the jewels just waiting to be taken from those warm Florida waters, and about his sweet ship, *Lilith*. They downed ale after ale, and long before the last patron left and Sam remembered his meeting with Prudence, they were both laughing, speculating, and drinking toasts to their futures—their very *affluent* futures.

"Sounds like a grand idea to me," Paul said. "And the sooner we depart for these southern seas, the better!" He noticed his companion was merely watching him with a devilish gleam in those fathomless black eyes of his. "And what do *you* think, my friend?" he asked, as he dug the last coin out of his pocket and bought the final round.

Sam touched his tankard to Paul's, "I think," he said slyly, "that yon Reverend Treat would deem us a *most* formidable pair!"

Chapter 2

Fate is a sea without shore.

SWINBURNE

S am Bellamy held his liquor well and prided himself on his ability to drink any man in Eastham under the table. By midnight, however, he was cursing himself for doing just that, for his head ached and he'd long since hit the bottom of the pockets of his fine gray broadcloth coat.

He had to hand it to the Rhode Islander. Paul Williams had tried desperately to match him ale for ale. Now, he snored drunkenly in a chair beside the tavern's dying hearth. Paul wasn't the first person to think he could outdrink him, and certainly wasn't the first to find out otherwise. Yawning, Sam stood up, stretched the stiffness from his cramped limbs, and made his way toward the door.

The brisk wind off the sea slapped him in the face as he

stepped outside, refreshing him, invigorating him, and whetting his appetite for that which Prudence had offered. He was getting impatient to be back at sea, eager to leave the stagnant, docile land behind. Not that Sam found such threats as Indians and wild animals docile, but as one who'd spent his lonely childhood watching the ships going in and out of Plymouth in all of their majestic splendor, the sea was in his blood. And long ago, on that cold February day when he'd turned nine years of age, and neither his father nor his siblings remembered—or cared—that it was his birthday, he'd left his family behind and shipped aboard the Royal Navy frigate *Brittania*.

So long ago . . .

He chased the memories from his mind. They weren't worth remembering. Aye, the ocean had been there waiting for him then, just as it was now. He could hear its echoes of freedom in the thunder of distant surf, could smell its nearness in the fresh, gusty wind: the tang of salt, the headiness of storm-stirred brine. Closing his eyes, he threw his head back and drew the scent deeply into his lungs. The sea had loved him and he loved it, and though it had been a hard master, it had taught him well. And now, its sirenlike call was so strong that he considered abandoning Prudence under her damned apple tree, walking the couple of miles to where the sand cliffs stood sentinel over the midnight ocean, and sitting there watching it, worshipping it even, as he'd done so many times as a lonesome little boy.

He sighed heavily. The sea would be there tomorrow. It was patient enough to wait for him. At morning light he'd walk out to those cliffs and watch the sun rise up out of the ocean in a burst of brilliant color. Unless, of course, it was raining again. . . .

He thought again of Prudence. It had been, after all, too long since he'd had a woman. Too damned long.

The tavern was far behind him now, the flickering candlelight in its windows lost to the forest as he wandered into the night. He passed a thick stand of scrub oak and looking up through their interwoven branches saw that the sky was clearing; a chain of stars, a thick, bright cluster of light in the velvet sky, peered down at him. He smiled. There'd be a sunrise on the morrow after all. He continued on, leaving the

oaks behind, making his way through the brushlike boughs
of pitch pine. Here, the scent of the ocean wasn't so strong;
here, the air was perfumed with the sweetness of pine, lilac,
and apple blossoms.

Ah yes, apple blossoms. Where the devil had Prudence
said that blasted tree was? She'd told him to pass the burying
ground—he'd done that—enter a small hollow, and it would
be right there. He paused, trying to get his bearings, then
continued on. From afar, he heard the distant song of the
sea, a faint, steady roar that he had to strain his ears to catch.
From somewhere near, the call of a nightbird, and the scuttle
of tiny feet through the carpet of last year's leaves as some
night creature, a rabbit probably, bounded suddenly away.
The trees thinned, then parted, and Sam found himself at the
edge of a moonlit clearing.

It was the hollow, all right. And there, he suddenly
stopped.

Singing? Could it possibly be? Yet there it was again. From
somewhere nearby came the high, clear notes of a beautiful,
haunting voice, as lovely and soul-stirring as the pealing of
a thousand bells. A faultless voice; a woman's voice, singing
a tune he'd never heard before. Enchanted, Sam stood where
he was, unwilling to step into the clearing for fear that the
vision that met his astonished eyes would disintegrate and
float away like some fragment of a fleeting dream.

In the meadow's center a gnarled apple tree spread a perfumed canopy to the night, and beneath it, the moonlight
painting her long hair silver, her slim figure tall and nymph-
like in the starlight, stood a girl. She was young—very young.
Sam frowned. He must've taken a wrong turn somewhere. If
he had any sense at all he'd get the hell out of here and go
back to the tavern. If he had any sense at all he wouldn't have
drunk so much ale that his besotted mind started conjuring
up visions of angels singing in moonlit meadows. If he had
any sense at all . . .

He stood where he was, watching her. The gentle hands
of the night wind lifted and tugged at hair that was long and
loose and shining, beautiful hair that flowed in thick, rippling
waves all the way to the enchanting curve of a tiny waist.
Moonlight bathed her neck in a silvery glow, flowed over the
hollows at the base of her throat, and made enticing shadows

beneath breasts that were high, firm, and proud. She went beyond beautiful, she went beyond exotic—she was something mystical, ethereal, as haunting and lovely as the sea itself.

He took a step forward, but confusion—and growing suspicion—kept him in the shadows of a stubby little pine. Reality returned, bringing a scowl to his swarthy features. What the devil was going on, anyway? He was supposed to meet Prudence here, not some virginal vision who sang songs to the stars. Granted, Prudence had been relegated to a forgotten corner of his mind, but he'd be damned if he'd dally with a girl as young as this one, no matter how enchanting she was. His frown deepened. And what the devil was she doing out here all alone in the darkness, *singing*, of all things? At *midnight*? There were others who weren't as honorable as he was, who might do her harm. Beautiful, foolish chit. Indians . . . wild animals . . . anything might happen to her out here! And he would tell her so!

Purposefully, Sam left the shadow of the pine and stepped into the moonlight.

There, the noise again. The crackle of a stick, the crunch of a leaf. Oh God, *he* was coming. Sam Bellamy—wicked, godless, devil incarnate—he was coming, and it was too late to run. Out of the mists that hung over the field, walking with steady, unwavering purpose . . . Maria reached for another apple blossom, her hand shaking so badly that she dropped the flower before she could place it in her basket. If *he* didn't kill her, Auntie surely would when she discovered her little attic bed empty! Oh, why had she let Thankful talk her into this?

Jonathan . . .

But was Jonathan really worth *this*? Surely, when Bellamy discovered she wasn't Prudence he'd feel cheated—and would probably be furious. The *last* thing he'd do would be to fall in love with her! But no, she'd come this far. She must go through with it! Jonathan's face began to waver, to dim, in her mind, and she clung to his image like a drowning woman, for it was all that was keeping her here in this moonlit meadow. Desperately, she tried to relax, to keep the melody—all part of Thankful's plan, of course—from dying in her throat like a death rattle.

He was just behind her now. The sound of his progress through the tall grasses ceased. Maria swallowed fearfully, took a deep shaky breath, and, turning, looked up into the wickedest, blackest pair of eyes she'd ever seen in her life.

In that instant, she knew that all of the things she'd heard about him were true. Her feet went numb, and she couldn't have fled if her life depended on it. The devil? Oh yes. Handsome? Oh God, yes. His face was chiseled, clean; flat muscle laid in just the right way over a classical bone structure; high cheekbones, a wide intelligent brow, a patrician nose. A jaw that was strong, almost square, now darkened with shadow. Black hair that was thick and waving, curling almost boyishly at the nape of his neck and caught in a seaman's queue that hung over his collar. Yet he had at least ten years on her, and there was nothing of the boy in him, nothing at all. Not in the hard set of that jaw, not in the span of those broad, capable shoulders, and certainly not in the way those bold eyes of his seemed to see right through her as he studied her with a casual interest that was fast melting the numbness in her feet.

And she was supposed to *kiss* him?

But if she wanted Jonathan she had to, didn't she? Gripping the basket so tightly that her nails bit into her moist palms, Maria took a hesitant step forward, seeing her life flash before her eyes as one does in that instant just before death, but his words stopped her, saved her.

"Is this some sort of a joke, woman?"

His voice was deep, resonant, and impatient. Had he seen her for what she was? A young, dim-witted girl embarking on a foolhardy mission?

"Joke?" Maria asked numbly, with a sense of foreboding. "What do you mean, sir?"

"I was supposed to meet someone here, a woman named Prudence. Perhaps you've seen her?" At the quick shake of her head his eyes narrowed thoughtfully, and she fought the urge to turn her face away from his penetrating gaze. "No matter, then. What the devil is a young girl like you doing out here all alone, anyway?"

"I—I'm picking flowers . . . for the breakfast table."

He gave her a sidelong glance and folded his arms at his chest. "Picking flowers? At midnight? A young innocent like you?" His dark brows came together in a frown, and she knew that he didn't believe a word she'd said; it was a flimsy excuse, even to her own ears. But he studied her long and hard—and suddenly he smiled, a wolfish grin that made her feel like a sheep going to slaughter. "Ah, now I think I understand." Thoughtfully, he rubbed his chin between his thumb and forefinger. "Perhaps you're not quite so innocent after all, are you?"

"Sir?" She didn't like the way he was looking at her, sizing her up, taking her measure. "I—I don't think you understand. . . ."

"I understand perfectly, my dear. And here I'd thought you to be nothing more than a sweet young girl, a child. But you really aren't an innocent, are you? I knew this situation was too contrived. No virginal maid would be out here in the darkness, and picking flowers, of all things!" He gave a short laugh, frightening her even more. "That's where you didn't fool me, princess. That, and the fact that your friend Prudence never did show up here as she was supposed to. That Pru, she's a conniver, isn't she? And you're one hell of an actress. Women and their infernal plotting!"

Maria paled, and the blood pounded through her veins until she could hear the frantic beating of her heart in her ears. This man was no docile, ruddy-cheeked Eastham lad. He was no simpering suitor. He was *Sam Bellamy*, for God's sake—and he hadn't been to church this morning.

Play with fire, and you're going to get burned. Her aunt's words, intruding upon her thoughts at a time when she needed all of her wits about her.

Impenitent sinners will writhe in Hell. Reverend Treat's favorite warning.

And Thankful. *All you have to do is kiss him.*

Kiss him. She would do it and be done with it! Before his annoyance turned to anger, before her feet took flight and carried her to safety. Closing her mind to everything except Jonathan, Maria squeezed her eyes shut and blindly raised herself on tiptoe. Awkwardly, she placed her lips against his, and before the first expression of surprise came into his eyes, jerked away as though she'd been burned. Yet that quick touch

was enough; enough to sear forever in her memory the feel
of his warm mouth, his rough chin, the taste of ale that still
lingered on his lips.

Waves of hot shame and cold fear swept through her, and
something else, too—something she couldn't identify, something that caused her heart to start whacking against her ribs
like a caged butterfly. Unable to face him, she averted her
eyes; but the touch of a rough finger beneath her jaw forced
her head up, and Maria found herself staring into eyes that
were as dark and twinkling as a star-studded midnight.

He was looking down at her, his lips quivering with laughter, one arching, dark brow raised in question.

"What the hell was *that?*"

She was shaking so badly it was a wonder he didn't hear
her teeth chattering. "It—it was . . . it was a k-kiss," she
squeaked.

"A *what?* You call that a kiss?" He threw back his dark
head and laughed. "You really *are* a good actress, aren't
you? No more games, my little 'innocent.' Let me show you
what a real kiss is!"

"No!"

But there was no way out. He leaned close, and Maria
shrank, feeling the coarse, knotted bark of the apple tree
pressing through her gown and against her spine, stopping
her flight from a man whose eyes pinned her like a hawk's
might a songbird. Sick with fear, and unable to move, she
brought the little flower up between her chest and his tall
frame as though it were a crucifix to ward off some real but
unknown evil.

But Sam only smiled and raised an arm that looked as
though it had been hewn from oak, each furrow that defined
the muscles, each bulge of knotted strength the work of a
carpenter's adze. Seaman's arms; seaman's hands. That arm
came up, that hand rested against the gnarled wood behind
her neck, and he leaned his weight upon it, trapping her. He
caught a length of her silky hair in his other hand and rubbed
it between his thumb and finger. The heat of his wrist against
her neck made her tremble. She could feel the soft hairs
at the back of it brushing her throat. He was close . . . too
close . . .

Run! her mind screamed, but she could not. She was a

rabbit in the talons of a hawk, a field mouse staring into the hypnotic eyes of a wolf—and she could not move.

"What's wrong, little songbird?" His gentle fingers were scorching the velvety skin of her throat now, his knuckles brushing the lobe of her ear. "Where's that lovely voice I heard just moments ago? Sing, princess. I want to hear you sing."

"Sing?" Maria shut her eyes, swallowing in fear. She felt her throat move against his warm, calloused hand. "I . . . I can't."

"Sure you can, I just heard you."

"I can't sing in front of a stranger!"

Again, that slow, easy smile. "But I'm not a stranger. Not any longer." He reached up, hefting her hair as though testing the weight of gold. Gently, he laid the thick gilded mass of it against her shoulder, smoothing it, caressing it where it lay in a soft wave of satin against her throat, her chest, her breasts. "I suppose that if you insist on playing the innocent, we'd both be better off if you told me your name."

"An innocent what?" she cried, causing him to laugh again. At the sarcastic quirk of his brow, she paled, swallowed nervously, and finally found her voice. "My name is . . . M-Maria. Maria"—she gulped—"Hallett."

"M-Maria?" Again, that grin, a rogue's grin of twin parentheses framing a sensual mouth and straight, even teeth, a grin that made her heart do a fluttering little dance within her breast. "Not something so common as Mary? But of course not, I shouldn't think so. After all, you're far from common. An unusual name, a lovely voice. Don't waste it on this cowardly pretense at fear. I won't bite, you know." He raised a hand, running a rough finger down her cheek, across her chin and down the satiny skin of her throat, where her pulse was beating wildly. "Now, sing for me, Maria!"

She closed her eyes in terrified agony. "I can't!"

"Then I shall make you," he murmured, and before she knew what was happening his mouth came down upon hers, gentle yet insistent, his lips as commanding as his eyes had been. Struggling, Maria found only the merciless trunk of the apple tree behind her. Her eyes flew open in horrified alarm, and whipping her head to the side, she tore her mouth from his.

"You go too far, sir!" Gasping, she turned to flee, but his fingers closed over her wrist. She struggled—and when he did not let go, whirled to face him with defiant, resolute eyes.

If he wanted her to sing for him, she would! And then she'd run home where she belonged, where she'd someday forget that any of this had ever happened. Yet although her eyes were steady, and her chin rose in determination, her voice betrayed her. "I shall s-sing for you, sir, and then you'll go away and never t-touch me again!" She opened her mouth, but before the first haunting note came forth, his fingers pressed gently against her parted, trembling lips.

"That is not the song I want from you, Maria."

His voice was calm, quiet, unnerving. Confused and flustered, and nearing tears, Maria stared at him in desperation. "But that is the song I was singing before!"

"Well, it isn't the song you will sing for me now." His dark head was bending to hers, his hand searing the soft flesh of her trembling breast through the veil of her hair, the thin barrier of her gown. Thick waves of shame—and something else, too—pulsed through her body, and she whimpered like a frightened animal. But his lips were against hers once again, his hand holding her jaw steady when she tried to tear away. His body was solid, hard, and unyielding, forcing her back against the tree. With terrifying gentleness, he dragged his fingers in a slow path from the curve of her fragile jaw, down the swanlike arch of her throat, and across the delicate embroidery and lace at her gown's modesty piece. It was no match for him. The fabric surrendered to his bold fingers until her breasts were against his hand, unprotected, unguarded, and all but trembling at his touch.

Paralyzed, Maria dropped the basket, and it landed with a soft thump at his feet. Pink and white blossoms spilled over the square toes of his shoes and lay fluttering in the grass.

"You're much prettier than Prudence," he murmured, his voice as warm and smooth as the bay at morning light. His breath tickled the sensitive skin behind her ear, and there was the barest hint of laughter in his voice. "I'm glad she sent you in her place. But tell me, Maria, why do you resort to playing the virginal maiden? You're too lovely for such foolish games. What, no answer? All right, then. If you insist on playing them, fine." Trembling, Maria shrank away as he nibbled her earlobe with his lips. "To be honest, I grow rather bored with these women who think they know every facet of lovemaking. You know, the brazen ones, the ones who try to seduce. How refreshing it is to find one who pretends quite the opposite . . . one who wants *me* to seduce her."

She still clutched the apple blossom, and now he gently ran his fingers over the soft skin of her arm until gooseflesh marred its smoothness. His warm, calloused hand closed over hers, encompassing it and the fragile little flower in her grasp.

Maria was so frightened that she felt sick. Yet he seemed not to notice, or perhaps not to care about her terror. But then, he thought she was acting, pretending! Pretending *what?* Thankful had said that one kiss would make him fall in love with her. Was this terrible thing he was doing to her love, then? Was this what was supposed to happen? Was this what Thankful had known all along that he'd do? Oh God, help her. And now he was raising her hand to his mouth, his lips warm against her fingers, his breath whispering against her knuckles, her palm. The little flower fell from her suddenly lifeless grasp and drifted to the pool of petals her bouquet had become. Reaching down, he retrieved it, brought it to his nose as if to test it, and presented it to her.

Her gaze darted behind him, looking for an escape route. The way he'd so brazenly taken her hand frightened her; the odd, tingling shivers that his touch created frightened her even more. He was making her uncomfortable in ways she didn't understand. Danger lurked in him, behind those penetrating eyes of obsidian, beneath that slow, lazy smile, within the touch of his fingers. Danger . . . not to her fair, untouched body, but to her very heart, now thumping so loudly within her breast that she couldn't hear herself think. For Thankful was right. Sam Bellamy was far more handsome than Jonathan.

Jonathan?

Just one kiss . . .

All you have to do is get him to fall in love with you.

And as he bent down to kiss her again, his tall form blocking the moonlight and casting the handsome planes of his face in facets of light and shadow, Maria's terror waned like dying ripples in a pond. She was trembling, yes—but now with a delicious mix of fear and anticipation, of sinful enjoyment and discovery. His touch was pleasant, enjoyable, strangely exciting. How could she be afraid of him, when he was causing these strange, wonderful feelings to flow through her body, to make her knees feel weak, to make her impulsively want to return his kiss?

Shyly, Maria reached up to touch his cheek, wondering at the slightly rough feel of his skin. She explored the hard line of his jaw, traced the lips that had sent her senses spinning beneath their gentle, insistent warmth. He was smiling now, a wicked grin that sent shivers pulsing through her body. His arm went behind the small of her back, and she didn't protest when he coaxed her toward him. On feet that weren't her own she stepped away from the tree, letting him draw her up against a solid male body that was no less hard and just as unyielding as the tree trunk had been. She raised her head and closed her eyes; she felt the press of his thumbs against her cheeks, felt him brush loose strands of hair from her lips. And then her mouth was against his, and nothing beneath God's heavens above had ever felt so good.

After a moment he drew back, holding her at arm's length. His dark eyes shone with the gleam of triumph. "That, Maria," he said huskily, "is the song I wanted you to sing."

And then she was in his arms, folded against his chest once more as he kissed her brow, her fluttering lashes, her dewy, heatflushed cheeks. She couldn't think—oh God, she couldn't think, but she had to, she had to run away. This was wrong. This was the devil's work. But Maria couldn't run. She couldn't resist him. She didn't *want* to. He found her mouth, gently forcing her small, pearly teeth apart until his tongue danced against her own and his teeth nibbled gently against her lips. Then his kisses were dropping sugar-sweet and warm against her neck, the tingling skin of her throat. He nuzzled the lacy modesty piece at her bodice aside, and Maria shuddered as his tongue traced warm circles around her throbbing nipples and the surging waves of sensation within her became a flood tide. Her breathing came ragged, her skin was flushed despite the cool night breeze that whispered against her breasts, and the blood was humming—no, *singing*—through her veins.

And she *was* singing for him, in a voice that only her

sweet, maidenly body could sing as she leaned against him, in a way that the soul does when it has found that happiness that is granted to only a chosen few. By the time he found and unfastened the tiny buttons at the back of her modest gown, she was trembling with an unfamiliar longing for something she didn't understand. The gown parted beneath his fingers, sliding from her shoulders and down her tiny, tiny waist until it pooled, forgotten, about her ankles.

And then he stood back, his gaze raking her from the top of her head to her toes, taking in every little hollow, every sweet, alluring curve. Yet standing there shyly before him, caught up in the magic of the night, in his strange, wonderful power, Maria felt no humiliation. Yes, she was sinning, but she felt no shame. She was innocent, but she drew the inborn sensuality that was hers as a woman like a cloak around her and faced him proudly. Trust emanated from her eyes; victory, from his. With a low groan, he unbuttoned her quilted petticoats, removed her lacy chemise. He kissed her again, more urgently this time, unfastening his shirt, shrugging out of it, and tossing it impatiently aside. Breeches, shoes, and hose followed until he stood proudly before her in all of the magnificent splendor that was his as a man.

Maria's eyes widened in proper, maidenly shock. But she had no time to think, for if he noticed her stare he paid it no heed. His mouth came down upon hers once again, hot and demanding, and she forgot everything but him.

The slickness of heated bodies, the mingling of hot breath, fingers pressing into sensitive skin and hardened muscle. Her nails made the barest indentation in his arm—and that was all. Beneath that skin it was solid rock. To Maria, who'd known softness all of her life—the silk of a cloth, the down of a little chick, the velvet of a flower petal—he was all hardness. Lean, hard planes beneath the swarthy skin of his face. Hard, strapping muscle cording his sinewy arms, knotting his strong shoulders, and rippling beneath the black wedge of curling hair that darkened his chest.

Above her, the branches of the blossoming apple tree sighed in the night breeze as he slid a hand behind her back and eased her gently, slowly, to the ground. There, he settled her upon a bed of soft, cool grass blanketed by a carpet of fragrant blossoms; there, he ran the palm of his hand down the concave curves of her waist, caressed her hips where they met her flat belly, worshipped the sleek softness of her long legs. He left no part of her untouched, trailing kisses where his hand blazed a trail across her trembling, virgin flesh. And when his fingers found and tested her readiness, Maria's breath burst forth in a gasp of wonder as shooting stabs of pleasure made her body quiver and writhe.

She was beyond reason, beyond thought; no fear, no shame, nothing; only sensation, sweeping over her in tides of pleasure that flashed hot and cold and then hot again. His mouth came down on hers with a fierce intensity, drawing the very breath from her; his hand slipped between her thighs and coaxed them apart. She moaned as he withdrew it, already missing the sweet, throbbing ache; and then there was only a hard, pressing, tightness filling her slick heat as he slowly entered her. Stars were exploding behind her eyes like the brightest meteors, and the ache pinnacled, spiralling upwards higher and higher until she cried out at the searing pleasure that tore through her in pulsing waves of sensation.

And hearing the cry he drove into her, spilling his seed deep within her and causing her cry to become one of agony as fire pierced her being like a white-hot lance.

Maria didn't see the stricken realization in his eyes as he collapsed upon her. She didn't see his dismay, his regret; she saw only the taut curve of his shoulder and tasted the salt of her own tears. His head dropped within the curve of her neck as he lay still, fighting to regain his breath. Then, with a muttered curse, he rolled off her.

"Damn my eyes, woman, why the hell didn't you tell me you were a blasted virgin?"

Her lower lip began to tremble. Tears of pain, hurt, and betrayal pooled in her eyes and made silvery, moonlit tracks down her cheeks. What had happened? Oh God, *what had she done?*

And then there was only his voice above her, soft, soothing, and instantly contrite. "There now, princess, my little one . . . don't cry. Please, don't cry. 'Tis my fault." He reached for his coat and she felt the softness of its lining as he wrapped it around her forlorn little shoulders. "All my fault. I'm a worthless blackguard, and I know it. I never intended to hurt you. I thought you were something you're not.''

With wounded eyes, Maria looked up at him. There was nothing left; no fear, no anger, just a bitter realization that she'd been cruelly betrayed by Thankful, by him, and by her own naive thinking. Oh, how stupid she'd been! Now she knew what it meant to have a man fall in love with her. Now she knew what her aunt was trying to protect her from. Now she realized just what the girls had meant when they'd whispered about virgins and maidenhoods. How they'd laughed at her because she'd had no idea what they were talking about. How they would laugh when word got around that she'd done that unspeakable, shameful thing that they'd whispered about—and not with a gentle, respectable Eastham man, but with a godless, wicked Englishman who wasn't even one of their own.

All you have to do is kiss him. . . .

With a strangled sob, Maria shoved his hand away as he tried to draw her into the comfort of his arms. Through a mist of tears she saw that his face was filled with regret, and his eyes, so challenging and bold just moments before, sympathetic with pity. She shrank from him like a wounded animal. ''Don't you touch me, you villain, you barbarian, you rotten, rutting animal!''

Ignoring her tearful outburst, he picked up her gown and shook the apple blossoms from it. Gently, he handed it her. ''Put this on, before you catch your death of a cold.''

She ripped it out of his hands, nearing hysteria. ''What do you care! After what you've done to me? A cold! Better that I die than have word get around that I'm a soiled woman!'' She swiped at falling tears, childishly passed a hand beneath her running nose. ''Why concern yourself with some young *innocent* who means nothing to you? You got what you wanted, now go away!''

But he wasn't moving, only studying her with eyes that were narrowing in anger and suspicion.

''Did Prudence put you up to this?''

Mutely, she turned her face away and struggled to put on her dress without exposing any more of herself to him than possible.

''Damnation, did she?''

It was a thunderous voice, cold and vibrant with anger. For Maria, it was too much. Forsaking her efforts to don the gown, she threw it to the ground, sank to her knees, and buried her head in her hands. Tears leaked between her fingers and watered the apple blossoms on which she knelt.

"God's bloody teeth," Sam muttered. Seeing that he was only frightening her, he pulled her into his arms once more. This time she didn't struggle but huddled there, sobbing quietly. "If Prudence didn't put you up to this, then who did? A friend? An enemy? Why the devil did you do it, Maria? Why did you lead me to believe you were some accomplished temptress playing a game of innocence?" He turned away, gritting his teeth. "And why the *hell* didn't you stop me?"

And in between broken sobs, choking hiccups, and a stream of tears, she told him about Jonathan and the plan to make him jealous enough to marry her, of Thankful's assurance that one kiss would make him—Sam—fall in love with her. She wept out her heart and her loss of innocence, wetting his chest with her tears and huddling within the protection of his thewy arms like the lost child she was.

The moon was beating a retreat into the western sky by the time she finally quieted. And Sam Bellamy, who'd always fancied himself a heartless rogue, was seized by a flash of honor that, three hours ago, he would've denied existed within his wicked, godless soul. He looked down at her bent head, the nagging voice of his conscience telling him that if he was truly as wicked as he liked to think he was he'd succumb to her innocent charms and take her once more. But he didn't.

"It seems that we've both been the victims of a cruel joke, my dear," he said quietly. Pulling a handkerchief from his coat pocket, he dabbed at her glistening cheeks, patting them dry with a tenderness he didn't know he had. His voice softened, became almost teasing as he tried to console her. "Now stop crying, little princess. Rant at me, curse me in a dozen languages, but please, don't cry. I can take anything but tears. *Anything.* Besides," he added, "things aren't so bad." He shut his eyes, knowing he was going to regret this. "I have a plan of my own."

Woodenly, she looked up, feeling dead and empty, used and ashamed. "There's nothing more that you can do for me."

But ah, there was, he thought. He had ruined this shy colonial maid. She'd never find a husband without her virtue. There was that flash of honor again, tormenting him when he wished with all of his black heart that it would go away and bother someone else. A wife was the last thing on earth he needed—or wanted. But what did it matter, anyway? It wasn't as though he'd have to be saddled with her; soon he'd be gone from Eastham, leaving her with only his name. But it would be enough.

That satisfied both his black heart and his unwelcome sense of newfound honor.

"Nonsense, my dear. There's plenty I can do for you. I may not be your Jonathan, but I'm . . . an honorable man." And then, with a teasing light in his eye, he tipped her chin up and looked down into her sweet angel's face. He brushed the last tears from her cheeks with calloused thumbs, and forced her to meet his gaze when she would've looked away. "We'll marry, Maria. And when I come back from the tropics and the hold of my ship is bulging with treasure from the Spanish galleons, I'll take you away and make you a princess of a West Indies island. You'd like that, wouldn't you?"

The brief spark of hope in her eyes died. She stiffened within his arms, looking at him coldly, distrustfully. Why should she believe him? More lies, no doubt. Fairy tales. The villagers had said that he had a way with words. And that was just what they were, pretty words, meant to persuade and confuse. Princess, hah! He was nothing but a rogue, a scoundrel. Only a blackguard would've done to her what he'd done and then have the audacity to propose marriage—and so soon after she had told him of her love for Jonathan!

The look she gave him was one she would've bestowed upon a wasp that had just stung her. "*Marry* you?" She tore herself out of his arms and flung the coat, still warm with the heat of her body, at his feet. "Arrogant beast, I wouldn't marry you if you were the last man on earth!"

"Maria, think of your reputation. My name is good. I only wish to spare you shame and humiliation."

"I know what you want! And it's not me!" She snatched up her gown and, with the protest of splitting seams, yanked it down over her head. "When I marry, 'twill be for love, not because someone feels sorry for me. Go away, go make your fortune, go make someone else your 'princess,' someone who's beautiful, someone who's smart enough not to let herself be taken and dirtied. Do you understand? Do you?'' And as she lunged to her feet, her small hand came up and dealt him a stinging slap to the side of his cheek.

Before the surprise left his eyes and his mouth tightened in a line of frustration she was fleeing, her light footsteps fading into the night. And then there was nothing but the forgotten basket of flowers at his feet to remind him that she'd ever even been there.

With a heavy sigh, Sam bent and picked it up. He studied it for a moment, then stared off toward the woods where she'd gone. Absently, he tapped a long finger against the woven handle. It was just as well, really. The years he'd spent at sea, his command of a privateer during the war—they'd not taught him about survival for nothing. He recognized danger when he saw it.

"Christ," he muttered, tossing a wilted little blossom to the wind. It was high time he got the hell out of Eastham.

Chapter 3

For she is what my heart first awakening
Whispered the world was; morning light is she.

MEREDITH

It was raining again when Sam opened his eyes the next morning. Sighing, he threw back the heavy woolen coverlet. No sunrise today, and it had grown cold overnight. The chilly spring air shocked his body to life, and shivering a bit, he turned his head upon the pillow to gaze out the window. The wind hadn't changed; one of those wretched little Cape Cod scrub oaks scratched against the panes, and its branches

were all bent westward. The word that he used to greet the
new day was a curse.

"Damnation."

He'd be stuck in this hellhole for another day then.

He ought to just crawl back down in this comfortable
feather bed, close his eyes, and go back to sleep. But he
didn't. From downstairs came the sounds of the awakening
inn: a sleepy fire being stirred to life, the booming laughter
of the innkeeper, the clang of a pail. He could smell something cooking; fish, maybe? And bread. *Hot* bread. His stomach gave a pleading growl.

But the real reason he didn't want to go back to sleep had
nothing to do with breakfast, nor the fact that he had a million things he ought to be doing. It was because he'd spent a
restless night plagued by dreams that, in the gray light of
day, seemed no less real.

Dreams . . . of an ethereal woman of silvery, moonlit
beauty; a woman whose hair was silk between his fingers,
whose sweet curves and untried flesh made him forget Spanish treasure galleons, turquoise waters, doubloons and bars
of silver . . . a woman who had lain in his arms, clinging to
him, sobbing—

His eyes shot open. It had been no dream.

The innocent room cringed beneath his most lethal curses
as he lunged out of the bed and stalked across the braided
mat that covered the floor's rough planking. Miraculously,
his cheeks and chin survived both the fervor of his attacks
on them with the razor and the anger that animated his use
of the linen someone—that goddamned Prudence, probably—
had left neatly folded beside the bowl and pitcher. *Christ*. He
hadn't been dreaming. She'd been real, all right, and he could
only guess what would be waiting for him when he ventured
downstairs.

The constable, no doubt. An avenging papa with a loaded
musket. Maria Hallett herself, with the decision to accept his
oh-so-honorable offer of marriage. . . .

"Christ," he muttered.

But he'd never been one to run from anything. His clothes
were slung across the back of a chair where he'd tossed them
a scant few hours before. Anger abating, he drew them on,

gave the rumpled bed a last wistful glance, and smothering a yawn, trudged down the narrow, steep flight of stairs.

But there were no constables, angry daddies, or visions in white awaiting him; just a warm fire, a room that reeked of stale pipe smoke and ale, and one of those damnable, buxom serving wenches who was doing her best to catch his eye.

She sauntered over with an inviting smile, her eyes bright beneath her starched mobcap. "Breakfast, Captain?"

He sank into the settle beside the hearth and held his hands out toward the fire to warm them. "Aye, and a good mug of hard cider, too, if ye have it."

She brought the cider first. He guzzled it seaman fashion—straight down—then handed the empty mug to her. The fire in the hearth warmed his skin; the cider, his cold, hungry belly. But he didn't see the flames, didn't appreciate the bracing tipple, and when it came, barely tasted the hearty breakfast of salt fish and buttered eggs, piping hot bread and bean porridge. How could he, when his mind was torturing his body with sharp images of last night, images that were bringing a certain part of his anatomy awake with all too obvious clarity?

A walk. He had to get out of here, had to get some fresh air. He wolfed down a second helping of bread, chased it with another mug of cider and jamming his three-cornered hat onto his head, stalked out the door like a sullen wolf.

The serving wench stared at him with the heat of Hades in her eyes, for he made a handsome picture indeed; his coat of gray broadcloth open to show a fine lawn shirt and crimson waistcoat embroidered with gold threads, the deep, turned-back cuffs displaying the lace at his wrists. Snug black breeches and silk stockings emphasized the thewy muscles of his long calves, and his high-tongued, square-toed shoes seemed almost new. She hoped he wouldn't be leaving today; maybe, just maybe, she could catch his eye. But Sam gave no sign that he noticed her brazen perusal of his long, muscular legs, the wedge of tanned skin at his throat, the breadth of his wide, powerful shoulders that tapered with masculine grace to narrow, lean hips. He'd about had it with alluring females—and this one, compared to what he'd had last night, was far from alluring.

But then, any woman would be after Maria Hallett.

He slammed the door behind him with such force that, upstairs, it woke Paul Williams to reminders of last night's indulgence and set him to cursing in agony. Sam stood for a moment in the drizzle. Overhead, the clouds were moving swiftly, tumbling over one another as they moved inland and dragging thick tendrils of wet, clammy mist with them. He'd about had it with this Cape weather, too. But the fresh, tangy scent of the sea moved like a live thing in the damp wind, the errant drops of rain that slashed against his cheeks cleared his head, and he was suddenly glad of the dreary day as he moved through the woods and headed east, leaving Billingsgate and the bay behind and walking across the narrow forearm of Cape Cod toward where the Great Beach of Eastham faced the open Atlantic.

As he neared the beach the rain tapered off and the trees thinned, too cowardly to withstand the ocean's harshness save for a brave little scrub pine here, a stunted oak there. His long stride quickened as he crossed bleak, barren moors carpeted with bayberry, poverty grass, and spurge that crawled everywhere in a gallant attempt to hold down the wind-driven sand. Beach pea and cocklebur grew in wild abandon. The wind was stronger here, the scent of the ocean sharper. He could see the frothy, gray line of it just over the last reaches of the windswept tableland now, could hear the hiss and roar of pounding surf. And just as it had done when he'd been a lonely little boy walking the beaches of Devon, the sight of it stirred his blood now and made his heart ache with longing.

Innocent, untamed beauty, as unspoiled and virginal as . . . Maria Hallett. Damn! Here he was, thinking about her again. By the gods, what the hell was the matter with him? He'd never been one to dwell on a woman for *any* length of time.

At the edge of the tableland he stopped. Beach grass rippled in the wind, and beneath his feet, the land dropped abruptly in a hundred-foot wall of gold and cinnamon-colored sand to the beach below. It was a gull's view, this; a vista of gray-green ocean stretching away to the north, the south, and forever before him. The wind tore caps from the waves, made the swell of tide pulse like a living thing, and thrust the tang of salt—and the stench of something burning—to his quivering nostrils.

Burning? It was a ghastly smell, too. And peering down over the cliff, Sam saw the cause of it.

No. Not again. He pressed his sleeve to his eyes, successfully blocking the sight—but not the smell. But it was her, no doubt about it, though what she was doing down there on the beach, burning something that made brimstone stink like the finest of french perfumes, he couldn't imagine.

Just as he'd been last night, he was drawn to her, though the stench was doing its damnedest to drive him clear back across the peninsula to Eastham proper. Slowly, he picked his way down the cliff, the surf's roar drowning the hiss of falling sand. Her back was bent, treating him to an enticing view of slightly rounded buttocks as she tossed something onto the fire. Still, she didn't see him, but the shaggy horse that stood nearby did, and so did the big brown-and-white dog that suddenly rose to its feet and stalked toward him with threatening, protective menace.

It was a pointer, and pointers, as anyone who knew a whit about dogs could tell you, don't bite. But of course, this one did—and it proved it by springing through the air like the graceful beast that it wasn't and sinking its pearly whites straight into the flesh of his calf.

His howl of pain and outrage brought Maria's head up with a snap, and she whirled, her hand going to her mouth as the dog trotted happily back to her, a piece of Sam's fine silk stocking dangling from its jaws like a prized pheasant.

"Good Lord," she breathed. Shame, embarrassment, and a thousand other emotions all fought each other for space at sight of him, for the previous night was painfully fresh in her mind. Sam Bellamy—what on earth was *he* doing here? And oh, he looked fit to kill something, maybe poor Gunner, who sat at—or rather, on—her feet, his haunches warming her toes, his tail swishing upon the sand, his eyes full of adoring canine happiness as he waited for her to take his prize of fine white silk. "Oh . . . good Lord," she murmured once more.

But when Gunner grew tired of waiting for her to take his prize, he got up and stalked back toward Sam. "By the gods, woman, call that damned beast to heel, would ye?" Sam roared as the dog began circling him. He drew his pistol. "I happen to value my leg, mind you!"

The sight of that fine flintlock pointed at her beloved pet shook Maria into action. "Gunner! Gunner, you come over here!" She clapped her hands to get the dog's attention, and with a last menacing growl, Gunner trotted back to her. She clamped a hand around his collar, not so much to hold him but to comfort herself. The collar was something solid and warm to hold on to, something to anchor her racing thoughts. The dog was real; she wasn't at all sure that last night had been. But the lingering ache between her thighs was. The peculiar way her heart had begun to pound was. And the man who was walking toward her, slowly tucking the pistol back into his coat pocket, most *certainly* was.

His every well-honed survival instinct warned Sam that he was a fool for staying here. The dog was eyeing him coldly as he limped toward her—and so was she. She held a bleached clamshell in her hand—a pitiful, far less effective weapon than that snivelling canine—and now, she tossed it onto the fire, where it quickly blackened like the heap of others that were already there. Ah, so that was the stench, then. Burning clamshells? . . . Moving upwind of the fire, he squatted down in the sand, stretched his leg out before him, and examined the injured flesh.

" 'Twas a fine pair of stockings," he murmured absently, and then flashed her a forgiving smile that caused her to frown in confusion and loosen her hold on the dog. Sam froze, but she grabbed its collar just in time.

"Gunner, that's enough," she said, somewhat shakily. "Now, be off with you!" She waved her arm, and like any well-mannered, adoring beast, the dog acknowledged the command with a happy wag of its tail, shot Sam a final look of promised malice, and galloped off toward the flock of gulls that dotted the beach a half-mile distant.

Sam visibly relaxed with Gunner's departure, his chest rising and falling beneath his elegant waistcoat as he let out his breath in a sigh of relief. Maria wished she could do the same. Like a wary bird she approached him, concerned about his leg—after all, it had been her dog's fault—but ready to take flight in an instant. She tried desperately not to think about last night, hoping that he attributed the color of her

cheeks to her embarrassment over Gunner's naughty behavior
and not to what had transpired between them mere hours
before. "Your leg," she murmured, squatting a safe distance
away and peering at his bruised, sulking calf. "I'm so sorry.
He *never* bites. . . . Does it hurt very much?"

"Oh, like the devil," he lied, smiling, for she was quickly
making him forget about her damned dog, his bleeding calf.
By the light of the moon, Maria Hallett had been breathtaking. By that of day, she was nothing short of beautiful.

And she was far from ordinary.

Lashes sprinkled with gold dust. High, almost exotic
cheekbones set beneath guileless eyes whose lucid shades
mirrored the Caribbean on a sunny day. Nature had used the
same paint on her perfectly drawn mouth as it had used on
coral, or maybe seashells. Flawless skin showed neither
blotches nor freckles, and was so clear that the golden slash
of her delicately arched brows seemed to have been brushed
on with an artist's hand. And her hair . . . Sam caught his
breath. It was the color of sunlight on fresh hemp, or wheat
ready for harvest—as bright and shiny as a Spanish doubloon,
as thick and lustrous as the finest silk, tumbling in rippling
yellow waves all the way down her back, where the ends
curled against the curve of her waist, enticing him, inviting
him to twine them around his fingers. He thought about how
soft it had been . . . how sheer . . .

Damnation!

He averted his eyes so he wouldn't have to look at that
enchanting face, that silky hair, but his gaze fell on her trim
little body instead and that was far more damaging to his
already strained control. Her blueberry-colored gown of
sheerest corded dimity hugged her slim frame and lay open
in front, revealing her quilted petticoats like a wedge of fresh
snow; a handkerchief was knotted around her graceful neck,
discreetly draping the ripe, full breasts that had brought him
such pleasure just hours before; at her elbows, the sleeves of
her chemise hung like bells; and her small, graceful feet were
clad in Indian moccasins.

He swallowed hard and cursed beneath his breath, for
Maria Hallett was a burst of sunlight in the oppressive gloom
that was Puritan Eastham.

God help him.

She'd gathered the courage to lean forward now, though hesitantly, and rogue that he was, it was suddenly of utmost importance to feel her sweet little hand upon his calf, examining it.

Pulling the torn silk away, Sam bared the wound. "Hmm . . . I wonder if it'll grow infected," he mused, flexing his calf muscles in the hope of forcing a bit more blood out. But that well had gone sadly dry; the bite was really not as nasty as he suddenly wished it was. "What do you think?"

"Oh dear . . . I don't know," she said, all embarrassed and ashamed. Gunner—sweet, lovable Gunner—why, he never bit anyone! She peered a little closer, unaware that he was studying her beneath the thick black sweep of his lashes all the time he was pretending an interest in his leg. "Perhaps I should take a look at it. I *am* somewhat of a medicine woman, you know."

Ah, how convenient, Sam thought. "Would you mind terribly? I'd hate like hell for it to turn ugly. . . ."

Her face was not only warm now, Maria knew, it was blazing. She'd practiced her knowledge of Indian medicine only on herself, her stodgy old aunt, and a few trusted, *female* friends. Examining a man, especially one as handsome and virile as this one, and one whose reputation as a scoundrel had preceded him—and proved itself last night—was something that set warning bells to ringing in her head with a clarity that rivalled the most ardent of Reverend Treat's sermons.

"On second thought, I really don't think you have anything to worry about," she said quickly, drawing back and shrugging her shoulders in a nervous, birdlike gesture. " 'Tis barely bleeding."

"But it hurts like the blazes." He tilted his head, peering at her sideways. His eyes were hypnotic, persuasive; she could lose herself in those black depths. "Surely, you could just *look* at it. . . ."

Maria cast a quick glance about her. The beach was, as usual, deserted; there was no one to see her. Gunner was within calling distance if he tried to force himself upon her again. Surely no harm could come of it.

"All right," she reluctantly agreed. But her mind had other ideas. *Don't,* it screamed. *Remember last night. . . .*

Remember? How could she forget? The feel of those strong, rough-palmed hands gliding over her trembling flesh, the solid, masculine weight of him pinning her helplessly against the tree, his lips, stealing the very breath from her body and driving her to return his kisses with an ardor that shocked and now embarrassed her. Her face was steaming; she must look like a sunburned fool. It shouldn't matter what he thought. After all, it was Jonathan she had to impress, not Sam Bellamy. Yet she hadn't thought of Jonathan at all in the agonized hours she'd lain awake in her bed last night, her mind going over every shameful, wicked thing she'd done with this handsome Englishman. She couldn't imagine doing those things with Jonathan. She didn't want to imagine them. And it startled her to realize that making a good impression upon Sam Bellamy *did* matter—it mattered quite a bit.

She was no different then, than the Knowles girls, or the other women of Eastham who were all competing with each other for this man's attentions.

"Stretch your leg out so I can look at it," she said more abruptly than she intended, and bent down to peer at the wound. Her hair fell over her face in a rippling curtain of gold, screening his penetrating eyes from her, hiding her flaming cheeks from him. She cringed as she touched his flesh, for the skin was warm beneath her quivering fingers; the muscle beneath like bedrock, the hair that grew there soft, almost silky. Trying to keep her thoughts focused only on the wound. was like spinning wool from flax; it just couldn't be done. But oh God, she was trying.

And he, sitting there so placidly, wasn't helping any, either. His black-eyed gaze was heavy upon her. At the corner of her vision she saw his sun-browned hand hanging casually over his bent knee. Her face grew hotter yet, and nervousness beat its wings against her stomach, making her queasy. Uncomfortably aware that he probably noted her discomfort and was inwardly laughing, she heard herself rambling on, trying to drown that nervousness with words. "I know, you're probably wondering about the clamshells, right? I'm sorry they smell so bad. Actually, they're for my aunt. She gets these boils on her—" Maria's face flamed hotter than a potter's kiln and her hands fluttered quickly over his calf—"well, she just gets them. So I burn these shells, grind them up into powder, then I mix them with grease to put on the boils. It's the only thing that brings Auntie any relief''—his muscles jerked as she hit a tender spot—"oh, dear me, I'm so sorry, how careless of me—"

"Maria." He grasped her wrist, stilling it. Startled, she glanced up into his swarthy face. "Don't worry about my leg. I've endured far worse and survived."

"Honestly, I'm sorry! I didn't mean to hurt you."

"You didn't." She was staring at him like a frightened doe, and Sam found the guilt—and the rising feelings of desire—were not worth the tease of those sweet little fingers against his calf. God's teeth, why was his conscience bothering him so? "It doesn't hurt, really. I was . . . jesting. Maybe you could just tell me what to do about it, and I'll take care of it myself."

She snatched her hand back, gratefully. "Are you sure?"

"Aye. Most sure, princess." He got to his feet, brushing sand from his clothing and favoring her with a benign, friendly grin. "But where did you learn such an art, anyway?"

"From the Indians." And when he looked at her, no doubt puzzled that she kept company with heathen savages, she hurriedly explained. "You see, I'm quite"—she cast about for the right word, too humble to give herself the credit she deserved—"uh, proficient at weaving, and"—she glanced down at the sand, blushing wildly—"needlecraft. The Wampanoags love bright colors, pretty designs, and when they found out I could weave scenes and pictures into blankets when they couldn't, they begged me to make some for them." She was too modest to tell him the Indians weren't the only ones who couldn't duplicate her patterns; try as they might, the village women couldn't either. "And in trade for the blankets, they teach me about their medicines."

She had him intrigued again. A woman who sang in the moonlight, wove blankets that even the Indians couldn't duplicate, and stood here tossing clamshells into a fire. She was full of surprises. Hell, maybe it'd be nice to stay in Eastham for another few days after all. "And what would these Indians advise you to do for dogbite?" he asked.

She looked up, caught his eye, and grinned. "Shoot the dog, probably."

And then they both laughed, he with a deep rumble of appreciation, she with a nervous little twitter. But some of the tension was dispelled. "Actually," she said on a more serious note, "you could collect some of the bayberry's bark—it grows all over the dunes—dry it out, pound it into powder, and use it as a poultice. Of course, by the time you do all that the wound will have healed, so maybe that's not such a good idea. Or, you could get some plantain and mash the leaves into a paste, and put *that* on your leg, instead. 'Tis wonderful for preventing infections."

The wicked rogue in Sam was rearing its troublesome, familiar head. "And do you have any of this dried bayberry bark?"

"Well . . . uh, actually, yes."

"Maybe we could go back to town and get some. You have it at your house, I presume?"

"Yes, but good Lord, if I brought you home Auntie would probably beat me to within an inch of my life!"

"What, can't you have any suitors, princess?"

"Suitors?" She let out her breath and picked at her sleeve. "I've never had a suitor in my life. Auntie won't allow it until *she* feels I'm old enough. And if she did, you, Captain Bellamy, are the last person she'd allow me to see."

"Hmm . . . I wonder why that could be," he mused, idly stroking his handsome chin and giving her a look that told her he knew very well why.

"I don't think that needs explaining," she said, thinking of last night and growing uncomfortable all over again. By the light of the moon what they'd done had been sinful; by that of the sun, even its memory was shameful and embarrassing. She couldn't meet his gaze. Coloring deeply, she looked away.

Her fears that those keen black eyes of his could see right through to her soul and read her mind were proved with his next words. "Listen, sweeting," he said, reaching out to tip her delicate little chin up. He gazed down into her eyes, now widening in fear at the familiarity of his touch. "I'm sorry about last night. I really am. What I did to you was unforgivable, and—"

"Please, Captain Bellamy. I . . . I don't want to talk about it."

The ever-present stain that bloomed on her creamy cheeks spoke for itself. He nodded in understanding. "As you wish, princess," he said, recognizing her maidenly embarrassment. Poor little thing. He'd been a dastardly beast, hadn't he? He really ought to make it up to her. "And your 'friend,' Thankful? You didn't tell her what happened, did you? I fear 'twould be your undoing, my dear."

Was he actually concerned, or just making conversation? Maria wrung her hands together, wishing he'd change the subject, or better yet, just go away and leave her alone. She couldn't take this kind of discomfort. "No, I haven't told her—though she was at my house at sunup, asking me about . . . about what happened. Probably so she could go tell everyone, and gloat about making me the butt of her latest joke."

"And a damned cruel joke at that! What did you tell her?"

"I told her that her plan didn't work. That you wouldn't kiss me because I wasn't pretty enough."

He laughed incredulously. "Not pretty enough? Like hell!" And then, seeing her grow uncomfortable at his curse, he tried to look contrite. "I'm sorry, Maria. I'm a man of the sea, not accustomed to the genteel company of a well-bred maid. I fear I'm not very good at watching my language. Please forgive me." His dark eyes sparkled. "But I must say, if your, er, *friend* believed that excuse, then she's even more gullible than you are."

"Gullible? I'm not gullible!"

He merely raised a brow and gave her a sidelong glance.

"Well, I'm not!"

"All right." He bent down, picked up a brightly colored pebble, and sent it skipping out over the wave crests that clawed their way toward the beach. "Why don't we just say you're not as gullible as you were before you met me?"

He was smiling, in a coaxing, teasing way meant to put her at ease. "Agreed," she said, "and not as stupid, either."

"Nay, you were never stupid, my dear."

The way he said it warmed her, sent liquid honey flowing through her veins. She looked up at him. Oh, he *was* handsome, and if it was possible, he grew more so every minute that she warmed to him and realized that maybe, just maybe, he wasn't as much of a heathen scoundrel as the good reverend made him out to be. His hair held just enough curl to look slightly tousled, and she knew that if he loosened the plait of his seaman's queue it would fall in rich, glossy waves all the way to those wide shoulders whose strength must rival Atlas's. It was the kind of hair that invited touch; the kind of hair she wanted to run her fingers through, just to see what it felt like.

But it was the twinkle in those wonderful black eyes, and the smile—especially the smile—that did it. More than just a slight pulling back of sensual lips over straight, even teeth, but a charming, almost boyish expression that framed that handsome mouth and softened the slightly austere look of his dark face. Surely such a smile would not have graced a wicked man. Surely a wicked man would not have offered to marry her last night. A wicked man would not have held her in his arms while she sobbed out the agonies of her heart. And a wicked man would not have politely pushed away her tender ministrations to his injured leg.

Jonathan had never offered to marry her. Jonathan had never held her in his arms. And Jonathan had never been polite to her, because Jonathan had never even bothered to notice her.

But Sam Bellamy had.

A fierce sort of protective defense of him suddenly overwhelmed her, for this man had been unfairly judged by the "righteous" citizens of the parish. The depth of the feeling startled, shocked her. Who were they to say such mean things about him? She would not be like them. She would not judge him on what had happened last night. After all, she'd been as much to blame as he was—maybe even more so, she now realized. And now, here he was, the most proper of gentlemen, apologizing for his bad language, paying her gracious compliments that she didn't deserve, and bestowing upon her the kind of attention that made her feel wanted, needed.

She really ought to do something about his leg. . . .

"I can't let you come back to my aunt's," she said, "but if you like, you can help me gather some plantain while we're here. I'll prepare it for you, and you can put it on when you get back to town."

"Really? You'd do that for me, princess?"

"Yes, but under one condition."

"And that condition, my dear?"

"That you don't breathe a word of it to anyone."

"I know. Your reputation is of utmost concern to me."

"My reputation?" She laughed then, a wonderful, bell-like sound that quickened his blood and made him wish that he was devil enough to take her again, right here and now upon the windswept sands of the beach. " 'Tis not my reputation that concerns me, Captain, but my skin!"

For if Auntie found out that she was walking across the moors with the notorious Captain Samuel Bellamy, chaperoned by nothing more than a brown-and-white bird dog that never, mind you, bit anyone, she'd have more than her reputation to worry about.

With a brave little smile, she offered her arm and together they retraced his solitary footsteps in the sand.

Chapter 4

If love were what the rose is,
And I were like the leaf,
Our lives would grow together
In sad or singing weather,
Blown fields or flowerful closes,
Green pleasure or gray grief;
If love were what the rose is,
And I were like the leaf.

SWINBURNE

The wind had changed by the following day, blowing out of the west in stiff, fresh gusts that would've swept *Lilith* far out to sea had her master decided to raise her old gray sails to catch it, for Paul Williams had given him not only his friendship, but the financial backing he'd sought in East-ham as well. And the wind stayed thus day after day, eager, wondering, growing confused, impatient even; but to *Lilith's* crew, who wiled away the hours in the local taverns, and her captain, who wandered the moors gathering the prettiest, most colorful wildflowers he could find, the wind had ceased to matter.

Sam had never courted anyone in his life; he'd never had to, for finding a woman willing enough to spend the night with him had never been a difficult matter. But to court one? How the hell was he supposed to do that? He had no idea where to begin. And speaking of courting, why on earth should such *sickness* infect him now, when *Lilith* was tugging at her anchor cables and a thousand miles away the Spanish treasure ships waited?

Because he was a fool, that's why.

Courting. Images of rich, foppish dandies came to mind, all scented and powdered, with bouquets of roses in one milk-white hand, confections in the other. He grimaced. He had no roses, and if Maria Hallett liked confections she'd be as fat and blacktoothed as the rest of the Eastham wenches.

So here he was, wandering the dunes, hoping that the rain would hold off, and that the bearberry flowers he'd picked, pristine white and tip-kissed by splashes of pink, would do. Their colors reminded him of Maria's complexion. And thinking of her sunny hair, he plucked a few of the poverty grass's tiny, star-shaped yellow blossoms and added them to his bouquet, too.

A shadow fell across his hand, wringing a curse from him as he glanced skyward. Thick, black clouds were rolling toward him across the glistening line of water that was Massachusetts Bay, and unless he missed his guess—which seldom happened, for as a seaman he knew the sky's moods as well as he did his own—it would be raining soon. He'd have to hurry if he expected to beat it. God's teeth, the damned flowers would probably be wilted by the time he finally got them to her.

The sky was darker than pitch by the time he reached the King's Highway leading back to town. What a fool he must seem, he, a seaman, traipsing across the moors with a handful of flowers while his ship lay waiting and Paul Williams grew more and more impatient to leave. He smiled. Ah, damn the lot of them. They weren't going anywhere . . . so what the devil was the big hurry, anyway?

After all, there was more in life than just Spanish gold.

Back in town it was raining again, but the fire that burned in the huge hearth made the room toasty warm and cast flickering tongues of light across the cast-iron cooking pots, the herbs that hung from the rough-hewn beams, and the shape, made eerie by the leaping shadows, of Maria's loom. She sighed and straightened up from her work, listening to the steady, lulling beat of water upon the roof, trickling down the windows. It was enough to put a body to sleep, that rain. She rubbed at her aching back with weary fingers. At least the blanket she was taking such special pains over was almost finished.

As usual, she'd made a mess. Yarn spilled in a pleasantly disorganized but colorful heap from the basket beside her spinning wheel. They were bright, cheerful yarns of wool she'd carded and dyed over the winter and flax she'd spun into linen, and their colors came from dyes that Maria had made herself: deep shades of red obtained by boiling pokeberries in alum, yellow gleaned from the barberry root. She'd simmered berries and iris petals to make a purple regal enough for a king and had gotten rich browns from the bark of oak trees and walnut shells. Indigo was the only dye she had to buy, and this Maria usually used sparingly. But not now, for this was a very *special* blanket. . . .

It was to be for Sam Bellamy.

She passed her hand over it lovingly and rose to her feet, stretching her stiff limbs and kneading the small of her back. *Sam Bellamy*. She said the name aloud, letting the words roll off her tongue, savoring the sound of them, the feel of them. A week had passed since that night beneath the apple tree . . . a week of stolen walks across the dunes with him, a week of making excuses to her aunt, a week of getting to know him and growing more and more . . . fond of him. She berated herself. Who was she fooling? She was more than just fond of him.

Maria flushed with prickly heat all over. The fire was suddenly too hot to bear. She went to the window, where water streamed down the diamond-shaped panes and blurred her view of Auntie's vegetable and herb gardens, the cattle in the far pasture with their rain-darkened hides, the robin that stood on the lawn playing a furious game of tug-of-war with a hapless worm. She pressed her face to the glass, savoring the coolness against her hot cheek. Vapor quickly fogged the pane and spread out over the window until she couldn't even see the robin anymore.

Sam Bellamy. Oh, she was more than just fond of him. With a secretive little smile, Maria put a finger to the glass and drew a small, careful S in the vapor beside her nose.

But what did he think of her? Did he care one whit for her? He'd certainly spent a lot of time with her during the past week; and when the wind had changed, he hadn't taken advantage of it to sail for warmer waters, but had stayed in Eastham. Why? For her? An odd little shiver raced up her spine at that delightful thought. And he'd been the perfect gentleman too, never laying a hand on her, always conducting himself within the rules of propriety—although there were times when she saw a hot, lupine gleam in his eye when he thought she wasn't looking, times when she'd turn abruptly and find a lazy, admiring smile curving his handsome mouth that made her remember the way he'd looked at her that night beneath the apple tree.

But he never mentioned what had happened beneath that tree, instead keeping to safe, benign subjects that didn't make her feel uncomfortable. His plans of salvaging the Spanish ships. The wild moors of Devon he'd all but forgotten until they'd begun to walk Eastham's barren dunes and boyhood memories, long relegated to a dark, cobwebby corner of his mind, stirred within him. Her weaving, her interest in the Indians' medicine—

A sharp rap on the door brought her musings to an abrupt halt. Hastily, Maria obliterated the telltale S from the foggy pane with a swipe of her palm and hurried across the room. It was probably Thankful, who, suspecting she hadn't been given the whole truth about Maria's "encounter" with Sam Bellamy, had grown increasingly waspish of late. Well, she wasn't going to find out any differently now. Resolutely, Maria lifted the latch, pulled the heavy door open—and gasped in surprise.

Sam Bellamy stood there, rain streaming from his black hair and trickling through his brows, his lashes, and down his swarthy cheeks. His seaman's jacket was dripping, his full canvas skilts, belted at the waist with a thick strap of wet leather, were splotchy and dark with water, and his shirt was plastered to his chest. That soggy shirt was nearly transparent; beneath it the mat of hair that darkened his chest showed through with startling clarity. His muscular calves were encased in woolen stockings, and his shoes were spattered with mud.

"May I come in?" he asked, one dark brow sliding up his forehead in question.

"Sam! What are you doing here?"

He smiled and brought his hand from around his back. In it was a colorful—but wilted—bouquet of wildflowers. Maria squealed in delight.

"Oh, they're beautiful!" Pressing them to her breast, she dashed across the room, searching for a bowl to put them in.

Sam was grinning foolishly and he knew it. But oh, it was worth it just to see her as happy as a child on Christmas Day, her features sunny and bright and making him feel all warm inside. Maybe this courting idea wasn't so foolish after all. . . .

Suddenly she remembered him standing in the doorway. "Oh, do come in out of the rain!" she exclaimed breathlessly, her eyes glowing with happiness.

"Why, thank you." He closed the door behind him and shuffled his feet upon the braided rug to dry them. " 'Tis a beastly day out there, princess."

"I know. And what compels you to be out in it is beyond my understanding. Let me guess—a seaman's wont, to be drenched to the skin and shivering like a wet cat? Here, give me your coat and go stand next to the fire."

His jacket was heavy with rain and smelled pleasantly of sea salt and wool. She hung it on the peg beside the door and watched as he stalked across the room, warily checking the shadows and the far corners.

"Where's that blasted dog of yours, anyhow?"

"Gunner? Auntie took him with her to the reverend's."

"Thank God. Don't you feed that animal? I get the feeling he sees my poor leg as a chunk of beef."

Laughing, Maria plucked one of the wildflowers from the bowl and ran it lovingly across her cheek. In her innocence, she had no way of knowing that the simple gesture only tantalized her guest all the more. A mischievous twinkle brightened her young eyes. "Surely, Sam, you didn't come here just to discuss my dog."

"Nay, I did not."

She went to the hearth and ladled something out of an enormous black pot whose savory aromas didn't have a prayer of holding his attention when it came to competing with more delightful temptations. The taut curve of her buttocks. The shimmering beauty of her hair, the nip of her tiny waist, the flashing tease of a trim ankle beneath her petticoats. . . .

She returned and offered the bowl to him. Steam drifted up, tickling his nose. He wrapped his hands around the hot, curved wood and let the delicious warmth seep through his fingers. "Let me guess," he teased. "Clamshells boiled in water. Clamshells with carrots. Clamshells—"

"Venison stew," she declared saucily. "I hope you like it."

"No clamshells?" he asked with mock disappointment. "Why, I certainly wasn't expecting dinner." Nevertheless, he dug his spoon into the bowl like a starving man and, grinning, looked up at her with a wicked light in his black eyes. "Don't you know, my dear, that if you feed a stray he'll always come back for more?"

She drew up a chair and arranged her skirts over her knees. "That's true, Sam. But that stray will only hang around until he finds something better at the next house."

His eyes met hers over the top of the bowl. "Well, this stray is perfectly content to stay right where he is. If"—he took another sip of the stew—"you get my meaning."

"All too well. But mind that the stray doesn't stay so long that he's set out on his ear when Auntie comes home."

The spoon thunked down into the bowl and he reacted with swift, unexpected anger. "Confound it, Maria! Do you really think I've ever cared what she—or anyone else, for that matter—thinks? Sneaking around like a damned whelp so no one finds out, keeping my feelings for you a secret—I've put up with this idiocy for long enough! It's about time we stop this farce, don't you think? Time we stop hiding from everyone!''

Maria bit her lip as he dropped his tall frame into the settle beside the fire and rested his head against its back. He stretched his long legs toward the crackling flames, glanced at her, then softened his outburst with a confident, self-assured smile. ''I think I'll just wait right here 'til your aunt comes back. That's the proper way, isn't it?''

''Proper way? For what, pray tell?''

''Why, to ask her permission to court you, of course.''

''Court me?''

''What, do you find the idea disagreeable, princess?''

''No—it's just that . . .'' She looked at him, wringing her hands in despair. ''Oh, Sam, you don't understand! I can't *have* suitors. Not Jonathan, not Ben Nickerson, not you. *Especially* not you.''

His sigh broke the weighty stillness and he stared up at the beams above his head in frustration. His voice was tinged with bitterness. ''Yes, *especially* not me.'' Springing to his feet, he began to pace the little room like a caged animal. ''I'm poison, aren't I? Ravisher of young innocents, stealer of maidenly virtues. A wolf among little lambs.'' He stopped and spun around. ''Damn them for a pack of bloody hypocrites! Should I be tried and condemned because I find you beautiful? Is my blackened blood the only kind that runs hot at sight of a lovely woman? Am I so damned evil that I'm to be condemned for having feelings that are quite . . . bloody . . . *normal?*'' He stalked to the window and stood leaning against the sill, jaw set in anger, eyes hard, hands gripping the wood. He felt her eyes upon his back and knew that his anger—justified though it was—was probably frightening the blazes out of her. He forced himself to take a deep breath. It had taken a full week of hard work to win her trust, to convince her that he wasn't the disreputable rogue the townsfolk still believed him to be. He had to control his anger.

That in mind, he turned, gently grasping her shoulders and gazing down into her eyes.

''Sam, I—''

He put a finger to her lips, silencing her. ''No, hear me out, lass. I've put up with this nonsense long enough. No more sneaking around. No more hiding. You deserve to be courted like the beautiful woman you are, and that's something your aunt is just going to have to accept.'' The finger dropped below her chin, forcing her to hold his gaze when she would've looked away. ''Now, when do you suppose she'll be back?''

Maria swallowed thickly. ''I . . . don't know.''

''Fine. I'll just wait here until she returns.''

''She's not going to allow it, Sam.'' Her tone was flat and devoid of spirit, for her certainty of Auntie's reaction dampened the excitement his words brought, excitement she longed with all her heart to feel. Why get her hopes up, just to have them crushed? Tears of desperation welled in her eyes, and quickly, she blinked them back. ''You can talk to her all you want, beg her even, but she'll refuse you. I know her, Sam. She's—''

''Maria, stop fretting, will you? I will placate her.''

''My aunt cannot be placated! It'd be best if you didn't say anything at all. She's just going to refuse you, and then she'll be so suspicious of me that she won't let me out of her sight, and if that happens we'll *never* be able to see each other! Let's just continue as we have been. I don't need to be courted. I don't mind if she doesn't know—''

''I do,'' he said quietly.

She stared at him. ''Why, Sam?'' she whispered. ''Why does it matter so much?''

The words were out before he even realized he'd said them. ''Because I want to marry you, princess.''

And after they were out, he didn't regret them a bit. It felt as though a great weight had suddenly been lifted from his shoulders.

''Marry—''

''Aye, marry.'' He folded her little hands in his own and rubbed his thumbs over the smooth skin of her knuckles. Her eyes had filled, were now brimming with what he hoped were tears of happiness, not dismay. Lightly, he said, ''And it wouldn't do to have one's future husband sneaking under the table like a puppy after the crumbs now, would it?''

She turned away, hoping he hadn't seen her tears.

''Maria?''

She felt his strong, wonderful hands gripping her shoulders, turning her to face him. She looked up at him. There was the briefest flicker of worry in his eyes, or perhaps uncertainty. No doubt, he was already regretting his offer. He was probably offering to marry her not because he loved her, but because he felt sorry about the way he'd treated her. But she loved him. Oh God, she loved him, and she would not burden him with a wife he didn't want.

"I . . . I cannot marry you, Sam."

He stared at her, his brow darkening.

"I . . . Oh Sam, Auntie would never permit it. And you could do so much better with someone else, someone more like you. Someone who's smart, and brave, someone who's . . . who's as pretty as you are . . . handsome."

"Who the hell said you aren't pretty?" he demanded, growing angry once more. "Your aunt? To protect you from men who might be interested in you? Men like me?"

"No . . . I just know that I'm not, that's all."

His sigh was one of exasperation. "And how old are you, Maria?"

She looked away. "Fifteen. . . . I'll be sixteen next month."

"Ah, the wisdom of a fifteen-year-old. Do you think you know everything, then?"

"Nay! I never said that. But I'm not stupid, either!"

"Well then, we're making progress, aren't we? At least you'll admit to one of your attributes, and I can assure you, my dear, that you have many. And as for your being suitable enough for me? Hah!" He threw back his head, his deep laughter filling the little room. "Now, there's a joke. And here I was, afraid you'd think me not good enough for *you.*"

She said nothing, only stared at her feet. She wanted to say yes to him, wanted to be his wife more than she'd ever wanted anything in her life! But it was a futile dream. Auntie would never allow it.

"Maria," he said softly. "Remember that night, after we made love under the apple tree? Don't turn your face away," he said, when she flushed crimson and averted her eyes. "You told me that your, uh . . . *friend* . . . said that one kiss would make me fall in love with you. And you believed her."

She shuffled her feet. "I was a fool," she whispered.

"Nay, not a fool, Maria. Did you ever stop and think that maybe 'tis true?"

"No. She lied to me, you said so yourself."

"Perhaps. But then again, maybe not."

Maria looked into his dark eyes, now earnest, serious. "Are you saying . . ."

"That I love you?" He grinned, showing fine, strong teeth. "A beastly thought, isn't it? To have caught the eye of the worst rogue to ever sail into Eastham. A wicked sinner, a rascally dog. Poor, poor Maria. How much happier she'd be if she settled down with one of these white-faced milksops. Good God, to think her strapped with a godless fiend, a—"

"Stop it, Sam," she said, unable to prevent herself from smiling at his light, teasing tone.

"Ah, life would be terrible with me, wouldn't it? But yes, I love you. At least if the symptoms of this god-awful plague indicate that particular sickness, then I'm infected. Sleepless nights. Thoughts of nothing but you. Christ, picking flowers. Can you imagine? *Me?* Picking *flowers?* God's teeth, I thought the day would never come."

And as he dropped his tall body into the settle once more and leaned his head against its high back, it was all she could do not to throw herself into his arms and sing for the pure joy of it. As for Sam, he was smiling as he let his eyes drift shut in contentment, for now he knew what had been eating at him for the past week. *He loved her.* 'Twas the truth, plain and simple. To hell with courting. He'd just marry her and be done with it!

Her soft, melodious voice was one he could listen to all day, one he wanted to listen to for the rest of his life. "Don't make yourself too comfortable," she was saying. "Auntie's going to be angry enough about finding you here. Don't make her more so by falling asleep."

One dark eye opened lazily. "I have no intention of falling asleep, my dear."

He opened one eye to wink at her, then let it fall shut again, allowing Maria to study—and admire—him without facing the knowing perusal of his dark gaze. Even seated, he seemed to fill the room. He was charismatic, he was exciting, he was magnetic. And handsome, with his hair drying in gleaming waves of sable, curling enticingly behind his ears and against the strong column of his neck. How powerful his chest was, rising and falling steadily with his breathing. How long his legs were, stretched toward the fire, and how boyish he looked, vulnerable even, with his eyes closed and his long lashes lying upon his swarthy cheeks.

Suddenly, Maria wanted to get up, walk over to him, and touch those lashes, just to see what they felt like. She wanted to comb the thick waves of his damp, black hair with her fingers, to smooth the tiny crow's-feet that crinkled the corners of his eyes when he smiled, to sit beside him and once more touch her lips to his, to feel those strong arms, now in careless repose, wrap themselves around her body and crush her to him until her breasts lay pressed against his wide, hard chest, to—

The latch rattled and the door swung open. Aunt Helen swept into the room, her hair already working itself loose from the knot she'd made of it atop her head.

Maria gasped and clapped her hand to her mouth. Across from her Sam merely opened his eyes, smiled lazily, and straightened up.

"Reverend Treat sends his gratitude for weaving such a pretty blanket for him," Aunt Helen said. Once, she'd been a beautiful woman; now, age had drawn a fine spiderweb of lines upon her cheeks and at the corners of her faded blue eyes. "Heavens, when is this rain ever going to stop? I know we need it to water the flowers, but if this keeps up 'twill surely drown them!" She shook out her soggy cloak, turned to hang it upon the peg—and froze, her jaw falling open at sight of the sea jacket that hung there.

"What on earth . . ."

Maria's heart skipped a beat. "Auntie—"

But the old woman was already sweeping into the room. Seeing Sam in quiet repose upon the settle, she came to a halt, her eyes bulging with shock.

"You!" she gasped, clutching her throat and beginning to turn an alarming shade of red.

Sam rose, giving her an elegant bow that was more suited to grace His Highness's court than the presence of this frowning Medusa. "Captain Samuel Charles Bellamy, madam, at your service."

"What in God's name are you doing in my house!" The cords in her birdlike neck stood out as she pierced Maria, who sat trembling in her chair, with a look of outrage. "What is the meaning of this? Explain yourself, Maria, or so help me God, I'll have Justice Doane down here so fast—''

"Here now," Sam said calmly. Maria had indeed spoken the truth about this wizened old witch. "Spare your niece your anger, and save it instead for me. She asked me to leave, but I insisted on staying."

"Well, if she asked you to leave, then why didn't you?"

His disarming smile only infuriated the old woman even more. "Because I wished to speak to you," he said mildly, his dark eyes boldly meeting hers until even the stoic Aunt Helen was hard-pressed not to look away. This was the man whose name had been whispered in church, at Patience Nickerson's quilting party, at afternoon tea. She'd known he'd be handsome, but never had she met a man as virile and well made as this one—and didn't he know it, too, she thought. And never had she seen such eyes; eyes that shone with intelligence, astuteness, and even a bit of laughter—smoldering, black eyes that seemed to see right through to her very soul. A rogue's eyes. *The devil's eyes.*

"I want you out of here this instant," she cried, "and so help me God, if you ever set foot near Maria again you'll find yourself in the gaol so fast you won't know what hit you!" With that, she lunged for the musket on the wall.

But the dog that appeared in the doorway behind her concerned Sam far more than the gun did. Nevertheless, he caught its muzzle as the old woman swung it around with enough force to take his head off, pushing it away with unruffled calm until it was pointed at the thick beams above their heads.

"Really, madam. There's no need for such dramatics. I can assure you that my intentions are quite honorable."

"Someone of your sort wouldn't know the meaning of the word *honorable!* Reverend Treat says you're a Royal Navy deserter, and anyone who would leave the king's service—''

At precisely that moment Gunner made his attack, hurtling through the air in a flash of brown and white. Maria screamed, Sam jumped back, stumbling over the settle—and the gun went off with a terrible, deafening explosion.

The earsplitting roar was the only thing that saved him from the beast's jaws. Gunner froze, the gun dropped from the old woman's startled hands, and Maria lunged forward to grab the dog's collar. With as much dignity as he could command given the circumstances, Sam picked himself up from the floor.

"See, even the dog doesn't like you." The old woman's voice was barely more than a whisper. "Get out of here, unless you wish Maria to turn him loose!"

But Maria was dragging the dog, still growling, toward the door. She put him outside. "Auntie . . . Captain Bellamy said that he wishes to speak to you. You could at least give him the courtesy of listening to what he has to say!"

"I don't care what he has to say!"

"Ah, but I think you will," Sam said, calmly brushing wood chips and ash from his clothing. In the fireplace a log fell and sent up a shower of sparks. "I came here to ask your permission to court Maria." The old woman's eyes widened in outrage, but Sam, undeterred, went on. "But I've since changed my mind. Instead, I should like to marry her."

Aunt Helen turned even redder. *"Marry her!"*

Sam folded his arms across his chest. "With your consent, of course."

It took all of two seconds for Aunt Helen to find her voice. "How dare you," she said slowly, trembling with outrage. "Just who do you think you are, anyway? You sail into town, set it astir with your talk of treasure hunting, and then come here asking for my Maria's hand. Never in my life have I met anyone so arrogant! A knave you are, a libertine, and a rogue, to boot. And just what have you been doing with her behind my back, you son of Satan? I've seen your likes before, all charm on the outside, and as vile as a viper on the inside!"

"Auntie!" Maria cried. "Sam has done nothing to deserve your hatred of him!"

"Maria, stay out of this!" the old woman barked. "So it's 'Sam,' now, is it? Already on a first-name basis?" She glared fearlessly up into his impassive features. At any other time, he would've found her courage amusing—but not now. "I want you out of here by the time I count to ten," she said, "or God help me, I'll put a hole in that black heart of yours so fast that Satan himself won't have time to prepare a proper welcome!"

Sam held up his hands in a gesture of truce. "Madam, I only ask for your niece's hand. Good God, is that reason enough to murder me in cold blood?'' He chuckled softly. ''If so, then I'm afraid the coroner will have his work cut out for him, for you'll have to shoot every young pup who comes knocking at your door. Maria's everything a young woman should be. How can you blame me for wanting her as my wife?''

Aunt Helen's eyes narrowed to chips of blue ice. ''Captain Bellamy, I don't *care* what you want. You will not take Maria as your wife, and you will not court her. *You . . . are . . . not . . . good enough for her!*''

The words were careful and calculated. For the first time, Maria saw a flicker of emotion in Sam's dark eyes. Hurt.

''Not good enough?'' he asked, unable to prevent the derision from creeping into his voice. ''And pray tell, madam, what do you mean by that?''

''When my niece marries, 'twill be to someone respectable. Someone *I* approve of. An honest farmer, a hardworking fisherman. A God-fearing man. You, sir, are neither. I'd rather her become an old maid than marry you. What do you have to offer her? Nothing! Nothing but heartache! Oh, I know the lot of a seaman. Leaving his poor wife at home for months at a time, her belly fat with child while he's off carousing in every port he docks in. Wenching, gambling, drinking. Well, that won't happen to Maria! She deserves better than that!''

Count to ten, Sam thought, clenching his fists at his sides and staring out the window as he fought desperately to control his temper. An angry muscle twitched in his jaw. Eyes flashing, he turned to the old woman. ''Is that your final answer, then?''

''It is my only answer! *No!*''

''Then perhaps you should ask the lady in question what she would like.''

''Maria doesn't know what she wants! She's only fifteen!''

'' 'Tis a marriageable age.''

''Auntie, you're being unreasonable,'' Maria pleaded, glancing between the two. ''Sam would make a good husband!''

''No man of the sea makes a good husband! My answer is no, Captain Bellamy. Don't make me repeat myself!'' She hefted the flintlock in her hands. "Now, I advise you to fetch your coat and get out of here. *Now*. I'm counting!"

Smiling darkly, Sam crossed the room. "Very well, then," he said with a dispassionate shrug. "You win—this battle maybe, but certainly, I can assure you, not the war." Maria's eyes flooded with helpless tears as he reached for his damp coat, drew it on, and faced the old woman with eyes as black as midnight. "You haven't seen the last of me, madam, I promise you. Good day."

And then he opened the door, stepped out into the rain, and was gone.

Chapter 5

Pains of love be sweeter far
Than all other pleasures are.

DRYDEN

When her aunt gruffly asked her to take a sack of corn to the mill to have it ground into meal, Maria was more than happy to escape the stifling, uncomfortable tension that had sprung up between them since Sam's visit two days past. Her errand done, she also wasted no time in turning the protesting mare—who would much rather have returned to the barn—off the King's Highway and westward across the marshes toward Billingsgate Harbor.

She was a sinner—disobedient, willful, and wicked—and if Auntie found out that she was on her way to see Sam Bellamy, God only knew what she'd do. But Maria was undeterred. Surely, something that felt so right could not be a sin, could it?

But as Jilly's sorrel haunches churned before her and the cart bumped over tufts of grass, Maria's defiance began to turn to trepidation instead. Never had she defied her aunt so blatantly before. And worse, what would Sam think of her brazenness?

The scent of ripe marshlands strengthened, the wind brought whiffs of salt and sea to her nose. Massachusetts Bay appeared before her, serene and well behaved in comparison to the thundering surf of the Great Beach, a few short miles across this narrow arm of the Cape. Maria could see the masts of a few ships now; one of them was probably *his*. Her hands grew damp upon the reins, and unconsciously she began to worry her lower lip, cursing herself for a brazen little fool.

But the harbor stretched before her and there was no turning back. Fool she might be—but she wasn't a coward . . . was she?

No. Not a coward. A sinner, a fool, a brainless little idiot— but not a coward. And indeed, as Maria drew up to the quay and scanned the collection of vessels moored in the harbor, her heart was not pounding out of a fear that her aunt might find out, or that Sam would think her brazen—but from a sudden terror that *Lilith* might have already sailed.

"Mistress Hallett!"

Startled, Maria whirled at the sound of the male voice. Jilly, taking advantage of the opportunity, drove toward a clump of marsh grass several feet away, sending the reins burning through Maria's palms. It was Paul Williams, sweat glistening upon his ruddy face and causing the powdered curls of his full-bottomed wig to cling damply to his brow and cheeks. He wiped his forehead with the back of a grimy hand and, grinning, came forward. "What a pleasure to see you again!" he said amiably. "And a fine day to be out for a ride! Did you come down to see the boats?"

"No, I . . . I, uh . . ."

Now what? It wouldn't be proper to admit the real reason she'd come. But Paul Williams noted her averted eyes, her fidgeting hands, the way the color was creeping above the loosely knotted kerchief that concealed the top of her bosom. "Then you must be looking for someone, eh?"

"No. No, I . . . I merely went out for a drive, that's all. I really shouldn't tarry."

Coward . . .

His friendly brown eyes began to sparkle mischievously.

"Well then, I won't detain you. I just thought you might be looking for someone. . . . An Englishman, perhaps?"

She felt her cheeks go from pink to scarlet. "No!" she declared, a bit too emphatically. "I told you I'm merely out for a drive! I'm leaving now."

"No wait," he said, laughing and putting a restraining hand on Jilly's bridle. "Stay right here, and I'll get Sam for you. He'll be glad to see you."

"No, honestly—"

"Oh, he won't mind. He's been doing the work of ten men and could use a break. I'll go tell him you're here."

"Mr. Williams, please!" Maria cried desperately.

It was bad enough that Sam would think her bold, brazen. But now Paul Williams probably did too—as well as the men aboard the sloop who'd stopped what they were doing to stare at her with leering, undisguised interest. Oh, God. She wanted to slink off into the woods. She wanted to slap the reins against Jilly's back and send her away at a full gallop. She wanted to race back home before her aunt found out. She wanted—

Coward.

A muscle began to shake involuntarily in the back of her calf. Her mouth went as dry as November leaves. It was too late. Paul was already walking out on the dock, calling across the water to the anchored sloop.

Oh God, *why* did I do this? she thought.

And then she saw him. He was high in the rigging, so high that her heart lurched with a sick kind of dread. As she watched, horror-struck, he grabbed a line, plummeted to the deck, and landed as lightly as a mountain cat. "Paul!" His distant voice was good-natured, teasing. "Idle hands won't get us out of this hellhole. Am I the only one working around here?"

Someone handed him a bottle of something, wine probably, and she watched as he lifted it to his lips and drank deeply. His sleeves were pushed up to his elbows, his forearms dark against the sun-brightened whiteness of his shirt. The mild breeze flattened its billowing sleeves against his arms, outlining the detail of muscle beneath. Full canvas skilts reached to his knees and a scarlet kerchief was knotted carelessly about his neck. She watched as he tugged it off and mopped his forehead with it.

At the sound of Paul's voice she wished desperately for a place to hide. "Idle hands, eh? Ho, no doubt yours shall soon be. Look yonder, my friend. You have a visitor."

Sam turned his head. Seeing her, his face brightened and he lifted a hand in greeting, but Maria, too embarrassed and ashamed of herself for coming out here so brazenly, could not return it. Fidgeting uncomfortably, she swallowed hard and looked down at her toes peeping from beneath the hem of her yellow dimity gown.

Risking a glance up, she saw him descending the Jacob's ladder to the little boat bobbing alongside *Lilith's* weathered, peeling hull, the muscles of his powerful muscles flexing as he sent the craft through the waves toward the dock. His bare feet thudding softly against bleached planking, he strode past crates of chickens and casks of water awaiting their turn to be loaded onto *Lilith* for the voyage south.

And then he was there, before her. "Maria!" He took her hand, sending sparks and heat flooding through her. She blushed furiously, and the sight of him—so handsome, so obviously happy to see her, only tugged the color all the way up to the roots of her hair. "Is everything all right?" He frowned suddenly. "Your aunt—by God, she didn't punish you did she?"

"No," Maria said, dropping her gaze once more.

Something wasn't right. And then Sam saw the quick, guilty glances she threw toward his sloop and correctly interpreted at least part of the reason for her discomfort. "Carry on, lads," he called, in that deep West Countryman's voice that sent butterflies beating their wings against Maria's nervous stomach. "Ye've work to do if we're to sail on the morning tide!"

Morning tide? Was he leaving that soon?

"I was worried about you, princess." A trickle of sweat ran down his temple, and Maria looked up in time to see him shake out the handkerchief and blot the moisture away. "You were right about your aunt. God's teeth! Even that damned dog of yours is friendlier than she is!"

She glanced up, her eyes worried and apologetic. "Oh, Sam, I feel so awful! There was no reason for Auntie to be so mean to you. Those things she said—they were unkind, unforgivable—"

"Here now, what are you apologizing for?" Fondly, he took her chin in his gentle fingers and lifted it. He was smiling, the little creases drawn by sea and sun fanning out from the corners of his eyes, and the total effect—his easy charm, his warmth, and the feel of his rough fingers against her sensitive skin—turned her heart to pudding. "Ah, Maria my little worrier. Always concerned about other people's feelings. Don't make excuses for your aunt. You're responsible for your actions, not hers. Besides, can you blame her? I'm not exactly something to take home to Mama—or rather, Auntie." His grin deepened. "It must've been a hell of a shock for her to come home and find *me* sitting by her fire!"

"Now *you're* making excuses for her."

"Am I?" Taking her elbow, he guided her to a nearby stand of pines, out of the sun, and away from the curious eyes of his crew. He sat down, leaned his back against a tree trunk, and stretched his long legs out before him. A sparrow flitted in the branches of a nearby elm, and he watched it for a moment before looking up at her with concerned eyes. "Are you *sure* you're all right, Maria?"

"I'm fine. 'Tis just that . . . oh, Sam, why does she have to be like this? Why does she have to hate you just because you're a sea captain? My father—her brother-in-law—mastered a ship, and he and Mama loved each other deeply. I was a little girl when he died, but I remember how they'd say kind things to each other, how happy Mama would be when he came home from a voyage. And then one day he didn't come home, and she cried and cried. . . . They told us his ship went down in a storm. I can still remember how angry Auntie was, how she held Mama all through those awful weeks, and later, when the sickness came—"

"Angry? Whatever *for?*"

"Well, Papa was seldom at home to begin with, and now would never come home again. And Auntie always believed the worst of him, saying he spent so much time away because he loved other women in other ports. He didn't, though. I have all the letters he wrote Mama during his voyages to prove it. 'Twas just that he was a seaman and seamen are, well, always on voyages. But Auntie still believes Papa's death was what caused Mama's . . . that she pined away from grief.''

''Well then, besides her objections over my . . . *deserting* the Royal Navy, 'tis obvious why she hates me,'' Sam said. ''She doesn't want you to suffer the heartbreak her sister did.''

''Oh, Sam, don't be silly. You're not going to die in a shipwreck like Papa did! Besides, you're making excuses for her again.''

''Nay, merely observations.'' He patted the soft carpet of pine needles, inviting Maria to sit down beside him. Drawing her knees up to her breasts, she modestly pulled her skirts down to cover her ankles, encircled her legs with her arms, and propped her chin upon her kneecaps, all the while fully aware of how near he was. Her heart, quickening in tempo, was aware of it too.

They sat together for a moment, listening to the sigh of wind through the pines, the birds singing above their heads, the gulls crying, the distant chatter of the men aboard the sloop as they went about their work. *Ah yes,* Maria thought sadly. He was leaving. The thought made her feel empty and alone. She picked up a little clump of rusty pine needles and twirled them between her fingers, afraid to meet his gaze, as though doing so would confirm what she already knew to be true. But she had to know. At length, she gathered her courage. ''You're getting ready to leave, aren't you?''

He glanced at her, surprised. It was an innocent enough question, but she was too young to know how to hide her feelings behind her words. He looked at her for a long searching moment—and then, for the first time since that night beneath the apple tree, he took a liberty with her. Raising his arm, he rested it across her drooping shoulders and pulled her closer to him. At first she stiffened, then relaxed, and he saw the glimmer of tears before she quickly looked away.

''I know what you're thinking, princess.''

She said nothing, only put a knuckle to her eye.

''You're thinking that I was going to sail away without coming to say good-bye, aren't you?''

Maria nodded, swallowing hard.

''Ah, love. I thought ye had more faith in me than that.''

She sniffed, feeling wretched and miserable as she turned

her face toward him. "But I heard you say you're sailing tomorrow."

"I am. But did you think I wouldn't have come tonight to say good-bye?"

"Auntie would never permit it."

"No, but the tree that stands so close to your window certainly would."

"Sam!" A smile broke through the clouds that shadowed her face, but he merely grinned, a wicked, wolfish grin she'd come to know well. "You're not afraid of anything, are you?"

"Certainly not old women with guns. Just snivelling whelps with a penchant for my blood—and my stockings." He drew her closer, his hand burning against the soft, satiny skin of her arm. Maria trembled, unsure if she should allow him to touch her so but unable to deny herself the pleasure those warm, gentle hands brought.

By tomorrow at this time he'd be gone. Tears sprang to her eyes once more and it was all she could do to blink them back. If only Auntie had consented to his request for her hand. If only things could've been different. But then—perhaps they could be. Hesitantly, Maria raised her head and looked up at his clean, handsome profile, her eyes suddenly hopeful. "Sam, I don't *have* to marry who my aunt chooses."

"Don't worry, my dear, you shall not."

"I mean—"

"You'll marry me," he said, and there was something in the way he said those three words that both excited her and confirmed her suspicions that Sam Bellamy was a man who was accustomed to getting—and taking—exactly what he wanted. And he—handsome, bold, and dashing—wanted *her*. Maria's blood went to butter and shivers coursed up her spine. She glanced up at him but he was staring off past his sloop, just visible through the trees, and toward the sea beyond. "I'm sailing tomorrow, Maria," he said quietly. "The Spanish ships are waiting. Oh, I used to think it would be a grand thing to do, a way to have some fun and make some quick money. But not now. Now, those wrecks mean something entirely different to me. One of the reasons your aunt dislikes me is because she knows my wealth doesn't extend beyond this sloop and the clothes on my back. Well, when I return to Eastham, I'll be a rich man. Richer than anyone in this

parish—richer, even, than everyone in this parish put together. Your aunt will not refuse me then.''

He glanced at her lovely face, so near to his own, and the
ache that had been gnawing at his heart grew so strong he
didn't know if he could stand it. This wanting. This all-
consuming desire to have her, to possess her. She, with her
gentle innocence, her ethereal beauty, had managed to strip
away every layer of protection he'd put on over the years to
guard himself against the clutches of the female race. She
made the idea of marriage seem not like vinegar, but hot
buttered rum. And she, sitting there beside him—sunlight
filtering down through the trees and dappling her shining,
honey-gold hair, her wrists graceful and elegant beneath the
frothy white lace of her chemise sleeves, her young breasts
pressing against the bodice of her pale yellow gown—was a
sight he wanted to remember forever—or at least until he
returned to Eastham to claim her. He tucked every little detail
into his mind, to be pulled out and cherished when he was
far away and the nights were lonely and quiet. The coral
shades of her full lips. The faint colors of raspberry that
lingered in the hollows beneath her high cheekbones. The
clear, beautiful shade of her eyes as the light shone through
them and cast the shadow of her lashes across the irises. The
graceful arch of her throat—

Christ.

He couldn't resist.

Even a gentleman is human, and it came to Sam—who'd
always taken utmost pride that such behavior was, thank the
gods, something that had never bedeviled him—that he'd been
acting like one for the past agonizing weeks. And that was
just what those weeks had been—torture.

He could put up with it no longer. Gently, he wrapped his
fingers around her wrist, fully encompassing it in his large
hand. Maria swallowed and looked down at that hand; at the
fine black hairs that sprang up on its back, at the long, well-
defined muscles of his forearm that glistened with a sheen of
sweat. Like a well-planned painting that leads the eye into it,
those muscles led hers upward to his elbows, where the cuffs
of the shirt lay wrapped and rolled; to the bulge of his upper
arms beneath his full sleeves; to the wedge of dark skin at
his throat; and then, finally, to those obsidian eyes, hot and

intense and conveying his desire for her in a way that made her mouth go dry and the little butterflies uncage themselves within her stomach once more.

"Sam?"

He drew her against him, and Maria—though it was within her power to do so—did not resist. " 'Tis just an experiment, princess," he murmured huskily, though they both knew it was anything but. His dark face loomed above her. His strong, thewy arms enfolded her slight body. She could smell that wonderful, masculine scent that was his alone, of salt and sea and ocean wind. And then it became the most natural thing in the world to melt against him and let her body do as it had been begging to do ever since that night beneath the apple tree.

She raised her face to his. Her eyes drifted shut and sunlight warmed the inside of her lids. And then she felt his hand cupping the back of her head, his thumbs tenderly smoothing the hair away from her hot cheeks, and his lips, gentle yet hard, sweet yet demanding, against her own. Her senses exploded, her heart shooting here, her brain there, leaving her body as a lump of jelly, puddling somewhere above her feet. She twined her arms about the rock-hard trunk of his neck, and didn't protest when he drew her onto his lap, where she could feel him, hard and unyielding, pressing against her hip. And he was doing things with his tongue that both shocked and excited her; tasting her, touching her teeth, running it across the inside of her mouth until at last the tinglings in her breasts and between her thighs grew so strong that she began to squirm against him, unwittingly inciting his own passion to swell until, unable to stand it any longer, he tore his mouth from hers.

Eyes closed, he let his head fall back to rest against the tree trunk, his breathing as ragged and harsh as if he'd just run from here to Eastham and back.

"Sam?"

"Keep that up, woman, and I promise you 'twill be more than just an experiment."

For a moment, Maria stared at his quickly rising and falling chest. Her palm lay pressed against the mat of soft, moist hair there, and beneath it she could feel the frantic thud of his heart. Why, to look at him, he seemed to be in pain! And then it came to her that *she* had brought him to this state; *she*, Maria Hallett. The truth was right there in front of her eyes, beneath her hands—and under her hip.

It wasn't pain. Oh, no, not at all.

He desired her.

He wanted her.

And with that knowledge came the sweeping, wonderful feeling of power that comes to every woman: *she* had the means to make a man's heart race, to make him swell formidably beneath her hip, to make his eyes smolder with passion beneath his half-closed lids; *she* had done this to him. And sinfully, wickedly—but compelled by that same newfound sense of heady power, Maria took the "experiment" one step further.

Slowly, she reached out and touched the charcoal-black line of his eyebrow, finding it soft and silky beneath her fingertips. And then she did as she'd been longing to do for a fortnight—she smoothed those tiny crow's-feet at the corner of his eye, letting her finger trail downward until she felt the hard bone of his cheek just beneath and the muscles of his jaw, now clenched as he visibly fought for control.

His breathing quickened, grew ragged. "Stop, Maria. . . ."

But her fingers were drifting down to trace the line of his lips. Shivers coursed through her as he looked up, pinning her in a simmering black gaze that mirrored her own desire.

He caught her hand. "I said stop, lass."

"But Sam—"

"Stop."

"Don't you like me to . . . to touch you?" she asked, hurt in her eyes.

Perspiration sheened his brow. "I like it very much. *Too* much."

Her hurt look only intensified as he placed his hands on either side of her ribs, hoisted her off his lap, and plunked her down on the pine needles beside him. He shut his eyes, fighting to control the throbbing ache in his loins before he lost all control.

"But—"

Hoarsely, he said, "Maria, remember what I said about that tree that grows outside your window?"

She swallowed hard, wistfully eyeing his handsome face, his strapping arms. "Yes."

"Well, keep your window unlatched tonight, all right?"

He opened his eyes. They were very black and very bold, his meaning very clear. Returning his gaze, Maria blushed. And then, fidgeting, she smiled, a slow, shy smile of agreement. Of course, he didn't want to dally with her here in broad daylight. But in the privacy of her little room in the attic . . .

"Sam," she said softly, reaching out to touch his lips, "not only will I leave it unlatched. I'll leave it as wide open as it will go."

Their gazes locked in mutual understanding and consent. He took her hand, pressed it against his mouth, and kissed each knuckle, his eyes never leaving hers even as she shivered and blushed harder and her breathing grew raspy and labored. Then he folded each finger down upon itself and rose, pulling her to her feet. Covering her hand with his, he guided her back through the woods and towards the beach.

Jilly was where Maria had left her, for it would've taken nothing short of gunfire to get her to move from where she stood sleepily blinking in the sunlight. Maria climbed up into the cart, her blood humming, her heart pounding in expectation of the coming night. The seat was warm with sunshine, the day unfairly beautiful. But the night . . . the night would be more so.

She gathered the reins in one shaky hand and looked at Sam. He stood in the typical stance of a seaman: legs planted slightly apart, hands clasped behind his back. He was smiling, but it was a lupine smile and it reached all the way up to his fathomless dark eyes.

"Don't I even get a good-bye kiss to hold me over, princess?"

Princess. Suddenly, she knew why he called her that. Princess . . . *of a West Indies island.* She flung herself out of the cart and into his arms. It didn't matter that his crew had stopped working again and now stared at them with great interest. It didn't matter that she was likely to face an inquisition when she got home. It didn't matter that the sun had crested the zenith and would soon set on Sam Bellamy's last night in Eastham. Nothing mattered, except being in his arms. . . .

And this final, upcoming night.

All too soon, the kiss was over. With effort, Sam drew back, tearing himself away from her and leaving nothing but a lingering throb, and then an empty coldness, where his lips had clung to hers. She shut her eyes as he touched the back of his hand to her cheek, then stepped away from the cart. " 'Til tonight, then?" he murmured.

She opened her eyes, met his inviting gaze. " 'Til tonight," she whispered. And then, before she could go into his arms once more, she leaped into the cart, dug beneath the seat for the blanket she'd made for him, and thrust it into his arms.

And as she slapped the reins against Jilly's back and sent the startled mare off at a gallop, she couldn't know that his dark eyes followed her until the cart turned a bend and disappeared behind a grove of pines. She didn't know that he stared at that empty spot in the road for a long, long time. And she didn't see the expression that came into his eyes as he finally looked down at the beautiful blanket he held in his hands.

And of course, she couldn't know that he wasn't thinking of the blanket, nor of Spanish treasure—but of the tree that grew tall and straight just outside her window.

He came to her a half hour before midnight. He didn't use the tree; he never made a sound. One moment she was sitting on her bed, her arms around her shivery body, her mouth dry, her ears attuned to any sound from a night dominated by the distant roar of the ocean; the next, there was a soft scraping noise at the window—

Her head jerked up and she saw him, just pulling himself over the sill in much the same manner a buccaneer might board an enemy ship. His eyes gleamed, his hair was as black as the night behind him, and clamped between his teeth was a single fragrant rose.

She ran lightly to the window to help him in. "You look like . . . like a *pirate!*" she exclaimed.

He stood up, tall and handsome, his head nearly brushing

the rafters. "But I feel like a thief." With a flourish, he presented her with the rose, the touch of their hands sending shivers through both of them. As she went into his arms and molded herself to his chest, he buried his face in her silken hair and inhaled its sweet fragrance. "Besides, no pirate in his right mind would carry a flower between his teeth. He'd carry a knife."

"Are there no pirates with romantic tendencies?"

"Nay. Just no roses growing in the middle of the ocean."

"Oh, Sam!"

"Shh, lest your aunt hear us!"

She muffled her laughter against the broad expanse of his warm chest, thrilling to the sound of his heart pounding beneath her ear. His nearness, the wickedness of what she was doing, and the danger of discovery sent flutters through her heart and raised the goose bumps on her arms. But oh, she didn't care, *didn't care!* He had come to her, *he was here,* and that was all that mattered. She felt his hands cupping the back of her head, stroking her hair, holding her close to his powerful body and allowing her to feel the hard, honed length of him. She heard his heart quickening in tempo even as hers began to beat so madly that the resulting roar of blood through her veins rivalled the distant song of the sea. Sighing, she nuzzled the linen of his loose shirt aside. "Took you long enough to get here."

"I wanted to make sure your aunt was abed."

"My aunt goes to bed an hour after sunset. You wasted a lot of time, Sam!"

"And I shan't waste any more by standing here mincing words when I could be making up for that lost time."

His voice was deep and husky. She felt his hand roving down her back, sending tremors down her spine that radiated into her arms, her legs, and down into her womanly regions until she was forced to clamp her thighs together to try and stem the hot, burning sensation his touch evoked. Deftly, he unbuttoned her gown, sliding it off her moonlit shoulders and letting it fall to her waist. His rough palm seared her shoulders, her nape, the knobby protrusions of her spine. The wind sighed through the open window, making her hair dance against her arms and gooseflesh rise on her skin. She shut her eyes, fearing that her trembling legs wouldn't support her

and knowing it was only a matter of time before they would
not. Swaying, she felt his mouth cover hers, gently demanding, then not so gently, and as he drove her slowly backward
toward her bed, her legs *did* give out and he swept her up in
his strong, steely arms before she could fall.

"Sam. . . ."

He lifted her, hoisting her up so that she clung to him with
her legs wrapped around his hips, her arms around his neck.
They stood there for a long moment that wasn't long enough,
his hot gaze roving over her face, down her throat where the
pulse beat so wildly, across her creamy shoulders, and finally, lingering on her bare breasts and tight, taut nipples
with an intensity that made them even more so. Her heartbeat
quickened; moisture gathered between her thighs and she
clasped them to his hard hips and tried not to squirm. But
she couldn't help herself, and as blood began to singe their
veins and burn through their hearts, she felt his manhood
stiffen beneath her, against her. His gaze roved her body,
touching her as boldly as his hands might, and eliciting the
same response.

"I want you . . . Maria."

She swallowed, feeling feverish, feeling dizzy, throbbing
in places she didn't know she had and shivering in areas that
were far from cold. Sensations assaulted her: his rough hands,
burning against her back; night wind kissing her hot and moist
skin, wafting across her tight nipples, caressing her aching
breasts. Her gown was still wrapped around her waist; it
floated on the sweet, mild breeze that sighed through the
window and grazed her thighs like a lover's kiss. . . . And
Sam. All raw power and male majesty, strength and fire and
splendor. . . .

He bent his head and drove his mouth against hers, plunging his tongue between her teeth and into the honey-sweet
recesses of her mouth. She moaned deep in her throat and
let her head fall back under the onslaught, her hair tumbling
down and tickling the base of her spine, flowing over his
arms, brushing the floor. Her legs tightened around his hips,
her arms around his neck. And still he kissed her, one hand
bracing her back while the other stroked downward, cupping
her buttocks and pressing her closer to the rigid shaft that

even now strained against his breeches and sought the closeness of her eager young body.

He began to move toward the bed once again, slowly, tantalizingly, his kiss going on and on and on. Dizzily, she felt herself being lowered; faintly, she was aware of the mattress beneath her, the cornhusks rustling as they took her weight and then his; acutely, she felt him cover her trembling body with his own hot, rock-solid one. The wind murmured through the trees outside, bringing with it the sound of the sea, the taste of salt. It whispered over her bare flesh and stirred her hair, purred through the room and filled it with the magic of the night. Maria felt all of it, felt none of it. She knew only him.

"Ah, princess," he murmured into the curve of her neck, "knowing you'll be here waiting for me will hasten my return. You *will* wait, won't you?"

His lips grazed her collarbone, the hollows of her shoulders. "Oh, Sam, never doubt that I'll wait for you. . . ."

"And when I come back I'll have a hold full of treasure, just for you, lass—jewels, silver, gold." She shivered as his mouth dragged across her throat and toward one aching breast. "I *will* take you away from here, make you a princess of a West Indies isle, where the sun is always hot, the wind never cold . . . I promise. So help me God, I promise. . . ."

She silenced him with her lips, her arms, her body. Clothes were shed, tossed to the floor. Gentle kisses became urgent, slow caresses grew desperate. Hearts thudded wildly against each other, separated only by skin and bone and blood, and then a slick layer of moisture that lay between their hot bodies and heightened the pleasure when he began to move slowly against her.

"Sam. . . ."

His harsh breathing stirred the tangled hair behind her ear, his lips burned the sensitive skin there. She moaned as his teeth grazed her earlobe, her neck. "God, Maria, you're beautiful. So cursed, bloody, *beautiful* . . . ." She felt him parting her thighs with his knee, then stroking them with his hand, gently at first, then roughly. She gasped, then groaned as he cupped her soft, moist curls, teasing her, tantalizing her, causing her to pant, to moan, to sob.

"Sam, please. . . ."

His finger slipped within her moist recesses.

"Oh God, Sam—"

His mouth came down over hers and muffled her cries; his hands brought her young body to the peak of ecstasy as he rubbed and rolled the aching bud of her womanhood between thumb and forefinger until she thought she would die from the sheer, sweet agony of it. She bucked wildly beneath him, thrashing madly until he finally caught her flailing arms above her head and drove himself into her slick heat, thrusting hard, thrusting long, and impaling her with a sweet, rippling agony that bordered on pain in its intensity. Faster and faster he moved, deeper and deeper he drove, until, until, until—

"Sam!"

He exploded into her, burying his face in her damp curls even as she convulsed and spasmed and drove herself upward to meet him. She felt his seed pulsing hot and warm inside her, and the beauty of it was so intense, so magical, that she couldn't stop the sobs from choking her throat, the tears from spilling down her face and wetting the tangled fan of her hair on the pillow beneath her. They clutched each other, rolling on the little mattress as one, their breaths mingling, their lungs heaving, their arms and legs tangled in damp, crushed sheets and trussed blankets.

Outside, the trees murmured in the wind.

Downstairs, Aunt Helen slept on.

And in a cornhusk mattress tucked beneath the eaves, two lovers lay in each other's arms, dreading the dawn and the parting that it would bring.

She stood at the very edge of the sea cliffs that faced and held back the wide Atlantic, the sun warm against her face, the wind a gentle caress that raked the sea, made a banner of her golden hair, and dried the tears upon her cheeks. Swallowing tightly, she watched as *Lilith's* sails grew smaller and smaller.

Lifting her chin, Maria hugged her arms to herself in a futile attempt to hold the pieces of her breaking heart together. Her lip trembled as she slowly raised her hand and waved in farewell.

And aboard the sloop she saw a movement, tiny with distance, as he returned the gesture. Moments later, the ship was just a speck on the southern horizon; then, it was gone.

And so was he. Taking a tremulous sigh, Maria turned, blinked back the tears, and began the long walk over the lonely moors back to town.

Chapter 6

*The Music in my heart I bore
Long after it was heard no more.*

WORDSWORTH

By August, Maria knew that something was wrong.

By September, she suspected she was pregnant.

And by October, she knew for certain that she was.

And so did Aunt Helen who, upon noticing Maria's thickening middle—went into a dead faint, a screaming rage, tearful hysterics, and finally a sulking silence. In exactly that order.

But that was all past, thank God. Now, there were only three things she had to contend with: daily reminders of her wickedness which came in the form of tiresome speeches on her aunt's part that dragged on longer than Reverend Treat's sermons, impassioned pleas not to tell a soul about her condition, and nightly prayers to the Lord above to send Sam back to her—and soon.

The latter, of course, was the easiest. It was too bad that Auntie didn't feel the same way. To her, the only reason to have "that hellspawn" back was so that he could do right by Maria and marry her, for no matter how much she hated Sam, she moaned in despair at thoughts of Maria suffering the disgrace that was sure to come when the villagers found out about her condition.

To Maria, it seemed like a century ago that she'd stood at

the top of the sand cliffs and waved good-bye to him, eons since they'd lain together beneath the apple tree—and, despite his original intentions, that last night in her attic bed with her cornhusk-and-straw mattress rustling beneath their hot, straining bodies. But the memories were never far away. His keen, commanding eyes. His hair, black as a crow's wing and just as glossy, his hands . . . oh, especially his hands. She could still feel them, so rough against her smooth stomach, her aching breasts, her tingling thighs. . . .

Funny how all she had to do was think about him and the wicked, delightful feelings that had brought her to this condition in the first place throbbed within ·her like an ever-present ache.

But he'd be back soon—any time now, probably. Even now, he was probably filling *Lilith's* hold with Spanish gold and silver reales. Even now, *Lilith* must be riding low in the water. Even now, he must be on his way back to Eastham, back to her. . . .

Of course, Maria could not know that her visions were the furthest things from the truth. For Sam Bellamy had as strong a penchant for trouble as Gunner did for his fine silk stockings, and he'd long since given up on Spanish treasure ships in favor of other, more lawless pursuits that would've shocked the wrinkles right off Aunt Helen's weathered face. But Maria, on her way to the village green this fine October morning, was blissfully ignorant of any of that. And it was just as well.

The baby was still four months away. Four more months of hiding her telltale figure beneath woolen cloaks and keeping her secret from the villagers, four more months of trekking to the Great Beach, where she would sit for hours upon end with her eyes trained on the empty horizon. Watching. Waiting. Alone, except for the sigh of the wind and lonely cries of the gulls, straining her eyes as she prayed for a ship to hove into sight. Not just any ship but a small, weathered sloop whose hold contained riches beyond her wildest imaginings, and upon whose decks stood the handsomest man in the world. . . .

It didn't matter that Auntie thought she was wasting her time going up to the Great Beach, for Auntie, of course, was quite adamant in her belief that Sam was never coming back.

But Maria clung fast to the knowledge that he would. He'd made a promise to her. And wouldn't it be nice if he came soon, so that she could share with him the beauties of the season before the weather turned bitter and cold. They could hold hands as they trudged through a sweet-smelling carpet of crimson, russet, and gold leaves. They could gather the bayberries together, make candles to light their home with. They would eat squash and pumpkin pies, string apples up to dry, and go to bed snuggled beneath piles of thick, woolen blankets. . . .

"Oh, Sam," she said aloud. But the place where he should've been walking beside her was empty, and the only voices that answered her were those of the bleached cornstalks, shaking themselves in the wind and rustling like old bones.

She shivered, drawing her scarlet cloak around her and huddling within its warmth. At least she didn't have much farther to walk, for the meeting house was just ahead. Auntie would have a fit, of course, if she learned that she was in town—after all, what if someone saw her? But Maria had grown tired of being a recluse, tired of limiting her excursions to the woods, the marshes, and the wild, lonely moors as she gathered everything from pine bark to seaweed to make her Indian medicines. Not that she had anyone to practice them on, of course. She hadn't even seen Thankful lately, thanks to Auntie's "excuses" that she was ill, or absent, or whatever else she happened to dream up to keep would-be visitors away. And how lonely it was when the only time she got to see anyone was at Sunday service, where everyone's attention was on Reverend Treat and not her gently swelling belly.

"Maria! Maria, wait!"

The high, excited voice put an abrupt end to Maria's musings, and self-consciously she hugged her cloak tightly about her middle and hoped her stomach was as well hidden as her fear that someone might see it. But it was only Thankful, running past the stocks that sat ominously upon the faded, not-so-green grass of the village green. "Maria, I've been worried about you! You aunt says you were sick. A cold, but she didn't want me to catch it and bade me to stay away!"

Breathless, she studied Maria's face, thank God—and not her stomach. "You *are* all right, aren't you?"

"Much better, thank you," Maria assured her. She shifted the bundle in her hand, holding it over her stomach just in case.

"Oh, thank God. We were all so worried. Haven't seen much of you lately, you know."

"I've been uh, making blankets," Maria said, glancing down at her bundle. "This one's for Reverend Treat."

"Oh, can I see?"

With reluctance she handed it to Thankful, who eagerly shook it out, held it up, and gasped with delight. "Oh, Maria! 'Tis *beautiful* . . ." She looked up, her eyes excited, almost reverent. "He's going to *love* it. I've always said it's not fair that God gave you such skill at the loom, and denied it to the rest of us. Why, look at this!" She pointed to the gentle lambs, the calves with their soulful eyes, so lifelike that it looked as though they might actually walk right off the blanket and join them on the dirt road. "They look so *real*. And the baby Jesus! Oh, you've captured every feature, every detail—*a-a-a-a-h!*"

Shouts, screams, the thunder of pounding hooves. Whirling, they saw a riderless horse, its red nostrils flaring, its eyes wild and ringed with white. Stirrup irons banged against its empty saddle, a crowd of villagers were in hot pursuit—and it was heading straight for them.

"Thankful!" Reacting first, Maria shoved the girl out of the road but was too late to save herself. The horse veered off, trying to avoid her, but could not have anticipated that Maria would do the same. A glimpse of wild eyes, the stinging lash of flying mane, and then its shoulder hit her hard, snapping her head back and knocking the breath from her lungs. The world tilted crazily, she felt space moving beneath her and then dirt and stones digging into her cheek.

"Maria! Maria, are you all right?" Dizzily, Maria looked up. Thankful's pale face swirled before her eyes, focused, stopped spinning. The hand she thrust toward Maria was white. "Oh, what a terribly brave thing you did! Why, you could've been killed!" Thankful glanced up at the gathering crowd, who'd abandoned their pursuit of the horse and now pressed close in concern. "Did you see what she did? She saved my life!"

Their shadows fell across Maria, and doors slammed as people raced from their homes to see what the commotion was all about. She heard voices, saw familiar faces, caught a whiff of pipe smoke as Justice Joseph Doane shoved his way through the crowd. "Are you injured, Mistress Hallett? Here, let me help you up." Shoving the pipe into his stern mouth, he stretched out his hand.

"Honestly, I'm all right." She felt rather foolish with all of this attention. But Thankful had her other hand, and her squeal rang through Maria's dizzy head as she grasped her palm and turned it upwards.

"Oh, look, you've scraped yourself!"

Maria gained her feet, thanking the good Lord above that she hadn't broken any bones. " 'Tis naught but a scratch," she said. "Nothing to worry about, really." She reached down to brush the dust from her clothing and hastily pull her cloak, which had fallen open, about her.

But she was too late.

A dozen faces, all staring in shock and horror at the once-trim waist that had been the envy of every woman in Eastham. For a moment Maria could only stare back; and then she felt the heat creeping up her neck, suffusing into her face, spreading from hairline to earlobes like a rush of fever. Just as abruptly the color drained and she went white. Her hands were shaking uncontrollably as she reached out to take the blanket from Thankful's suddenly nerveless fingers.

"Thank you," she said hastily, with all of the poise she could muster given their accusing, horrified stares. Already, the whispers were starting, already their eyes were hardening, growing malicious and cold. She had to get out of here. *Oh, God,* she thought. "I—I think that I'll just be on my way. . . . I made this blanket for Reverend Treat and . . . and I, uh, must bring it to him."

They turned on her like a pack of wolves.

"A blanket for the reverend, huh? Mistress Hallett had best save it for herself!"

"Aye, she's in a family way, all right!"

"Shameless hussy!"

"Whore!"

Their awful words mingled, became a roar, until at last Justice Doane's gruff voice cut through the din. "I don't approve of you going to see the good reverend in your condition." He clawed the pipe from his mouth once more. "You ought to be ashamed of yourself, girl, insulting him like that. Someone as clean and holy as he shouldn't be exposed to someone as dirty and sinful as you."

Dirty? Sinful? Surely this wasn't happening to her! Confused, Maria felt hot, scalding tears brewing in her throat, behind her eyes. "But . . . but I have a gift for him!"

"Then I suggest you burn it. He'll have no use for the fruits of your soiled hands." Doane's eyes narrowed, pinning her helplessly in their accusing stare. Behind him the others clustered, gawking at her as though she was a freak of nature or worse yet, the plague. "And by the way, Mistress Hallett . . . who soiled *you?*"

"I—I . . ." She bit down hard on her lip, trying desperately not to cry.

"Out with it, girl! Whose babe are you breeding?"

"I can't say!"

"You can't say. . . ." He towered over her, his smoky breath filling her face. "And why not? Doesn't your aunt know about your wickedness?" He shoved the pipe between his teeth and glared at her with intimidating fierceness. Terrified, Maria tried to turn away, to run, but his fingers dug into her shoulders and spun her around to face him. She cried out in indignation and pain. "In the name of God, you'll tell me who the father is! I'll not have anyone in this parish soiling a young woman and then leaving her to bear the consequences alone!"

But she couldn't tell him. What grew within her womb was something sacred and special, something that she and Sam had made together, and to expose it to their vileness, condemnation, and hatred before it was even born was something she couldn't bring herself to do. She would not tell them, would not let them make a crime of the love she had for its father, would not stand here and listen to them tear Sam apart and call him all sorts of evil, terrible things.

Doane cruelly pinched her shoulder, his voice thundering in her ear. "I'll not ask you again, Maria Hallett! Who fathered that babe?"

"I told you, I can't say!" Her words were drowned in sobs, and blindly her mind groped for an excuse, an answer, anything. "I can't tell you because . . . because . . ."

"You want to know why she can't name that babe's sire?" A woman's shrill, high voice pierced the silence. "I'll tell you why! She can't name him because she doesn't *know!* And the reason she doesn't know is because *he's the devil!*"

The crowd went as still as death. One by one, they turned their white, corpselike faces toward the woman who had spoken.

"Oh, blind fools, can't you see?" she wailed, her voice rising to near hysteria. "She doesn't *know!* Just as Mary, the most beautiful virgin, conceived Jesus, our *Maria* here"— she paused, allowing the crowd to note the similarity between the two names—"the most beautiful girl in Eastham, has conceived a child—by Satan! Oh, to think we envied her beauty! Didn't we always know it would be her undoing? *Wasn't it obvious?* Oh, what did I tell you? She's too pretty for any mere man of earth to possess! Only the devil could have her!" Her wild eyes swept the crowd. "And do you know what that makes our Maria?"

Hushed silence.

"It makes her a *witch!*"

"No. . . . No, 'tisn't true!" Maria cried, but she was too late. The woman was already fleeing down the street, her words still ringing in everyone's ears. " *'Tisn't true!* You've known me all my life! How could you believe such nonsense?" But already they were backing away. Another woman broke from the circle and fled. And then another, dragging her crying child with her.

And now even Justice Doane was stepping away from her. "Daughter of the devil," he whispered. "In the name of God, stay away from me!" He held up a shaking hand as she lurched toward him, ignoring her imploring eyes, her chalky face. "I said stay away from me, witch!"

"Please, Justice Doane, *please* listen to me! I can explain!" Cold, ugly terror writhed like a snake in the pit of her stomach. This wasn't happening to her! It couldn't be!

But it was. And now, they were growing defensive.

"Then why did my cow suddenly go dry?"

"You think that's bad, huh? Now I know why my hens

stopped laying. And no wonder my poor Sarah can't find a husband! The witch put a hex on her, she did!''

"A heathen, I tell you!''

"And no wonder she can turn out such beautiful patterns on her loom when the rest of us can't!''

"The devil's work!''

"The devil's own!''

"Do you think that dog of hers is her familiar?''

It was all laid at her door; the rancid butter in Mrs. Knowles's churn, Tommy Cotter's foot pains, the rabbits that had wiped out Abigail Nickerson's vegetable garden three months past. Through the awful, ugly haze of unreality Maria heard their prayers as they called upon the Lord to save them, saw them shielding their faces to avoid looking at her. And now their voices were no longer accusing, but rising with fear.

"Get away from us, witch!''

"Blasphemous whore!''

"Bride of Lucifer! Consort of the devil! You're unfit to walk amongst us!''

The tears welled up and spilled over, trickling down her cheeks and making twin spots of moisture upon her scarlet cloak. In desperation, Maria started toward the one person she knew would stand by her—Thankful. But the girl knelt, groped in the dirt, and came up with a stone clenched in her fist.

"Stay away, Maria!''

The tears froze in her eyes. "Thankful, I'm your *friend!*''

"Not anymore you're not. I don't keep friends who are witches!''

But I'm not a witch!

Others picked up rocks, hefting them in their hands. And now it was Maria who backed away, turning to flee as they advanced upon her.

The first stone glanced off her arm, bounced away into the dirt. Another buried itself within the folds of her cloak with a dull thud. Then another, slamming painfully between her shoulderblades. She cried out, stumbled and fell. Her cheek slammed against the hard-packed dirt and she tasted blood. Through the blur of tears she saw the beautiful blanket she'd

labored so hard over lying in a heap in the road, saw it
stamped into the dirt and crushed by angry heels.

"Witch! Begone, daughter of Lucifer! And stay out of Eastham if you know what's good for you!"

More stones. Struggling to her feet, sobbing in pain and
terror, Maria ran blindly, their shrieks and prayers ringing in
her ears. She raced out of town and down the King's Highway, oblivious to all but her destination. Pain knotted her
calves. Fire seared her lungs. Blackness came and went,
swirling behind her eyes. But she didn't stop.

At last she reached the Great Beach. Here, wind swept
across miles of ocean, wind that might've filled *Lilith's* sails
and touched *his* skin, his hair, his clothes a thousand miles
away, wind that blew on and on until at last it carried that
tiny bit of him to where she stood upon the high plateaus of
sand overlooking the vast ocean.

He was here. Somehow, some way, he was here.

Hugging her arms to her breasts, Maria sank to scuffed
and bloody knees and cried out her despair, her fear of what
would become of her, and her overwhelming, aching loneliness. She sobbed until there were no tears left. She sobbed
until the terror and agony congealed into a big chunk of cold
clay that sat heavily within her stomach. She sobbed until she
was no longer crying about the way the villagers had treated
her, but because the one man that she loved, the one man
she would ever love, was a thousand miles away.

And then she lifted her head, staring out to sea across an
endless expanse of tossing waves and white foam. The tears
returned—for the horizon, cold and gray and stretching into
forever—was empty.

That winter was a hard one for the people of Eastham, and
would long be remembered for its vast amounts of snowfall.
It was also the winter that old Reverend Treat, beloved by
all, died. They had to dig tunnels through the snow just to
get him to the Burying Acre, and no one would ever forget
the crowds—both villagers and Wampanoag Indians alike—
who stood sadly beside his grave on the cold, wintry day that
he was laid to rest.

It was also the winter that the Sea Witch of Billingsgate had her baby.

Maria was afforded none of the luxuries of companionship that Reverend Treat, even in death, enjoyed; she birthed the baby all by herself, for her aunt was unable to get across the stormy, snowy moors to be with her, and her nearest neighbor—who happened to be male, anyway—lived two miles distant. Only Gunner, lying beside the fire that cold, stormy morning as the snow piled up on her thatched roof and the wind rustled beneath the clay-clinked rafters, was with her when she brought little Charles into the world; only he heard her screams of agony and pain, and then her sobs of joy when it was all over and Maria beheld a tiny face and soft, curling hair that was as black as his bold, handsome father's.

Sam. . . . She thought of him often; nay, constantly. She remembered the heat of his lovemaking as she sat by her crackling fire, felt again the shivers his touch had elicited as February's cold winds swept off the ocean and blew kisses against her wind-whipped cheeks, and felt her loneliness in the mournful howl of the wind as it whistled and sang around the walls of this little hut upon the wild dunes and sand cliffs she now called home.

But Maria had grown accustomed to loneliness, and if asked—as she often was by her well-meaning aunt, who, remorseful over her treatment of her niece and perhaps even a bit lonely herself, came often to visit—would've admitted that she'd come to prefer the solitude of living out here all by herself on the windswept dunes. Here, she could walk the miles of shoreline with her gaze turned seaward; here, she could keep up her constant vigil, watching, waiting; from the top of the sand cliffs, from the flat moors of the tableland, and even from within her little hut, where she'd positioned her loom beside the window for an unhampered view of the ocean. She didn't need the villagers; she didn't need anyone except Sam, and here, at the edge of the sea over which he'd gone, where even now he sailed, she felt closest to him, and never alone.

Maria hadn't set foot in Eastham since that terrible day last fall when the villagers had driven her out of town. Oh, she was allowed to go as far as the town limits, where she traded her beautiful blankets for much-needed supplies, and frequently some of the bolder—or more hypocritical—villagers would venture out to this little hut she'd built with the help of some friendly Indians, to seek her skills as a medicine woman, for as a witch, everyone knew she could cure everything from sore throats to gout. She was self-sufficient and independent, and those who saw her wandering the sand cliffs that stood sentinel over the ocean, her hair whipping in the wind and streaming out behind her and her gaze trained on an empty horizon, thought her a bit eccentric. But only her aunt knew why Maria wandered the dunes, the cliffs; only she knew why her niece always had an eye trained upon that distant horizon where sea met sky.

But for the past two weeks Maria hadn't been able to go farther than her front door. Little Charles demanded every bit of attention she had to give and then some. And while Maria could cure fever, set a fracture, or even make an herbal concoction guaranteed to ensure fertility, what she couldn't do was get him to stop crying long enough to give herself some much needed rest. And now, staring out the window of her little hut while Charles whimpered in her arms, the idea of seeking Auntie's advice in forbidden Eastham was beginning to seem more and more appealing.

Outside, snow still sifted out of leaden skies. Wind drove it into thick drifts, piled it on the boughs of the little scruff pine at Maria's westward window until the weary branches sagged and groaned beneath the weight. But the peaceful scene was shattered as Charles began to wail incessantly, his cries growing louder and louder until Gunner, raising his head and heaving a great sigh, padded to the door and nuzzled the latch.

Maria let him out and watched as he disappeared into the swirling veil of snowflakes. She rested her cheek against her baby's, kissing him, rocking him, soothing him. His little face was puckered and red from crying, his tiny fists balled and flailing. Frustration welled within her. Was she a success as a healer only to be a a failure as a mother? She'd fed him, changed him, cuddled him, had done everything she could think of to make him comfortable; but still he cried, on and on, until the nagging fears of a mother's intuition—that he *wasn't* just colicky, that something was wrong, terribly wrong—outweighed any perils that the storm, or the hostile villagers might offer.

Auntie. She'd know what to do. Maria bit her lip and shot a quick glance toward the raw, gray sea beyond her window. Still, no sails. But then, she hadn't really expected to see any through this snow . . . had she? So why not go to town and seek her aunt's advice? If she hid little Charles in a pile of blankets and pulled the hood of her cloak up to cover her face, no one would recognize her. . . .

The baby wailed again.

She made her decision. Determined now, Maria checked the fire, donned a heavy woolen cloak trimmed in fur, and grabbed her muff before she could change her mind. Wrapping the baby in the warmest blankets she had, she took one last look about the hut's single room and stepped resolutely out into the cold.

She stood for a moment, long tresses working their way out from beneath her hood and whipping in the wind. Snow whispered out of a black sky, settling upon her flushed cheeks and melting there like a lover's kiss. Oh, should they go?

Here and there, the wind had swept the moors bare, leaving clumps of dry beach grass poking up through the snow and making her trek easier; but for the most part the desolate, wintry dunes held drifts that engulfed her all the way to mid-thigh when she sank into them. Dauntless, Maria trudged on, a small, forlorn figure in a sea of emptiness, of barren land made even more so by winter's hand. An hour went by before the storm kindly let up and a watery sun peeped through a thin spot in the clouds. And by the time she finally reached the King's Highway, that same sun was orange and burnt with the age of the day.

She had to stop and rest constantly. Her feet were numb with cold, her arms aching from holding the baby. The sunset lit up the sky, turning the snowy fields surrounding her to crimson, purple and gold. Maria sighed in relief as she crossed the town limits, for here the snow was hard packed and easier to walk in. She could still see scuff marks and pieces of bark here and there where the villagers had cleared the snow from the road by dragging a huge log behind a team of horses. Her weary, agonized legs sighed in gratitude as she continued on.

It was near dark by the time she saw the Knowles's barn ahead. In the gathering gloom it was only a shapeless block in a snowy, empty field, but it marked a shortcut through these endless pastures that would bring her to Auntie's house that much sooner. It would be hard, slow progress through the field, and late by the time she reached her destination—but the chances of anyone seeing and recognizing her in a darkened field were far slimmer than they'd be if she remained on the well-traveled road. She shuddered to think what the villagers would do if they saw her, not to her, but to little Charles, still snuggled in her arms and for the moment, thank the Lord, not crying.

The fence that marked the path was just ahead. Maria quickened her pace and had almost reached it when she heard voices. Her heart skipped a beat and instinctively she clutched the baby to her breast. Coming around the bend was a group of school-age boys, laughing and yelling and hurling snowballs at each other. Their voices, loud in the brittle, frosty night, abruptly ceased as they caught sight of her.

Panic chased the color from her cold-reddened cheeks.

"Look! It's the Sea Witch!"

Their frosty breath made plumes in the cold air. "She's not supposed to be in town! Justice Doane said so himself!"

A murmur of fear, of open hostility. "Are you sure it's her?" she heard one of them ask.

"Oh, it's her, all right. My mother warned me about her, told me to stay away from her. She said she'd put the Evil Eye on me if I got too close!"

"Do you *really* think she's a witch? She doesn't look like one."

"Well, what do you expect? A wart on her nose and the ugliness of an old hag? The devil works in strange ways to fool God's chosen ones. That's what the Reverend Treat used to say, God rest his soul. And that's why she's so pretty, just to fool people into thinking she's innocent. She's a witch all right, and if you know what's good for you, you'd better stay away from her!"

Desperately, Maria eyed the distance to the path. Oh, this had been a fool's decision! Her arms tightened about little Charles. Let them do to her what they would, but she'd allow

no harm to come to her baby! Thinking that if she acted boldly
they'd leave her alone, she lifted her chin and tried to continue.

"Let me pass," she said firmly. "I mean you no harm."

They stepped back, eyeing her distrustfully as she hurried
past them. She felt their eyes upon her, heard their hushed
whispers, and it was all she could do not to break into a run.
Please God, she breathed, *oh please, don't let them see
Charles*. But before the words were even out of her mouth
the loud, highpitched wail of a baby pierced the silence.

Oh please, not now. . . .

"Did you hear that?'Tis the devil-child!"

"And she's bringing it into town! Quick, stop her!"

Shouts. The crunch of snow behind her. A sifting of cold
powder as a snowball whirred overhead, barely missing her.

Frantically, Maria grabbed her heavy skirts in one hand,
clutched the crying child in the other, and bolted for the
path. There was no time to thank God for the darkness, for
snow engulfed her all the way to her knees as she left the
road. Stumbling, she almost fell, then picked herself up to
flounder through the cold drifts. The shouts behind her grew
louder as the boys stopped to hurl poorly aimed snowballs
through the gloom. But not all of them were in pursuit; she
could hear their cries as most of them raced toward the
"safety" of the village. That they were running to spread the
alarm, to warn their neighbors that the Sea Witch of Eastham
was coming, Maria had not doubt.

And the first place they'd search for her would be at her
aunt's house. She couldn't bring little Charles there now. Oh,
the unfairness of it all! Why had she come to Eastham? She
should've stayed home!

But she couldn't stop now. Her lungs burned as she gulped
the brittle-cold air. Fatigue threatened to overcome her, but
the baby's incessant crying and the sounds of pursuit drove
her on.

She had to find a place to hide. *The barn*. Choking out a
prayer of thanksgiving, Maria half ran, half stumbled to it,
flung open the door, and slipped quietly inside.

Within, it was dark and cold. She collapsed against the
door, trying to control her frantic, pained breathing. Somewhere in the gloom a horse nickered softly then went back
to its hay, the steady grinding chop of its teeth oddly com-

forting to her. Slowly, Maria's breathing returned to normal and her eyes began to adjust to the darkness. And for once, Providence favored her, for at that moment, the moon peeped from behind the cloud cover and in its silvery light Maria saw stairs leading up to the loft.

Holding the baby close to muffle his whimpers, she clambered up the stairs as fast as her numb feet and ice-stiffened skirts would allow. Loose hay was scattered everywhere, and she shuffled through it until she reached the wall at the far side of the loft. Outside, the shouts grew louder; she squeezed her eyes shut and held her breath until they faded, became distant, and at last disappeared into the night.

Moments passed. Hours. Charles quieted and slept at last, growing heavy in her arms. From below came the peaceful sounds of the horses, from somewhere out in the darkness, the hoot of a snowy owl. At last, they were alone. And safe.

With a grateful sigh, Maria nestled within the hay's sweet, fragrant warmth, never realizing that the sleeping bundle in her arms was not only silent but still. Cuddling the baby lovingly, fatigue and worry finally claimed her and she sank into the dreamless sleep of pure exhaustion.

She woke a half hour later to the sound of voices. Shrill and excited, they penetrated the innocence of slumber and disturbed her dreams. . . . Something stabbed through her cloak and prickled her back, and disappointment flooded her when she realized it was only hay, not marsh grass. The brilliance against her closed eyelids was not spring sun washing the Great Beach but a shaft of light streaming in through a barn window. . . . And it wasn't Sam's long-muscled, warm body beside her, but the little one of the baby—

Warm body?

Maria's eyes shot open. There *was* no warm body beside her—only an empty coldness. With a terrible sense of foreboding she looked down in the hay where the baby lay—and froze in horror.

There he was, still swaddled in the blankets; but his tiny face was contorted, still, and tinted an unnatural shade of blue.

Her fist slammed against her mouth. A strangled scream

burst against her fingers. She knew he was dead before she even reached out a trembling finger to touch him.

Cold.

Bile welled up in her throat. Her vision blurred, a strange buzzing swept through her head, and she came close to fainting as her very soul left her body then slammed back upon her heart so hard that she was violently, horribly sick.

"Maria! Maria Hallett! Come out of that barn this instant! We know you're in there!"

She never heard them. In a daze, her movements wooden and numb, she reached down and very gently picked up the lifeless form of her baby.

"Oh . . . my God, no . . ."

Realization sucked the very breath from her lungs.

"No . . . Please God, no . . ." Her voice rose to a keening wail. Clutching the little body to her breast, her head fell forward and her outcry of pure agony pierced the stillness of the barn.

"Oh, S-a-a-a-a-a-a-a-m!"

"Maria Hallett! In the name of God, come out of there *now!*"

Her sobs were terrible, heart-wrenching wails that sent shivers up their backs by the time Justice Doane, Mr. Knowles, and the people of Eastham fearfully entered the barn. And as they rushed up the creaking old stairs to the loft, the very hair at the napes of their necks bristled and stood tall.

They were unprepared for what they found. For there was Maria sitting forlornly in the hay, cradling something in her arms, rocking it back and forth, and shrieking in agony. Her sobs had stained her complexion a bright crimson, tears fell incessantly upon the bundle of blankets in her arms, and her long golden hair was tangled and matted with pieces of hay. And as she looked up at them, her eyes dazed and red-rimmed, Justice Doane saw just what she was holding.

"Oh my God . . ." he whispered.

Behind him the ladder creaked and groaned as others joined him, the rustle of hay sounding like gunshots in the deathlike stillness. Gathering his courage, Justice Doane shoved his pipe between his teeth and took a wary step toward her.

"Let's go, Maria. I'm taking you to the gaol. Until the

evidence is sorted out and examined, I hold you personally responsible for the death of this child.''

She heard his words through a fog of unreality. Crying harder, she buried her face within the blankets and swayed back and forth in her misery.

''Oh, leave her be,'' someone said. ''After all, 'twas only the devil's child. In His wisdom and grace, the Lord saw fit to deliver us of its evil. Goodness has prevailed. . . .''

Murmurs of assent, fearfully uttered ayes. Justice Doane turned toward them and quieted them with a hard glance. ''Devil's child or not, it doesn't matter. What *does* matter is that she defied us all and came to town to spread her wickedness!'' He reached down to pull Maria up, loathe even to touch her, for after all she *was* a witch. ''Come along, Maria. And hand over the babe. I'll see to it that Mr. Freeman gives it a decent burial.''

Her head snapped up. Eyes flashing, she clutched the little body protectively to her breast. ''Nay!'' she shrieked. ''I'll never give up my son to you, never let you lay your filthy, murdering hands upon him! Do you think I forgot what you did to me last fall? Do you think I shall *ever* forget it? 'Tis all your fault that he's dead! If it wasn't for you I wouldn't have had to hide here! If it wasn't for you I wouldn't have had to—to''—her eyes filled—''leave town in the first place!'' She burst into tears once more, her voice rising as it tried to keep up with her sobs. ''Go away and leave me alone! Do you hear me? I said go away and leave me *alone!*''

Doane stepped forward. His hand closed over her arm and Maria lunged back, teeth bared, a cornered animal defending her young. But he didn't let go. Wildly, she fought him with fingers curled into claws, then fists. He released her with a startled gasp, watching in horror as she stumbled away through the hay, sobbing, to retreat to a shadowy corner of the loft.

''The woman's mad,'' someone whispered.

And as he tried once more to restrain her, there was a sudden commotion behind him.

''Leave that child alone!'' Aunt Helen raged, bursting into the hayloft and impaling Justice Doane with eyes as cold as the icicles that hung from the rafters just outside. ''Can't you see she's been through enough? May God condemn the lot of you for the miserable, heartless mob that you are!''

Her voice seeped through the fog of Maria's numbed mind. *Auntie?* . . . She had come at last. She'd make everything all right, would know what ailed little Charles. . . . But then the fog cleared, mercilessly, laying everything bare as a windswept dune. Auntie couldn't help little Charles now. Even Sam couldn't help little Charles now. *No one could.* For he was . . . dead. *Dead!* ''Oh, Auntie . . .'' Stumbling through the hay, Maria threw herself into her aunt's outstretched arms and buried her streaming face against the old woman's frail shoulder. Gnarled old hands smoothed and caught in the tangled river of gold that flowed down her back, gentle fingers plucked bits of straw from that dishevelled mane, and Aunt Helen's throat worked as she fought to contain her own tears.

Justice Doane, uncertainly watching this disturbing scene, cleared his throat. The villagers exchanged nervous glances. The Sea Witch blamed them for the death of her child . . . what stopped her from putting the Evil Eye on them?

But their trepidation was the last thing on Maria's mind as she trustingly, tenderly relinquished Sam Bellamy's son to her aunt's arms. She gazed for a long moment into the little face, then reached a shaky hand up to tuck the folds of the blanket about him, as though he might be cold. Only then did she see the wetness glistening on her aunt's lined cheeks, the shaking of her proud shoulders. She swallowed hard, making several unsuccessful attempts to speak before the words finally came out. ''Y-you won't let them touch him will you, Auntie? You'll take him and . . . and b-bury him—''

She couldn't finish, abruptly turning away to sob fresh tears into her cold, white hands. Knowing the fight had finally gone out of her, Justice Doane pulled her wrists down from her face and bound them with an old piece of rope. And then he led her away from her aunt, away from the hayloft—and away from the last part of Sam Bellamy she had.

The villagers parted to let them pass. Staring woodenly ahead, her eyes dead and lifeless, Maria followed him down the stairs, past the row of curious horses and out to the sleigh that waited to take her to the gaol.

Chapter 7

*Thou hadst a voice whose sound was like
the sea,
Pure as the naked heavens, majestic, free.*

WORDSWORTH

If Maria did not languish during her two-month stay in the
gaol, perhaps it was because she didn't actually spend
much time there.

She was as wild as the wind, the villagers said, for the Sea
Witch was more apt to be found wandering the sand cliffs
overlooking the ocean than in her little cell. It wasn't as though
she was treated badly, or that life there was unbearable, for
her aunt brought her good things to eat and plenty of blankets
to keep her warm. What Maria *did* find unbearable was the
thought that Sam might return while she was confined and
that she would not be there to greet him. Desperate and determined to free herself, it didn't take her long to discover
that the key to freedom had been hers all along.

Feminine wiles, Thankful had once said. *Use them to get
what you want.*

And she *did* use them, shyly at first, then with bold confidence when it became apparent that all she had to do was
plead and sob and turn helpless eyes on her gaolers and they'd
swing the great, creaky door open wide to let her out. She
wasted no time racing up to the Great Beach, where she would
walk the wild dunes and strain her eyes for the sight of a sail.
Her faith that Sam *would* return never wavered, even when
ships bound from southern climes put in at Billingsgate and
brought word that the young Englishman had abandoned treasure hunting and turned to piracy, instead. The news shocked
her at first, but she didn't despair. Not that she would ever

marry a pirate, of course, but surely she could set him back on the path of righteousness in no time; after all, he *had* said he loved her, hadn't he? She could change him; she was sure of it.

In March, Justice Doane, who, like everyone else, didn't know what drew Maria to those windswept sea cliffs and didn't *want* to know, finally grew so tired of finding the gaol door open, listening to his men's lame excuses, and trudging up to the Great Beach to drag her back that he finally opened the door himself and left it open for good. And about that time, when winter still hung on by its fingertips, far, far away—where snow didn't pile upon the rooftops and cold winds didn't set the teeth to chattering—Captain Samuel Bellamy turned the prow of his ship north, toward Cape Cod.

Springtime was knocking on winter's back door, eager to be about its business as that ship nosed its way up the coast, past the capes of Virginia, past New York, and finally, toward the dangerous shoal waters huddled protectively around Cape Cod. But the vessel in whose cabin Sam reclined was not *Lilith*. The decks above his head were not those of a little sloop but those of a great three-masted ship, dressed out in war clothes and groaning beneath the weight of twenty-eight loaded, hungry guns. And though the holds of that ship were nigh to bursting with Spanish silver, gold, and all other manner of glittering treasure that would've made a beggar—let alone a *princess*—weep, the riches hadn't come from the sunken stashes of a fleet of Spanish galleons but from the holds of ships that had been very much afloat—English, French, Dutch, and Spanish.

For Captain Samuel Bellamy—ex-privateer, Royal Navy deserter, adventurer, and now self-proclaimed enemy of mankind—had become a pirate.

It hadn't taken him many days of backbreaking, fruitless work to convince him that the riches of the sunken treasure wrecks were naught but a dream. The Spanish had beaten him to them, and so had the governments of Bermuda and Jamaica, crowds of enterprising treasure hunters, and a horde of pirates thicker than flies around a dead carcass. But the idea of going back to Eastham empty-handed had been unthinkable. So when the leader of that prowling pack of sea wolves, one Benjamin Hornigold, recognized a kindred spirit

in Sam and offered to take him—and the all-too-eager Paul
Williams—into his pirate crew, Sam had given up *Lilith* to the
sea and, over a Bible and an axe, signed the articles of the
Brethren, the Brethren of the Black Flag.

Old Ben Hornigold had thought himself pretty damned
clever for recruiting Sam Bellamy into his pirate crew, for in
his young protégé he'd recognized an abundance of those talents that make a good pirate a great one: sea savvy, reck-
lessness that knew no bounds, and a growing disregard, nay
hatred, for anything governmental. But what he hadn't recognized, or had perhaps misinterpreted, was Sam's natural
charisma and leadership abilities, a mistake he paid for dearly
two months later when his own crew booted him out and put
the outspoken young West Countryman in his place.

And so it had happened that Hornigold sailed away with a
small band of loyal men and Sam Bellamy found himself in
command of a tight little sloop named *Mary Anne* and a
hungry pack of rowdy, hard-drinking sea tars clamoring for
silver, gold—and always, a fight.

And as his new ship, *Whydah*, drove onwards toward Cape
Cod, Sam smiled up into the gloom of the cabin, watching
the mist and fog swirling around the skylight and making the
room almost as dark as night.

Maria.

In a matter of hours, Cape Cod's bleak shoreline would
hove into view above the horizon. In a matter of hours *she*
would be in his arms, her honey-sweet lips clinging to his
with the passion of a year denied, her silken thighs wrapping
themselves about his hips as he took her with him to the very
ends of pleasure. . . .

Just a few more hours, after a whole bloody year. . . .

Lying on his bunk, he crossed his arms behind his head
and felt a nervous little flutter in what he proudly considered
his very black heart. Was it excitement? Trepidation? What
if she wouldn't have him? What if she'd found someone else?
The idea that she might reject him because of his recent,
infamous acts against honest seafaring folk never entered his
mind, for as far as he was concerned his actions were perfectly justified. After all, if there were those who could afford
big ships and wealthy cargoes, well then, they could afford
to lose them, too. Let the wealth be spread around a bit,

right? Robin Hood style. He grinned, idly stroking a handsome chin that was now buried beneath a black, well-trimmed beard. But his grin hardened somewhat as he considered the *real* reason he embraced piracy with such ardor. He'd always been a recalcitrant, a trait that had earned him a brutal flogging that should've killed him—and nearly did—during his service with the Royal Navy. Piracy provided the means to vent his revenge upon a system that hadn't tolerated his disobedience to authority, a system that protected the rich and the privileged, and damn well got what it deserved from those who were neither.

He forced such dark thoughts from his mind. Excitement at seeing Maria again brought the softness back to his hard smile, and as he thought of the wonderful treasure stored belowdecks, he dreamed of just how it would be.

Whydah, plunging onward through the seas, the ocean parting beneath her graceful bow, foaming about her beakhead, sweeping over her elegant teak decks . . . *Whydah,* bursting free of the mists and bearing down on Cape Cod in all of her majestic splendor, wind bellying every taut, bulging sail, every gun run out in brazen challenge . . . And he, Sam Bellamy, no longer just a no-account seaman, but a prince— a free prince, as his men called him—in command upon the quarterdeck, his clothes as fine as any London lord's, the devil himself the only entity that didn't fear and respect him. And Maria . . . How her eyes would light up when he took her hand and led her aboard this wonderful ship of fairy-tale stuff, how she'd squeal with excitement when she saw the great sacks of Spanish reales, the chests of gold doubloons, the chunks of emeralds, the diamonds that were so brilliant that when the sun caught them it was hard to look at them. Indigo, ivory, beautiful silks, satins, cloths. They were all there, safely tucked away somewhere beneath him, enough riches and splendor to buy . . . a princess.

And soften a shrewish aunt.

How that wizened old witch would react when he boldly brought *Whydah* straight into Billingsgate—or better yet, Provincetown Harbor—and set the town on its ear was a vision worth every bit of treasure stored below, and then some. His mouth quirked in a smile and he chuckled, his deep laughter soft and self-contained. The aunt aside, just imagine setting close to two hundred pirates loose among those bloody Puritans. . . .

He thought back upon the past year. Of the plundering, the hell-raising, the blasphemies and curses that had followed him throughout the Caribbean like the wake of his proud galley. Of giving the old *Mary Anne* to Paul Williams when he'd moved on to bigger ships, better ships, including the one he sailed now.

Ah, Whydah. . . . Absently, he fingered the coin that hung suspended from a chain of beaten gold around his neck and now lay atop the relaxed muscles of his chest. *Whydah,* with her majestic spread of sail and tall masts that scraped the very clouds. *Whydah,* with her carved, proud figurehead— the bird of paradise—dipping toward the foamy seas with every plunge of her long, graceful bowsprit. *Whydah* . . . by God, how he'd wanted her, vowed to have her when she'd shown up in the salt-smeared field of his glass as they'd skimmed through the Windward Passage. For three days he'd chased her, shouting encouragement to his just-as-eager crew until his throat had gone raw and even mugs of spiced rum could no longer soothe it. And on that third day, when her captain had struck her colors to his Jolly Roger after firing a halfhearted shot from her chasers that had deterred the pirates about as much as a minnow might a shark, Sam had been so elated at getting *Whydah* intact and unharmed that he'd rewarded the man with the pick of the cargo, a ship, and enough sterling to see him back home to England.

Aye, he was a rogue all right, and now a damned good outlaw as well, but never let it be said that he, Sam Bellamy, was not a generous man.

But this afternoon he was a weary one, for he'd spent the better part of last night tossing and turning beneath the warm blanket that Maria had made for him so long ago, and the remainder of it adding another prize ship to his growing collection. But God's teeth, had he really expected to find sleep when the following day would bring his long-awaited reunion with Maria? Images of her hair, as bright and glittering as the chains of gold he'd soon drape her graceful neck with, had taunted him. Her gold-dusted lashes, the innocent, sea-green pools beneath them that he could very well drown in.

Curves as lush as a rain forest, ardor as hot as a tropical afternoon—ah, they were all waiting for him.

Just a few more hours. . . .

Somewhere around six bells of the mid-watch, thanks to the help of a bottle of dark Jamaican rum he'd relieved his last prize of, he'd finally fallen into a brief, restless slumber that had managed to last until the crack of dawn, when cries from the masthead announcing a prize had jarred him rudely awake. But Sam, tired and short-tempered, hadn't shared his crew's eagerness to take the little pink, a type of vessel with a fat, stubby hull and a rounded stern, especially when he learned that its cargo consisted solely and simply of that one commodity valued almost (but not quite, mind you) as much as the Spanish silver that made every good pirate's mouth water—tipple.

But his rambunctious young wildies had no headaches knocking on their skulls from overindulgence and lack of sleep, no lovely lasses awaiting them in Eastham, and no reason this side of hell not to add another ship with a fat cargo of Madeira wine to their little fleet even if she was just a leaky old pink. As all decisions were made aboard pirate ships, a vote had been taken—and so had the wine pink.

A bothersome move, Sam thought, although at any other time he would've enjoyed a ship full of tipple as much as the next man, if not more so. In fact, if it wasn't for the Madeira he wouldn't have thought twice about scuttling the wine pink and sending her to the bottom where her grave was already waiting, for she was so damned leaky that she now lagged astern of them by a good mile. 'Twas a damned pity they hadn't been able to get the cargo out of her. But the pipes of Madeira had been packed in tighter than fleas on a beagle, and her crew had thoughtlessly prevented anyone from bringing them out by leaving the anchor cable coiled over the hatch. Unwilling to waste time over it, and eager to get to Eastham, Sam had put a prize crew aboard her with orders ringing in their ears to follow in the wake of *Whydah* and *Anne*, a Scottish-built snow he'd taken a fancy to somewhere off the capes of Virginia, and hoisted sail once more.

Aggravations. And if that wasn't enough to put him into one of the moods that had helped earn him his sobriquet of Black Sam, there was the additional bother of the pink's captain, one Andrew Crumpstey, who'd been stupid enough to insult Sam's quartermaster and was now paying for it by spending a very unhappy tenure chained out of harm's way below until Sam could decide just what the devil to do with him. And to top it all off, there were the additional headaches—seven of them, to be exact—in the form of the pirates he'd put as a prize crew aboard the wine pink. No doubt they'd broken into her cargo before her topsails had even filled; no doubt, they'd be so damned far into their cups by the time night fell he'd be lucky to ever see them again. And with a storm grumbling on the eastern horizon, that was just the sort of aggravation he didn't need.

Headaches. For now, he'd just forget them. For now, he'd just pull this blanket with its pattern of the northern sky's constellations up over his bare chest, close his eyes, and steal a few minutes of rest. For now—

The door banged open. ''Cap'n?''

He sighed, opening his eyes to stare up at the deck beams above. ''What is it, damn you?''

''Mr. Davis 'as spotted a sloop bearin' down on us from the south'rd, sir. Prob'ly ain't seen us yet.'' The pirate, a meddlesome lad named Stripes, cleared his throat as his captain turned his aching head upon the pillow and regarded him with a half-opened, impatient eye. Behind him stood Peter Madigan, a sad-eyed orphan with a broken grin and a nose covered with stray freckles. ''Crew's clamorin' to come about, sir, an' sneak up on 'er before she can turn tail an' run.''

Christ. Sam swung his long legs off the bunk. Obviously, he was not going to get any rest this afternoon.

''Shall we give chase then, Cap'n?''

''Has it been voted upon?''

''The crew's waitin' fer yers, sir.''

''Fine. I shall be up momentarily.''

Stripes nodded, made a hasty exit with Madigan and left Sam to his headache, his black mood, and the aggravation that came with being the leader of two hundred sea tars who were as unruly and quarrelsome as a pack of terriers thrown into the same pit. He went to the stern window and leaned against the long barrel of one of the four-pounders there. The gun now sat quietly in its red carriage, having earned its keep as a chaser many times over. But there was nothing to see in the foggy mists swirling beyond the salt-smeared windows; nothing but his own thoughts, his fears, and yes, his worries about what he'd find when he got to Eastham.

With a heavy, resigned sigh, Black Sam Bellamy, pirate captain, slung a brace of pistols around his neck, retrieved his cutlass, and made his way to where his men awaited him on the quarterdeck.

Small, sturdy, and well built, the sloop *Fisher* boasted many leagues beneath her keel and a suit of sails that were all but lost in the thick clouds of fog wrapped about her lonely mast. Sea-wise and salt-eaten, she wasn't much to look at and didn't carry a fabulously wealthy cargo, yet the majestic galley that had slid like a ghost out of the mists just south of Cape Cod had a very obvious interest in her.

Her master, one Robert Ingols, stood nervously upon her bleached quarterdeck, one hand wrapped around a tarry shroud, the other sweating so badly he had to use the skirts of his fine new coat as a towel. His normally stoic face was now a study in apprehension. That apprehension peaked as a flag slithered up the galley's mainmast to join the proud English colors already there. And for every foot that banner gained his heart sank one, until nothing thrived within his chest but cold, raw fear—for staring him down from that black banner's field of death was a grinning white skull atop a pair of crossed bones.

The Jolly Roger.

"Guess you're right, sir," said Ralph Merry, beside him. The fear that shook the seaman's voice was reflected in the chalk-white pallor of his face. "Pirates. They say Black Bellamy's been seen in these waters lately." Ralph craned his skinny neck, trying to see through the last tendrils of mist. "Shall we strike our colors, sir?"

"Unless we want to be blown from here to Hell, I'd say that's a very wise decision," Ingols muttered, sliding a finger beneath his sweat-drenched, suddenly-too-tight stock. "We haven't a prayer of outsailing them. Their ports are open, and—Jesus! How many guns do they *have* on that thing?"

Ralph peered through the fog at the oncoming galley.

"Good God!" he exclaimed with a low whistle as he made a hasty visual count. "Twenty-eight? Thirty, perhaps? And look, they've mounted swivel guns, too. The ship's a damned arsenal!"

" 'Tis a wonder she's still afloat with all of that cannon. Yes, get the colors down and be quick about it. No telling what these devils'll do if we resist them." Ingols stole a glance at the patches of sky now visible through the lingering clots of fog. A thick bank of clouds sat on the horizon to the east and overhead; several gulls were winging their way toward shore. "Just what we need, a damned storm to complicate matters," he muttered, half to himself. "Yes, we'll give them what they want, and if we're lucky, damned lucky, maybe we'll be able to make port before it hits."

Ingols nervously tapped his foot upon *Fisher's* rolling deck as the galley slid closer, her pennants and topsails lost in mist, her sleek hull glistening with spray, her billowing sails majestic and proud. She was a graceful, soaring hawk, a predator—beautiful, free—and just as deadly.

And now she was so close that he could hear the shouts of her crew, the rumble of cannon being rolled into yawning gun ports, and the chilling sound of the pirate musicians' band as they beat upon drums and sounded trumpets in an act meant to intimidate him into surrender. But he needed no encouragement. The sight of that bristling warship alone was enough to make him quail in his boots.

And now, sliding out of the tail of the fog bank were the distinctive shapes of two more ships following in her wake.

Heavens, did these pirates have a cursed navy behind them?

"For God's sake, get that flag down now!" he barked.

Fisher's colors sank slowly in defeat. Men worked furiously to furl her sails. The sloop lost headway, stalled, then lay rocking in the choppy seas. Helplessly, Ingols watched the pirate ship drink up the distance between them, the curl of water and sheets of spray at her bow falling abruptly off as she shortened sail and hove to.

And now the sounds coming from her made his blood run cold. Random pistol shots, raucous laughter, a gleeful curse. And then, the clipped voice of an Englishman, ringing out in unquestionable authority across the water.

"Greetings, lads! We are of the sea! Where are ye from, and where are ye bound?"

Ingols searched for the speaker, his eyes sweeping the horde of rowdy, feral young men milling at the pirate ship's rail. And then he saw him.

He stood atop a cannon with a foot propped casually against the gunwale, but the restless rock of the ship appeared not to bother him in the least. Tall and handsomely made, he seemed too well dressed to be a pirate, for his coat of wine-colored velvet was lavishly decorated with gold braid, a generous array of brass buttons trailed down its open front, and its skirts, stiffened with buckram, flared fashionably out at the waist. But while he might have resembled a blooded aristocrat, no pompous nobleman in London looked, as this man did, like the devil incarnate.

A thick, magnificent mane of windblown black hair fell devilishly unkempt and wild to wide, powerful shoulders. An ebony beard with mustache to match framed a gleaming smile that was all direct contrast to the darkness of his hair, his skin, his eyes. And those eyes! Keen and bold and black, yet shining with a clever, calculating light, a glimmer of some barely-hinted-at knowledge, a flicker of arrogant self-confidence that was echoed in his proud stance, the hint of a smile, the casual way in which he held that wicked-looking cutlass.

Ingols knew it was the legendary Black Sam Bellamy, knew it even before the current swung the pirate ship's stern toward him and the name across her counter confirmed it—*Whydah*.

"Lord help us," he prayed, but was not granted the opportunity to study the man further.

"God's blood, I asked you your port and destination! Answer me, damn you, or pay for your insolence with your life!"

Ingols's voice sounded pitifully feeble compared to the pirate's commanding tone. "I am Robert Ingols, sir, and the sloop is *Fisher*, out of Virginia and bound for Boston. Our cargo is naught but tobacco and a shipment of hides—nothing of great value."

"I'll be the judge of that. Are ye her master, then?"

"Aye, that I am."

The pirate captain leaned forward, propped an elbow upon his bent knee, and thoughtfully kneaded his bearded chin.

His black eyes grew speculative, cunning even. "For Boston, ye say? Why, I'll bet ye've sailed these very waters more times than ye can count."

"Aye, that I have," Ingols said slowly, wondering what the pirate was leading up to—and unknowingly digging his own grave, though it would be hours before that fact became apparent. Clearing his throat, he wiped the sweat from his brow and gathered his courage. "Look, if you want our cargo, take it. I don't mean to offend you of course, but I really haven't the time for small talk. There's a storm coming on, and I'd like to reach safer waters than these before it's upon us."

One of the pirate's black brows rose haughtily. "Let me clarify something for you, Captain Ingols. Whether you do or don't have the time for talk is no longer your concern, but mine. I too would like to reach a safe harbor. And speaking of *small talk,* aye, why *don't* we talk about the weather, which, as we both know, is about to turn bad!"

Ralph Merry leaned close to Ingols's ear. "I wouldn't anger him if I were you, sir," he advised. "I, for one, would like to live to see tomorrow."

"Quiet," Ingols said in a strangled voice.

The pirate captain ignored their exchange, idly studying the blade of his cutlass in a manner that was meant to heighten Ingols's fear. He looked up and smiled innocuously. "Besides, it's not your damned cargo I want, but your sloop. That, and your help in guiding my fleet through these shoal waters and into Provincetown Harbor." He glanced down at his cutlass, then lifted his black gaze once more to study Ingols in a most disconcerting way. "Shouldn't be too difficult, should it, lad? Do that, and do it to my satisfaction, and perhaps I'll even give ye your sloop back."

"Is that all he wants?" Ralph whispered eagerly. "For you to lead him and his fleet up the coast? Tell him yes, Cap'n! For God's sake, *please!*"

Ingols offered a wary smile to the pirate. The smile was returned. Obviously, the Black Bellamy had him right where he wanted him and knew it. With an apprehensive glance at the distant cloud bank Ingols took a deep, steadying breath. "I suppose I have no choice but to comply, do I?"

"Not unless you'd rather be dinner for the sharks lurking

beneath your keel,'' the pirate returned, his words belying his bland smile.

"Yes, yes, of course I wouldn't *think* of refusing,'' Ingols sputtered. "Indeed, sir, I'd be honored to assist you in any way that I can.''

"A wise decision, lad.'' The corners of those black eyes crinkled in good humor. "Hoist out your longboat, Ingols, and come across before the seas get any rougher. Perhaps you and your mate would like to join me for a bit of tipple while we discuss the situation.''

It was not a question but a command. A rogue, an outlaw, a *pirate,* with the manners of a nobleman. And the arrogance, too.

Ingols yelled for his longboat to be prepared, but his men, terrified of Bellamy and his bristling, belligerent mob, were already at the task. Swallowing hard, he looked back toward the *Whydah,* where the pirate captain—nay, the pirate prince, he corrected himself, for that was just what this man appeared to be—had leaped down from his cannon throne and was striding through his pack of outlaws like a ruler among his subjects. A glimpse of his retreating back, the colorful flash of his pleated coat, and then he was gone, leaving only a crowd of unruly, unkempt ruffians in his wake.

With a sense of doom, Ingols turned, climbed over the gunwale, and descended the Jacob's ladder to where the longboat awaited him in the restless waters below.

By the time he stepped onto *Whydah's* glistening teak decks Ingols's entire shirt was drenched with sweat. He was greeted by a pirate in a ragged shirt and blue-and-white-striped cotton trousers, who dropped from the shrouds and thrust a wine bottle in his face. Mischief danced in the pirate's brown eyes, his closely shorn hair was the color of chocolate, and his sun-toasted face was young and not unhandsome. "No need fer ye t' look so scared,'' the pirate said, taking back his bottle when Ingols declined it. "The cap'n's a man of 'is word. He'll give ye yer ship back if ye do 'is bidding.''

Reluctantly leaving his mate on deck, Ingols followed his guide through the mob of men who reeked belligerence as surely as they did the combined fumes of wine and rum. The

pirate, chattering nonstop, informed him that his name was
Stripes, leaving Ingols to wonder whether he took that odd
moniker from the striped breeches he wore or from possible,
if not probable, scars upon his back. Wisely, he decided not
to ask.

They made their way across decks that were surprisingly
neat given the fact that *Whydah* was a pirate ship, Stripes
guzzling his wine and Ingols's shirt pasting itself with cold
sweat to his back. He was on his way to share a drink with
the infamous Black Sam Bellamy, and whether he would exit
the pirate's cabin in the same state that he would enter it—
alive—only the gods and Black Sam himself knew. Trying to
muster his courage, Ingols commented on the galley's tidy
decks and clean lines.

"Aye, this 'ere *Whydah* ain't nothin' t' trifle with," the
pirate warned, wagging a finger in Ingols's face. "Ye can see
why Black Sam wanted 'er. Laid those black eyes of 'is on
'er an' swore by every god in the Good Book that 'e was
going t' have her if he had t' fight the very devil 'imself t'
do it." He leaned close, washing Ingols in a bath of rum
fumes. "An' ye know somethin'? If Satan had dared take up
'is own sword I do believe our Sam would've run 'im through
an' tossed 'im t' the sharks!"

Ingols had no doubt about that.

Outside the door his escort turned. "Now, don't ye be
goin' and doin' anythin' t' make Black Sam mad, ye hear?
He ain't been in a good mood lately."

Ingols gulped.

"Well, here we go, int' the lion's den!"

Black Sam was seated at a knife-scarred desk, a quill pen
in one hand, a half-empty bottle of wine at his other. Above
his head a lantern swung with the roll of the ship, casting a
warm glow upon his dark hair and throwing eerie shadows
across the papers on which he wrote. Even seated, he was no
less intimidating than he'd been standing on deck. And though
his wind-tousled, magnificent black mane had been loosely
queued at the nape with a bit of black ribbon, on such a
redoubtable man the effort seemed a hopeless attempt at re-
finement.

"Ingols, lad! Make yourself comfortable." He tossed the
pen aside, slid the bottle across the table, and leaning back,

crossed his arms behind his head. "We took a ship full of Madeira just hours ago, and I couldn't resist a small sample. Here, have some."

The "small sample" consisted of two empty bottles and another that was more than half finished.

Ingols eyed the bottle uncertainly. "Uh, no thank you," he said, wondering if the pirate might have poisoned it.

"Very well then." Uncoiling himself from his chair, Sam rose and crossed the room, the top of his head almost scraping the deck beams above. Ingols glanced at the pirate's feet, hoping to find part of that commanding height donated by a pair of silver-buckled shoes with the high, blocky heels that were so popular among seamen. He was sadly disappointed. Black Sam's feet were tanned, well-formed, and bare. And before he could ponder such an odd mix of polish and barbarity, his host returned with a Queen Anne–style tea server complete with an ebony handle and a spout fashioned in the shape of a dragon's head. The beauty of the object caused Ingols to let out his breath in admiration.

But Black Sam was obviously accustomed to entertaining prisoners, for he seemed very much the gracious host as he poured tea into one of two pewter mugs, and the remainder of the wine into the other. He slid the first across the table to Ingols. "Here ye go, lad. To our health, eh?" He quaffed the wine with a flourish and noted Ingols's chalky features. "So, I suppose Stripes must've filled you in on what a villain I am?"

"On the contrary, sir. He had nothing but praise for you."

"Oh?" Black Sam's smile seemed a bit rueful. "Well now, that's rather odd . . . not like the lad at all." He pulled out his chair, settled his lean frame into it, and propped his bare feet upon the table, much to the shock of his guest. "Did he talk your ear off, then?"

"Aye, sir, that he did."

" 'Tis more like him. I'll warn you to watch what you say around him. He's a harmless wretch, but his tongue's looser than a New Providence whore. Why, I've lost count of how many times my poor quartermaster has had to settle disputes caused by that man and his gossipy ways. By the gods, he's worse than an old woman."

Ingols frowned in confusion. Topside, Black Sam had been

arrogant, haughty even. But here in the privacy of his cabin he seemed amiable, perhaps even pleasant. Ingols wondered if the arrogance he'd displayed earlier was for the benefit of his crew.

"How's the tea?"

Ingols set the mug down. "Very good, sir."

"How about a spot of rum in it?" He grinned. " 'Twill cover the taste of the poison, ye know."

Ingols glanced up in surprise. Could Black Sam read minds, too? He stared for a moment at his host. He hadn't thought that humor could sparkle in such black eyes, but it did. "Thank you, but I must decline," he said, rather sheepishly. "As loathe as I am to admit it, spirits don't sit well in my stomach during rough seas. I'd be of little help to you if I were lying abed seasick."

Sam's teeth flashed white against the darkness of his beard. "As you wish, then." Absently, he studied his own mug for a moment, drained it as if to prove he had no such weaknesses, then slammed it down upon the table. Unexpectedly, he rose to his feet once more and stormed across the cabin, and Ingols realized that he was a man who was quite adept at hiding his moods when the need suited him. Unlike others, who might've entertained a guest with no small degree of distraction if their minds had been elsewhere, Black Sam had quite skillfully led him to believe that his full attention had centered upon his prisoner's comfort. Now, it was all too obvious that it had not been.

He shrank in his chair as the pirate flung open the door to bellow up into the crowd of men on deck. "Damn ye for a pack of irresponsible whelps! Where the hell are Julian and Lambeth? Do they think I have all day to sit around and wait for them?"

So far, Stripes was right about one thing. His captain's moods were as unpredictable as Cape Cod weather and just as inclement.

Ingols said nothing, trying to maintain his courage as Black Sam stalked back across the cabin and flung himself into his chair once more. But his anger seemed to have spent itself like a bluster of wind and now he seemed only weary, or perhaps at the end of his probably limited patience, as he leaned his forehead into his hands and kneaded his temples with thumbs and fingertips. "A damned nuisance, those two," he said, then looked up at Ingols as though such was the bane of every ship's master. "I tell ye, I must've been daft in the head to hire them on as pilots. One an eternal drunk, the other an Indian barely out of diaper clothes." He lifted his gaze to stare out through stern windows that were caked with rivers of dried salt. "Said he knew this coast well though, grew up on Cape Cod and knew it like the back of his hand. Hah! *That* remains to be seen. He has yet to show me he knows the coast of Cape Cod *from* the back of his hand!"

"So that is why you wish me to pilot for you."

"Aye." Sighing, Sam tipped his chair back and shot Ingols a weary, hopeless look. "The abilities of those two are questionable in fair weather, let alone in a stormy night with a lee shore off our larboard bows. I'll be damned if I take any chances with my ship or the lives of my crew."

Like a restless panther he rose, began to pace the cabin, and finally ended up leaning against one of the big guns that stood leashed to the bulkhead. Hazy light shone through the stern windows, gleaming dully off the scrollwork of their iron barrels. Black Sam's cabin, Ingols noted, was not a room designed for comfort, but for war: just a scarred table, chairs and desk, a bunk covered with a beautiful blanket that seemed oddly out of place in this warlike setting, a cutlass hanging on a peg in the wall and dominating the room, the two stern chasers that looked ready and willing to do business.

Black Sam reached out and ran a palm over the iron barrel of the one on which he leaned, almost lovingly, Ingols thought. "Since our friend Stripes deems himself such a font of information today, did he think to tell you just how generous I can be when someone pleases me?"

"No sir, I'm afraid he did not. But you did say you'd grant me my freedom if I guided you into Provincetown Harbor. . . ."

"And so I shall. Do you doubt my word, Ingols, because I'm a pirate?" He grinned as Ingols averted his eyes. "And here I'd hoped you might find our life far more . . . shall I say, *rewarding,* than that of a simple merchant captain's."

Ingols didn't miss the shrewdness behind those black eyes. "Are you forcing me to join your crew, then?"

"*Force* you? Don't be vain, lad, it doesn't suit you. We don't force anyone. We simply give them a taste of what they might have if they sail with us, and most are quite willing to sign the Articles."

"I—I'm not sure I would find the calling to my liking," Ingols said nervously.

"Ah, but I think you would. In truth, Ingols, piracy has other rewards besides wealth and a life of ease. Those things are rather material, when one considers the true scope of it." He crossed his arms at his chest. "The laws of no country govern us; the only rules we follow are our own. We pledge loyalty to no nation save ourselves. And if you doubt my word, ask any member of my crew from whence he hails. He won't tell you England, Ireland, or even Scotland. D'ye know what he'll say?"

Ingols shook his head.

"He'll tell you, 'From the sea'! For *her* laws are the only ones we heed. No more serving aboard His Majesty's ships, where you're rewarded with naught but a crowded, stinking berth, little pay, and the sting of the lash for the smallest misdemeanor. No more tyrannical captains who are dictators, not leaders of men. No more serving anyone but ourselves! Our mistress is the sea, our master naught but our own wants and desires. Do ye think I really give a damn about the riches, the treasure stored below? Bah, there's more to this calling than that!"

Ingols met the pirate captain's defiant black eyes. "And that is?"

"Freedom!" Sam declared, beginning to pace once more. "And I, lad, am its most faithful advocate!" He hefted a bottle of Madeira and took his cutlass down from the wall. "Now then, let us get down to business." Ingols felt his hackles rise as he eyed that wicked length of steel. A wicked light sparked in Black Sam's eye as he raised his hand, the cutlass catching the lanternlight and spilling it, as he sent it slashing down—

Ingols's strangled scream pierced the room. His eyes shot open in time to see the neck of the wine bottle flying through the air as Black Sam lopped it off with easy skill. It banged upon the deck, rolled crookedly, and disappeared beneath the carriage of one of the guns. Laughing, the pirate captain replaced the cutlass on its peg with lordly nonchalance.

"A real devil, aren't I?" he declared, still chuckling at Ingols's reaction. "Gets them every time."

Ingols sat back and shut his eyes.

Serious once more, Sam shoved a yellowed chart beneath Ingols's nose. "Here ye go, lad," he said casually. "I know you're familiar with these waters, but I'd rather you study this chart anyhow. And study it well, mind ye. Any mishaps and I'll be practicing on *your* neck next time instead of a wine bottle."

And with that he rose to his feet, swept up the bottle, and headed toward the door. There he turned and bestowed an innocuous smile upon Ingols that didn't fool him a bit. "And when you've memorized that chart, then please join me abovedecks. I'll be at the helm. That, my lad"—the smile deepened—"is an *order.*"

Chapter 8

*Where beyond the extreme sea-wall, and
between the remote sea-gates,
Waste water washes, and tall ships founder,
and deep death waits.*

SWINBURNE

Ingols did indeed study the chart, although he was more than familiar with the shoals huddled around outer Cape Cod—and their breakers that could smash a ship to bits should she venture too close. He waited a long moment to be sure the pirate captain was really gone and then, with a treachery in his eyes he could never have hidden from the astute gaze of the Black Bellamy, shoved the chart away from him. He had no need to study it further. For Ingols, law-abiding 'til the end and determined not only to save Provincetown from the ravages of the pirates but, if need be, to die a martyr's death, had already plotted *Whydah's* course—straight toward the harborless shoreline of Cape Cod's great Outer Beach. And if the storm came on as it appeared it would, by the time the pirates realized his betrayal it would be too late. . . .

Topside, *Whydah's* bell tolled mournfully as the watch ended. Off the larboard bow the distant, thin line that was Cape Cod appeared, vanished beneath a large swell, reappeared. To the east, massive black thunderheads began to thrust themselves over the horizon.

And as darkness fell and the rising wind whipped up the sea and pulled streaks of foam from the breaking waves, a figure stood silently at the helm, his dark eyes filled with excitement and anticipation as far ahead of him *Whydah's* bowsprit, a long, dark silhouette spearing the night, rose and fell, rose and fell. . . .

Sam Bellamy wasn't worried about the storm. He wasn't worried about anything. For in several more hours, he'd be with Maria.

Nightfall brought the storm on in full force.

They heard it coming when it was still a good ten miles away, the low rumble of thunder rolling across the water, the distant, eerie flickers of lightning upon the horizon; and then an unholy, deafening roar as rain exploded out of the sky, instantly darkening the sails and ricocheting off the monstrous black barrels of the guns like grapeshot.

At the helm, Sam, Ingols, and the pilot Lambeth stood shivering as the seas rose and *Whydah* kicked up her heels like a skittish filly, making it nearly impossible to keep their footing on decks that were already awash with frozen spume and seawater. The wind gathered force, snapping the masthead pennants this way and that until they barked like gunfire over the howl of wind and rain. The night grew blacker than pitch, snuffed out the lights of the three ships in their wake and scattered them to the darkness. A lantern swung madly in *Whydah's* shrouds, another at her stern, but neither they, nor the red glow of the binnacle, could pierce the darkness of the stormy night.

But *Whydah's* nervous crew needed no light to see the black, angry ocean thrashing and boiling around and beneath them. The storm rose in intensity, screaming its lungs out and raising the waves until they clawed at the mainyard. Wind ripped the foam from the toppling crests, drove it against raw cheeks and into eyes that were already blinded with salt, sleet, and driving rain. Coats grew heavy and sodden, froze on cold-numbed bodies. Hands became reddened and raw. Ice formed in brows, whiskers, and hair.

Coffee in hand, Sam stood knee-deep in the frigid black seawater that surged over the decks with every dip and plunge of the ship, cursing the storm, cursing the gods, and now cursing his crew's incompetence. His discerning eye spotted a cannon that hadn't been properly lashed down and seawater surging in great foamy floods through an open port. His patience snapped like a strained backstay.

A group of men huddled about the mainmast got the brunt of it. "You there! Have ye nothing better to do than stand around like a flock of bleating sheep? Damn ye, get that gun hauled in and lashed down before it breaks loose and kills someone!"

Beside him, Lambeth fought back his seasickness enough to yell through chattering teeth, "She's fighting me, sir! I'm afraid I can't hold her!"

"Just keep the helm down and make damned sure ye hold her head to the wind!" Sam grabbed madly at a line as *Whydah* took a sudden nosedive, nearly throwing him off his feet and spilling scalding coffee down his coat, his breeches. His mug went flying, and with it, his temper.

"Madigan!"

The freckle-faced lad fought his way across the heaving decks, his shock of red hair standing straight out from his head in the wind. "Cap'n?"

"Where the bloody hell is Julian?"

"Below, sir!"

"For God's sake, think I don't know that? I want him on deck, now! What the hell's he doing down there?"

"The last time I saw him he was in the wardroom!"

"Doing what?"

Whydah bucked madly, throwing Sam to his knees once

more. Salt water flooded his nose and he clawed himself to his feet.

"Uh, teaching knife tricks to one of the black slaves you freed—"

Coughing and sputtering, Sam bellowed, "You tell Mr. Julian that unless he wants me to demonstrate them on *him* he'd best get his carcass up her *now*!"

Lazy pack of wound-licking curs! Sam was about to go looking for the pilot himself when Julian, clutching a rum bottle, melted out of the darkness.

"When I give an order I expect it to be obeyed, is that understood? Take your place at the helm, *Mr.* Julian! And you, Lambeth, cut yourself loose and go seek your berth!" But the pilot couldn't move, for ice had glued his hands to the wheel. Swearing once more, Sam grabbed the bottle from Julian and dumped rum over Lambeth's frozen fingers. The pilot screamed in agony. Shoving him toward Madigan, he yelled, "Take him below and soak his hands in rum 'til they thaw out!"

"Aye, Cap'n!"

He'd rotate the two pilots, swapping them for a turn at the wheel while he sent the other below to rest. But for him there'd be no rest, no shelter, no warm berth—nor bed—'til harbor was reached. The storm, a leftover from a brutal winter, was worsening, and though spindrift and spray drove hard over the rail, biting through his heavy greatcoat, his clothes, his clammy skin, and into his very bones, Sam dared not leave his place at the helm. Too much was at stake. He wasn't about to trust his ship and crew to a drunkard, a half-wild savage, and a man he'd met only hours before. But they were his only hope. *Just get us to Provincetown*, he thought, *and I'll do the rest.*

But Lambeth was too sick to be much help, Julian lacked experience, and Ingols, who was whiter than bleached bones, seemed more skittish than ever. Clawing the streaming, wind-whipped hair from his eyes Sam yelled, "Ye sure ye know where you're going, Ingols?"

"If we hold course we should make harbor by midnight!"

"Well, mind that ye keep a close eye on our bearings! I've no care to make our glorious entrance as just another shipwreck against the Outer Bars!"

"Aye, sir!" Ingols yelled, growing whiter still.

Somewhere out there in the darkness beyond the lee rail lay Cape Cod, with its dangerous shoal waters, its harborless shoreline—and Maria Hallett. Above, Saint Elmo's fire sizzled between main and mizzen and flooded the decks with pulsing, purple light. Thunder exploded around them and the very seas trembled in awe. *Whydah* heeled so far over that her rail was buried in the foaming black water racing past, the tip of her mainyard scraping the monstrous combers that heaved all about them.

Stripes stumbled out of the darkness, pressing a hot tankard of buttered rum into Sam's hand just as a terrible slice of lightning cracked the sky and slammed into the sea a mere hundred feet off the larboard bow. Ingols let out a startled scream. Stripes dove for cover. Julian shut his eyes and cried out in his native tongue. And then the thunder came, blasting out of the heavens with such terrible, awful force that it stunned their senses and smothered their screams. And as that terrible report gave a last mighty boom before fading into the roar of rain and shriek of wind, they heard their captain's voice.

And he was laughing. *Laughing!*

Aghast, they stared at the wild black mane that streamed down his back and framed his grinning face—and into dark eyes now glinting with exhilaration. Black Sam, they concluded, must certainly have gone mad.

"Ye pack of hen-hearted whelps, what ails ye? A bit of lighting, a scrap of thunder? Why, 'tis the gods, drunk on their tipple and having a bit of fun!" Thunder burst from above and he raised his tankard to the sky, shouting now to be heard over the deafening roar. "See, lads? Even they pay tribute to us! 'Tis a damned shame the seas are so rough I can't run out my own guns to return the salute!"

He downed the rum with a flourish and flung the tankard to the raging seas. But he wasn't laughing a moment later when the first indications that something had gone terribly, dreadfully wrong became apparent through the shrieking rage of the storm—a far off, rhythmic boom that was definitely not thunder. His head jerked up in alarm. The hairs on the back of his neck went stiff. And at the exact moment the sound registered in his brain, the wind flung the terrified cry of the maintop lookout down to the wildly pitching decks.

"*Breakers!* Dead ahead off the larboard bow!"

And then the others heard it too, heard it over the scream of wind and sleet, the terrible thunder that shook the very seas beneath them—the sound of giant waves breaking on a hidden sandbar. The storm had driven them too close to shore.

With sudden, awful clarity Sam knew why his prisoner had grown so skittish. "*Ingols!* God damn ye for a traitorous bastard!"

But killing his betrayer came second to saving his ship—for *Whydah* was about to make an entrance that was anything but glorious.

Staggering, slipping, going down into great floods of seawater and heaving himself to his feet, he raced across the decks, shouting himself hoarse as he tried desperately to rally his men. He grabbed a frozen shroud, hanging on for dear life as the deck canted and a giant comber broke over the forecastle, thundered down the deck, and all but drowned him beneath a wall of water so cold that it ripped the breath from his lungs. Choking, coughing, he saw his crew stumbling out of the hold in confusion, then wild-eyed terror as every damned one of them looked to him as though he was a god, as though he, and he alone, could get them out of this.

He would not disappoint them. By God, he wouldn't! Hauling himself to his feet, he bellowed to the heavens, "Ye want a fight? Blast your bloody teeth, 'tis a fight ye'll get! Get those bower anchors out, lads! And damn your hides, *move it,* else we'll all be tippling at Lucifer's table by midnight!"

His thoughts were racing.

Got to get the bowers out.

Got to hold her off.

Get the men moving.

Show no fear.

For God's sake, show no fear, can't let them see I'm as damned scared as they—

"Move, damn you!" he hollered at the top of his voice.

They responded, for his rage was the only thing that penetrated their rum-soaked, fear-clouded brains. Two thousand pounds of cast iron came tumbling from *Whydah's* bows, disappearing into the mountainous black swells, sinking down, down, down into the depths. The giant flukes hit bottom, caught, clawed for a hold in loose sand. *Whydah* swung around to face the storm, straining at her leashes and dipping her bow down toward the very pits of Hell itself. Great pillars of seawater rose up to smash over her bowsprit, her beakhead, her forecastle. She staggered, fought, choking in the seas, no longer able to fling the waters from her bow with her nose tethered so. And now—

Jesus, Sam thought wildly. The anchors weren't holding. Christ, *they weren't holding!*

A ton of iron—and that wall of foam thundering and boiling several hundred feet off their stern was getting closer and closer. . . .

"Captain! Captain, for God's sake help us!"

"She's dragging, sir!"

But he was already yelling himself hoarse. "Cut her loose, lads! Cut cables! Loose the stays'ls, mizzen, and main! We've got to get her back out to sea!"

But he knew, with a helpless sense of fatalism and doom, that there was no room to wear the ship, no room to get her turned around and headed back toward the safety of deep water. He watched cutlasses hacking at frozen hemp, saw the staysails fall, some exploding like gunshots in the hurricane-force winds, others hastily secured by panicky hands. *Whydah* took the wind, trying to crawl forward on the slight bit of canvas her captain had offered, but the storm was too much for her.

Steadily, it drove her backwards. . . .

Sam pounded across the deck, grabbed the wheel and put the helm down hard just as the anchor cables parted and *Whydah* gave a great, shuddering lurch. He never felt the rope go around his waist as Julian lashed him to the wheel, didn't hear the screams, the sobs, the prayers of his men. Every bit of his strength, every fiber of his will drove down his arms, through his fingers, to that icy, shuddering wheel and into the very heart of the ship herself. *Come on, sweetheart, ye can do it,* he crooned, coming about as close to praying as he ever had. *That's it, lass. Just for me. That's the way. . . . Good girl. Easy now . . . easy . . .*

But the beautiful galley never had a chance. The storm

caught her, flung her toward the breakers, and as she swept
stern-first toward impending death, a burst of lightning pur-
pled the sky and silhouetted the long, cliff-backed shoreline
just beyond them.

Fate couldn't be so cruel!

"No! For God's sake, *no-o-o-o-o!*" he roared, smashing
his fist against the useless wheel. But standing white against
the purple, then black sky, they were unmistakable.

The sand cliffs of Eastham.

Spray exploded from the breakers and rained down upon
them. Men shrieked, fell to their knees, screamed and sobbed
like children. And through the gale's hideous roar, the thunder of breaking surf, came their captain's voice as, shaking a
fist at the raging heavens, he bellowed at the top of his lungs:

*"So help me God, I'll see you, Maria, if I have to sail this
damned ship over the blasted dunes themselves!"*

And then they were in the breakers, their roar drowning
out all sound. With a sickening, grinding jolt, *Whydah* struck
the bar.

She hit stern-first, and those who lived through the nightmare would never forget her screams as the sea drove her into
the sand and crushed her very backbone beneath its terrible
fury.

Men clawed their way up canting decks, scrambling over
the gunwales as they tried to escape the thirty-foot waves that
towered over them and swept them away to their deaths. Others clung to spars only to be lost as comber upon comber
roared out of the sea and tore them from their last, precarious
holds on life. Terrified of drowning, those men that remained
began to surge belowdecks, bottlenecking at the hatches,
screaming, cursing, hacking at each other with knives and
cutlasses in their frenzied haste to escape the raging seas.
Others clung pitifully to shrouds that could no longer bear
the weight of the masts as *Whydah* groaned and began to
broach. And then the decks began to tremble and vibrate and
a horrible, unholy roar rose from the very depths of the ship
as cannon, breaking loose from their moorings, thundered on
wheels of death across the decks, crushing men, gutting the
ship, ripping through her supports and timbers and smashing

great holes in her hull before finally plunging into the angry seas.

Abovedecks, the scene was repeated. Tethered to the wheel and choking beneath wall upon wall of bone-freezing seawater, Sam looked up in time to see a six-pounder break loose and charge down the quarterdeck toward—

"Madigan!" he bellowed frantically, but he was too late. Sickened, he turned his head, but not before he saw the lad fall beneath the huge cannon, saw him impaled beneath the muzzle, saw his lifeless body slam into the bulwarks and vanish into the gaping hole where the sea thrashed below.

There was nothing left to do except try to save himself.

Numbed fingers found and tore the dagger from his belt. Over and over his arm slashed down, sawing and chopping at the frozen hemp that bound him to the wheel. The ship canted further yet. *"Give, goddamn you!* For God's sake *give!"* Sam felt excruciating pain as the rope dug into his belly, saw only darkness as a monstrous comber smothered the purple sky and felled him beneath tons of water. He came up coughing and choking, feet slipping on the tilted deck, fingers clawing desperately for a hold. Splinters drove deep beneath his nails. His lungs ached, threatened to explode.

And from high above came the popping, gunshotlike cracks of splintering wood.

He froze, clenching the knife as he stared up at a full hundred feet of wildly teetering mast. The sounds came faster and faster. Stays snapped like thread and writhed snakelike against the purple heavens. Sails were blasted to bits. With exaggerated slowness the mainmast was falling, and dragging a tangle of sails, spars, and rigging down with it.

Frantically, Sam tried to jump clear but the last threads of hemp that bound him to the wheel held fast. His desperate lunge threw him to his knees. A falling block crashed across his back, knocking the wind from his lungs and slamming him facedown into seawater and deck planking. Spars and pieces of frozen hemp rained out of the darkness around him. Gasping, he reached his knees just as the tip of the mizzen yard hit the wheel, smashing it into useless wreckage and sending chunks of wood and ice bursting in a brilliant shower about him. And then pain exploded behind his eyes as something struck him a glancing blow to the side of his head.

He staggered, fell. Nothing now but a humming roar that grew louder and louder. . . . No screams of his dying crew, no mournful tolling of the ship's bell, no thunder. . . . Just lightning spinning around him in a brilliant vortex of light. Numbness. Warmth on his cheek and running down his jaw. . . . With fading realization, he knew it was his own blood.

He sagged against the splintered wheel, defeated. *I'm so sorry, Maria . . . so very . . . very . . . sor—*

The knife dropped from his lifeless hand and was swept away by the sea. The galley shuddered, gasped, and died. And then the great mainsail came drifting down, a funeral shroud to blanket *Whydah's* remains and the body of her fallen captain.

Chapter 9

*Listen: You hear the grating roar
of pebbles which the waves draw back, and
fling,
At their return, up the high strand,
Begin, and cease; and then again begin,
With tremulous cadence slow; and bring
The eternal note of sadness in.*

ARNOLD

It had been a wild night, and sleep, when Maria finally found it, had been disturbed and restless. Rain hammering against her window, lightning flooding the room like daylight, peals of thunder that had sent her bolting straight out of bed. And the wind! She shuddered at the memory. Out there in the awful darkness of the storm it had sounded like human screams. Even Gunner had been nervous, standing three inches from her nose and panting his hot breath upon her face as she'd lain awake watching the lightning flicker beyond her window.

Some time after midnight she'd finally let him up on the bed, telling herself that were she in his place she too would rather sleep on a mattress filled with cornhusks and straw than a braided rug beside a hearth that had gone cold hours before. Her efforts had not been in vain. Gunner had quieted, warmed her feet with his big, heavy body, and at last, she'd fallen asleep.

Now, the storm had passed. Gray morning light crept through windows still speckled with water. Wind gusted around the mud-chinked walls of the hut, flinging rain against the panes and moaning eerily. With a lazy yawn, Gunner crawled off the bed, shook himself, and went to stand by the door.

Maria regarded him with a malevolent eye. It was too cold to crawl out from beneath the warm coverlet, and exhaustion seemed quite content to keep her there. But Gunner, persistent as always, nuzzled the latch and began to whine.

Shivering, she got up and padded across the room to let him out, rubbing the sleep from her itchy eyes with every step of the way. The floor planking was rough and cold beneath her feet, the air damp and raw. She did not look forward to going outside for wood to start the fire.

But Auntie always said that idle hands accomplished nothing, and here she'd slept away the better part of the morning when she could've been working on the blanket that lay sprawled on her loom. Now there was no way she could finish it by this afternoon, and she would just have to wait for the cornmeal, flour, eggs, and ham she'd planned to trade it for. And wasn't Mr. Harding, her nearest neighbor, who lived two miles distant, stopping by today for some chokecherry bark medicine for his sore throat? She'd promised she'd have it ready for him.

Sighing, Maria donned a heavy woolen dress, stumbled into her moccasins, found the red woolen cloak her aunt had given her for her last birthday, and pulling its hood over her head, stepped outside.

The wind tore the door out of her hands, forcing her to lean every bit of her weight upon it just to get it closed and latched behind her. "Good heavens," she said, and then turned her gaze—as she did every morning—toward the sea.

No sails upon that misty horizon . . . but yet another ship had come to grief on this vicious coast, and by the looks of it this one, lying smashed and beaten on the sandbar just offshore, had suffered a nasty death indeed. What was left of it was strewn as far down the beach as she could see. Maria leaned back against the door and let out her breath. Poor, poor souls. So then, the screams she'd heard last night hadn't been the wind after all. . . .

Forgetting the wood, she turned and went back inside. The blanket could wait, and so could the chokecherry bark medicine. If anyone had survived that horrible wreck they'd need her assistance more than Mr. Harding did his gargle-juice and she her cornmeal. Filling her arms with several blankets from the chest at the foot of her bed, she hurried back outside.

Only thirty feet of scruffy duneland separated Maria's hut from the ragged edge of the sand cliffs. Here she hesitated, a willowy figure against a sky clogged with clouds, a few strands of golden hair escaping her hood to whip about her wind-flushed face. The villagers. She should have known better. Already, they were down there on the beach, picking over the wreckage like a flock of hungry vultures. These were the same people who had hurled stones at her and driven her out of the parish, the same people whose mistrust of her had led to the death of her little baby. These were the same people who had thrown her into the gaol as if she was a common criminal. And the same people who, learning of her prowess as a medicine woman, were now showing up at her doorstep at night pleading for her to cure their various ills, and hoping all that while that their neighbors wouldn't find out they were seeking the services of the Sea Witch.

The Sea Witch. . . . Maria laughed then, but it was a bitter sound that held no humor. Should any of them glance up at the sand cliffs now and see her standing atop them, the wind molding the clothes to her thin figure, her golden hair brilliant against the scarlet hood of her cloak, they'd think so indeed, wouldn't they? Let them, then. She'd been banished from the South Parish, not her own backyard. Her chin came up in defiance, and resolutely she began to pick her way down the steep slope of sand to the beach below.

The villagers grew silent as she approached, the occasional wary glance sent her way over a toiling shoulder reminding her of a pack of curs guarding their suppers. They worked hurriedly, each man hoping to beat his neighbor to the best pieces of the wreck. Chunks of splintered wood and spars, forlorn bits of rope, tattered rags that had once been proud sails—all were flung with little dignity into carts already piled high with flotsam.

The wind was a freezing blast that nailed the cold to her very bones. Shivering, Maria ignored the villagers and fought her way down the beach. How warm it must be in the tropics, where Sam was. But no. *Don't think about him*, she told herself, *don't ever think about him again.* For rumor had it that he was a pirate now, and after a long year of waiting and unanswered prayers, she'd finally begun to accept what Auntie had insisted all along to be true—that Sam Bellamy was never coming back for her.

Swallowing hard, Maria continued on, the wind that knifed through her clothing as bitter and raw as her heart. Sand stung her face like needles, forcing her to bury it in the blankets every few moments to shield her eyes from the onslaught. Stray rain slashed against her cheeks, spume melted on her lips, and the taste of salt was sharp upon her tongue. She pulled the strings of her hood tight to draw the circle of fur about her face, bent her head, and continued on.

Some distance down the beach she saw Gunner, tail wagging furiously as he sopped up a villager's attentions like a dry sponge. Beside him, two placid, well-fed horses stood in stalwart defiance against the wind, their thick manes and tails streaming forward. They were familiar animals, and she recognized them as belonging to Timothy Hingham, one of the young gaolers who'd been so hopelessly enamored of her during her brief stay in the gaol. And as Tim straightened up and Gunner raced off to explore elsewhere, she saw that he was deep in conversation with Justice Doane and a tall, reed-thin man she knew to be the coroner.

The steady, continuous roar of thundering surf made any thoughts of overhearing their conversation impossible. Would Justice Doane try to apprehend her? Perhaps she ought to walk the other way instead. Maria paused, chewing her bottom lip. But no, she reminded herself. This wild beach was her home, and they would not drive her from it.

She continued on, hating herself for the glances she still cast toward the horizon when the wind let up long enough for her to raise her head. In its turbulent state, the ocean was breathtaking: huge, angry waves racing each other to shore and thundering against the beach. Wind ripping the caps from their crests and driving spindrift and spray before it. Foam mantling the breakers, thick as snow and just as white farther out, dirty and sudsy and churning with pieces of wreckage closer to shore.

But among the broken shells, pebbles, and handfuls of randomly flung kelp that were strewn the length of the beach was the sad evidence of just what the ocean was capable of. Some fifty feet of a mast that had been snapped like a twig, still swathed in sailcloth and knotted with twisted ratlines and rigging. Torn bits of hemp, tatters of what had been someone's clothing. There, a sailor's ditty bag, forlorn and desolate in the sand. A leather shoe, a broken sea chest . . .

She looked away. A group of children played amongst the debris, some wrapping tattered bits of sail around their little bodies and pretending to be ghosts. Their antics brought a faint smile to Maria's face and chased away some of the melancholiness that the shipwreck had brought on. But then her smile turned sad as she thought of little Charles. Had things been different, some day he too might have played upon this beach as he waited for his father to return from the sea. Maria blinked back the old, familiar tears. Charles was gone. There was nothing she could do for him now.

Yes, Sam's son, the only thing she would ever have of the man she'd loved, was gone, but she could still help the living. The little children might flee her, the villagers might shun her as a witch, but any survivors from the wreck would not.

If there were any survivors.

She saw the first body, eyes sightless and staring, belly hideously bloated, lying in a bed of seaweed just beyond the claws of the thunderous surf. Another, clad in the tattered remains of a seaman's garb, was sprawled brokenly, facedown in the sand. Maria turned away, fighting the lump of bile that rose in her throat. Bodies were everywhere. Floating in the surf, rolling over and over in the waves as the ocean flung them against the beach, then clawed them possessively back. . . . Bodies, with great wounds torn in their white flesh by the angry seas. . . . Bodies, half buried in the sand, some openmouthed in the eternal scream of a hideous death, some staring at her with sightless eyes as she passed.

She felt impotent, helpless . . . and sick. Shipwrecks were all too common on Cape Cod—especially this part of it—and Maria was well accustomed to the grisly sights they left behind. But never had she seen a wreck in which so *many* had died. She must've been daft to think there might be survivors. Already, the coroner was digging a trench at the base of the sand cliffs in which to bury the dead.

Tears of sympathy for these unknown men and their families burned the back of her throat. But oh, what good did it do to cry for them? All she could do was offer a silent prayer for their souls, hope that at least they'd found peace in death. That done, she wiped the back of her hand across her eye, took a deep breath, and continued on to where Tim knelt, digging something out of the sand while Justice Doane looked on.

Neither heard Maria's approach over the wind, the hiss of flying sand, the booming thunder of angry surf. As she came up behind them Tim pulled an object free of the sand, brushed it off, and handed it up to Justice Doane.

"What do you think, Joe? A pretty nice piece, wouldn't you say?"

Curious, Maria craned her neck to see. It was a long sword of some sort; a rapier, perhaps? Or maybe a cutlass. She watched as Doane took the weapon by the hilt, turned the blade over for inspection, and let out a low, admiring whistle.

"Well?" Tim repeated.

"Yeah, sure is a beauty. Far too nice for the likes of pirates. God only knows who they stole it from."

Pirates? Did he say . . . *pirates?*

"Let me see it again."

Behind them, the color was draining from Maria's face. Had she heard Doane correctly? Was that broken, gutted vessel lying in the breakers and strewn the length of the beach a *pirate* ship?

Just whose pirate ship was *it?*

Her gaze shot to that battered, capsized hull just offshore. She didn't have to see it in its original state to know that those crushed timbers had once been part of a sleek, beautiful ship—and Tim had told her that *his* ship had been fine, lovely. . . .

Her hand was shaking as she touched Tim's shoulder.

"Maria!"

She ignored Doane, the stares of the villagers, everything but the fear that clawed at her heart. "Tim . . . I heard you mention pirates. Was this"—she swallowed hard—"was this a pirate ship?"

He nodded enthusiastically. "It sure was!" His voice dropped to a low whisper so that Justice Doane couldn't hear. "Do you know how rich we'll all be if we can get these things off the beach and hidden before the authorities find out? Here, take a peek at this rapier. See those emeralds encrusted in the hilt? And look at that workmanship! Quite a beauty, isn't it?" Grinning, he held it out for her perusal but she ignored it.

"Tim," she whispered, searching his face and clutching the blankets to her heart as though to shield it from what she desperately feared to be the truth. "Just what pirate ship *was* it? And . . . and who"—she took a deep, shaky breath—"was its captain?"

And as Tim looked down into her sweet, upturned face, the eyes that glistened with what looked to be unshed tears, the teeth catching the lower lip to still its trembling—suddenly he knew.

How upset she'd been that day in the gaol when he told her the Englishman, who was still a subject ripe for gossip long after his visit to their town, had turned pirate. Beautiful, sweet Maria, who had birthed a love child and never revealed its father. Maria, who kept a vigil on this barren, lonely beach for reasons known only to herself. Maria, a forlorn little figure standing before him, misery clinging to her very being as she gazed up at him with tortured, anguished eyes. . . .

Fools that they'd been, the truth had been right there in front of them all along and none of them had seen it. Those tears streaming down her pale cheeks were not in sympathy for some seaman she'd never known. Now he knew why she'd refused his attentions, why she'd made a recluse of herself out here on these barren cliffs . . . for Maria loved—

"Sam Bellamy," Justice Doane announced smugly, answering her question when Tim did not. He drew on his pipe and stared down the length of his nose at Maria's stricken face. "That hell-raising Englishman. 'Twas his ship *Whydah*, and serves him right, too, having the audacity to sail it right up here to our very shores! Can you imagine? What in heaven's name is this world coming to?" He shook his head. "And now I'm told he was headed for Provincetown of all places! Can you imagine what he would've done to those poor people had he reached it? Murdered them in cold blood, probably! Thank the Lord above for taking mercy on us, for sending the storm to stop him, to deliver us from him and his evil intentions!" He jerked the pipe out of his mouth, disgusted at her stricken look. "Oh, don't you go feeling sorry for these wretches nor Bellamy, neither. Bad blood runs deep. Got what he deserved, I say!"

But Maria heard these last words through a thickening, choking haze. She broke out in a cold sweat, the world reeled before her eyes, and she knew that if she didn't faint, she was going to be violently, deathly sick. She felt Tim's hand upon her arm, heard his anxious voice coming from far, far away.

"Maria? Are you all right?"

And then the mist parted and the shock waves hit, slamming the blessed numbness from her stunned brain. "No . . ." she whispered, shaking her head. And then her voice rose in denial. *"No!* You lie! *You're lying, Doane, I know you are!* Tim, tell me he's lying! Oh, God, tell me he's lying, *please!"*

Justice Doane took a step backwards. "Good Lord, what's wrong with her?" he cried. "Maria Hallett! Don't you dare go putting the Evil Eye on us, do you hear?"

"You're lying!" she screamed.

Tim tried to shield her from the sight of the wreckage, the bodies. "No, Maria," he said softly. "He's not lying." And as she burst into tears, he looked down at the rapier he still held and with a helpless gesture tossed it to the sand. "I'm so sorry. If only I'd known."

"Known what?" Doane snapped, ripping the pipe from his mouth.

Maria thrust herself away from Tim, her eyes wild behind her tears. "Known that *he* was the father of my baby!" she screamed at him. *"He* was the one, do you understand? *My baby's father!* The one I was to marry!"

In a flash of gold and crimson, she whirled and fled.

"Now what the blazes . . ." Doane tore his eyes from Maria's retreating figure and frowned. "What's she babbling about?"

But Tim was nodding toward the wreck just offshore. "I think it's obvious," he said quietly. "You figure it out."

"Him?" Doane exclaimed. *Bellamy?* And as understanding hit him he nodded sagely, folded his arms at his chest, and began to smile. Jamming the pipe back between his teeth he said smugly, "Well then, seems as though I was right all along, wasn't I?"

"About what?"

"About who sired that babe," he chuckled, looking out over the waves to the pitifully smashed wreck. "Told you the father was the devil, didn't I?"

"And the devil got his due," said the coroner, who'd come up behind them. "Amen."

Maria watched the sudsy foam drying at the water's edge. Heard the surf's hollow roar, and then the hiss of pebbles as the undertow raked them back into the sea once more. Lonely sounds, sad sounds. A single wave, green beneath embroidered eyelets of foam, reached out to console her, swirling around her moccasins and kissing her toes before eddying back into the surf.

He had come back for her.

Just as he had promised, long ago, that he would.

Oh, God . . . She buried her face in the blankets, dug at her weeping eyes, and raising her head, beseeched the gray sky. Rain leaked down, joining her tears. *"Sam . . ."* she cried brokenly. "Oh, Sam. I'm sorry if I *ever* doubted you." Guilt assailed her, guilt that somehow, some way, she was responsible for this. For only she knew the real truth, knew it as surely as her heart thunked woodenly within her breast. The Black Bellamy hadn't been headed for Provincetown to sack and plunder it, as the villagers thought.

He'd come back to claim her.

She burst into tears once more, crying so hard she couldn't see the sand upon which she walked. Gunner came up to trot beside her and lick her hand. She no longer saw the tangles of wreckage, the pieces of things that might or might not have belonged to *him*. But oh, they had. *His* eyes had looked upon these once-proud spars and broken timbers, *his* will had commanded them. *He* might have touched that broken musket, or perhaps it might have hung on the bulkhead of his cabin. Those torn pieces of sail, those lengths of rigging, all of it—they had heard his mighty voice, responded to his orders, obeyed him. Obeyed him, until last night. . . .

Her steps carried her farther and farther down the beach, away from the villagers. *Scavengers,* she thought bitterly. Thieves. Tomb robbers, desecrating *Whydah's* grave . . . *his* grave. And with every body she came upon she dreaded to look down at its face, afraid of finding *him*, yet at the same time afraid that she might not.

For another mile she walked, eyes sightless and staring, like a sleepwalker trudging through the throes of a nightmare. Long habit coaxed her gaze toward the sea. *Wake up, Maria,* said a little voice in her mind. *Wake up and look around you. He's not coming back today, tomorrow, ever. Sam Bellamy is dead.*

"No - o - o - oooooooooo!"

Dead, dead, dead. She fled, wailing at the top of her lungs and trying to escape that voice, until her foot caught on something and sent her sprawling. Sobbing, she got to her knees. A large pile of debris had tripped her, undisturbed and undefiled by the villagers, the wind-driven sand against its base smooth and white. Nothing more than a lumpy mass of sail, hemp, planking—and a fluttering sheet of black fabric held down by the broken length of a spar.

The Jolly Roger.

Maria stared. She dug her hands against her mouth and bit down hard on her fingertips. And then, shaking, she reached out and reverently pulled that stained banner from the debris pile and, laying it atop the blankets, still in her arms, buried her face in it. "Why?" she cried brokenly. "Why, Sam?" She rocked back and forth, her voice breaking. "Why, in God's name, didn't you just s-stay in the Indies, d-damn

you? You should never have c-come back . . . come back . . .
t-to me now!'' And then, dropping her burden, she broke
down, beating her fists upon the sand, her hair whipping about
her face, lashing the tears from her cheeks and flinging them
to the wind.

He was dead. Dead, dead, dead, lying somewhere out there
beneath the waves, and there was no way on earth that she
could go on without him. It was hard enough when she'd lost
his child. But to know that *he* was dead—would no longer be
alive, somewhere, on this earth—was too much.

Picking up the pirate flag and her blankets, she got to her
feet, staring past the pounding surf and out over the endless,
heaving expanse of water toward a horizon that would never,
ever again hold any hope. The sea. Mighty, awesome, restless—and eternal. She felt its pull, heard her name whispered
in the crash of breakers upon the beach. It was calling her,
wanting her. *He* wanted her.

And this time, she would not deny him.

Trancelike, she stood up. Her feet moved. Her legs followed, as she drew closer to the pounding surf. Loose sand.
Hard sand. Wet sand. The pirate flag fell from her arms and
was claimed by the wind; the blankets followed. The water's
edge swallowed her foot. Another step and she was up to her
ankles. Her calves. Her knees. Another step, and then, at
that very moment, a thin spot in the clouds passed above and
sunlight—watery, weak, but full if divine hope—flooded
the beach. Maria paused, turning to take one last look at the
world in which she had known one brief moment of divine
happiness.

It was small, nothing more than a splash of color buried
beneath planking, sand, and the broken spar, but it had caught
her eye. Slowly, numbly, she retraced her steps.

Just a bit of wine-colored velvet dusted with drying salt
and grains of sand—yet her heart began to pound against her
ribs. Her brain awoke, screamed a warning. The sky darkened once more, and with a sense of doom, she tugged at
the sailcloth. It wouldn't give and she suddenly realized it
was held down by something heavy.

An arm.

She brushed away more sand, frantically now.

Another body, buried beneath the debris pile. She jumped back, reluctant to touch it.

But what if . . .

The velvet was fine. The lace at the wrist was exquisite, rich. *"No!"* she screamed, but her hands were already working feverishly, ignoring the warning. Planking came away, was hurled upon the beach. She tore at tattered canvas and flung it to the wind. And then she saw hair—black hair—sparsely covering a wrist and the back of a dark hand.

With a heart-wrenching cry, Maria tore the last bit of cloth away, brushed the wet, tangled hair off his brow, and looked down into the bearded, still face. . . .

Of Sam Bellamy.

Chapter 10

By the sea
She knelt and bent above that senseless me;
Those lamp-drops fell upon my white brow
there,
She tried to cleanse them with her tears and
hair;
She murmured words of pity, love, and woe,
She heeded not the level rushing flow.

THOMSON

Time stopped; the world stopped.

For a long moment, Maria could only stare, unable to move.

He lay sprawled on his side, one arm pinned beneath his ribs, his pale cheek lying on sand and pebbles, the sea-torn remains of what had once been a fine coat half on, half off his still body. Sand, blown by wind and pushed by wave, dusted his skin and eyelashes, and was strewn throughout the hair that clung damply to his cheek and brow and the salt-dulled beard cloaking his jaw.

Maria closed her eyes and took a deep, shaky breath. *No.* This wasn't the man who'd sailed into Eastham so long ago. This one had darker skin, burned to mahogany by a sun that was hotter than Eastham's would ever be. The unruly hair that flowed over his shoulders and onto the beach sand was longer, thicker, blacker. And that beard . . . though neat and well-kept, it was alien to her. No, this wasn't her Sam. . . .

But in the stillness of death, there was that same straight-bridged nose with its slightly flared nostrils, the long lashes lying against sculpted cheeks, the sensuous lips, now chapped and wind-blistered, peeping from between the blackness of that beard.

Sam. . . .

It was him all right.

Trembling, she reached out and touched those cold, parted lips, the salt-stiffened hairs of his mustache, his beard. *Sam.* She gulped. *Oh, Sam.* . . . Never again would those lips speak her name, kiss her into the passion that had forever changed her life. Never again would those laughing dark eyes tease her, never again would he smile down at her with that lazy, crooked grin she remembered so well. . . .

Sa-a-a-a-a-a-a-A-A-AAAAM!

Her grief burst forth in a deluge of tears and a forlorn scream of bitter, twisting agony that reflected the very limits of anguish a human soul can bear. She had killed him, just as surely as she had little Charles. It was all because of her that he'd come back, all because of her that he now lay dead beneath a coffin of splintered timbers, his burial shroud the black flag he'd sailed under, his tombstone the imposing cliffs of sand, his death knell the timeless crashing of the waves upon the beach.

Tears streamed down her face and dropped upon the torn shoulder of his handsome velvet coat. "Oh, God, not you! *Please*, not you. . . ." But there was no denying the truth. Hysterically now, she pulled his heavy body onto her lap. And as his head fell back against her arm, she saw something hanging from the chain of gold that circled his neck, something silver and shiny, something that looked like . . . a coin.

Spanish treasure.

"Oh, God!" she wailed, and buried her face against his chest.

Against her lips, the coarse braid of his buttonholes. Against her cheek, the knit of bone and muscle that made up his chest, and sharp grains of sand that cut into her skin. And against her ear, the faint thud of his heartbeat.

Weak, uncertain, but steady.

He was alive.

Her head shot up, a sob lying caught and forgotten in her throat. *Alive?* Slowly, very slowly, terrified of shattering the illusion, Maria reached out and reverently brushed the backs of her fingers against his cheek. She bit down on her wildly trembling lip and then, with infinite care, picked up his limp wrist and pressed a shaking finger against its underside.

It was no illusion. There was a pulse there.

Wildly, her heart burst the cage of her chest and leaped with savage, spinning joy! Her soul took flight and soared high above the wreck, the beach, the ocean. He was alive! Alive, alive, *alive!*

Oh, stupid fool that she was, couldn't she see that his skin didn't hold the iciness of death, but the surface chill of one who'd been exposed to the elements for too long? Those dark eyes weren't open and staring like the others—they were peacefully closed. No, he wasn't dead at all! She burst into tears again, but this time they were ones of joy and gratitude.

"Oh God, thank you, thank you, *thank* you," she sobbed over and over again as she took his cold, lifeless hand in her own and kissed it mindlessly. Her tears washed his skin, trickled into the hollows between his knuckles, raced down his arm. It was only his hand, but she worshipped that hand: the soft hairs there, the web of veins beneath the skin at the back of it, the hard calluses of his palm as she stroked it with her thumb. Tenderly, she pressed that hand to her cheek and rubbed it back and forth, smudging her tears with his knuckles. *He was alive!* He was here, with her. And for the moment, it was enough to feel the pulse beating in his wrist and know that after all these months, after all this pain—this *agony*—his life's blood now flowed just a hairsbreadth away from her own.

There would be a use for her blankets after all. Stretching to reach them, for she was unwilling to relinquish her grip on his hand, reluctant, in fact, to lose physical contact with him ever again, Maria pulled them across the sand and, tucking them beneath his shoulders, his back, and around his ribs, dragged his big body up against her own to warm it.

It was as she tenderly brushed the dried salt from his face that she heard voices. Her head jerked up. Two figures were approaching, still some distance down the beach.

Justice Doane and Tim.

"Lord, no," she breathed, her arms tightening protectively around Sam's torso. Oh God, what should she do? What *could* she do? If Doane saw that Sam still lived he'd take great pleasure in nursing him back to health just to make a spectacle of his hanging. But worse, if he thought he was dead, he'd bury him alive! Quickly, desperately, Maria made her decision. By a miracle, he'd survived the shipwreck and the wrath of the sea; she would not lose him to the laws of mere men!

"Forgive me, my love," she murmured, gently easing him back to the sand and drawing the blanket over his face. Seeing him shrouded so, as if in death, drove chills up her spine; superstitiously, she prayed the action would not be a bad omen. Like a mother grouse, should she leave him and therefore draw their attention to her instead? Or should she stay with him to try to protect him?

She stayed.

By the time they reached her Maria was a convincing picture of grief, her forced tears coming easily after all she'd been through, her hair billowing like a sun-washed sail about her face. She heard Justice Doane's voice above her. "Cease your snivelling, witch. 'Tis wearing on my nerves. Look at you, bawling your eyes out over some villainous blackguard who only got what he deserved. To think you'd waste—"

His eyes had found the blanketed form.

"Well, well, now! Just who do we have here, eh?"

"Leave her alone, Joe," Tim said quietly. He put a restraining hand on the justice's arm. "I think it's obvious who it is."

"But oh, I think I should like to see this scoundrel who wreaked such havoc up and down the coast," Doane said, sneering at Maria. And with that, he reached down and tore the blanket from Sam's unmoving form.

Maria's breath caught in her throat. She went deathly still. *Please God, please God, please God,* she thought. But Doane's lips curved in a satisfied smile as he stood up and let the blanket drop to the pirate captain's face. "And you're crying over *him?* This devil, this blackguard?" He shook his head in disbelief. "But then you *are* a witch, aren't you, Maria Hallett? Why should I be surprised?" He jerked his head toward Tim, dug his boot into Sam's ribs, and, bending down, roughly grasped his wrists. "Come on, Tim, let's take him away. He's naught but a pirate. Captain or not, he deserves no better a burial than the rest of these thieving wretches."

"No!" Spitting and clawing like a wildcat, Maria came alive. Doane jumped back as if he'd been burned by the fires of Hell, letting the pirate captain's wrists thud to the sand.

Maria's voice was high, her eyes wild, her hair a tangled, disheveled flag whipping in the wind. "Don't you dare touch him!" she cried, shielding Sam's body with her own. "He was too good for the likes of you! So help me God, if you so much as lay a hand on him I'll claw your eyes out of your head and feed them to the gulls. *Do you hear me?"*

Doane glanced down at Sam and took a step backwards.

From out of the curse they'd bestowed upon her, the answer came. Her voice grew low, threatening. "Touch him, Justice, and I'll . . . I'll cast a spell on you that'll make you old before your time! Yes, go ahead, try it! And remember me when your teeth fall out, your skin shrivels up like a dried apple, your leg ripens with gout—"

"Enough!" he barked, fearfully backing away. "I merely wanted to give him a *decent* burial! You ought to be thanking me for it, not cursing me! You want him? You can have him! Let him rot here to feed the gulls, then! See if I care!"

"I'll bury him!" she ground out, eyes flashing.

She didn't like the gleam that came into his eyes. "On second thought, no you won't. The coroner will. By tomorrow morning he'll have dug a hole big enough for all of these wretches and then, like it or not, your precious captain is going in with the rest of them!" He jammed the pipe back into his mouth, leaving Maria to wonder that he didn't break a tooth. Throwing her a last look of disgust, he spun on his heel and stormed off down the beach.

Tim stayed behind for a moment. "Don't worry, Maria," he said quietly. "He won't come near you; none of them will. Despite all of this, they're still terrified of you." He looked down at the dead pirate. "Bury your captain, and I'll keep them away so you can do it privately." Bending down, he drew the blanket back over Sam's face.

"Sure was a handsome rogue," he admitted, straightening up. "No wonder I never had a chance. 'Twould be hard to compete with a man like that, even if he is . . ."

"Dead," Maria finished, with just the right amount of grief in her voice. And he soon would be if she didn't get him off the beach and out of this damp cold. But not even to her friend did she dare to reveal that Sam was alive. "Thank you, Tim." She passed a knuckle beneath her lower lashes to wipe away a tear. "Thank you for letting me . . . have this time alone with him."

Smiling wanly, he touched her cheek and turned to follow Doane back toward the villagers.

The day seemed to stretch on forever, but she held him in her arms, close to her body, close to her heart. The sun peeped hesitantly from behind the clouds, fading in and out as morning grew to afternoon and, finally, to evening. Maria knew that Sam's chances for survival lessened with every hour he lay upon the cold beach and suffered the biting wind; yet with the villagers nearby she dared not move him, and could only sit in the sand, holding him close and shielding him from the cold with as many blankets as she could pile upon him.

The villagers. . . . 'Twas a blessing they thought him dead. Surprisingly, none of them, save for Doane and Tim, had come to satisfy their curiosity about the infamous Captain Bellamy. But of course, money and goods salvaged from a wrecked pirate ship were worth more than a look at its dead captain, she mused. But tomorrow . . . tomorrow, they'd be back, no doubt. To stare at him, to gawk. And, she thought fearfully, to bury him.

She shuddered with horror. But tomorrow was tomorrow,

and she had all of tonight. Somehow, some way, she'd have to get him to the safety of her little hut atop the bluffs—but how?

Doubtfully, she eyed those great precipices rising almost vertically from the beach, and knew there was no other way.

She would have to do it, unless she wanted to let him lie here and die. She *had* to do it, and when darkness settled in to conceal her labors, she *would* do it.

Already, the sun was beginning its descent behind those seemingly insurmountable escarpments. The wind was getting colder now, drying Sam's hair so that it fell in thick waves over her arm. If only he'd awaken and make it up those cliffs under his own power. He might have done the impossible in surviving a shipwreck, but she had her doubts if she could perform a similar miracle. And getting him up the sand cliffs would require nothing short of one.

The villagers were leaving, taking as much of *Whydah's* remains as they could pile into their groaning carts. A flock of gulls winged past in timeless flight, skimming low over the waves and casting purple shadows upon the water. To the east the sky was pink and mauve, the clouds that hung suspended there great hulking masses of slate and purple. The sea, still marbled with whitecaps, was now changing in hue from angry green to slate blue lacquered with pink and mauve to match the sky above.

And to the west, the sun finally sank behind the cliffs, snuffing the light from their steep, sloping banks, making silhouettes of the poverty glass that studded their plateaus.

Maria swallowed. It was almost time.

She ignored the complaints of her hungry stomach, her body's plea for dry clothes and warmth. Sam was all that mattered. Struggling with his weight she sat up, pulling him up against her and cradling his lolling head against her breast to shield his face from the punishing, wind-driven sand. She closed her eyes, leaned her cheek against the top of his head, and as she had once done with little Charles, rocked him slowly back and forth.

Finally, the last villager led his horse off the beach and disappeared into the twilight. The sea turned to liquid pewter, and the moon rose up through the clouds on the horizon.

She was alone at last, with only the wind's moan and rhythmic roll and clap of the waves to keep her company.

She sat there for a long moment, listening to the breakers slapping the beach and trying to summon her courage, her confidence. She heard the hollow, thundering pop of the undertow, and knew she could delay no longer.

With great effort, she managed to roll him onto one of the blankets and, taking its corners in one hand and his wrists in the other, dug her heels into the sand and pulled.

At first he didn't budge, and neither did she. It was to be a fight then, but Maria was determined. Trying again, she took a deep breath and put all of her weight into the effort.

He moved. One inch. Two. And then, as she gained momentum, the blanket began to pass sledlike over the sand. Breathing hard, Maria trudged toward the base of the sand cliffs.

There, she stopped, looking up at their steep faces that seemed even steeper in the darkness. Her lungs heaved in exhaustion, and despite the cold, sweat trickled from her brow and into her eyes. She'd managed to drag him a full thirty, maybe forty feet. The effort had all but sapped her strength, and as she gazed hopelessly up at that wall of sand, she knew there was no way on earth that she'd be able to get him up those cliffs.

But there was no way he should have lived through the shipwreck, either. And had God let him survive, just to let him die upon this lonely beach? Gritting her teeth, Maria took up his wrists once more.

She got him moving again, and with jaw clenched in determination, began to climb. But for every excruciating step she took, she made little headway. Her feet could not get a grip in the loose sand, and it only raced down like a miniature avalanche until it swallowed up her shoes and ankles and left the hem of her gown puddled around the spot where they should've been.

Blinking back tears of frustration, Maria sank to her knees, watching loosened sand trickle down to the beach. Her hands were slippery with sweat and sea salt. Doggedly, she wiped first one palm, then the other, upon her woolen cloak to dry them.

Taking a deep breath to restore her confidence, she tilted

her head back and looked up at that imposing wall rising above her. But the cliffs were no less intimidating than they'd been before and seemed to smile down at her, smug in their imposing majesty. Waves crashed upon the beach in timeless rhythm, mocking her. *You can't do it, Maria. . . . You can't. . . .*

"I *can!*" she cried to the night, her hair blowing wildly about her face. Dauntless, she faced the dark expanse of the sea and the wind swept her words out over its barren vastness until even the waves heard her impassioned vow. "I can, and I *will!* I didn't pull him from your reach just to let you have him back! He's mine now, do you understand?" She took his wrists once more. *"Mine!"* And planting her feet in the unforgiving sand, she gave a mighty tug and pulled for all she was worth.

And made slow, painful progress. She gained a foot, two, then stopped to rest. Climb and rest, climb and rest. Arms screaming in agony. Sand pooling in her shoes and clumping beneath the arches of her feet. Hands numb with cold, breath frosting the air—and still she climbed, somehow, with resolve, determination, and perhaps a kind hand from God himself, managing to move Sam.

One quarter of the way. . . . Halfway. . . . Ten feet from the top she paused, her breath knifing in and out of her lungs, her blood roaring in her ears. The beach was far below her now, the cliffs here almost vertical. She wiped her brow and again took up Sam's wrists. His skin was now as damp and hot as hers was. Maria could feel the fever raging inside his body. She managed to drag him another two inches, paused to wait for her heartbeat to slow, then started again, making another foot of progress. She took another step. Another. Now she was crying in anticipation and hope, for she could almost see over the top of the plateau. Another few feet and they would be there!

And then the sand gave out beneath her aching feet, throwing her onto her back and sweeping them both downward. Frantically, Maria drove her heels into the cliff, straining, screaming, until at last she managed to stop their descent.

She heard the soft sigh of the wind, the rustle of the breeze through the sea grass. And then the waves again, mocking her, laughing at her.

Told you so. . . . Told you so. . . . You can't do it.

Her arms aching with fatigue, her muscles jumping spasmodically, tears streaming from her tightly shut eyes, Maria threw back her head and beseeched the night sky above.

"Oh, please, please, ple-e-e-e-e-e-ase, God, help me!"

And this time, she found that last bit of desperate strength she didn't know she had. Now, she fought her way skyward with grim-faced resolution. Fervently uttered prayers tumbled from her lips. Her head fell forward as she crawled backwards up the slope. Below her, Sam's boot heels traced twin lines in the sand and sent a shower of loose granules down to the beach below.

But they were not losing headway.

Higher and higher she climbed, her breathing ragged, her heart swelling against her ribs until she thought it would explode. Sobbing in triumph, for the plateau was at eye level now, Maria took the last, agonizing step.

Her hand groped in the dark, closed around a rough clump of poverty grass. With a final, desperate lunge that sapped the last of her strength, she hauled herself and Sam's heavy body onto the firm sand that topped the cliff. There she lay gasping, her sides heaving like a winded horse.

She had done it.

Chapter 11

A mystic Shape did move
Behind me, and drew me backward by the
hair;
And a voice said in mastery while I strove,
"Guess now who holds thee?"—"Death!"
I said. But there
The silver answer rang: "Not Death, but
Love."

BROWNING

It's all your fault. All your fault. All your fault. . . .

"No-o-o-o-o!"

Madigan, his crushed body walking zombielike toward him out of the waves. Andrew Crumpstey, the ex-captain of the wine pink, still shackled below and unable to escape the rising water, cursing him until it finally rose over his head and choked off his strangled, gurgling screams. Lambeth, eyes accusing and cold in a face that was swollen, hideous, nightmarishly purple. . . .

"All your fault. . . . All your fault. . . ."

He was screaming now, his head whipping back and forth in the water, seaweed filling his mouth and choking him with moist, cloying tendrils that slid up and down his face. And still they came on, no longer his faithful crew but a vengeful pack of demons with dead eyes and hands that were stretching toward him. . . .

And now their arms were around his shoulders, holding him, pinning him down, forcing him back into the awful, death-cold seawater. Frenzied, he fought them, screaming in terror when he realized he was too weak to throw them off.

All your fault. . . .

He cried out again. Water. Oh God, the water, it was closing over his head, he couldn't breathe—and *they* were in the water, bloodless, hideous corpses—

"*Sam!*"

He struggled harder, going mad at the feel of their flesh against his skin, their hands pressing him down, trying to drown him—

"*Sam! Sam, wake up! 'Tis me!*"

He was dead now. He had to be. The demons were fading into the murky darkness. *Whydah* was sinking gracefully out of sight, down, down, down. . . . Peace drifted over him, and up from the depths a mermaid was swimming, yellow hair waving in the current like kelp, hands gentle upon his shoulders, sea-colored eyes wide with concern as she took his hand and pulled him up toward that bright, wonderful light. Her arms enclosed him. Her hair brushed his cheeks. And then, with the last of his strength, he gave a mighty kick and broke the surface.

His eyes shot open. There were no bodies. No sunken ships. No mermaids. Just Maria Hallett, her arms wrapped about his shoulders with gentle strength, the ends of her hair damp with his own sweat, her tears.

" 'Twas a nightmare, Sam," she said gently. "Nothing more." And as she smoothed the damp hair back from his brow, he knew that nothing this side of Heaven was as sweet as that gentle touch, that God had made nothing more beautiful than that lovely face with its softly bowed lips and pert nose, its exotic eyes that now seemed afloat in a puddle of tears. And as he stared dazedly up at her, wondering why he was here in Heaven and not in Hell, where he rightfully belonged, one of those puddles overflowed and a tear leaked from the corner of her eye, trickled down her cheek, and plopped upon the skin at the base of his throat.

"Sam . . ." she whispered. "Oh, Sam—" And then she burst into sobs.

He tried to speak, but his tongue was swollen and dry and seemed to fill his entire mouth. Her fingers touched his parched lips. "Shh, my love," she whispered, her sobs quieting as quickly as they'd begun. "You're going to be all right. I want you to rest now. You've been very, very ill."

"My crew—" he got out.

Soft fingers grazing his bearded cheek. Her voice, gentle, comforting, soothing. He closed his eyes and leaned his aching, throbbing head back against her supporting arms. Strange, but it seemed as though she'd been here all along. He *was* dreaming, of course. Yet the physical sensations were painfully real and becoming more so by the minute. The taste of salt when he passed his tongue over his cracked lips. The deep, searing pain that throbbed in every muscle and limb. The awful ache that rang in his head, the nausea in his stomach, the chills that were making his body tremble in the seawater—

Seawater?

His eyes shot open, and with sudden clarity he knew he wasn't dreaming. It was seawater all right, and he was sitting in a damned tub of it, an *icy* tub of it, and immersed clear up to his bare chest! And as he threw off the last smothering mists of unconsciousness, he realized there *was* something in his mouth, something bitter and foul tasting, something alien—

Cursing, he spat it out and lunged upward.

"Sam!" Her hands, not as delicate as they looked, pushed him back down into the tub. Icy water sloshed up against his neck and set his teeth to chattering. Was she that strong or had he grown that weak?

He, *weak?* Never!

"What the bloody *hell* am I doing in a tub of seawater?"

It was not the kind of reunion that either had anticipated; certainly not the glorious one that Sam had envisioned, nor the sweetly romantic one that Maria had dreamed about. "I told you, you've been sick," she declared, her hand pressing against his chest to hold him down and feeling deliciously warm against his cold, shrunken nipple.

"Sick? God's *teeth*, I wonder why!"

Her calm smile held the sort of wisdom usually reserved for those many years her senior. " 'Twas a fever, Sam, and if it hadn't been for the seawater you wouldn't be alive to complain about it at all. Now, please. Just sit there and be still."

"Be still? Are you out of your bloody mind? No wonder I had a fever! What normal man wouldn't, being dunked in ice water after nearly drowning in it?" He spat the last of the foul stuff out of his mouth. "And what the hell have you been feeding me?"

"Tea."

"Tea? Christ, I'll bet fish piss tastes better than this god-awful—"

"Sam, please. Your language." She touched his brow, relieved to find that the fever, thanks to the immersion in the very water he was railing about, had finally broken and his skin was pleasantly cool. Her touch seemed to calm him and his eyes drifted shut.

"Sure as hell doesn't taste like any tea *I've* ever had."

"I made it from bayberry."

"Bayberry?"

"The leaves and stems."

One dark eye opened to regard her with distrust.

"What, is it that bad?" The eye closed, and his weak nod sent little ripples spreading out from where the strong column of his neck rose out of the water. His handsome, masculine form reposed beneath the surface in crystal clarity; it was a form she'd labored over for a week, trying desperately to contain the life that sought to escape it; a form that, since he was awake, now brought a hot flush to her pale, tired features.

"I could go back to the goldenrod," she mused.

The eye opened once more. "Goldenrod?"

"Well, yes. I made a brew from it yesterday. You were pretty sick; I don't think you'd remember it."

Both eyes were open now, staring at her.

"Or maybe you'd prefer something else," she said hastily. "I made some tea from oak bark, another from birch—"

"Maria."

"Or perhaps I should try the elderberry—"

"Maria." Flashing eyes belied the patience that controlled his voice. "I don't want to know what you've been feeding me. I don't want to know what this greasy stuff is all over my chest. I don't want to know what crusty mess lurks beneath the bandages on my fingers, and I *don't* want—"

" 'Tis a poultice. I made it from plantain leaves to draw out the splinters—Sam, they were too deep! I couldn't get them out! I tried, but they were into the quick beneath your nails!"

His voice was no longer patient. "And I *don't* want to know what was sliding up and down my cheek a moment before I opened my eyes—"

At precisely that moment he saw the dog, curled up on a hearth rug and regarding him with laughing satisfaction in his brown canine eyes.

It was the final insult. "God's *bloody* teeth!" Sam exploded, leaping out of the tub. "Ye let that damned beast near me?" Water went everywhere, splashing onto the rough-hewn floor, spraying the crude furniture, soaking Maria's rumpled gown. But as he gained his feet Sam found that he *was* weak, weaker than a newborn kitten. He pitched helplessly forward, cursing as he fell heavily to the floor and lay there, as naked as the day he was born, in a puddle of cold water.

"Gr-r-r-r!"

His eyes shot open. Three inches from his face stood the dog—hackles raised, lips drawn back over white fangs—and eyes cold with clear, unmistakable malice.

He froze.

"Now, Gunner," Maria was saying, leaving him to lie there in humiliation while she went to the hearth and ladled something out of the cook-pot that hung from a rod across the fire. Good God, he thought, was this her way of teaching him a lesson? If so it was damned effective! His eyes rolled to the dog. It wasn't moving, only lowering its head so it could intimidate him all the more. "Now Gunner, you come over here and be a good boy. Gunner? Do you hear me?"

Jesus, Sam thought. He'd survived a year of piracy, a shipwreck, and Maria's "cures" only to have his throat torn out by an overgrown whelp.

"Gunner!"

Reluctantly, the dog padded back to the fire, its long tail wagging in an admission of guilt, but not regret.

Sam let out his breath in a heavy sigh. He tried to sit up but even that was too much of an effort for him. His eyes closed, and he felt himself sinking back down toward unconsciousness. This time he didn't fight it. But then her soft hands were sliding beneath his neck, lifting him. Her arms were cradling his head, her fragrant hair tickling his nose. It took all of his strength just to open his eyes.

"Come now, my fearless sea rogue," she said, not un-kindly. " 'Tis not a ship, you know. We can't have you sleeping on deck." His senses swayed dizzily as she made him sit up. Cursing his weakness, he let his head sag against her breast. Her fingers were gentle, stroking his hair and tenderly avoiding the painful area behind his ear. "Think you can get up?"

"Aye," he groaned, not so sure anymore that he wanted to. The softness of her breast beneath his cheek was more than pleasant. It was delicious. . . .

But she had other ideas for him. Her arms were beneath his shoulders, pulling at him, slipping against his wet skin. Afraid she'd break her slender back, Sam tried his best to help her, managing to get to his feet and leaning heavily against her as she toweled him dry and guided him across the room. Gratefully, he sank down onto a mattress filled with cornhusks and straw, sighing as she pulled the thick, warm coverlet up over his chest and tucked him in like a babe. He smiled, for even as a child, no one had ever tucked him in.

"You're forgiven," he whispered.

"Forgiven?"

"Aye, lass. For stuffing weeds down my throat. For drowning me in ice water. For slathering me in sticky paste and stinky greases. But not for wrapping my fingers up and binding them in two pounds of bandages. . . ."

He knew, without opening his eyes, that she was smiling. "And why is that, Sam?"

"Because you've robbed me of the pleasure . . . of touching you."

She sat on the bed beside him, the warmth of her body spreading through the coverlet and blankets to heat his chilled skin. "Perhaps, then," she said softly, blushing, "a good-night kiss will make up for that. . . ."

She took his hand, holding it gently and stroking the underside of his palm. And the sweet touch of her lips against his was the last thing he sensed before deep, peaceful sleep claimed him.

When Sam awoke several hours later he felt well enough to notice that which he hadn't before: the unfamiliar surroundings, the rhythmic roar of the sea outside, and of course, Maria.

He sought a more comfortable position upon the mattress, silently cursing the crackle and rustle of cornhusks beneath him. All he needed was for her to notice he was awake and she'd be shoving more weeds down his throat. Next time he might not be so lucky. Goldenrod? Bayberry? Christ, with his luck it would probably be poison ivy.

He watched her through slitted eyes. She bustled about, replacing bottles and jars filled with God-only-knew-what in the cupboard that dominated one corner of the room, stirring something in the big pot that hung over the hearth (God help him), coming over every so often to lay her cool hand on his brow. This he bore with a hidden smile, feigning sleep, and obviously satisfied she went about her business once more, humming now, as he secretly watched her.

Oh, princess, he thought, wishing he could be doing other things in this bed—not lying in it, sick. For Maria had fulfilled every promise her youth had held long ago. Her hips had lost their girlish lines and now curved in womanly splendor beneath her tiny waist. Her hair tumbled in soft waves all the way to the small of her back, and the firelight played off it the way candlelight does gold. Such a sweetly curving bottom, such delicate little ankles . . . and such pretty legs, the turn of her calves flowing enticingly into her moccasins. . . .

She turned then, caught his heated stare—and in that instant he realized that something else had changed about her as well. There was no longer innocence in those clear, exotic eyes, but nuances of something else, suggestions of the scars found in one who has experienced the trials of life . . . things like deep pain, betrayal, suffering.

He opened his mouth to ask her what had been going on in his absence, but her cheery words cut him off. "Ah, good. You're awake," she said, smiling sweetly and making a beeline toward the pot.

"No!"

She turned, frowning. "What's wrong?"

"I—I'm . . . not hungry."

"Oh Sam, 'tis only rice gruel. It won't kill you, I promise."

Oh, what was the use? Knowing her—and the unmerciful wench she'd apparently become—she'd probably shove it up his nose if he didn't open his mouth.

He steeled himself for the worst as she came to sit on the bed beside him, her slight weight bowing the mattress as she helped him to sit up against the fluffy pillows and pulled the blankets—brightly colored, embroidered ones that he recognized as her handiwork—up over his scraped, bruised shoulders. "Comfortable?" she asked.

"Aye. For the moment."

He shut his eyes, his stomach recoiling in apprehension as she dug a spoon into the bowl and nudged it against his lips. But she was right. It wasn't poison ivy, clamshell paste, or mashed goldenrod. Just rice gruel, and she'd been thoughtful enough to sweeten it with a few drops of molasses. "There," she said softly, her eyes shining as she gazed down at him. "That's not so bad, is it?"

That one mouthful had awakened his hunger. "Nay, princess." He grinned. "In fact, I think I might even survive another bite."

She complied, happy that he was eating. If the authorities didn't discover she had him up here she might be able to save him after all. Her eyes wandered over his gaunt, handsome face, the scratches on his neck, the ugly, purple-yellow bruises on his shoulders. And what a fight it had been, saving him. Endless treks to the forest to collect pitch from the scrub pines, heating the sticky mess into a salve that she'd spread over his chest in the hopes of preventing pneumonia. She thought of the terrible fever that had burned through his body the night she'd dragged him up the cliff and got him into bed, a fever that had battled her for his life and had left her dizzy with exhaustion as the days crept by and she'd tried one remedy after another to no avail. Her despair, her bitter tears of defeat, until she'd looked out the window at the remains of his dead ship and seen the ocean he loved so much, the ocean that had tried its best to claim him—and now offered the only hope she had of saving him. Lugging bucket upon bucket of seawater up the cliffs, she'd filled her tub with it, dragged his feverish, sweat-soaked body off the bed, got him into the tub, and lost count of the hours spent pouring the frigid water over his chafed, raw skin. And her prayers had been answered; against the mighty will of the sea, the fever hadn't had a chance.

Now that he was awake and no longer deathly ill, she could look at his battered body and feel pity. The gashes on his upper arms, the splinters she'd dug from beneath his nails, the bruises, the cuts, the skin scraped raw by a night in angry surf. She thought of all he'd been through, the terror, the suffering he must've endured. And she could think about how very, very close she'd come to losing him.

"Oh, Sam," she said, her voice catching on a sudden sob. He looked up, startled, then wrapped his arms about her as she put the bowl down and collapsed upon him, her tears flowing hot against his chest, pooling there and running across his shoulders and down his neck in little rivulets.

"Maria, lass! Here now, what's wrong?"

That deep, beloved voice. Those sea-roughened hands, weakly stroking her back. "Sam, oh Sam . . . you're alive. . . ."

"Aye 'twould appear so," he said, frowning as he wrapped his shaky hand around a tendril of thick, silken hair and pressed her down against him. She was deliciously warm, her body soft and pliant. "Is it something to cry about?"

"Stop teasing me!" she sobbed, raising her tear-streaked face. "Do you know how I felt when I looked out my window and saw that shipwreck? Do you know how I felt when I found out it was *yours?*" She paused, sniffing, reliving that awful agony. "You were as good as dead when I dragged you up those cliffs. You almost died this past week. And here you sit, teasing me about it, laughing—"

"Oh, princess. If I'm laughing 'tis only because I'm grateful ye didn't leave me there to die." The effort of stroking her hair was taxing his strength, and he finally stopped, letting his arm weigh heavily upon her shoulders and pinning her against his chest. "Anyone else would have, you know."

"And if anyone else finds out you're here, your fate will be the same."

"Ah, yes," he said thoughtfully. "That reminds me." He turned his head to glance about the unfamiliar room. "Just where is 'here,' Maria? I seem to recall that you lived in town, not near the sea. Yet I can hear it roaring outside, and I don't recognize anything about this room."

"I . . . I live here now, Sam."

"Live here? Where? Why?"

"I'll tell you . . . when you're stronger."

He frowned. What the hell was the big secret? "I *am* strong, and I wish to know now, Maria."

" 'Tis my home, Sam, all right? A one-room hut with mud-chinked walls and a roof of thatch, overlooking the sea here upon the Great Beach. There. What else do you want to know?"

He didn't like the guardedness in her voice. "Why you're here."

"When you're better I'll tell you." She sat up, reached for the bowl, and began to feed him the gruel once more. There was a tightness about her mouth, a flash of pain in her beautiful eyes. But now his curiosity was piqued, and she'd succeeded in igniting the first sparks of his volatile temper.

"Damn it, Maria, I don't like secrets!"

"No? Well then, if you don't like mashed goldenrod either, be quiet and stop asking questions."

"You'll have to threaten me with something more lethal than weeds, lass, to get me to stop!"

"Sam, *please*. Can't you understand? I don't want to talk about it!"

"I can assure you that my fragile health can withstand it!"

"Well maybe mine can't!"

He opened his mouth to retort, then fell silent, the now-cold gruel going tasteless as he wondered what the hell she was hiding from him, why she was so reluctant to talk about it. And now, damn it all, the tears were back in her eyes, and he had no wish to bring them spilling down her cheeks once more. But he'd find out, he vowed to himself, what the big mystery was. The devil take him if he wouldn't!

"Are you . . . comfortable?" she asked once more, awkwardly.

"Quite, my dear."

"How do you feel?"

"Like I've been run over by a team of stomping stallions and the coach as well."

His joking manner and devilish smile managed to dispel the sparkle of tears in her eyes. She put the gruel down, tenderly exploring the scrapes, the gashes, the bruises with gentle fingers. "It must hurt terribly," she mused.

"Aye."

Her touch was warming his blood, despite his weakness, despite the pain that throbbed in his head, his toes, and every muscle and limb in between. He gazed at her trim figure in appreciation. "Perhaps I should put some salve on these cuts so they won't fester," she said.

"They don't hurt that bad, Maria."

"Oh Sam, it's just a salve."

"I know. It's just that I don't want you to leave me. You'll have to get up, and I don't want you to. What I *do* want is for you to sit right here and take a little rest." He reached up and enfolded her hand in his. "You look tired, my dear. You've been running yourself ragged, haven't you?"

She looked away.

"You can't fool me. Besides," he added with a hint of his old, lupine smile, "the feel of your hands upon my skin is very, very . . . pleasant. I rather like it." He lifted her hand, pressing his lips against her knuckles while holding her captive in his black gaze. "And I would like the feel of your lips upon mine, if you'd be so inclined, my dear. . . ."

She smiled down at him, playfully now, her tears forgotten.

"Come now. A kiss for your future husband, lass?"

He didn't have to ask twice. She leaned down, her eyes closing, her lips seeking the familiarity of his, for during this past week she'd kissed those lifeless, feverish lips, traced their shape with trembling fingers, forced them apart to spoon tea and broth down his throat more times than she could count. But now they were wonderfully alive, gently demanding, and warm with life, not death. Now, they sought hers with the ardor of passion that had been a year denied, and Maria was lost, melting against him as his hands came up to thread through her hair, his bandaged fingers catching the golden strands and making them tug against her scalp. Her senses spun; warm currents surged through her blood. And beneath her, his breathing quickened as his own passion, fully alive and far stronger than his weakened body, responded to her.

Reluctantly, Maria drew back, fearful of hurting him.

"Princess?"

"You're not strong enough yet, Sam."

"Oh, *please*. Not this again."

"No. I want you to rest, regain your strength."

"Don't you love me anymore, dear?"

"Love you?" His words had been light, but beneath them she sensed the need for the truth. Did he doubt her feelings for him? Did he think that just because he'd gone off to become the most rascally scoundrel this coast had seen in recent years that she hated him? Oh, she was angry with him for it, furious even—but hate him? She gave a short, dismissing laugh. "Yes, pirate, I love you." And then, softly, "I always have."

"Then tell me why you're living here, all by yourself."

He was back to that again. "You're just not going to give up, are you?"

He smiled, that charming, lazy smile she remembered so well. "No, I'm not. Tell me."

"Later."

"No, Maria. *Now.*"

She looked at him, lying there waiting with arms crossed over his chest and black eyes beginning to flash with impatience. Despite his weakened state he was as demanding as a king. No wonder he'd been such a capable leader and captain. And God help her, she *did* want to tell him everything, every bit of it, but she couldn't tell him about little Charles just yet. How would he react if he knew he'd fathered a babe? What would he think if he learned she'd been accused as a witch? And worst of all, what would she do if he, like the others, turned away?

For Maria no longer dared to predict his reactions. She wasn't even sure she really knew him anymore, for this man was different, far different from the one she'd known a year ago. It wasn't the unruly black mane that flowed to his shoulders, nor the beard that made his swarthy face all the more dark. It wasn't the hoop of Spanish gold in his ear, nor even the regal, imperious manner in which he'd been dressed that gave him away. She looked down into his gleaming black eyes and knew instantly what it was. A wildness from within. His was an untamable spirit that had gone unchecked, allowed to run free without restraint; and Maria realized that although he hadn't gone looking for piracy, it was inevitable that it had come looking for him.

Bad blood runs deep. . . . The words of Justice Doane, echoing over and over in her mind.

And Tim, no less astute in his judgment: *He was a wild one, that Sam Bellamy. . . .*

She reached for the jar of salve. "We'll talk about it later."

"No, woman, we'll talk about it *now!*"

Maria's head shot up in indignation. "Don't think to play pirate captain with me, Sam! You don't scare me one bit, do you hear me? Not one bit! I'll tell you when you're fully recovered and when I'm good and ready, and not a moment before!"

He reacted as though she'd slapped him, the expression on his face registering surprise, then shock. Being put in his place, she realized, was definitely *not* something that he was accustomed to. As for Sam, he wondered just what had become of the shy little maid he'd known a year ago. Gone was that pretty girl, and in her place stood a woman—a flawlessly beautiful one—whose eyes flashed with defiance and dared *him* to challenge her!

He raised himself on one elbow, glaring at her beneath a dark scowl. "Maria, don't coddle me," he warned.

"And you, *Black* Sam," she said, shoving him back down upon the pillows, "don't try to threaten me! I told you, I am *not* afraid of you and your bluster, and need I remind you that Gunner does not like a commotion? Now, lie down and behave yourself. You've already made a mess of this salve."

Silently fuming, his jaw clenched in frustration, he did as she asked. But the salve felt wonderfully pleasant against his wounds, her little hand even more so. He relaxed, allowing her to work it into his scratches and scrapes. But there were questions burning in his mind, questions he wanted answers to, *now.* He'd be damned if he'd let her have her way! And it was obvious that force and intimidation, though they'd been quite effective in getting hardened sea captains to submit to him, were useless when applied to this mere lass. He had to try other tactics. . . .

Idly, he studied the colorful wall hangings that decorated the drab, mud-chinked walls. "Doing lots of weaving lately, Maria?"

"A bit," she said warily, very aware of the beat of his heart, the warmth of his body beneath her palm.

"Hmm. I notice your gown has lots of embroidery on it. . . . I like that. Something exotic about it, unconventional, even. I hate conformity, ye know."

"I know. As a pirate you proved that."

"Aye, that I did, didn't I?" He missed the twinge of irritation in her voice, or perhaps chose to ignore it. "That reminds me, lass. I hear the ocean. Are we far from the beach?"

"It's right outside. Why?"

"I was just wondering about my ship."

She'd just scooped a large glob of salve from the jar, and now paused with it an inch from his chest. "Sam, I really don't think you want to see it . . . at least, not yet."

His feigned geniality instantly vanished. "And why not? Do you think me some squeamish whelp? Damn it, I told you not to coddle me!"

"But Sam—"

Impatience glittered in his eyes. He sat up, thrusting her arm aside and hurling questions at her like rounds of cannon fire. "What became of my men? Did any survive? And what of the other ships in my fleet?"

"We'll discuss all that when you're better."

"Damn it, woman!" he swore, swinging his legs from the bed and hauling the blanket with him. "I'm tired of this, damned tired of it! Treating me like some convalescent invalid, keeping secrets from me, hiding things!" He was on his feet now, his tall body swaying and looking like it was going to go down at any moment, but he was doing it, lurching across the room, stumbling against the table, clutching the back of a chair as he finally reached the door and flung it open.

The sight hit him square in the chest and knocked the breath from his lungs. *Whydah.* His beautiful, lovely *Whydah,* lying smashed and beaten in the foaming surf, her tallowed underside and broken keel all that remained of her graceful hull. He sagged weakly against the door frame. The reality, the sight of what she'd become, was worse, far worse, than what he remembered from that awful night. He smelled the smoke from the fires the people had made to burn down her once-proud masts for their iron. He heard the chop of axes against her splintered timbers. He saw loose planking tumbling over and over in the waves, saw someone dragging what looked to be a body over the sand.

Dizzily, he turned his face against the doorway's rough wood. And then Maria was there, her arms around him as she quickly guided him away from the door and back to the bed before the villagers could see him. She said nothing, merely allowing him to lean heavily upon her before easing him down and quietly drawing the blankets up over the rise of his shoulders. And now, his nightmare was returning with sudden, hideous clarity. " 'Tis all my fault," he groaned. "Dead, every one of them, and it's all my fault!"

She found his hand, squeezing it in her own. "It wasn't your fault, Sam."

He was shaking now, eyes haunted as he stared up at the dried plants and herbs that hung from the beams above his head. "It *was* my fault! I was the one who took on another pilot, hoping that he could guide us safely into Provincetown. I trusted him, believed him. I promised him his freedom if he could do it! Oh, fool that I am! He never had any intention of keeping his word, as I did mine! He set our course right toward these shores, knowing the ship would be dashed to pieces in the storm—"

"Then it was his fault, Sam, not yours."

"You don't understand, Maria! The life of every one of those lads was in my hands. They were my responsibility, and I entrusted them to someone I didn't even know!"

Lightning dancing about the spires of the mast . . .

The cannon smashing poor little Madigan's chest like dry firewood . . .

The screams of the drowning, the dying . . .

It had all happened so violently, so fast—

And poor Captain Crumpstey—he'd never even had the chance to free him from his irons before the ship had gone down. . . .

All your fault. . . . All your fault . . .

He closed his eyes, his great, gaunt body trembling anew, reality slipping away from him once more. He didn't hear Maria get up and rush to the cupboard. He didn't feel her fingers quickly prying his jaws apart. And this time, when she forced a hot, strange-tasting brew down his throat, he didn't protest, only shaking and fighting the nightmares until at last the medicine took effect and the awful visions were smothered beneath the dark cloak of blessed oblivion.

Chapter 12

The many men, so beautiful!
And they all dead did lie:
And a thousand thousand slimy things
Lived on; and so did I.

COLERIDGE

Not only was he the most gravely ill patient she'd ever treated, but Sam Bellamy also proved to be the most difficult, irascible, and ungrateful one as well, sputtering and choking and cursing loud enough to wake the dead as Maria forced everything from apple bark tea to birch bark to mashed goldenrod down his throat. After several days of complaining, grumbling, and sulking, he finally flung the bowl clear across the room and began hollering for rum instead.

"God's teeth, woman, I'm sick of eating these weeds! D'ye think me a damned garden?" He leaped out of the bed, stubbing his toe on the table and howling in pain as he hopped about on one bare foot. Instantly Gunner was up, lips drawn back and showing a very capable set of gleaming white teeth. "Leave me be, ye bloody cur! Damn it, I can't take this anymore! I want real food! Potatoes! Beef! Bread and butter! Chicken pie—"

"Sam, eat your broth. 'Twill make you feel better."

"What, this refuse? I hardly think so, Maria! I shudder to think what it's doing to my insides! It's going to kill me yet!"

"I'm going to kill you if you don't get back in that bed and rest!"

"If I get back in this bed I can assure you it *won't* be to rest!"

He was just contemplating *that* idea when the door crashed open and slammed back against the wall hard enough to splinter the wood. Maria screamed, Sam grabbed a knife from the table, and Gunner—snivelling coward that he was—dove under the bed.

Snatching her musket from its cradle above the hearth, Maria never saw Sam lower his knife, fold his arms, and regard her with grinning amusement. She didn't hear the faint whines that came from beneath her bed. She only saw a man silhouetted in her doorway, and assumed the worst.

Her hands trembling, she raised the gun. "Wh-what do you want?"

"Why, Mistress Hallett. Is that any way to greet a friend?"

"Friend? None of my friends is so rude as to nearly break my door off its hinges! Now, who are you and what do you want?"

He stepped into the room then, sweeping off his hat with a flourish. Maria's heart skipped a beat and she lowered the gun in shaky relief. "Paul Williams," she breathed, not knowing whether to laugh or cry. Her knees had gone to water. For a minute there she'd thought he was one of the king's men, come to take Sam away. But out of the corner of her eye she saw Sam muffling his laughter with a broad palm, saw a flash of white as the courageous Gunner streaked across the room and shot out the door.

"Forgive me for intruding on such a . . . *cozy* scene," Paul remarked, for he'd heard Sam's voice raised in anger a moment before he'd made his singularly spectacular entrance. Glancing about the room, he took in the assortment of jars on the table, some nearly empty, others filled with dried leaves and flowers. Something wet and slimy slid down the wall—something that was dripping onto the rough-hewn planking of the floor and the bottom of an overturned bowl. His brow furrowed in puzzlement.

"Aye, cozy, isn't it?" Sam remarked. " 'Twas my breakfast, Paul, that you see gracing that wall yonder!"

One of Paul's lips curled in distaste. *"Breakfast?"* But his disbelieving eyes were on his friend, taking in the fading bruises on the broad chest and arms, the scratches and scrapes that, although healing nicely, covered the swarthy skin. "Black" Sam was leaner than he'd ever seen him, and his breeches were no longer snug and well fitting, but hanging loosely from his frame. "No wonder you're so damned thin. Pardon me for saying so but you look awful, my friend."

"And so would you if you'd had berries, branches, and twigs forced down *your* throat for nigh on two weeks!"

"Ungrateful cad!" Maria said, laughing.

"Aye, that I am. She saves my life only to torture me with food even a rabbit wouldn't eat! Christ, Paul, do ye know how much I long for a potato? A piece of bread? Hell, at the moment I'd even settle for a piece of salt beef off the ship!"

"Hmm . . . you must be pretty desperate, then."

For answer, Sam merely swore and began to pace.

Paul's laughter filled the room. "Good Lord, Maria, why ever did you bother? I would've let him die for all the appreciation you get for your troubles!" He pulled out a chair, tossed his three-cornered hat—complete with crimson feather—upon the table, and, leaning back, crossed his wrists behind his elegantly peruked and powdered head. "In fact, you'd have been better off trying to salvage the treasure that we all worked so hard for!" He turned to Sam, whose eyes had gone hard at the reminder of what he considered the greatest failure of his life. "Needless to say, my friend, you can imagine that word of the wreck was not very well received aboard my *Mary Anne*. What the blazes happened, anyhow? You're the last man to let his ship run aground in a storm. Rumor has it you took a wine ship that day . . . too much tipple, my friend?"

"No, damn you," Sam growled, his guilt over what had happened already eating a hole in his gut. "A faulty pilot."

"Ah . . . I daresay, if you want something done right you must do it yourself. So, Maria, do you have anything to drink? I'm a bit thirsty."

"Take your pick," Sam said acidly. "Birch bark broth, pine cone soup—"

But Paul, despite almost breaking her door down, was in good enough graces with Maria to earn himself a mug of cold, delicious cider. Sam eyed it with envy. "So tell me, just how did you find me?" he asked.

" 'Twasn't hard. I went to Maria's aunt's house to offer

Maria my condolences on her . . . loss.'' He gave her a sly wink. ''I knew she cared for you, you know. But did I find Maria there? Oh, no! Nothing but a wizened old woman who came after me with a gun and told me if she ever saw my likes again she'd blow my guts clear across Eastham!'' he tipped the mug to his lips, his obvious enjoyment of the tipple grating on Sam's taut nerves. ''Told me a rather strange story about witches and devils and a pirate who had the good graces to wash up dead at his lover's doorstep. Good thing she doesn't know you're alive, my friend. I'd hate to be at the receiving end of that gun.''

''I'd rather take my chances with the gun than that damned whelp of Maria's,'' Sam commented dryly.

''What, that harmless pup? Seemed friendly enough to me.''

''Gunner doesn't like Sam,'' Maria put in. ''And I'm surprised that Auntie told you I was out here.''

''She didn't. I made some inquiries along the way. Funny, but not one of those townspeople offered to show me where you lived. Acted like they were scared of you. Nothing but a pack of cold snobs, if you ask me.''

''I . . . don't get very many visitors,'' Maria said, pleading with her eyes for Paul not to disclose the things he'd no doubt learned from the villagers. Now was not the time to discuss the witchcraft business, little Charles or any of the other things that, with each passing day, grew harder and harder to bring up. And Sam, uncharacteristically quiet about the issues, had not pressed her. But then, he'd been so occupied in torturing and blaming himself for the shipwreck that he'd thought of little else; not even of her, nor of sharing a bed with her. . . . The rejection hurt.

''You know,'' Sam was saying, helping himself to the cider and daring Maria with his black-eyed stare to defy him, ''you're taking a foolish risk in coming here. That beach is crawling with the king's men. If they see you, you might as well put the noose around your own neck.''

''Come now, do I look like a pirate captain?'' Paul asked innocently. And indeed, as Maria took in his clothes—stolen, no doubt, but fine nevertheless—she would never have put him in the same league with the rogues who'd been terrorizing the coast of late. Beneath his silver-trimmed hat, a

Ramillies-style wig hung in a long plait past his shoulders and was tied with black ribbon bows at nape and tail. His coat was well tailored, his boots reflecting the hearthlight. No, he didn't look like any pirate captain she knew . . . but then, she knew only one—and he and Paul were as different as night and day.

"No," she said softly, with a wistful glance at Sam. "Indeed, you do not."

"You've yet to answer my question," Sam snapped irritably.

"Ah, yes. Why I'm here." Paul swilled his cider, smacking his lips in appreciation. "Actually, my men were complaining about the wreck, driving me so crazy with their whining that I finally decided the only way to shut them up was to come here and let them see it for themselves. I thought we might be able to salvage some of the treasure, but that's a hopeless quest if ever there was one. The seas are so rough I can't even get near it."

"Neither can Southack," Sam said, smirking.

"Southack . . . now why does that name sound familiar?"

"Captain *Cyprian* Southack? His Majesty's Most Honorable Servant?" Sam's lip curved in a derisive sneer beneath his mustache and beard. "Protector of this coast, defender of its people from the horrible misdeeds of piracy, ex-commander of the *Province Galley*—"

"Ah, *that* Southack," Paul said, nodding sagely. "Good God, I hope he doesn't find out *you're* here!"

"He shan't," Maria declared, never ceasing to be amazed that among seamen everybody knew everybody, no matter which side of the law they walked—or sailed—on.

Idly, Sam went to look out the window, his keen gaze taking in the glistening, but empty, sea. "Well, I'm glad ye had the sense to take the *Mary Anne* elsewhere."

"Aye, she's up the coast a bit." Paul held out his tankard, allowing Maria to fill it once more. "But I hope you don't take offense if I make this a short visit."

"I'd think you a fool if ye didn't."

Paul downed the cider in a few hurried gulps. "Good. Well then, I should be off. I've seen what I've come to see. Oh, by the way, I'll leave these with you. With Southack sniffing around outside, you might need them."

Grinning, he pulled two pistols from his bandolier and laid them on the table. They were beautiful weapons with brass escutcheons, their buttcaps each boasting the face of a snarling lion in raised relief. "Took these off a naval man," Paul said, smirking. "Kind of ironic that they end up in the hands of the most legendary pirate to sail this coast since Kidd, isn't it?"

Sam's laughter matched Paul's as he picked up one of the pistols and ran a finger over the lion, symbol of the might of England. Ah, how he loved to mock authority, especially that of the bloody English government, which didn't do a damned thing for anyone except make its members' coffers all the fatter! "Aye, most definitely," he agreed. "Though they'll do the pirate no good if he hasn't the powder and shot to go with them!"

"Good God, you're a greedy rascal. Take all you can get, won't you?" Paul chuckled and tossed his leather ammunition pouch to the table followed by a fancy dagger with an emerald-encrusted hilt. "Here, take this too. What else do you want? My cutlass? My ship? The clothes off my back?"

Sam placed the dagger on the table and grinned. "What? Those foppish garments? No thank you, my friend. And as for the *Mary Anne*, don't forget she was once under *my* command until I so generously gave her to you. Oh, and do keep the cutlass. . . . I wouldn't want to leave you *totally* defenseless on your way back to her."

"A thoughtful bastard, isn't he?" Paul complained.

"And most ungrateful, too," Maria added, overlooking Paul's harsh language as she'd been trying to do with Sam's. "Thank you, Paul. We shall remember your kindness."

He picked up his hat, twirling it on one finger as he went to the door. "My pleasure. Good day to you, Maria. And Sam? I'm sure I'll be seeing you again . . . soon."

Sam raised the pistol in casual salute. "You can bet on it, lad."

With that, Paul opened the door and slipped outside, leaving Sam caressing the pistols and Maria wondering suspiciously what he'd meant by his last remark.

'Twas said that on dark, stormy nights the ghost of the Whydah's *captain wandered the dunes of the Great Beach in search of his witch lover. . . . When the moon rose pale and bloated over the sea, you might catch a glimpse of his dark shape as he strolled through the silvery waves breaking along that endless shore, waiting for the skeleton hands of his drowned crewmen to toss a lost coin or two up from the depths. And if you listened closely—very closely—you could hear his deep, rolling laughter in the night wind as it sighed over the vast, barren moors and deserted cliffs of the Great Beach. . . .*

They weren't entirely untrue, those legends. Captain Bellamy did indeed haunt that beach at night. Yet it was in the flesh, not as some ghostly apparition, and the laughter the villagers heard in the wind was nothing more than the product of easily frightened, overactive imaginations, for the pirate captain did not find much to laugh about as he wandered the dunes and gazed at what remained of his once proud ship.

It wasn't long before the people of Eastham started locking their doors against the night and trying to chase the darkness away with bright, blazing fires in their hearths. And when the Sea Witch ventured to the edge of town to trade a blanket or two for supplies, or to sell a potion for this ailment or that, no one dared question her about the ghost who roamed the Great Beach. And no longer did anyone make the long trek to her little hut to seek her medical advice or renowned cures.

But that was all well and good as far as Maria was concerned. She made no move to put talk of the ''ghost'' to rest, for it gave Sam what he needed most of all: safety, protection, and time to regain his strength.

Despite her dismay that his guilt over the *Whydah's* loss claimed his every thought, as well as his moods, Maria tried her best to make him happy. She abandoned her dreadful cure-alls in favor of more sustaining foods that strengthened and nourished Sam's gaunt, fever-ravaged body: baked apples with cinnamon, Indian pudding smothered in molasses, wild strawberries, fish chowder, dried pumpkin slices, shellfish, and as much hard cider as he wanted. This he consumed by the jugful—upon rising in the morning, as refreshment during the endless pacing of the little room that filled his days, and late at night while he walked the beach. She could not remember him drinking so much when he'd come to Eastham last year, but, she kept reminding herself, Sam Bellamy had a lot on his mind—and a lot to forget about.

She only wished that he hadn't forgotten *her,* for she had only to look at his proud, strengthening body and desire for him would swell her breast 'til she thought her heart would burst. But he remained aloof, and her heart went out to him. He didn't belong here, confined on land; he belonged on the quarterdeck of a mighty ship, for her pirate captain was a creature of the sea, and belonged to it as surely as did the sharks, the gulls, and the mighty whales that swam past the Great Beach now and then. It was a painful truth, one that she realized every time she found him standing silently in the shadows of the doorway, his dark eyes lingering wistfully upon the great, shimmering surface of the ocean.

With every day that passed, he sank further into his own private hell of grief and self-blame, and the tension between them became so palpable that Maria began to find it uncomfortable to be in the same room with him. The idea of confiding her past troubles and lingering heartache over little Charles became unthinkable. In his brooding, easily angered state, that was a subject she thought it best to avoid.

But at least he'd said nothing about returning to piracy, and she blissfully contented herself with the knowledge that his lawless days seemed to be over. And as she sat before the fire this mild night, making a new coat of blue broadcloth for him while he walked the beach, she gave thanks for that.

She was just sewing one of the last buttons on when the impatient rattle of the door latch startled her. Hurriedly, she shoved the coat behind her—after all it *was* to be a surprise. The door opened and Sam came in, bringing with him the heady, salt-tanged scent of the sea and a draft of cool air that made the fire jump, flare, and finally settle back down again as he closed the door behind him.

But she needn't have feared that he'd seen the coat. His dark eyes were distant, shuttered. Obviously, he was in no better spirits tonight than he'd been for the past two weeks. Withdrawn. Unapproachable. Needing comfort, but unwilling to ask for it.

Disinterestedly, he indicated the blue fabric she'd been trying to hide. "What are ye making?"

He was far more astute than she would've given him credit for. "A . . . new dress."

"Oh. Nice."

He didn't ask to see it. Maria swallowed tightly, feeling relieved, but somewhat hurt. "You've been down to the wreck again," she stated quietly.

"Aye." He stood on one foot, the other absently rubbing the sand from his wet ankle.

Maria sighed hopelessly. "Why do you torture yourself so? You can't bring them back."

"No. But dammit, how I wish I could!" He began to pace, that awful, back-and-forth motion that was starting to drive her crazy. "Those bloody villagers," he snarled, his temper rising with the speed of his pacing. "I'd like to carve their blasted gullets out, every last one of them! Have ye seen what they've done to my ship? They've robbed her, desecrated her! And that damned Southack, he's even burning her masts down to get at the iron that rings them!"

She winced at the thunder in his voice. "Sam, please. We're fortunate that you're *alive*."

"You call this fortunate?" he exploded. "To be stuck in this damned room all day just so that bloody idiot sent by the goddamned governor doesn't see me, let alone your addlebrained villagers? To be stranded without a ship? And just how long do you think it'll be before Doane ventures up here to check out the rumors of my ghost? Or Southack himself? God's teeth! I can't stand this confinement any longer! I have to get out of here!"

Helplessly, Maria watched as he paced back and forth, back and forth. But oh, the magnificence of him in such a fine rage: black eyes snapping, lips drawn tight, head high, and spine as straight as a frigate's mast. "Sam, please. Come here and sit down. I don't like it when you act like this."

"Like what?"

"Angry."

"And why the hell not?"

"Because it frightens me, that's why."

That, at least, brought a smile to his dark features—the barest quirking of his lips, but a smile nonetheless. But then he grew sullen again as he dropped down beside her and sprawled before the hearth, his head resting upon her knees, his eyes staring up at the ceiling in frustration. Hoping to calm him, Maria smoothed his neatly trimmed beard.

"I'm sorry, princess," he said morosely. He caught her hand and brought it to his lips. His kiss was tender against the sensitive skin of her knuckles, the wiry softness of his beard eliciting little shivers as he pressed her palm against his cheek and held it there for a long time. "I don't ever wish to frighten you. Others, maybe, but never you."

The silence stretched, the fire calming him and mellowing his temper. At length, Maria murmured, "And I'm sorry, too."

"For what?"

"For the fact that you're stuck here in this little room all day with nowhere to go, nothing to do. For feeding you weeds. For . . . for everything."

" 'Tisn't your fault," he said at length. "I don't want you to be blaming yourself for anything. If it hadn't been for you, and your weeds," he added with a smile, "I'd be dead now. Besides, one of these days Paul will be back. Today, tomorrow—who knows."

Maria stiffened. "Does that mean you'll be . . . leaving?" Tears sprang to her eyes, for she didn't have to be a prophetess, a soothsayer, or even a witch to know what his answer would be.

"Aye, I'll be going with him."

Thick silence followed. She shut her eyes and bit her lip, her dreams disintegrating like vapors from a dying fire. He had no plans of making a life with her. He had no intention of becoming an honest man. She'd been wrong about him—dead wrong. Sam Bellamy was a pirate, and a pirate he'd remain. Her hand, still folded within his and pressed against his bearded cheek, began to tremble, and then she heard his voice, soft, quiet, and demanding as he looked up at her and saw the single tear that trickled from her eye.

"I want you to go with me, princess."

She opened her eyes and stared down at him, unable to think, unable to speak. Go with him? Aboard a . . . *pirate* ship? Oh, God, she couldn't. *Don't ask this of me,* she thought. *Please, Sam, don't do this to me.* She would stand by him, follow him anywhere. Anywhere, that is, but onto a pirate ship.

"Don't you like ships, Maria?" he asked, a frown marring his brow as he looked up at her stricken face.

"I . . . I like them very much."

"Are you afraid to leave home?"

"No. No, 'tisn't that either. There's naught for me here, anyhow."

"Do you no longer care for me then?"

She gazed down at him helplessly. "Oh, Sam. What do I have to do to prove how much I love you? Don't you understand? It's not you, it's not the ship. It's—it's the way of life."

"Aha." Thoughtfully, he began to knead his chin with thumb and forefinger. "Piracy. Is that it, lass?"

Maria nodded.

"It bothers you that much, then?" And when she didn't answer he smiled, as though that was the least of his problems. Her spirits sank as she realized that in all probability, it was. Sitting up and reaching for his cider, he said, "Pirate or not, Maria, I'm still the same old Sam. The same one who will marry you."

"No, Sam. You're not the same," she said tightly.

"Granted, I've been a bit under the weather lately, but I'll be all right once I have a deck under my feet and a ship to command."

Her despair was mounting by the minute, denial of her shattered dreams making her reckless. "No, you've changed. You used to smile, to tease me, to laugh. You used to be friendly, but not anymore. Now you're moody, unpredictable. You remind me of a shark caught in a tidal pool!"

He laughed then, for that was exactly how he felt. "You can hardly blame me, Maria. How would you feel—"

"There was a time when you'd take me in your arms and love me 'til I couldn't think straight, but not anymore!" she cried, shoving a lock of hair out of her face. "You haven't made one move toward me, Sam, not one since you've been back, and don't tell me it's because you're not strong enough yet! You're out there walking that beach every night!"

"*What?*"

"All you care about now is a dead ship, dead men, and *tipple!* I hate it, Sam! Hate it!"

He set his jaw, for he hated being ruled by his guilt, too. But the *Whydah's* loss was eating a hole in his gut and the last thing he needed was for her to make that guilt even worse by reminding him about it—let alone condemning him for it. "I know I've been preoccupied lately," he said tensely, "but as I told you, once I get a deck under my feet I'll be all right."

"And what kind of deck? A *pirate* ship's deck?"

He clenched his fists at his sides.

"Piracy! That's *all you think about!* You're obsessed with it, and look what it's doing to you, to *us!* We don't talk, we don't touch, and everything I say seems to anger you! It's to the point I don't even want to be in the same room with you! You could care less about us! Now you drown yourself in cider, you're wearing a hole in the floor with that awful pacing, and nothing I say or do makes a bit of difference. You used to have dreams, ambitions—now, all you can think of is what was, what might've been. They're gone, Sam! *Whydah,* your crew, piracy, all of it!"

"Nay, not piracy," he said with a wicked gleam in his eye.

"Why? Why must you return to that thieving life?"

"And what do you find so distasteful about it, my dear?"

"Distasteful?" she cried, leaping up and no longer caring that he might see the coat she'd hoped to surprise him with. "For God's sake, a pirate is the worst kind of criminal the devil ever created! Enemy of the Crown, threat to honest commerce, opposer of sane, lawful government, and thief, murderer, and defiler of everything God stands for all wrapped up in one dirty, stinking package! You expect me to *condone* it?"

By the stubborn set of his jaw and the way he began to tap his empty tankard against his kneecap she knew he was on the verge of losing his patience with her. "Come now, Maria. Is that all you think we did, sail around killing people?"

"Well, didn't you?"

"Hell, no! We robbed them, for Chrissakes! And if they surrendered their ships without a fight there was no need to harm them!"

"I don't care! What has it brought you? Your entire fortune lies buried beneath the waves and all but two of your crew members are dead, and you want to go *back* to it?"

He frowned, staring at her. What had she said? That not

all of them had died? But she was in a full-blown fury now, her accusations hammering at his taut nerves, his ebbing patience. "Oh, you think there's nothing wrong with it, do you?" she raged. "Do you seriously *believe* that? What about the robbing? Did you ever stop and think about the poor people you stole from? 'Tis wrong, Sam! *Wrong!*"

Oh, she'd done it now. Anger was flaring up in those dark eyes, making them gleam like cold obsidian. "I'll have you know, Maria, that those we robbed from were far from *poor.*" His voice was cold, expressionless. "Scoundrels they are, men who don't give a bloody damn for those who are starving in the streets as long as their own tables groan with food. Men who turn a blind eye to the abuse, the mistreatment heaped upon those who sail their stinking ships. They make laws to protect their interests and then make *more* laws to punish those who are bold enough to break the first ones! If anyone is 'poor,' 'tis the lads who serve aboard their ships! I've been there, Maria! I know what it's like! *And by God, I'll never serve such scurvy, scum-ridden bastards again!*"

With a savage oath, he flung the tankard across the room, where it smashed against the wall and clattered to the floor. "And people think that men take up piracy for the riches alone? Hah! Riches be damned! At least we treat our own well!"

"Just because someone is rich doesn't give you the right to steal from them! I'm sorry, Sam, but nothing you can say will change my feelings!"

"And nothing you can say will change mine! Now, are you going with me or not?"

"Nay! I'll not go with you and participate in such evil!"

"Dammit, Maria! Do I have to show you a ship full of ill-treated wretches to make my point? England treats her seamen worse than anybody and I have the scars on my back to prove it!"

"So I've noticed," she said dryly. "And how did you get them? As punishment for thievery? Mutiny? *Stealing?*"

"No, damn you! Insubordination!"

"Somehow, I'm not surprised," she said with sweet acidity.

He turned and slammed his fist into the door so hard she heard the wood crack beneath the blow, then he leaned his forearms against it and stared at the floor in a last, desperate attempt to control his anger. She remembered the clean-shaven, faintly disreputable—but honest—man she'd known a year ago. A man who'd promised to return to her, and had; with a hoop of gold in his ear.

He muttered something she didn't catch, something she wasn't so sure she wanted to hear.

"What?"

"I said, I did it for you."

Mutely, she watched him until at last he straightened up and faced her with tortured eyes. It never occurred to her that his anguish sprang from the fact that she wouldn't accept him for what he was—and not that he couldn't make her see his point. "Did it all for you," he continued, baring his heart, his now-dead dreams to her. "With every ship we took I thought of how your eyes would light up when I gave you my share of the spoils. How happy you'd be, how excited, how much you'd . . . love me." He turned away from the lingering accusations in her eyes. "I promised I'd return with enough silver and gold to make you a princess, didn't I? And it would've been yours, every damned bit of it."

He glanced at her, sitting there so quietly, the long, loosely plaited rope of her hair curling in her lap like a coil of hemp. Her lashes were lowered, and he saw the sparkle of a tear on their fringes. But when she looked up at him, her eyes were steady, firm, and resolute.

"I wouldn't have wanted it, Sam."

"*What?*"

"I said, I wouldn't have wanted it."

Nothing she might've said could've wounded him more. Her words hit him like a slap across the face. "What do you mean, you wouldn't have wanted it? I spent a whole year amassing that treasure!" Blind rage surged within him, and savagely he turned on her. "A whole bloody year, and this is all the thanks I get for it?"

"I just told you I didn't approve of piracy," she said sadly. "How could you possibly think I'd accept its ill-gotten spoils?"

"Because I'd forgotten just what a sickening model of righteousness you are!" he exploded, the thunderous timbre of his voice making her shudder with fright. "And had I remembered, I sure as hell wouldn't have come back here just to lose everything I worked so damned hard for, to have it all thrown back in my face by an ungrateful wench who'd just as soon poison me with birch bark! Go ahead, live by your stupid, righteous rules, but 'twill be a cold day in Hell before I do the same!''

He stormed to the bed, flung the pillows aside, and snatched up the two pistols that Paul had given him. Maria watched in horror as he began to ransack the room. The cupboard doors were flung wide. Bottles of herbs and plants went crashing upon the floor. Cursing, he slammed the doors shut, then attacked the chest at the foot of the bed.

Maria lunged to her feet. ''What are you doing?''

''Looking for something!''

''What? If you'd bother to ask before tearing my house apart maybe I'd tell you!''

''Like you've told me everything else I've wanted to know?'' He spun on his heel to face her, his face a dark mask of rage. ''My dagger, woman! The one that Paul gave me! Where is it?''

''What dagger?'' she said with an innocence that didn't fool him at all.

Dark eyes narrowed. He lashed out and grabbed her arm, his fingers biting into the tender flesh. Rage burned in his eyes and Maria could see there was no sparkle in those black orbs now. Was this the pirate captain who'd walked the decks of the *Whydah*, then? The real ''Black'' Sam?

Bravely, she said, ''So, is this how you intimidated those who dared defy you, *Captain?*''

He yanked her forward by the bodice of her gown. *''Where . . . is . . . my . . . dagger?''*

She'd be damned if she'd tell him! ''And where are you going that you can't live without it?''

Her syrupy tone enraged him all the more. ''To rescue my men!''

''What men?''

''The two that you said survived the shipwreck! No doubt they're being held in some bloody gaol, and if I don't get them out no one will! Now, where the hell is my dagger, damn it?''

But Maria wasn't moving. Angrily, she returned his hard

stare. "To rescue your men, huh? Well then, you'd better take more than just a pair of pistols and a dagger! There are more than two who need your *noble* services!"

He loomed over her. "What the hell are you saying?"

"That ship whose name you called out in the midst of your delirium while you lay thrashing in my bed with fever? The one who I thought was another woman, of all things—"

"What about her?" he snarled.

"Only that the seven pirates you put aboard her are also alive!" And as he stared at her she went on with uncharacteristic nastiness, the loss of her dreams making her say things she knew she'd regret. "That wine ship, a pink, went down the same night as your *Whydah* did, but at least *those* fools had an excuse for wrecking their ship, when you did not! They were drunk! Drunk on Madeira wine!"

He went deathly quiet. His knuckles whitened around the pistols. His nostrils flared above his dark mustache. Never, ever before had Maria seen him look so fearsome. Afraid now, she began to back away.

Very, very quietly, his voice dangerously low, he asked, "And where, my dear, might these men be held?"

"In . . . the Boston gaol."

"And where," he continued in that same frightening, menacing tone, "were they kept before that?"

"In the Barnstable gaol," she said in a small voice.

"And you didn't tell me?"

"It wouldn't have done any good! You were in no condition to rescue them!"

"Damn you for the conniving little witch you are!" he railed. "If ye'd told me about my men earlier I could've gotten them out! But no, you deliberately waited 'til it was too damned late for me to do anything here! Now I have to go all the way up to Boston!" His foot lashed out, sending a chair slamming against the wall; another vicious kick and her blanket chest spun halfway across the room. The lid popped open and blankets tumbled out onto the floor. And then he was upon her, shaking her, while curses and angry threats filled the air above her head.

And this time, she truly *was* afraid.

"Stop it, Sam!" she cried, terrified in the face of such a violent temper.

"My dagger, woman!"

Unbidden, her gaze darted to the blanket chest; deliberately, his followed, and a wicked, knowing gleam entered his black eyes. She felt the blood drain from her face, for not only was the dagger in that chest, but little Charles's things as well. Desperately, she tried to twist free of his painful grip on her arm. "Unhand me, you—you savage! You're hurting me!"

But he didn't let go, merely yanked her forward to crash up against the solid wall of his chest. He glared down at her, his eyes fierce. "You should have *told* me where it was, Maria, and I would've gone easy on ye! Miserable, stinking pirate that I am, I always reward those who offer no resistance! A bit of gold, a chest of silver, makes no difference to me!" He yanked her closer, his flashing black eyes mere inches from her own. "But ye don't want those things, do ye? Not if they're gotten by piracy! What the hell do ye want, then? What, no answer? If you'd told me where that damned dagger was I'd give ye something far richer than a sack of damned coin! Something ye've been begging for all along!" His black gaze locked onto hers. "Something you're *still* begging for!"

And she knew by the smoldering gleam in his eyes that silver and gold were not what he offered. She remembered that hot, simmering look, knew it well—and had no illusions about what he was implying.

"Damn you, Sam Bellamy! You're nothing but a scoundrel, a rogue, an ill-bred—"

He didn't allow her to finish. His deep, mocking laughter filled the air, and before she could twist her head away, his mouth came crashing down upon hers, bruising her lips and sending hot, pulsing sensations tearing through her body despite her terror, her own anger. He drove her head back, stabbing his tongue within the recesses of her mouth, taking her lips, her mouth, her very heart just as he had any other prize he'd ever wanted: ruthlessly, mercilessly, and giving no quarter.

"Ye think me not strong enough, eh?"

"No! No, Sam, please—don't! Not this way!" She turned her face away, but he was deaf to her pleas. Looming over her, he forced her backwards toward the bed, fingers ripping at the buttons that held her gown together, his mouth slashing brutally down upon hers. There was no love in this act, no tenderness. Nothing but lust, born of anger. The backs of her knees came up against the bed and she fell, twisting to the side in an effort to escape him. But his body fell upon hers, trapping her, pinning her down, his steely arms an enclosure that at any other time she would never have fought. Futilely, she kicked, struggled, beat upon his hard chest with useless fists.

Stop it. Oh please, for the love of God, stop. . . . Tears of despair, terror, and grief over the loss of the man she'd loved spilled down her cheeks in two fat, shimmering drops of crystal. The last buttons that held her gown together gave way, and then his hands were hot upon her flesh.

She was pinned like a butterfly. A sob caught in her throat and she bit down on her lip, squeezing her eyes shut to block the sight of his dark head as he tasted one swelling, pink-tipped breast.

"No, Sam," she sobbed brokenly. "Not this way, please. I beg of you, please, not like this—"

But he was already unfastening his breeches, and she saw that he was swollen, erect, and ready. Crying, she dug both palms into her eyes, wishing she could block out this vile, awful act he was about to commit. But that stabbing thrust never came. A moment passed, two. Slowly, she opened her eyes to stare tearfully up at him. His face was paling, his eyes widening with the horror of what he'd been about to do. With a bitter curse, he rolled away, his heavy breathing and her quiet sobs the only sounds in the deathly quiet room.

"Oh, God," he moaned, shame and disgust at his loss of control flooding through him. This time his temper had carried him too far. He bent his head, leaning his brow into both hands while he waited for the denied fires in his blood to cool. Behind him Maria lay unmoving, the pillow on each side of her white face damp with tears. Moments passed, long moments of thick, uncomfortable silence. Finally he got up, drew on his breeches, and turned to look down at her. Where there had been violence in his eyes before, now there was only agony and a desperate plea for forgiveness.

He leaned down and touched a finger to her wet cheek. But Maria flinched as though he'd burned her, and squeezed her tearflooded eyes shut, too hurt, too sickened by what he'd done—and by what he'd been about to do—to look at him.

His fingers were warm against her cheek. Gently, he traced the track of her tears, wiped them away, dried them with a soft corner of the blanket. She felt the bed shift as he sat beside her, heard his heavy sigh when she didn't respond, and then she felt his touch no more.

"I'm sorry. So sorry, my little princess."

She opened her eyes. He sat at the edge of the bed staring morosely at the floor, elbows resting on his knees, head bent, hands clasped behind his neck. Black hair flowed over his fingers. There was no triumph in his stance, just regret.

"I'm sorry, Maria. I have no excuses, save that your beauty holds me even in anger, your sharp tongue goads me to do things I would never consider in less . . . trying circumstances." He lifted his head with great effort, his eyes filled with anguish. "Maria, love. Oh, what have I done?"

She sat up then and rose from the bed. He needed her—oh God, he needed her love, her comfort—but she did not go to him. Woodenly, she fastened what remained of the buttons at her nape, took her cloak down from its peg near the hearth. With stiff, detached movements, she put it on.

"Maria?"

She didn't look back until she reached the door. "It isn't what you've done, Sam. *It's what you've become.*"

The door opened, closed behind her, and then she was gone, leaving him with only the howl of the mournful wind outside to keep him company.

Sickened, Sam looked at the shambles he'd made of her home. The chair leaned sadly upon a splintered leg. Blankets lay in crumpled little heaps upon the floor. The tankard, its handle twisted, its sides dented in, huddled in the corner. She'd called him a savage, a brute . . . and God help him, she was right.

He had almost raped her.

Sam Bellamy, pirate captain, leaned his face into his hands as silent tears of regret, self-disgust, and remorse leaked through his strong fingers and dropped softly upon the floor.

Chapter 13

*I love thee, all unlovely as thou seem'st,
And dreaded as thou art!*

COWPER

Maria had a single destination in mind and she didn't care that she'd have to pass straight through the middle of Eastham to reach it—the apple tree where she'd first met Sam. Why she was heading there, why she even *wanted* to go there, she didn't know. There was nothing like adding salt to a wound. But as she stormed across the dark, lonely moors she could only attribute such self-torture to a determination to purge that beast from her heart once and for all.

Dawn broke as she reached the King's Highway, but she found no joy in it. On she walked, moccasins weaving trails in and out of a jumble of day-old wheel ruts and hoofprints. She heard the haunting call of a cardinal, the screech of a jay, the songs of a hundred birds as the sun rose higher; but now such happy twittering sounded hollow and empty to her ears, perhaps even mocking. When a squirrel rebuked her from a pine's scruffy branches she didn't look up, and even the bearberry shrubs whose bell-shaped white flowers lent a serene beauty to the dunes seemed bleak, somewhat sad.

I will not cry over him. That silent vow became a marching chant with every step she took. *I*—step—*will*—step—*not*—step—*cry*—step—*over*—step—*him.* He'd already caused her enough heartache in the past year alone to last a lifetime. Yet the resolution not to cry was easier said than done. Where her heart had been there was only a hollow, aching hole of grief, for the Sam Bellamy she'd once known and loved was as dead as if he truly *had* perished with his ship.

And in his place walked a monster.

Just what sort of evil had she resurrected from the *Whydah?* Had she been out of her mind? She should've just left him there to die!

But no, never! Never, never, *never!* Even in its anguish her heart rebelled violently at the thought. For no matter what Sam had done to her, no matter what he'd become, there was one thing she couldn't deny, try as she might to do just that.

She still loved him. Always had and always would.

"Damn you, Sam Bellamy!" she cried, to no one but the clouds that floated in a sea of blue high overhead.

She'd been mad to nurse him back to life. Insane! She wouldn't have wasted the effort on a dying shark, a wounded wolf, so why him, a pirate, no less dangerous and surely more of a predator than either? But she knew that if a wolf should limp to her doorway, she'd bind its leg. If a shark lay thrashing in the surf, she would guide it back to sea and hold it until its mighty gills flared and it vanished in a swirl of foam.

She made a formidable sight as she crossed the town limits and boldly entered Eastham, never looking more like the witch she was thought to be, Satan's wayward daughter grieving for the devil himself. Her golden hair swirled in wild, defiant glory about her face, her eyes were haunted. The people stared, some fleeing into their homes and dragging their children with them, others merely gaping as she passed. But no one made a move to stop her.

Passing Higgins Tavern where it lay tucked among the gnarled oaks and scrubby pines, she turned off the road and trudged through last year's dead, rustling leaves. Sunlight filtered down through the trees, and the earth grew soft and doughy beneath a blanket of pine needles. The trees thinned, the land sloped gradually downward, and there, its branches dressed in clothes of spring green and dripping with infant apples, stood the tree.

She sank down and leaned against its comforting, stout old trunk. Sunlight dappled her hair, the patches of skin at her nape where missing buttons left gaps in her gown; it played against her eyelids and made her sleepy. A sparrow flitted into a knothole high above her head, and she heard the incessant peeping of baby birds, the steady drone of a bumblebee. Here, where she'd thought to purge herself of anguish, the peacefulness of the meadow triumphed and dulled the sharp edges of her pain.

She plucked a blade of grass and rolled it between her thumb and forefinger. Serenity, peace . . . oh, if only it could banish the awful, nightmarish memories! Sam. He was naught but a pirate, a beast of prey, who could give her nothing but heartaches and a lifetime of pain. Auntie had been right all along. She was better off without him! She didn't need him!

It was too bad she couldn't believe her own lies—for thoughts of a life without him brought the tears back to her eyes with more sting than ever. And suddenly the meadow wasn't so peaceful anymore, but lonely and sad and full of memories that had never died, and never would.

Maria awoke to long shadows and a fiery, muted sky. She was groggily aware that something bad had happened—and then the memory of the previous night slammed up against her heart and jolted her fully awake.

Sam.

But there was no sadness now. Indeed, while she'd slept, something else had arrived to arm and strengthen her. Anger. She stood up, brushing bits of grass from her skirts, remembering the last time she'd been beneath this very apple tree and had had to do the same thing. Then as now she'd been hurt, angry; then as now she'd felt abused and taken advantage of. And then—as now—Sam had been the cause.

But then, she'd been a frightened child. And Maria, who'd endured far too much to ever be called a child again, made up her mind to stop acting like a little girl, stop feeling sorry for herself, and return to her home. To think Sam had driven her from it in the first place! That she had *let* him! Oh, she hoped he was still there when she got back, because if he was, she was going to let him know exactly what she thought of him!

Bold and domineering he was, but he would not intimidate her! She'd meet that awful temper of his with unruffled calm, would arm herself against his praise of piracy with God, the Good Book, and her own heartfelt beliefs. Oh, she wouldn't let him frighten her! Bully! Beast! *Pirate!* With a determined gleam in her eye, Maria slapped the wrinkles from her skirts and by the last light of day struck out across the darkening meadow and shadowy woods.

She saw candles flickering in its windows long before the dim outline of the tavern came into view through the trees. Guffaws of laughter, the clink of glasses, whiffs of pipe smoke drifting out of the open doorway. A pang of loneliness welled up inside her. Envy filled her as she listened to those happy sounds, and she suddenly wished that *she* could go to church and hear the pastor's sermons, or sit in a circle with the other women and sew, or share cold cider with the villagers during autumn's husking bees. She wished that she had a friend. They were all futile wishes. She was an outcast.

Thank you, Sam. . . .

Her chin came up in fresh ire, and her long golden hair thumped rhythmically against her buttocks with each angry stride. In no time she reached the road, a starlit path through the trees that led back to the flat, lonely moors that were her home.

So caught up was Maria with thoughts of what she'd say to that—that *barbarian* that she never heard the footsteps behind her. And it wasn't until a voice called out through the darkness that she realized she was being followed.

"Why, if it ain't the Sea Witch of Eastham, out for a nightly stroll! In a hurry, Mistress Hallett?"

The voice was thick and slurred with the effects of ale, the laughter that accompanied it even more so. Maria spun around, suddenly uneasy. Despite the choking gloom, she recognized the two men immediately. Adam and Freddie Morse. They'd come here from Boston two years ago, and where they'd lived before that was anyone's guess. When they weren't out fishing in the bay—which wasn't often, given their aversion to hard work and their penchant for drink—they could be found in the tavern. Neither was well liked by the people of Eastham, and even Prudence had complained about these two, for they'd never been ones to leave her with an extra coin for her efforts.

And here she was, the tavern a quarter mile behind her and an empty road stretching before her into the darkness. Her heartbeat quickened and she stepped up her pace.

Behind her their footfalls hastened, matching hers. "Don't you wanna talk to us, Maria? We happened to see you walkin' oy as we came out of the tavern and thought you might like some company. The roads ain't safe for a young thing like you to be travelling on at night, 'specially seein's how you're not even supposed to be in town in the first place!''

"Yeah," Freddie added. "He's right. They ain't safe— 'specially for a . . . *lady.*"

"Hell, they ain't safe for no one! Not even poor, unsuspecting souls like us! Never know who you might meet up with . . . Indians, wild animals—maybe even a *witch,* if it's your unlucky night!''

"Or your lucky one," Freddie said slyly.

Bursts of laughter followed. Maria fought down panic and the urge to run. To do so would be foolish, would admit her fear of them—and invite them to chase her. Bravely, she stopped, raised her chin, and faced them. "Yes, Adam, you're quite right. I *am* a witch and therefore I have no need of your . . . protection. Now please let me pass, or I promise that you shall regret it.''

Sour fumes of ale hovered about them like a pungent cloud. Their unwashed bodies stank of dead fish and sea brine, their hair lay greasy and matted against their heads. And to her dismay, they did not back away, but only laughed.

"Aw, Maria," Adam said, baring his black-stained teeth in a smile that could only be described as a leer. "You don't really think we believe those ol' wives' tales now, do you? A witch! We ain't as dumb as the others, y' know!''

"Oh, really?" Her attempt at a sarcastic purr sounded more like the mewing of a frightened kitten. "Then why did you throw stones at me like they did?''

"Stones? What stones?''

Freddie elbowed him in the ribs, and leaned toward him. "She means that day last fall.''

"Oh, that!" Again that awful leer, and now, drunken laughter that frightened her all the more. "How could I have forgotten? Tell her why we did it, Freddie.''

"No, you tell her!''

"Me? Hell, we just did it 'cause it was fun, that's why!''

"Fun?" Involuntarily, Maria took a step backwards. It was bad enough that the villagers had hurled stones at her because of their beliefs—but these two had done so for a reason so awful, so terrible, that her gentle heart could not

comprehend the very evil of it. They had done it for fun?
Because they'd *wanted* to cause her pain and see her suffer?

Dear God, what would they do to her now?

It took all of her strength not to panic, all of her courage
to maintain the height of her chin, the steadiness of her voice.
''I think you've just proven that you're exactly what I've always thought you to be—nothing but a pair of demented,
nauseating beasts, both of you!'' And as she turned away,
their laughter rang in her ears and a thick, beefy paw caught
her arm.

''Why don't we show the *lady* how demented we really
are, Adam?''

''No!'' Struggling wildly, Maria fought to throw off Freddie's arm. ''Unhand me this instant! Let me go!''

She screamed, the awful, perverted sounds of their laughter ringing in her ears. She saw Adam's fingers go to his
waistband, felt cruel hands gripping her jaw and forcing her
to watch. Frenzied, she drew back her hand and with a
strength born of desperation, struck him full across his dirty,
sweating face.

Without waiting for a reaction she bolted. Pain ripped
through her shoulder as fingers caught her arm and yanked
her viciously back. She caught a glimpse of Adam, one hand
against his cheek, the other holding his breeches up at the
waistband. His eyes were ugly, narrowed with malice, and
as she struggled wildly in Freddie's grip, he took a threatening step toward her.

As she opened her mouth to scream, a voice rang out behind them, cold, ominous, and familiar.

''Touch her, and so help me God, I'll slit your throat from
chest to chin.''

Adam turned to ice. Slowly he looked up, the color draining from his face like sand from an hourglass. ''Sweet Jesus,''
he breathed, staring past her.

Maria followed his gaze. And there, standing calmly in
the road not thirty feet away, was Sam.

His face was thunderous, his lips a hard line of fury, his
eyes blacker than death and perhaps even colder. Moonlight
glinted against the pistols hanging from his neck. Not only
was he wearing the coat she'd meant to surprise him with, he
had indeed found the dagger and now had it clenched in one

very capable hand. But Sam did not require any weapon to inspire terror—the savage, murderous wrath that emanated from him was enough.

"Jesus, Freddie, *it's the ghost!*"

And now he was striding purposefully forward, the devil straight from hell, tall and forbidding and full of deadly intent. Screaming, Freddie bolted off into the darkness, leaving Adam trying desperately to fasten his breeches.

Sam's voice was cold, flat. "Take one step and you're a dead man."

But Adam, suddenly sober and paralyzed with terror, could not have moved if his life depended on it, and at the moment, it very well did. If there was ever any question in his mind about just who this apparition was, the way it stood—with legs braced slightly apart in the seaman's way as though still in command of the quarterdeck of a mighty ship—quickly dispelled any lingering doubts. And now disdain, and something very like amusement, flickered in those cold, black eyes as they watched Adam's fumbling attempts to fasten his breeches.

But it was all too obvious that Sam Bellamy found no humor in the situation. A muscle twitched in his grim, hard jaw, and Maria, backing fearfully away, saw no little creases fanning out at the corners of his eyes.

He thrust her behind him in a sudden, fluid movement, his gaze never leaving Adam. His lips curled in disgust as he watched Adam's pitiful attempts to close his breeches. "Don't bother," he said, his voice cold, casual, and devoid of feeling. "You won't be needing them."

"Please, sir, don't hurt me! I didn't mean it, any of it! Honest, I swear—"

"Shut up, damn you!"

Cringing, and about to disgrace himself in the very breeches he was struggling to hold up, Adam whimpered like a child as the pirate captain began to walk a slow circle around him, making him feel like a market swine about to be butchered. Dark fingers tugged at that black beard, perhaps thoughtfully, more likely not, for Adam knew with a sinking feeling in the pit of his suddenly ill stomach that there *was* no thought involved, no deliberation—his fate had already been decided. Tears streaked his filthy cheeks; he closed his

eyes, smelled the stink of his own fear. And then he heard
the distant sound of voices. Patrons, no doubt alerted by his
brother's screams, were pouring out of the tavern and heading
up the road. The pirate had heard it too, and by the way he
was smiling—a slow, hellish grin that was not meant to reassure but to bode ill—it was clear that he, unlike Adam, had
been aware of the approaching villagers for some time.

"My, my, looks like we're going to have some company,
doesn't it, lad?" Black eyes bored into him like nails, and
the fingers that had, a moment ago, been stroking that hea-
thenish beard now stroked—no, *caressed*—the bejeweled hilt
of the dagger. "And seeing as how you were so intent upon
. . . displaying yourself, I'm sure you'll find this a most op-
portune moment to demonstrate your talents. Surely, your
neighbors will appreciate them far more than Mistress Hallett
would have, don't you think?" Again that cold smile, the
merciless humor that backlit those devil's eyes. "As for
me"—he crossed his arms and began to stroke his beard once
more—"I think I shall enjoy what promises to be a very . . .
amusing performance." The grin widened, showing teeth that
were unfairly white and straight, teeth that were the only spot
of light in a face made all the more dark by a moon that had
suddenly, wisely, taken shelter behind a cloud.

Unable to comprehend the implications of the pirate's
words, Adam could only stare at those thewy, strapping seaman's arms crossed so casually over that broad chest, at the
dagger peeping beneath one bent elbow whose subtle appearance was anything *but* casual. Droplets of sweat popped
out on Adam's brow, raced down his temples, and mingled
with the dirty tracks of his tears.

"Now, step out of your breeches."

"*What?*"

"Ye heard me." Sam gestured with the knife. "Step out
of them."

And now Adam understood. His bloodless face went the
color of ashes. "Sir, no. Please, oh *please*, I beg of you—"

"Maria, dear, please turn your head." Sam's voice was
too calm, too casual. And then, unexpectedly, he exploded.
"I said off with them, ye blithering, stinking cur!"

Behind him, Maria slunk into the woods, her knees weak,
her hands shaking. She heard Adam's sobs, the soft scrape

of fabric sliding down his legs. She waited for the agonized scream—but there was only Sam's derisive laughter and the voices of the villagers as they loudly made their way up the street.

"Ah, listen . . . your friends are coming." Again, that unnerving, deadly calm. " 'Twould be a shame to keep them waiting, wouldn't it? Now go, and show *them,* not an innocent young woman, what a pitiful excuse for an organ you have!"

"Sir, *please*—"

"Now, damn you, before I lose my patience and geld ye where ye stand!"

The knife flashed in the starlight, but Adam was already fleeing, his bloodcurdling screams hideous enough to raise the dead, his shirttails flapping wildly around his bare buttocks like a loose sail.

From down the road came howls of laughter, the horrified shriek of a woman.

The faintest of grins flickered across Sam's austere features. Damned, miserable, filthy, stinking cur! Feeling somewhat satisfied, he turned and shoved the dagger into its scabbard. "Maria?" he called. But the road behind him was empty. "Maria? Where are ye, lass?" And then he heard the crackle of underbrush, a sharp cry—and silence.

He found her lying on her side, her face damp with tears, her hand gripping her ankle. She looked up at him. Her lips were white with pain, the lower one trembling, and in her wide eyes he saw apprehension, fear, and absolute misery.

"Oh, Sam . . ." She burst into sobs. "They—they—he was going to—"

"I know, dearest." Wordlessly, he bent down and gathered her up in his arms. She was a featherweight, all legs, gown, and not much else save for the tumble of hair that draped her tear-streaked face. He pulled a damp strand of it out of her eyes, kissed her lids, and held her face against his chest. "Little fool," he murmured, rocking her, and the words were both an endearment and an unspoken plea for forgiveness.

But he need not have asked it. Childlike, she nestled against his chest as he carried her, her little hand pressed trustingly against his sternum, her golden head tucked beneath his jaw. She never asked where he was taking her. She didn't care. All that mattered was that he was here; she was safe, and the arms that shielded her from the horrors of the world were sweet and gentle once more.

Chapter 14

*If I leave all for thee, will thou exchange
And be all to me?*

BROWNING

Branches clawed at the starry heavens, brambles tore at their clothes. Sam skirted the marsh, avoiding the mud that ripened the night air with the pungent scent of rotting vegetation, salt, and the heady stench of low tide. Cattails and rushes engulfed them, rough grasses swished against Maria's legs, but he didn't stop until he reached the glass-calm waters of Billingsgate Harbor.

Down the beach he carried her, and straight out onto the wharf that melted into the darkness cloaking the bay. Past boats sleeping in the harbor and nudging the wharf, where starlight gleamed faintly against darkened hulls and the tide sucked and lapped around them, between them, and at the poles supporting the pier. The darkened silence was disturbed by the sharp sound of Sam's boots striking rhythmically upon bleached planking. His face gleamed in the darkness, set with determination. Finally, he halted, and silence reigned again as the night breathed around them.

His arms tightened around her. She heard his breath moving harshly through his lungs, felt the dampness of his chest as it rose and fell against her cheek. The long trek through woods and marshes had been too much for him, but never would he admit it and never would she provoke his temper by reminding him that he was not fully recovered. But as she waited for him to set her down his breathing steadied, his heartbeat levelled out beneath her ear, and she felt the weight of his chin upon the top of her head.

He held her thus until the silence between them finally grew louder than the gentle sounds of the night. Burying his lips in the soft, fragrant sweep of her hair, he said softly, "Aren't ye going to curse me to Hell and back? Scream at me, rage at me? I deserve it, you know. Anything but this silent treatment."

"What would you have me say?"

"Oh, I don't know. There must be some pretty foul thoughts of me running around in that sweet head of yours. Say them. Let them out. I can take it."

"I'm afraid the thoughts I have of you at the moment would do nothing but inflate your pride, so I prefer to keep them to myself."

"Is my pride so inflated that it will burst given a bit of reassurance?"

"No. But you're right. You hardly deserve it."

Her words, had she not delivered them in such a gentle manner, would've cut deeply, for she was right—he deserved her anger, her disgust, and more. In fact, he *wanted* her to lash out at him, to hurt him. Perhaps it would ease his guilt over the way he'd treated her. But as she tilted her head back, sending her hair spilling over his forearm, he saw only gratitude, love, and an apology of her own reflected in the luminous pools of her eyes.

"I'm sorry—" they both began, and the ridiculousness of it all struck them at the same time. They burst into shaky, nervous, but healthy laughter, dispelling both Maria's lingering hurt and the guilt that had been festering in Sam's conscience like the plague. It washed away the bad feelings, smoothed out the rough edges. It was something they hadn't shared since Sam had first come to Eastham over a year ago, and now they both succumbed to it until they clutched each other for the pure joy of it. She wrapped her arms around his neck and he swung her around and around until they both grew dizzy and nearly stumbled off the pier and into the dark waters of the bay.

Finally, he set her down. "Did you see Adam's face?" she gasped, still giggling. "I thought for sure he was going to faint dead away! Oh, Sam, if you could only have *seen* yourself! You looked more forbidding than the devil himself!''

He stroked his beard. ''Did I, now?'' he asked with a crooked smile, obviously pleased.

''Oh, absolutely. Heavens, no wonder poor Adam thought you were a ghost. What *that* little scene will do for your legend!''

He sobered somewhat. ''Too bad I can't stick around long enough to find out.''

Her laughter was squashed like a bug beneath a boot heel. The happiness fled her heart in a dizzying rush, creating a vacuum that sucked the breath from her lungs. Horror swept in to take its place. ''Leaving? What do you mean, leaving?''

''Be serious, Maria. After tonight, you don't really think I can stay here, do you? They're probably searching your hut already. And you read the governor's proclamation—anyone found hiding, harboring, or nursing any survivors from the *Whydah* will share in their punishment. If they'll hang mere pirates—and I can assure you, my dear, that they will—just think how they'll deal with me, their captain. Delightful thoughts, aren't they?'' He gave a short laugh at her involuntary shudder. ''Sorry, lass, but that's one risk I'm not willing to take. I love you, but whatever punishment they intend for me is something I will *not* share.''

Devastation was merciful; it didn't bring pain, agony, or tears—yet. Just a spreading numbness that drained the warmth from her bones, her blood, her skin, her very heart. Gooseflesh stood up on her arms. From far away she heard her own plaintive, quivering voice. ''But they don't know you're alive. . . .''

''Nay, but they will if I stay here long enough. 'Twill take only one bullet to prove that a 'ghost' is naught but flesh and blood.''

She stared at him. He was right, of course. And the villagers would be swarming over her hut like a cloud of angry hornets; they could not go back, not even for Gunner. If Sam was caught, he'd be sent to Boston for trial and certain execution, and she, who had nursed him back to health and now accompanied him, would be tried right along with him. Eastham was no longer safe for either one of them; they *had* to leave.

And now they heard shouts, calls, and the sounds of the villagers moving through the night.

"Let's go," he said, taking her arm.

But Maria hesitated. What about Gunner? What about Auntie? What about her memories of little Charles, of her parents, her childhood, of—

"Come on, Maria, we haven't all night!"

What about the fact that Sam was a pirate?

"But Sam—"

"What, dammit?"

"I . . . I can't!"

He swore beneath his breath and stared beyond her to the woods. The villagers were getting closer. And closer. "Goddammit, we don't have time to sit here and talk about it. *Now come on!*"

"I'll not go anywhere with you as long as you remain a pirate!"

He swore again, harder this time. Lanterns were shining through the trees now, the voices getting louder. Any moment now the villagers would discover them. Desperate, Sam took the only course open to him—he lied to her, telling himself it was for her own damn good. "Dammit, Maria, I'm not going to stand here and argue about it! If piracy's what's needling ye I'll give it up, all right? Now Christ, let's go!"

"You'll give it up? Honestly?"

He gritted his teeth. *"Yes!"*

She was reluctant to believe him; but she trusted she could talk him out of going back on his word if indeed he tried.

And as he scooped her up once more and raced down the wharf with her, he thanked the gods above that she knew nothing of his *real* plans, for if she did, she wouldn't follow him farther than the edge of this warped and weathered pier. In fact, she'd probably push him off it. But he'd die before he'd leave her alone in Eastham, especially after tonight. Reaching the pier's edge, he eyed the fishing boats that lay quietly in the harbor until he saw one that would suit his purposes. "Now, dry those tears," he said, tenderly smudging a track of moisture into her cheek with one callused finger. "I'll have no wet-nosed brats in my crew!"

Just then Gunner came racing out of the woods, across the beach, and down the pier.

"Gunner!" Maria cried.

"Oh, for God's bloody sake!"

"Sam, we *have* to take him!"

Swearing, he vaulted down into the hapless little boat, his boots making a hollow, thudding sound against its empty hull. That was all he needed, a damned dog along! A woman aboard ship was bad enough, but a dog—

Ah, hell.

Impatiently, he reached up for her, easily maintaining his balance in the small craft. Lights were shining upon the beach now, stretching toward them across the water.

"Call the snivelling whelp and let's go!"

But her face was paling, her eyes going doubtful. "You don't really expect me to get into . . . *that,* do you?"

"It would most certainly be helpful!"

"But . . . 'tis so small! And what if it should storm and the seas grow rough? It'll capsize!"

"Trust me, princess," he snapped, arms still outstretched and fingers beckoning.

"But Sam, we can't do this! This is just a little fishing boat! Besides, it isn't yours, and to take it would be stealing! It's . . . it's—"

"Piracy?" he supplied helpfully, quirking a dark brow and giving her one of those lazy, devilish smiles that sent flutters of sensation shooting upward through her belly. "I prefer to think of it as . . . survival." His voice grew firm, his motions hurried. "Now, come on. We're wasting time."

He was right. What choice did they have? The only safe, sure way off Cape Cod was by way of the ocean. Gunner was already in the boat, looking expectantly up at her. But as Maria stared down at the black, black water that lay calmly reflecting the stars on its mirrorlike surface, fear seized her heart and glued her moccasins to the dock. Even here in the safety of the harbor the little boat seemed dwarfed by the vastness of its surroundings; she didn't want to think about this tiny craft out on the open ocean. She didn't want to get into it, didn't want to be out on the sea in it. She didn't want to end up like one of the poor souls from the *Whydah.* . . .

"Maria, my arms are beginning to tire."

"I . . . I can't!"

"Dammit, I don't have time to play games. Now, come on!"

"But Sam—"

He rolled his eyes in exasperation. "Now what? Are you afraid to leave Eastham?"

"No."

"Are you afraid of *me*, then?"

"No!"

His patience snapped. "Then what the hell *are* ye afraid of?"

"The boat," she said in a small, embarrassed voice.

"The *boat?*" He looked at her incredulously. Then he began to chuckle, and finally threw back his head and let his laughter roll across the still waters of the bay. "The boat! You, a Cape lass, afraid of a bloody *boat?*"

Maria looked down at her feet and shuffled uncomfortably. "Yes."

"Oh, I've heard everything," he said, still chuckling. "Absolutely everything! But tell me, lass, what frightens you more? The boat, or the hangman's noose?"

"I'm afraid of dying either way," she said, looking down at him. "Be it drowning *or* dangling."

"Well, if ye deliberate much longer, I promise that the choice will be denied you. Now, give me your hands." Taking her wrists, he looped her arms around his neck, where they fastened themselves like barnacles to a keel. "That's it." And before she had time to protest further his hands were around her ribs, lifting her.

"Sam, I'm *not* a sailor!"

"But I am. Relax. I've got you."

She swallowed tightly, squeezed her eyes shut, and nearly choking him, clung to his neck for dear life as he lifted her off the pier and set her down in the boat in one swift, easy movement. There she stood, too terrified to move, her precarious balance threatening to upset the little craft until Sam finally pushed her gently down onto the seat. "Now just sit there," he ordered, "and *don't move.*"

Untying the mooring line and shoving an oar against the dock, he sent the boat gliding out into the waters of the bay in a gurgling swirl of foam. Although Gunner stood in the prow, he needn't have worried that Maria would upset the little boat's balance; indeed, she was too nervous to do more than sit stiffly on the hard seat and watch as black water rushed past and waves sluiced against the seemingly fragile hull. The sight terrified her; she looked away from it, trying to relax, and stared down at her moccasins instead. But that was no better, for in staring at her feet came the awful realization that thin planking was the only thing that stood between them and fathom upon fathom of inky depths that would show her no more mercy than it had the dead souls from the *Whydah*. Her palms grew moist as she gripped the seat, her knuckles whitening as the safety of the wharf grew more and more distant and finally melted into the darkness altogether.

"Sam . . ." she began.

But he was at home, in his element, sure and at ease and in total control of the situation. He handled the boat with skill, letting the boom swing freely in the gentle breeze as he raised the sail. And he was humming—oh, God, he was *humming* as he secured the halyard, loosely gripped the mainsheet, and settled himself at the windward side of the boat. Grinning devilishly, he took up the tiller. "Still scared?"

"Oh, you think it's funny, do you?"

"Sorry, princess, but the sight of you, sitting there all pale and shaking like a jellyfish, is more than I can bear!"

"We're going to drown, I just know it!"

"Nay, lass," he assured her in a quiet, knowing way that almost had her believing him. "We're not going to drown." And indeed, he'd never seen the ocean so calm, so serene, almost as though it was penitent for the way it had treated him, the way it had behaved the night of the *Whydah* disaster. No, tonight the sea was begging his forgiveness. They would not drown.

But Maria, unlike her pirate, took no comfort from the black water as she stared at the frothy stream of foam trailing past the bow and wondered what sort of sea creatures lurked in those awful depths waiting to devour her should she fall overboard. The wharf was lost to the night; whatever safety there was now lay with Sam. And to make matters worse, the boat, picking up speed as it slid out of the harbor and angled into the bay, was now heeling over on a starboard tack

and some of that black water was reaching across the gunwales and finding its way into the hull. . . .

She heard Sam's teasing voice through the numbness of
her fear. "You can come sit by me, if you like."

He didn't have to ask twice. On shaky legs Maria raised
herself to a half crouch, crossed the short distance between
them like an arthritic old woman, and gratefully sat down
beside him.

"Better?"

"Yes, much," she said, huddling against him and burying
her face in the folds of his sleeve to block the sight of those
dark waters racing past. He wouldn't let anything happen to
her. He would keep her safe. And as his arm came up to lay
heavily across her shoulders, pulling her against him and providing solid, comforting warmth, she at last dared to open
her eyes.

And it really wasn't that bad. Sam was perfectly relaxed,
the wind tugging at his hair and revealing his handsome profile. The motion of the little boat was peaceful, the sound of
water gurgling against the hull oddly comforting. The moments passed, and no awful leviathan reared up from out of
the black depths to devour them, no storm clouds marched
in to choke out the light from a billion stars above. The boat
continued steadily forward. Gunner curled up and went to
sleep. Relaxing somewhat, Maria rested her head against the
solid warmth of Sam's shoulder and let herself appreciate the
peaceful beauty of the night.

Coward, she berated herself, thinking of the hundreds of
ships that even now lay somewhere on this peaceful sea, of
the sailors who made the ocean their life and called it home.
She thought of the *Whydah*, this time not as it had been in
death, but as it must've been in full, vibrant life with nearly
two hundred pirates running its decks, Jolly Roger snapping
in the breeze, white sails filling the sky. She thought of it
gliding over a night sea like this one, whose surface reflected
these very same stars while its crew sang bawdy songs with
drunken abandon; she imagined its sleek hull cutting through
the moon's silvery path. And then her heart swelled with
pride as she thought of the man beside her, and how he
must've looked in command of the quarterdeck, proud and
handsome and ruler of not only that fine ship but the very

seas beneath his feet. Yes . . . the free prince of the seas, they'd called him. And suddenly, it became all-important to know what that life had been like.

"Sam?"

"Hmm?" His voice sounded almost sleepy.

"What was it like?"

"What?"

His fingers rested on her arm. She reached up and touched them, finding them moist with sea spray. "Piracy."

"I thought you didn't care to hear about it."

"Well, now that it's behind you, I think I could bear to."

He bit his lip, wondering if he should dispute *that* particular fact. He decided not to. "Well, what do you want to know?"

She snuggled closer to him, blissfully content as he absently caressed her arm through the gauzy fabric of her sleeve. "What it was like. How you lived, the adventures you had. . . . Was your crew really as bloodthirsty and ferocious as everyone says they were?"

"No more so than I," he said evasively.

"Tell me about them."

With a fond smile of remembrance, he did. About Tom Baker, cocky and arrogant, who'd walked with a swagger and had dreams of becoming a captain himself some day; about Stripes, who knew every man's business and made sure everyone else knew it too; about Simon Van Vorst, with his shock of blond hair and his great booming laugh, and poor Thomas Davis, the frightened, unwilling carpenter they'd forced to join them because his skills were so badly needed. And he told her about old Ben Hornigold, whose reluctance to take English ships had cost him his captaincy, and Ned Teach from Bristol, his friend and shipmate aboard Hornigold's sloop who'd had great aspirations in his eye and wasn't afraid of the devil himself. *Ah, Teach.* . . . They'd had some fine times together. He wondered what that fearless rascal was up to now.

"So . . . none of the *Whydah's* crew ever killed anyone?" she was asking, somewhat relieved that Sam had not, at least, committed that unforgivable sin.

"Oh, I wouldn't say that," he mused. "We did have some

bloodshed among ourselves once. Things got a bit carried away before I could put a stop to it.''

"What happened?'' she asked, lying back against his chest, pillowing her head in the cradle of his arm and staring up at the ceiling of stars above. The Milky Way was a chalky path through an already breathtaking vista, the summer triangle seemed close enough to reach up and touch. The weight of Sam's arm across her ribs was a comforting one, and she had never been happier or more content as she rubbed at the soft hairs that furred it and traced the muscles, relaxed now, that lay just beneath.

"Well, we had a lot of time on our hands,'' he said, his gaze lingering on the tempting swell of her breasts just inches from his fingers. He forced himself to look away. After that scene in her hut he had no idea how she'd react. He would not force himself upon her, had no wish to disrupt this pleasant mood they now enjoyed. Perhaps Maria had forgiven him, but beneath those guileless eyes he knew she still harbored distrust and certainly it would take more than an hour of peaceful talk to banish the strain of that last, awful encounter in her hut. No, it was best to go slowly. He gazed out over the darkened bay, trying not to think of her tantalizing nearness, the sweet, ripe curves of her body that begged to be touched, caressed, kissed; instead, he tried to lose himself in his story.

"There wasn't always a lot to do, you know. Oh, we'd dice, or tell tales over a pot of rum. If things got too slow we'd fire off a cannon or two just to hear the noise. Well, one day, someone thought up the idea of staging a play on the quarterdeck.''

"A play?'' Maria asked, looking up at the dark outline of his chin against the starlit sky.

"Aye. 'Twas a good way to pass the time; we did it often for lack of anything better to do. Well, this one was about Alexander the Great. I still laugh when I think of the men, ransacking every chest in the hold for material to make costumes out of. You should've seen them. They went belowdecks dressed in ragged breeches and torn shirts, and came up wearing silks that looked more like harem costumes than togas. . . .''

"So, what happened?'' she asked, half listening to the

tale. Already, her breasts were beginning to ache with sweet longing at the nearness of his fingers to them, and she wished she had the courage to guide his hand to their burning peaks. But no . . . after the way she'd reacted to him in the hut, she dared not do anything so bold. Surely, he'd think her hypocritical. Besides, he was too caught up in his story to notice her longings, longings that were beginning to make themselves known in her slight fidgeting and the quickened thump of her heartbeat. She wondered if he could feel that rapid pounding beneath his fingers; she could certainly *hear* it, for the blood seemed to be rushing through her ears and from her head with a speed that nearly made her dizzy.

"Well, the rum punch was pretty strong that day," he was saying, "and whether it was the potency of the tipple, or damned good acting, one of the gunners who was in the audience got carried away. Seems he thought the hero of the play was really going to be killed. Before anyone knew what he was about, he found a grenade and threw it among the actors. Caused one hell of a mess, but oh, it didn't end there. Before I could stop it, everyone was rushing into it, thinking to save the poor 'hero,' who had no idea what to do." He paused, smiling faintly in remembrance and sadness, for the gunner, the rowdy audience, those who'd played Alexander and the hero were all dead now. "As it happened, one lad broke a leg, one lost an arm, and another lost his life. Needless to say, I decided it was the last time *that* play would ever entertain the *Whydah's* lads."

"Did you punish the gunner for starting it all?"

"Aye, but not severely. After all, he was feeling the punch. I couldn't blame him for getting carried away. Besides, the play's 'hero' was a pirate playing, of all things, a pirate. 'Tis the way of the Brethren to look after their own."

His poignant memories reached out to her. Suddenly, she wanted to reach up and touch his face, to wipe away the glistening drops of sea spray that beaded upon his brow, his bearded cheek. She wanted to share his pain, wanted to comfort him, wanted to banish his guilt and sadness over the shipwreck forever. She started to sit up, but at that moment the sail luffed, then drooped lifelessly as the breeze finally fell off. "Damn," Sam muttered, waiting for the wind to come back up. But the faithless breeze wasn't the only thing he cursed. Maria, lying so trustingly and innocently against his chest, was far too tempting for her own good.

With irritation spawned by the lack of control he had over his own desires—and the kind of reaction he'd surely get from her if he gave in to them—he lifted her from his lap and stood up. Perhaps if he got away from her for a moment or two he'd be all right. On pretense of attending to the sail, he moved away.

"What are you doing?" she asked innocently, raising herself up on one elbow.

"Lowering the sail. Might as well just drift for a while. The wind's gone, anyhow."

The gruffness in his voice confused her. Wondering what she'd done wrong, Maria sat up, tucking her feet beneath her skirts and wrapping her arms around her knees as she regarded him with hurt in her eyes. His movements were more than just purposeful, they were brisk, annoyed even, as he lowered the boom and let it settle across the larboard seat. Powerless, the boat drifted peacefully on the sea's quiet surface. The air was dead, but looking up, Maria saw a tiny, high cloud scudding across the heavens, momentarily blocking out the summer constellations as it headed eastward. She glanced at Sam, who, despite the quickness of his actions, seemed to be taking an unusually long time to tend to the boat. It was obvious by now that he was doing so to deliberately avoid her—but why? She could stand it no longer.

"Sam?"

"What?"

She thought quickly. "I'm . . . cold."

He sighed heavily in obvious annoyance and came back to her, unaware that she was not as guileless as he believed her to be. Maria was far from cold. She wanted to be close to him, wanted him to take her in those strong seaman's arms and make love to her without the shadow of the *Whydah* tragedy hanging over his head. But she would not, she vowed, force herself on him like a shameless hussy—and so it was in frustration that she watched him remove his coat, wrap it around her shoulders, and take a seat, not beside her as she'd hoped, but across from her.

"Better?" He asked, somewhat irritably.

"No. I'm still . . . cold."

"Well, what do ye want me to do, build a bloody fire?"

Instantly, a shadow passed over her sweet face and he cursed himself for his shortness. But undaunted, she raised her head and looked him in the eye. "I want—" She looked out over the surface of the sea, a deep, glass-calm mirror that reflected the thousands and thousands of stars above. Waves lapped peacefully against the little bow, and the night was placid and magical. And they were alone, wonderfully, blessedly alone, a tiny speck of life in a vast expanse of night. "I . . . want you to come back and"—she swallowed hesitantly—"and hold me."

"Christ." He retreated to the bow, yanked and tugged at the bundle of extra canvas and netting there, and shook it out until he'd made what looked to be a bed in the bottom of the hull. With an annoyed growl, Gunner got up, bounded to the stern, and went back to sleep.

"Sam—"

"Look, Maria. I'm not in the mood to play games. Either tell me what's bothering you or don't—but I'm too damned tired to sit here and try to draw it out of you. I haven't slept in two days, and I'm exhausted. Good night."

She stared at him desperately. "But Sam, what if something happens?"

"Like what?"

"Well, what if the wind comes up? Or . . . or, we drift too close to shore? What if—"

Again, that exasperated sigh. "Maria, I don't sleep like the dead. I *can* be woken. Do not hesitate to do so if you see the need."

Helplessly, she watched as he stretched out on the pile of canvas, crossed his arms behind his head, and lay unmoving and stiff as a corpse. How could he be so cruel? How could he thoughtlessly ignore her? And as the moments passed and his breathing did not grow heavy and rhythmic but was, instead, a series of sleepless sighs and curses that reflected exasperation rather than weariness, she realized the plain and simple truth: he just didn't want to be near her.

Her gaze swept longingly over that unfairly handsome face, the bulge of forearm beneath that dark head, the lean, hard form of his body, and down toward—Suddenly, the answer came to her with a clarity that didn't need a woman's intuitiveness to confirm it. *Stupid fool, Maria!* she thought. Oh, he *did* want her, that was the problem! And he—undisputed prince of piracy, sinker of ships, anarchist, rogue, recalcitrant—was too much of a gentleman to cause her any more pain and hurt than he already had.

It was almost laughable.

She was a woman. And if that fact could reduce his good spirits to withdrawn irritation, it could most certainly do other things as well. She'd waited a whole year for him, had fought the devil for his very life these past several weeks—and won. She was not about to give him up to his own tortured hell of guilt, self-hatred, and remorse. No, it was time to put the bad feelings behind them, starting with what had happened last night.

"Sam?"

No answer.

"Sam?" she tried again.

He could ignore her no longer. "What, Maria?" he asked wearily.

"If you won't come here, can I come over there? I'm still cold."

Another sigh. "Aye."

He heard her get up, felt the little boat rock precariously with her unbalanced footsteps as she stepped gingerly around the boom. But she made it to him without causing any mishap, and he groaned inwardly as she settled down beside him and snuggled her sweet young breasts up against his damp chest.

"Maria, must you lie there? So . . . close?"

"I told you, I'm cold."

"Well, here. Take my shirt then, as well." Rising up on one elbow, he began to shrug out of it, and almost had it off when her little hand came up to stay his.

"Sam, I don't need your shirt," she said softly.

"I thought you were cold."

"I'm not, really. I . . . just wanted to be next to you."

She swallowed, unable to tear her eyes away from the tempting display of dark skin and chest muscles that were sheened with a film of starlight. Slowly, Maria pushed the shirt over his strong, hard shoulders and down past his elbows, his arms. Her hand came up, her fingers trailed through the soft hair that roughened the smoothness of his chest.

There, she traced the hard curve of muscle and the damp hollows between them. Her palm roved across his collarbone, then down to his tiny nipples before coming back toward the center of his chest, where the Spanish eight-reale coin still hung against his sternum. Her hand closed around the coin, the warmth of his skin emanating from it and heating her palm. For a long moment she held it, as though to trap that warmth and grasp it to herself; then, she let it fall softly back against his chest. Only then did she dare to look up into his eyes, afraid of what she'd see in them; but they were filled with love, as soft as black velvet, and she thought she would drown in their depths. Encouraged, Maria smoothed the dark waves of hair back from his brow, let her fingertips trail down his temples—and then did as she'd been longing to do—gently, slowly wiped the sheen of salt spray from his cheeks with the pads of her thumbs.

"Maria?"

With a sly, impish little smile, she placed a thumb in her mouth and sucked at the salt droplets in a way that sent Sam past any hope of control. She heard him catch his breath. Wickedly, she said, "I told you I wanted to be close to you, Sam."

"Jesus, woman, just *how* close?"

She smiled, a tempting, alluring sea siren with damp hair streaming down her breasts and spilling over his arms. "Close enough to hear your heartbeat," she said, her soft, musical voice full of promise. "Close enough to feel your blood rushing through your veins. *This* close." And then she lowered her golden head, pressing her lips against the warmth of his chest while she prayed silently that he would not push her away, that her deep-rooted feelings of shame and sinfulness wouldn't rise up and drown these new, womanly yearnings before he had the chance to nourish them and make them blossom. But as she nuzzled the soft mat of his chest hair, inhaling deeply of the scent of him—sea salt and ocean wind—she knew that giving her love to this strong, wonderful man could never, ever be wrong.

His voice sounded strained, hoarse. "Oh, princess, don't torture me so. . . . I can't take it." He shut his eyes as though in pain. But she had him in her power now, and that knowledge was the most wildly exhilarating sensation she had ever known. Shamelessly, she took his other hand, feeling the strength in the knit of bones and muscle beneath the rough skin, and guided his callused palm to one throbbing, aching breast.

"But I'm not angry with you anymore. . . . What must I do for you to believe me?"

"Christ . . ." he rasped. "If this is how you intend to prove it . . ." But the rest of his words were lost as he leaned back against the bow and reached up to pull her down atop him, protecting her from the dampness of the boat with his long, sinewy body. She raised herself so that she could look down into his handsome features, and felt one warm, rough hand caressing her nape, the other kneading her taut nipple through the soft fabric of her gown.

Flames licked outward from her breast and sent blood burning through her veins. His voice was strained, his breath hot against her ear. "Is this what you want, lass? Are ye sure?"

"What do you mean, am I sure?"

"After last night . . ."

"Would you please *forget* about last night?" Her lips feathered against his neck, his ear. "If you were as much a monster as you think you are you wouldn't be feeling so guilty about it." Her hand was grazing the taut flatness of his belly, and indeed, he *was* forgetting it, forgetting the shipwreck, forgetting everything but her and the wonderful things she was doing to him. "Show me that you're still the man I fell in love with a year ago. Show me that the real Sam Bellamy did not die with his ship but is very much alive, powerful, and full of strength . . . show me that he's not a dream from which I'll some day awaken, but here, really here. . . ."

Through the sweet torment he managed to gasp. "Ye love me, even after last night?"

"Powerful . . . strong . . . and *deaf.*" She raised her head, eyes shining as she looked down into his. "Yes, I love you, Sam. Let me prove to you how much."

"Sweet Jesus," he moaned, "I love you too." And then his lips were in her hair, against her temples, kissing her eyelids, her sea-dewed cheeks, and finally her softly parted, trembling lips. His hand went around her neck, tracing the slight hollow at her nape before fumbling with the buttons of her gown. She felt the hot roughness of his hand against her shoulders, her back, and then her breasts as the gown fell open and their starlit swell was bared to his hungry eyes, his hands, his mouth; he nuzzled the fabric aside and took first one creamy globe into his mouth then the other, teasing, sucking, stroking her swollen nipples with his tongue until her breathing grew harsh and ragged and her heartbeat thudded wildly in her ears.

Beneath her, his body was as hard as rock. Wantonly, Maria raised herself on both arms, allowing her streaming hair to tickle his bare chest, shamelessly letting her breasts hang tantalizingly in front of his lips. Sea air was cool against the moisture his tongue had left—and then his mouth was against those sweet peaks once more, sending delicious sensations rocking through her body at the contrast between cold and hot. Her head went back, and the starry heavens above blurred, reeled, then faded as her eyes drifted shut and his name fell from her lips. She felt the sweet tug as he pulled her nipples into his mouth, felt his tongue flicking around the swollen tips, and then his hand was sliding down her back, parting the closure of the dress, caressing the curve of her buttocks, and finally, the soft curls of her femininity as he gently stroked her fires to the point of conflagration.

"Sam . . ." she breathed, overwhelmed by the glorious nearness of him, impatient to feel him filling her very soul, eager to wrap herself about him and clasp him to her with all of the fervent abandon her body and heart demanded. She felt movement as he swiftly unbuttoned his breeches, and then his hands were hot upon her hips. Gently, he lowered her, his rigid manhood like velvet sheathing rock as he entered her.

He swelled within her, completely filling her until her head was swimming and she wondered, with a detached sense of bliss, if the exquisite agony was more than she could bear. Both strong hands still braced her hips, holding her poised atop him, and now his mouth claimed hers in fervent, hungry possessiveness. She cupped the sides of his bearded jaw, wanting to explore the hard muscle beneath every inch of skin, wanting to lay kisses upon every part of him until her lips knew him as well as her hands did. But in him, she sensed a desperate urgency that matched her own, and slowly, tantalizingly, he began to move her up and down against the length of him, up and down until she thought she would die from the sensations that were screaming through her body and pounding up against the confines of her hot, dew-sheened skin.

Faster and faster he moved her, taking her up and down and up and down until the fire in her blood flared to fever pitch and her fingers clawed at the skin of his damp, hot chest. Her head fell back to beseech the night sky, and then the stars above exploded into a million spinning lights as wave after wave of pleasure washed over her. Her thighs tightened spasmodically about him, and he gasped out her name as he shuddered, yanked her roughly down atop him one final time, and drove himself deeply within her.

Chapter 15

Not for a moment could I now behold
A smiling sea, and be what I have been:
The feeling of my loss will ne'er be old;
This, which I know, I speak with mind
serene.

WORDSWORTH

During the night the wind returned, at first as a gentle whisper, and toward dawn a more insistent breeze that stirred the calm surface of the sea, lifted the heavy silk of Maria's hair, and brought Sam awake when those soft, corn-colored strands tickled his cheek and caught gently in his beard. He swiped at his face as though to brush away an insect, opened his eyes, and greeted the morning with a smile when he saw that it was Maria, still cuddled against him, her head resting in the curve of his arm and her hair all but obscuring her sleeping face. Stifling a yawn, he sat up, propped his back in the bow, and carefully pulled her against his chest so as not to awaken her.

Awake, she was a thing of beauty, a strange mix of the exotic and the innocent; asleep, she might've been a slumbering angel, so perfect, so exquisite was every painstakingly made feature of her delicate face. Her skin, soft as an infant's, was like alabaster in the faint starlight, her lashes dark crescents feathering her cheeks. Softly parted lips tempted him with their unconscious appeal, the little hand that rested trustingly upon his chest penetrated the tough knit of skin, flesh, and bone to reach his very heart until it swelled with a protective sort of love that was strangely alien, yet pleasant to him. Softly, he rubbed his cheek against her hair, wishing he had the heart to wake her and the courage to tell her what he had not earlier—that his pirating days were far from over.

For directly across this gentle bay was Boston, where the remnants of *Whydah's* crew would rot in the gaol until someone had the mercy to toss a rope around their necks and end their misery. Never one to trust things completely to fate when he could have a hand in altering it, it was Sam's intention to rescue them before someone troubled himself to do just that.

But how?

Grimly, he assessed his current situation. Warship: a tiny boat that stunk of brine. Crew: a worthless whelp and a trusting girl who slept innocently in his arms and was likely to mutiny when she found out her captain's plans. Armament: two pistols slung around his neck, a knife tucked in his belt. Black Sam Bellamy, scourge of the Atlantic, free prince of the seas. Fearsome as ever, wasn't he?

He cursed and wished he had Paul, Louis Lebous, or even Ned Teach to help him. . . .

But he'd been in hopelessly bleak situations before. And as long as he was alive he was not powerless. Of course, it was common knowledge that *Whydah's* haughty captain had gone down with his ship, and this belief was one he didn't care to disturb, if only in the interests of Maria's well-being should his rescue attempt fail. No, 'twould be better to hoist the old flag under a new name, a simple one that smacked of evil and subtly mocked the idiots who'd never figure out who he *really* was. He tossed a number of aliases around in his head before he hit upon the right one. Black Sam, his men had called him. Why not Sam Black? *Sam Black*. He smiled, liking it. Ah, perfect mockery! And if his plans should go awry, Maria would be protected from the consequences of his real identity, for Sam Black was innocent of any crimes against the Crown . . . for now.

He leaned back against the bow and stared up at the sky, fading magically from black to purple with the coming of dawn. "Ah, lads, the situation is not hopeless," he said aloud to the night. His surviving crew might think him dead, but by the gods, he was *not!* He was still their captain, the man they'd elected to lead them, protect them, guide them—and as such he couldn't just desert them. He *wouldn't!*

And as he idly stroked Maria's hair with a calmness that belied the swift turns of his mind as it raced from one rashly bold plan to another, a sudden thought struck him and tugged a sly, gleaming smile from his saturnine features. The devil take him! Why hadn't he thought of it earlier? There had been *three* ships sailing with *Whydah* on that dreadful night, and only one of them, the pink carrying the cargo of wine, had been lost. But what of the other two? What had happened to Ingols's sloop, *Fisher*, and *Anne*, the two-masted square-rigger, similar to a brigantine, known as a "snow," that they'd taken early in April?

No doubt their prize crews had followed his orders and sailed on to Monhegan, a stark, mostly uninhabited island eleven miles off the Maine coast, where they'd all agreed to rendezvous if the storm should separate them. With any luck they'd still be there, if news of *Whydah*'s loss on that awful Friday night a month past hadn't reached them. Laughter rumbled up from Sam's chest, soft, cunning laughter that was already secure in victory. All he had to do was find those two ships, take command, get to Boston, and storm the gaol.

That laughter died just as quickly as another thought sobered him. *Maria*. He could hardly see her lending support to such a scheme. But he could tell her later, and for now keep his plans to himself. Ignorance was bliss. When her trust in him was solidly rooted and her love was strong enough to withstand it, he'd explain everything and pray to God that she'd understand.

But would she? Her rigid set of morals had been nourished

in a Puritan town, her upbringing was of the strictest. Sinless as a lamb, unstained as virgin snow. Well, *almost*. She had accepted *him* into her life, and into her pure little body too, for that matter. He looked down at her sweet face once more, so trusting, so damned innocent, and drew the coat up over her shoulders. His fingers brushed against the softly rounded spheres of her breasts. Again, he felt that familiar stirring in his blood, a fire that surged to life and began to roar through his veins, sparked by nothing more than that gentle touch. God help him, he was damned all right. Even while she slept he couldn't keep his hands off her. Touching her parted, coral-pink lips, he felt the whisper of her kitten's breath against his finger until at last she moaned softly, turned her face into his chest, and drifted back to somnolence once more.

Let her sleep. At least in slumber there was innocence—and ignorance. With a heavy sigh, Sam rubbed a strand of her hair between his fingers one last time, hung his arm over the gunwale, and trailing his fingers in the chilly seawater, looked up at the fading stars once more.

Daylight was an early explorer, painting the eastern sky pink and glowing softly upon the peaceful waters of the bay. Cape Cod's distant shoreline was now just a faint line on the horizon. He wasn't sorry to see the last of that cursed place. Too many bad memories. Too many reminders that he was a man, not a god. He turned his head toward the open waters of the bay. Too many—

The smile froze on his lips, his thoughts hanging suspended, forgotten in his mind. His chin came slowly up and he stared with the fixed intensity of a wolf, suddenly awakened and oblivious to all but its prey.

By the bloody gods. . . .

She was a trim, sleek little sloop, her extended bowsprit two-thirds her hull length, her single mast raking the faint stars above. She had a huge mainsail, and a topsail that caught and held the colors of dawn. The flag of England snapped at her masthead, and reflections from her running lights—one at her bow, another at her stern—reached across the still-dark water like ghostly fingers. She was a mile away, maybe more, but her sounds, achingly nostalgic and that of a ship pulsing with life, carried clearly and made his blood race in excitement. Seamen's voices raised in a timeless chanty . . . the hollow thunder of hungry canvas . . . the creaking of yards, the banging of blocks as the wind sprang to life with the coming of morning. . . .

His palms grew moist with nervous excitement. Obviously, someone—the devil, in all probability—had heard his desperate thoughts and favored him with an opportunity that he wouldn't have dreamed up in his wildest imaginings. The sloop was too lovely and unscarred to be a pirate ship, too gracefully delicate to be a Royal Navy hound dog sent to sniff out sea wolves of his ilk. From the looks of her she'd never seen battle; her jib was white and streaked with spray, her hull gleaming with morning light and a fresh coat of black paint.

Fortunately, Maria wasn't awake to see Sam's slow, cunning smile, nor the hungry gleam in his black eyes. For here was the answer to getting his men out of the gaol. Here was a way to Boston, to the open sea, to Paul Williams, Monhegan, or wherever the hell else he felt like going. Here was the return of the freedom that had been so cruelly stolen from him with *Whydah*'s death.

For this nimble, sweet little ship would navigate the shoal waters that had been *Whydah*'s downfall with ease. That square topsail would let her fly before the breeze, that fore-and-aft rig against it, and with her, he could lurk the offshore islands, the inshore coves, the bays, the harbors, even the open sea, with no one to say him nay!

She was spirited, lively, and convenient; and in her, Sam saw a pirate ship.

"Maria, lass, wake up!" he whispered, urgently shaking her shoulder, his gaze still locked on that oncoming thing of beauty.

Maria opened her eyes, stretching with unconscious feline grace in an attempt to rid her joints of the stiffness brought on by moisture and sea air. Reluctant to face the chill of the morning, she drew the heavy weight of Sam's coat tightly around her and snuggled back within its delicious warmth. But the hand on her shoulder was persistent. Mumbling sleepily, she stretched again, knuckled her sleepy eyes, and dragged them open.

Sam was in profile above her, the hues of dawn—gold, orange, crimson—coloring the black waves of his glossy hair, sheening his beard, and casting him like a rigid statue against the glowing brilliance of the sky. He was staring intently at something over her shoulder. Raising herself on one arm, Maria followed his gaze and saw a distant but oncoming cloud of white.

She shoved a hand to her mouth. "They've found us!"

He gave a short laugh that managed to sound assured and triumphant at the same time. Without tearing his gaze from the ship, he said, "No one's found us, princess. D'ye think any of your precious neighbors could afford anything so fine?" Thoughtfully, he studied the twin curls of seawater foaming from the sloop's bows, the stainless canvas on her long nose. "Nay, I'd say she probably belongs to someone who has far more wealth than any of your *former* neighbors."

"Where do you think she's from?"

"Look closely and you'll see her colors. British."

"Not a navy ship!" Maria cried, her fear succumbing to stark terror. "Oh Sam, if it is, they won't even bother to give you a trial before they hang you from the bowsprit—"

"Yardarm," he corrected her with a self-absorbed smile.

"Yardarm, bowsprit, whatever! I know naught about ships, but I *do* know about the navy's tactics for dealing with pirates!"

But Sam was pleasantly unconcerned. "She's no pirate hunter, lass. I can count her guns on one hand. 'Tis my guess her captain might be using her for something a bit shady— smuggling, perhaps. She's certainly fast enough." He rubbed his beard, stroking it between thumb and forefinger. "But then, I may be wrong. She might be totally innocent. One never knows."

"Maybe she's a pirate ship," Maria speculated, with some distaste.

"No." And to himself: *But she soon will be.* . . .

The sloop's lookout had spotted their boat, and Maria saw early sunlight flashing against his glass as his call drifted across the water. Nervously, she watched as the ship turned toward them and shortened sail, the magnificent sheets of spray at her bows dying to twin clouds of white foam. Sensing movement beside her, Maria turned. Sam was picking up the silk scarf with its pistols, loading them with a speed and expertise that both fascinated and appalled her. He slung them around his neck, shouldered his ammunition bag, and drew on his coat, concealing both weapons and pouch. Almost as an afterthought he removed the hoop of gold from his ear and dropped it into one of his pockets. But it was not that, nor the way he was caressing his dagger, that gave him away—it was the calculating smile that had no right being there in the first place.

"What do you think you're doing?" she cried.

"I'm sorry, lass. I didn't tell you the whole truth before. For you, princess, I swear I'll give up piracy—but not until I free my men from the gaol."

"But Sam!"

"Look, Maria, I have the deaths of nearly one hundred and fifty men on my conscience, and while I can't bring them back, I *can* do something about those in the Boston gaol. If piracy's the only way I can do it, then so be it!"

His voice was determined, his tone final. And with that, he stood up to face the oncoming sloop.

Speechless with disbelief and overwhelming, red-hazed anger, Maria watched the sloop come closer and closer, her huge mainsail blocking the view of everything behind it, sunlight now gleaming all the way up to the truck of her eighty-foot mast, where a pendant fluttered in proud innocence. She passed them in a rush of foaming water that rocked their little boat and made Maria clutch the gunwales, yet did absolutely nothing—unfortunately—to upset Sam's balance. It fleetingly occurred to her to shove him overboard, but that idea was lost as some doomed sailor gave the order to heave to. Didn't he know what he was getting himself into? Didn't he know that Sam was a *pirate?* And now the unsuspecting ship was turning her graceful nose into the wind, her great sails luffing as she stood floating in the gentle swells.

Angrily, Maria spun on Sam with mutiny in her eyes. "How can you even *think* of doing such a vile, disgusting thing? These men have done us no harm!"

"Please don't preach to me, Maria," he said with infuriating insouciance. His gaze, as sharp as a freshly honed knife, absorbed everything from the sloop's glistening figurehead—

a leaping dolphin—to the bit of giltwork decorating her counter. Sixty feet from stem to stern, maybe a tad more, with a beam about twenty. *Perfect,* he thought. Ignoring Maria's white-lipped face, the anger in her eyes, he conveniently shoved from his mind the fight he knew was coming. "Now, just sit there like a good girl and keep quiet," he ordered, "and let me do the talking."

"I'll do no such thing! This is madness, do you hear me? 'Tis absolutely"—she cast frantically for the right word— "*obscene!* Here you have a chance to make a new start on life, and what are you doing? Throwing it away! How can you even *think*—"

He cut her off with casual indifference. "Keep your voice down, princess. Sounds carry across the water, you know."

"I won't stand idly by and watch you kill someone!"

"I said, *quiet!*" Her tirade was sucking the last drop from his shallow well of patience. "Like it or not, you're going aboard that ship, and I'll have no more arguments from ye. Is that understood?"

"You can't intimidate me!"

"Can't I?" His tone was a warning one, his expression daring her to argue with him. "Now, stop wasting time. Lie down, up against the bow, and pretend you're ill."

"On your life I will!"

"Do it!" he said softly. "Or would you have them kill me?"

Gritting her teeth, she did as he instructed, hating him for what he was making her do, hating him for deluding her into thinking he was anything but what he was—a knave, a rascal, a blackguard. A *pirate!* What a blissful idiot she'd been to think that he'd change just for her. Angry tears of frustration burned the backs of her eyes. Nails digging into the soft flesh of her palms, she pulled her skirts clear of the dampness that lurked in the bottom of the boat and glared at him through the veil of her hair. "If you think that I'm going to—"

He cut her off, his voice low, urgent, and authoritative. "Not like that. Put your hand over your stomach. And close your eyes. You're supposed to look ill, not dead."

"I will *not* be a party to this madness!"

"Goddammit, Maria, you're trying my patience!"

"I don't give a damn about your patience! All it's ever

brought me is grief, hurt, and heartache! Beast! Barbarian! *Parasite!*''

He caught her jaw, holding it in his firm grasp and searing her with the flash of anger in his obsidian eyes. To those on the ship, the gesture appeared to be the concerned perusal of a lover; to Maria, it was anything but. "I'm warning you," he said dangerously. "Keep it up, dear. Just keep it up." He released her suddenly and glanced up at the men clustered at the sloop's rail.

Blinking back tears of anger and despair, she clamped a hand over her stomach and shut her eyes. She would go along with this . . . this *lunacy,* if only to protect his life and nothing else!

"Damn you, Sam Bellamy," she whispered through clenched teeth.

But he only laughed softly, ignoring her curse as he took up the oars and rowed the little boat into the purple shadow of the waiting sloop. Through barely slitted eyes, she saw him stand with feigned awkwardness, one hand hesitantly leaving the gunwale and ready to grab it should he lose his balance, his body towering above her as he answered the vessel's hail. *Oh, what an actor,* she thought bitterly.

Shading his eyes, Sam gazed up at the wall of black, sea-dewed planking to where men hung curiously over the rail. "Hello! Hello, there!" he called in a stranger's voice, one that held none of the West Country cadences with which Maria had grown familiar. She came close to grinding the enamel from her molars; his awkwardness in the boat wasn't the only thing he was feigning. "Thank the gods ye saw us! Lost I am, just a poor knave takin' me young bride and her puppy-dog out for a day 'pon the water. Guess I ain't no sailor, eh? And now the poor lass is seasick. I'd hate fer her t' catch her death of a cold, what with the little boat leakin' and all. Would ye be so kind as to let us come aboard ye?''

"Sam—" Maria hissed, disgusted.

An older man appeared at the rail, roughly shoving the others aside. His steel-colored hair was severely queued, his face, deeply seamed with a spiderweb of lines, shadowed by a three-cornered hat. His eyes flickered over Maria, and in them she saw hardness, cruelty, and something she was rapidly beginning to recognize as lust. Suddenly, she wasn't afraid for the crew of this graceful little sloop, but for herself and Sam. Did he know what he was getting them into? And to make matters even worse, another had joined him at the rail, a young man with fancy clothes, and brown eyes that should've seemed friendly, but didn't. For a moment, the two conversed in hushed tones.

Sam's whisper was urgent. "Goddammit, woman, groan! You're supposed to be seasick!"

A voice from the rail above cut off her retort. It was the older man, and Maria's assumption that he was the captain proved to be correct. "I suppose we can assist you and your bride, sir. I am Captain John Smuttynose, master of the free-trading sloop *Dolphin*, and this is, uh . . . my first mate, Malcolm Hastings. And you, sir? Where are you from?"

"Most recently from London," Sam answered without hesitation. "Though I just arrived in Boston a fortnight ago. Thought I could find me some land, start a farm or somethin'. Guess I should've stayed there, eh?" His laughter would've convinced the devil himself. "Don't know a thing about sailing, but it looked so easy, thought I'd give it a try. Little lass was begging me to, ye know. So I rented me a boat, took it out in the bay, but wouldn't ye know the damned wind came up? Next thing I know we're out here in the middle of the ocean. Guess we did a bit of drifting, huh?" He scratched his chin, looking at the empty sea around them. "How far are we from Boston, anyway?"

"About ten leagues or so," said Smuttynose in a lofty, condescending way that made Sam itch to reveal his true identity. But their safety, indeed, their very lives, might depend on how well he could fool this hard-eyed bloke and the well-dressed fop beside him.

"Well, I told ye I wasn't no sailor. Next time the little lady takes it into her head to do a bit of sightseein' I'm renting me a horse and carriage!" He bent toward her, pretending to keep his balance by nothing more than some precarious thread of luck. "Are ye all right, m' dear?" he asked, purposefully loud enough that his voice carried to those aboard the ship.

His concern had the desired effect. "All right, come aboard if you wish," Smuttynose said, waving back his men in a way that seemed almost angry. "You can tie up your boat at the stern and we'll tow it to Boston. But be quick about it. I'm already two days behind schedule because of the ineptitude of this damned crew.''

"Why thankee, sir,'' Sam said with a grateful smile. "I quite understand. We'll not hold ye up.'' And as he glanced up at Smuttynose's hard eyes and the sullen faces of the crew, his keen eyes and quick mind took in the situation at once; here was a hard master, a crew of ill-used men who obviously hated him, and a fast ship engaged in something that, given its sharp, predatory lines, was probably illegal. Oh yes, he understood, and understood quite well. Under such circumstances, it should be an easy task to overpower the master and take command. On falsely wobbly legs, Sam reached for the boat's mooring line and tossed it up to a waiting seaman, all too aware that Maria's sea-green eyes were narrowed at him in anything but illness.

"Give me yer hand, my dear,'' he said, taking her stiff hand in his own large one.

"You can dispense with the cowcrap where I'm concerned, *Captain!*'' she hissed, her eyes speaking betrayal and a hurt that tore at his heart. He hardened himself to it. Now was not the time.

"Fasten your arms about my neck,'' he commanded, hauling her to her feet and reaching for the rope ladder that was tossed down to them.

"Fasten them? Oh, believe me I will, but mind that I don't strangle you while I'm about it!'' But Maria understood the gravity of their situation and did as she was told. His hard back pressed against her stomach like a slab of rock, reminding her all too sharply of the bliss they'd shared just hours ago, a happiness that had dissipated with that shrewd smile and the reminder of just what those pistols hidden beneath his coat were really for. His flowing hair brushed her arm, and she felt the strength and determination in his hard, bearded jaw against the top of her laced fingers. There was no timidity in his climb, but nothing in the way that he ascended, hand over hand up the swaying, unsteady ladder, to give his ruse away, either. Opening her eyes, Maria saw tiny drops of water on black planking descending from her view, and made the mistake of looking down.

By the time they reached the sloop's deck, she didn't have

to feign illness any longer; the sight of their little boat bobbing in the waves far below had done weird things to her stomach and the gentle roll of the sloop only reminded her of its fragile claim to majesty over a sea that could be, when it wanted to be, quite merciless. But for Sam, having a good, solid deck beneath his feet was exhilarating, and with the reassurance of the pistols hidden just beneath his coat he felt as though he could conquer the world.

Setting Maria down on the deck, he stepped forward. And as his eyes found and held the captain's gaze, any misgivings he might have had vanished, for meanness and cruelty glittered in those pale, watery eyes, and his crew stood cowed behind him like a pack of beaten dogs.

As unobtrusively as possible, Sam put Maria behind him. Smuttynose, with interest and then a frown of suspicion, was eyeing Sam's fine boots of Spanish leather, the perfectly struck eight-reale that hung against his chest, the emerald ring on his finger that would've brought enough money to buy this sloop and ten more like her. Sam was quick to recognize the hungry gleam in those mean little eyes as they flashed from the ring and then back to the eight-reale—for after all, the coin was a royal strike, reserved for the aristocracy of Spain (and stolen from the coffers of one of her galleons), and in itself would command a fortune.

Just to be sure the man didn't look too hard, Sam reached beneath his coat, grasped one cold, deadly pistol, and casually trained it on Smuttynose.

Air whistled through the gap in the man's yellowed teeth as he sucked in his breath. "You—you *lied!*" he snarled, tearing his eyes from the coin to the pistol's black mouth. "You're no landsman from Boston!"

"Right you are, lad," Sam said with a genial smile. "I'm not. But thanks for your offer of assistance. Maybe next time you'll think twice about who you invite aboard as a guest." The smile faded, to be replaced with a cold, hard look that the *Whydah*'s lads would've known well. "Now, call forth your men."

Eyes blazing, Smuttynose didn't move.

"If I have to repeat myself, 'twill be the pistol that does the talking," Sam said offhandedly, "and I'd hate like hell to splatter your guts all over these spotless decks." Smiling as though he'd find enjoyment in doing just that, he cocked the flintlock and steadily raised it to within an inch of Smuttynose's heavy surcoat.

Such tactics of intimidation, one of the very first lessons a pirate learns, rarely fail to bring about the desired results, and with Smuttynose it was no different. Staring at the weapon, he croaked out an order to the men clustered in terrified confusion behind him. "Do as the scoundrel asks, you bunch of wet-nosed dogs! And hurry up, will you? He's about ready to put a ball through my heart!"

Slowly, uncertainly, several came forward, their eyes wide and fearful. Like frightened sheep they milled about, and Sam wondered just what cruelties this hard master had inflicted upon them to bring their courage to such yellow-livered wretchedness.

"Ye know," he said pensively, keeping the pistol trained on Smuttynose while he raked this simpering crew with black eyes that made them tremble, "when I was a pirate—a long time ago, mind you, as I've since given up such *unscrupulous* pursuits"—he chuckled, keenly aware of Maria's glare cutting into his back—" 'twas a custom to walk among the crew of a new prize and put a question to them." He took Smuttynose's arm, jabbed the pistol against his ribs, and began to walk among them, looking down with an innocuous smile into each cowering face, every frightened gaze. "We'd go to each man, just like this"—he reached out and grasped the jaw of a lad who couldn't have been more than ten years old and forced the boy to meet his gaze—"and ask, 'What sort of bloke is your master, now? Is he a good captain, kind and fair and unselfish with rations, pay, and most importantly' "—another chuckle—" 'grog?' " He thrust the young jaw away from him, not ungently, and continued on with measured strides. "Or"—he stopped, staring into the sheepish eyes of another until the seaman's gaze dropped—" 'Is he a hard man, quick to taste of your back with the cat, to tear the flesh from your spine for the most petty offense?' " He felt Smuttynose's arm go rigid beneath his tight grip and smiled. "And now, my lads, I ask the question of you. What manner of man is our friend Smuttynose, eh?"

Maria, staring angrily at the shadow between Sam's shoulderblades and the long, muscled calves beneath the flared skirts of his coat, could not prevent a flash of appreciation for his tactics. He was too crafty, too shrewd. He could hardly take over a ship with nothing more than two pistols and a dagger—or so she'd thought. But Sam was a master of persuasiveness, let alone intimidation. He was a pirate; he'd been trained by the best, had usurped the best, had become the best. He knew very well what he was about. If he could win the sloop's company to his cause—and by the way Smuttynose had obviously treated them, *that* shouldn't be too hard— there was nothing to stand in his way.

But at that moment a small noise and a flash of color out of the corner of her eye made her turn her head. Whirling, she saw a man vaulting down the companionway ladder and pounding toward them; too late, she saw the raised pistol, the gleaming cutlass in one sun-browned hand.

"*Sam!*" she screamed, and then everything happened at once.

Chapter 16

Never love unless you can
Bear with all the faults of man.

CAMPION

Sam whirled on reflex, not thought, and in that brief instant Smuttynose yanked his rapier from its scabbard and went for his unprotected ribs. Maria screamed, a pistol barked behind her, and dazed, she watched as Smuttynose let out a guttural howl of pain, dropped his sword, and stood clutching his shattered, bloody hand.

Everyone turned to stare at the slight figure who came forward, no longer running, but swaggering as he twirled the smoking pistol by its bronze trigger guard. His umber-colored eyes were dancing, and the deck fell quiet with tense expectation as the men waited to see how the pirate would deal with their newest crew member. But after two days of sailing with him, they should've known better than to think he'd have anything but the first word.

"Mother o' God!" he exclaimed. "Why, scald me balls if it ain't Black Sam 'imself! Jee-sus, Cap'n, I thought you was dead! Last time I saw ye, ye was sprawled flatter than a ten-year-old's chest. Tried t' help ye, I did, but a wave caught me an' threw me by the board. Thought I'd seen the last o' ye!"

"We should all be so fortunate," Maria muttered acidly.

Sam ignored her. "Stripes." His teeth flashed in a grin of genuine pleasure. "How in God's name did you end up here?"

"Same as you, I'd wager. Someone up there"—he pointed heavenward—"or down there, more likely, was watchin' out fer me." Clearing his throat, he cast a baleful glance at Smuttynose, whose face was twisted in agony as he stood clutching his injured hand and glaring at Sam. "Stayed on the Cape fer a bit, then made me way t' Rhode Island and signed on with this dog a couple o' days ago. I'm tellin' ye, Cap'n, had we the crew we once 'ad, they'd've worked this one up good. 'E's a mean one, I tell ye."

Smuttynose erupted in rage, earning him fearful looks from his crew and the threatening stare of Sam's pistol once more. "You mean to say *you're* a pirate too?" And at Stripes's nod, he snarled, "Damn you, damn both of you! When the authorities hear of this—"

"The *authorities?*" Stripes mocked, arms akimbo and coffee-colored brows sliding up his forehead. "Why, I'll be glad t' tell 'em *everythin'*, Cap'n *Snottynose.*" He grinned at his own joke. "Oh, don't look so surprised. I know all about yer little activities. Like the rum ye got hidden in that false hold below, hidden 'cause it's contraband and ye won't claim it as cargo. Smugglin's a crime too, jus' like piracy! And I know about lots o' other things, too. Go 'head, go t' the authorities, if ye like. But I'll be sittin' there right beside ye, tellin' 'em everythin' I know, too!"

Maria wondered if Smuttynose was going to have some sort of attack; his face had gone the color of radishes, his throat was working like a dying fish. Sam did not share her concern. Deliberately, he struck a relaxed pose at the rail and leaned against it, keeping his pistol trained on Smuttynose's chest and watching the men behind him with a thoughtful eye. One of them had already brought Gunner aboard; now, the dog stood among them, bewildered. "Hmm. How very interesting," Sam said, tugging at his beard. "Smuggling. 'Tis a most hateful trade, eh, Stripes?"

"Aye, most certainly is, Cap'n. Why, I'll—"

"Hateful? You have the damned audacity to stand there and talk about hateful trades."

Wordlessly, Sam pulled the trigger, and a lead ball plowed a groove in the deck two inches from the toe of Smuttynose's high-tongued shoe. "I," Sam said blandly, "do not care to see a man interrupted when he's trying to say something. Please continue, Stripes."

Accustomed to his captain's ways, Stripes went on without missing a beat, this exercise in discipline not fazing him in the least. "Oh, you ain't heard all o' it, Cap'n! I could tell ye stories—"

"Just how do you know so damned much, anyhow? You've only been on this ship for two days!" Smuttynose snarled, forgetting himself. He leaped backward as Sam casually produced another pistol from beneath his coat.

"I have me ways," Stripes said slyly. "Don't I, Cap'n?"

"Aye, lad. That you do." Sam smiled wryly. "Worst damned busybody I ever laid eyes on." His gaze swept the crowd, taking in the frightened faces, Maria's uncertainty, the absence of the foppish first mate who'd been standing on deck a short time ago. He turned to Smuttynose once more. "Where's that weasel ye had in your confidence? Hastings, I believe his name was."

"I don't know."

One of the men detached himself from the crowd. "I'll tell ye where he is. Belowdecks, probably in the cabin swilling wine and hiding beneath the table. Spineless as a jellyfish, that one is. Supposed to be some high-falutin' lord or something."

"Oh really." Sam stared hard at Smuttynose. "Pray tell, what persuaded him to lower himself from such an exalted status to serve as *mate,* my friend? The taste of illegal rum?" He dismissed Smuttynose's hasty excuses with a wave of the pistol. "Never mind. I grow tired of your lies." He turned to the seaman who'd spoken. "You, lad. What's your name?"

"Flanagan, sir. Billy Flanagan."

Sam nodded. "Mr. Flanagan, why don't you and Stripes go below and fetch His Bloody Lordship? We wouldn't want him to . . . miss anything."

"Aye, sir."

"You'll never get away with this," Smuttynose growled.

"Oh?" Sam arched a dark brow. Waving the pistol, he motioned Smuttynose to the rail. "There's the ladder," he said. "I'm sure, despite your little injury, that you'll be able to climb down it. You have exactly five minutes in which to do so."

"*What?* This is *my* ship, damn you—"

"Sir, wait!" Braver than his peers, another man stepped forward, his balding head sunburned and ringed by a half-circle of wispy brown hair. "What are you going to do with the captain?"

"He's no longer your captain," Sam said, "unless you choose to go with him. If not, then you may address me by that title. Now, which of you faithful pups wants to join old— what was it that Stripes called him?"

"Snottynose," came a high, timid voice from the rear of the crowd, and Sam was hard-pressed to choke back his laughter as he spied that same young lad he'd singled out earlier.

"Ah yes. *Snottynose,*" he echoed, lips twitching, corners of his eyes crinkling in amusement. He glanced at the crew. "I believe you all have *four* minutes left in which to make your decision before our good man takes his leave."

Several men exchanged wary glances and the rest merely looked down at their feet. Silence stretched on, the tension growing thicker and thicker. Finally, the balding one stepped forward. "I'm not staying with him," he declared, casting a hate-filled look at his former captain, "and I think I speak for all of us. As to your question, pirate, allow me to answer it. Smuttynose is a hard man and a cheat besides. Promised us good wages, but we've yet to see them. For a share of that rum and fair treatment, I believe that most of us would be happy to stay on with you."

"Fair treatment?" Sam echoed. "Good wages?" He threw

his head back and deep laughter rumbled up from his chest. When he looked back at them, his eyes were alight with good humor. "What do ye think I'm going to do, *pay* ye? Hell, lad, there are no wages on a pirate ship. Just equal division of everything. The more prizes we take the richer ye'll get, and that's all there is to it. And if ye think a pirate captain rules his ship with the hand of a bloody king, then think again. Piracy is a democracy, ye know, not a monarchy. Every man is his own master, free to do as he wishes. Ye want to dice and drink 'til four bells of the mid-watch? Be my guest. Spend your afternoon in drunken slumber? No one's stopping ye." His white teeth flashed in his swarthy face. "Aye, like that, don't ye? Can't ask for treatment fairer than that. And as to me, I think ye'll find"—he glanced at Stripes, who had come up on deck with a frightened Hastings in tow—"that I am indeed a very fair man. Just ask my former crewman here."

"Aye, Black Sam speaks the truth. And not only is 'e fair, but ye'll find yer pockets lined with gold if ye sail with 'im. He's the best there is, ye know."

"There ye have it." Unwilling to give them any more time to think about it, Sam called on intimidation once more. Glancing nonchalantly up at the boom of the sloop's great mainsail, he called out, "Three minutes."

"Wait!" It was the balding man again. "There's nothing to decide. We'll go with you. Smuttynose is a mean old bastard, and I'd rather dance the hangman's jig than spend another day working for him!"

"Aye, me too," added Flanagan, nodding.

Sam folded his arms across his chest, wanting to laugh with joy and triumph at his good fortune. It was all he could do to maintain his cool indifference, especially with Maria glaring at him. "And the rest of you? Are ye with me, or Smuttynose?"

"With you, sir," one man said, and several others nodded in agreement. And then the young boy stepped forward, regarding Sam in wide-eyed awe. "Are you really a pirate, sir? A real, honest-to-goodness pirate?"

Silence. And then Maria's voice, clear and sweet but filled with scorn. "Yes, he's a real pirate. Get a good look at him now, before he finds himself dancing at the end of a rope!"

Sam laughed her comment off with a wink. "These young brides. . . . You know how they are. Takes a while to teach them good manners." Ignoring her once more, he glanced at Smuttynose and said, "Two minutes."

"I'd like to stay too."

Hastings stood there in his fine clothes, carefully shined boots, silk stockings, and lace at his wrists, looking like he hadn't seen a day of work in his life. *"You?"* Sam burst into laughter. "Sorry, lad, but I don't care to have foppish *lords* on my ship." He turned to Smuttynose. "I believe your five minutes are up. Happy sailing, lad. And before ye curse me to Hell and beyond, remember this: we went easy on you, hard master that you've been. But I'm feeling merciful today. Now, off with ye before I change my mind."

Hastings was already down the ladder and waiting in the boat. Vowing to see Sam in the Hell from whence he'd come, Smuttynose followed, his one-handed progress painfully slow. Sam propped his elbows upon the rail's smooth wood, leaned his chin into the heels of his hands, and watched him with a wicked smile. "Oh damn, I almost forgot. Mind you watch that last rung, lad. 'Tis a bit on the slippery side!"

A curse, a cry, sounds of a body thudding into an empty hull. Silence, and then more curses that quickly died as Smuttynose looked up and saw that the pirate captain had braced a wrist against the rail and was calmly sighting down his arm. The pistol's sharp report smothered the old man's strangled scream, and the tether rope between little boat and sloop parted cleanly beneath Sam's unfailing aim. From the ship came hoots and howls of jeering laughter, and much back-slapping. A moment later, seamen were scrambling up the shrouds and the sloop was turning, catching the breeze in her awesome spread of canvas once more.

Slowly, she began to move away. The two men in the boat heard the pirate captain's deep, rolling laughter ringing out over the water. And then, in a final gesture of arrogance, he snatched up Smuttynose's rapier, and with the rising sun behind him, raised it in mocking salute.

With the wind fresh on her quarter, the sloop glided out of the peaceful waters of Cape Cod Bay, past the curving tip

of Cape Cod and the port of Provincetown that Sam had tried
so desperately to reach just weeks ago, and out into the chop
of the open sea.

"North by northwest, Mr. Flanagan," he called to the
tawny-haired lad at the helm, and the sloop angled into the
wind on a close-hauled tack. Her bowsprit stabbed far out
over the long, foam-flecked waves rolling toward them from
the open sea, and Sam revelled in the feel of spray against
his skin, wind against his face. Ah, how had he ever survived
without a deck beneath his feet, the song of the shrouds and
lines humming above, this heady feeling of utter freedom?

"Hold her steady, Mr. Flanagan!" Out here the waves
were higher, the wind brisker. But with the wind hardening
her huge mainsail and stretching her jib taut, the sloop responded like a veteran, causing Sam to wonder just how close
she could sail to it. "Put her a point more to larboard," he
added, thoughtfully rubbing his chin.

"Aye, sir!" Flanagan moved the tiller and the sloop responded. Spray hissed through the air but the little ship did
not slow her pace, only picking up speed and fighting for
more. Sam's smile widened to a grin of boyish excitement.
Lilith? Mary Anne? Whydah, even? They'd all be helplessly
in irons by now, every damned one of them! None of those
fine vessels had been as weatherly as this little sloop! He
threw back his head for the sheer joy of it and let the flying
spindrift cool his sun-warmed cheeks. *Ah, life was grand!*
"Let her fall off two points to sta'b'd!" he called, and then,
turning reluctantly from the rail, made his way to where the
crew had gathered around the mast.

Stripes was there, standing barefooted atop an overturned
barrel and entertaining an audience whose attention—whether
because of the fervor with which he spoke or the subject
matter itself—he was having no trouble holding. ". . . and
then 'e looked up, just as this blazin' bolt o' lightnin' crack-
led out o' the sky, and d' ye know what 'e said? Why, 'e said
'e was sorry 'e couldn't run out the guns and return the salute!"

Sam sighed in exasperation. "Please, Stripes," he said,
"another time, if you will. There are some things that must
be settled."

"Aye, sir! I was jus' tellin' 'em about that thunderstorm and how ye defied the gods above—"

"I know. But there are Articles to be drawn up, officers to elect, courses to be plotted. You can regale them with all the stories you like—afterward."

"Did you *really* say that?" asked the boy, eyes huge in his pale, young face.

For answer, Sam merely shot an annoyed glance at Stripes, strode to one of the sloop's few guns, a gleaming four-pounder, and leaning against its long, iron barrel, contemplated his new crew with a mixture of apprehension, speculation, and amusement.

They were an unusual group. Stripes: thinner, leaner, but as loose-tongued as ever. The boy, Johnnie, staring at Sam with something akin to idol worship. Billy Flanagan, his tawny hair like a lion's mane around his sunburned face, standing at the tiller with Silas West, who'd wrapped a crimson scarf around his prematurely balding and sun-blistered scalp. Sam scanned their young faces: seaman's faces all, some already weathered by salt and sun, some showing scars of long-ago fights or drunken brawls, but all alight with animation and excitement. Nathaniel Paige carried one of those scars just below one laughing hazel eye; he'd been among the first to rush below to bring up a hogshead of contraband rum, and because he'd also been the first to shove his mug beneath its spigot, Sam had no illusions as to how that scar had been obtained. And then there was Phil Stewart, who, with his dark skin, long mustache, and curling black hair, looked like a Spanish don. Phil had carefully chosen a pistol from the weapons chest, his emotionless eyes lighting up only in appreciation of the fine weapon. Now, with several more knotted in a sash around his neck and two daggers thrust into his belt, he reminded Sam of his crewmate aboard Hornigold's sloop, Ned Teach, who'd shown an appreciation not so much for the quality of his personal weaponry, but the quantity.

And there, sitting just outside the ragtag group, was the most unlikely crew member of all—Maria. Her eyes were accusing, wounded, betrayed. *Christ,* Sam thought, already dreading the moment when matters were settled and he'd have to take her aside and try to reason with her.

But first things first. He turned to West, suppressing a grin at the comical way in which the red bandanna blended with the man's sunburned pate. "How much more rum is below, Mr. West?"

"Barrels and barrels of it, sir."

"Good. Bring up another hogshead or two, if you please. I fear this one won't last the night."

"You mean we can drink freely of it? What about rations?" asked Phil Stewart, looking up from where he'd been polishing one of his pistols with a square of linen.

"Rations? We're pirates, lad, not navy men. Take as much of it as ye please." And as several men exchanged brief smiles before rushing below to bring up more rum, Sam's gaze sought out Maria once more. She had wandered to the rail and was gazing out over a sea that was dazzlingly bright with sunlight, her slim figure and golden hair causing his heart to thud wildly in his chest. Feeling his eyes upon her, she turned, but the glance she gave him was enough to freeze the very fires of Hell. Lifting her small chin, she returned her gaze to the sea.

"Damn," Sam swore beneath his breath, unable to tear his eyes away from the golden hair that streamed in the fresh breeze and whipped about her wind-flushed cheeks. The wind molded her gown against her body in lovely detail, and he didn't need any imagination or recent memory to envision the lush curves just beneath. God's teeth. He hoped he could ease their differences soon. He wouldn't be able to stand much of this sort of torment. His annoyance grew when he caught several of the men staring at her just as longingly.

Stripes's hushed whisper managed to penetrate the veneer of Sam's ill humor. "Ain't she a looker? Told young Johnnie 'er name's Maria. She's the one Black Sam lost the *Whydah* over. Mother o' God, I can see now why 'e was so eager t' get back to 'er!"

Phil Stewart raised his head, his long black ringlets blowing in abandon about his face. "He lost a ship over her?" Uncertainty tinged his voice as his eyes went to the slim figure at the rail. Slowly, he said, "Maybe we all should've left with old Smuttynose. Everyone knows it's bad luck to have a woman on board a ship. No wonder it went down."

Stripes raised a hand. "Wait a minute, Stu. Ye've got it all wrong." He caught Sam's eye, realized his captain was about to strangle him, and hurried on before he could. "We lost the ship 'cause the lady was *on shore*. Ye see," he said, dropping his voice to a loud whisper, " 'tis rumored she's a witch. A few o' the Eastham folk told me so themselves, an' they oughta know, bein' 'er neighbors an' all. Anyhow, aside from me and a couple o' others, the cap'n was the only one t' survive the wreck. And d'ye know why 'e did?"

At the rail Maria froze. Her heart stopped and her blood went to ice water. Slowly, she turned, her face draining of color. They were all staring at her, every last one of them— the boy, the balding man with the bright scarf, even the Spanish-looking one with the curly mane of tangled hair.

And Sam.

Shock and astonishment shone briefly in his black eyes before dark lashes swept down to mask them. He shot a hard-eyed glance at Stripes. Oh God, she hadn't wanted him to find out this way! Please, God, not like this! Fear, not unlike that she'd experienced that awful day when the villagers had stoned her out of Eastham, gripped her heart in icy talons, but this time there was no place to flee.

"I'll tell ye why the cap'n didn't die, and 'twas a miracle 'e didn't, out cold an' trapped b'neath the mains'l like 'e was! 'Twas because *she* didn't want 'im to. *She* brought that ship onto a lee shore all right, *she* caused the storm—but only t' bring the cap'n back to 'er. She never 'ad any intention of lettin' 'im die!"

"How dare you!" Maria cried, nearing tears. They were all staring at her just as the villagers had, their eyes reflecting wariness, distrust, fear. And Sam? Thunderclouds were gathering on his brow and his dark eyes were beginning to flash.

"There ain't no need fer you blokes t' look like a goose jus' shit on yer graves. There ain't nothin' t' fear, now, I tell ye. With *her* aboard, hell, nothin' can 'appen to us. Bad luck? My arse! She 'ad the powers t' raise the seas and cast the *Whydah* up at 'er very doorstep, all 'cause she wanted the cap'n. Now she's got 'im, she'll keep 'im safe. She'll keep *all* of us safe, long's we stay with 'im. An' if she can raise a hurricane, jus' think how far she'll go t' protect us from the king's ships!"

Sam was no longer relaxing against the cannon. "What the devil are you blabbering about, lad? *Witchcraft?*"

''Aye! Heard about it in one o' the taverns back in Eastham. Everyone's scared t' death of 'er, they are!''

Sam turned on Maria. ''Is this true?'' he demanded, grasping her arm.

''Sam! How can you believe I'm a witch!''

''Dammit woman, I *don't* believe you're a witch, I want to know if you were accused as one!''

''Yes! Yes, I was! And if you weren't so caught up in your own troubles you might've realized that things weren't the way they should've been back in Eastham! But nay! Instead, all you thought about was piracy! Plotting and scheming the whole time, weren't you? Oh, you're lower than a snake! I told you I wanted no part of this, told you how I felt about piracy, but still you dragged me onto this—this *tub!* You're nothing but a beast, a knave, and I rue the day I set eyes on you!'' And then, bursting into tears at the stares of the men around her she tore herself from his grip, raced down the companionway, and in a blur of color, fled belowdecks.

''Uh-oh. She's mad now,'' Stripes said.

''Cease your goddamned prattle!'' Sam raged. ''I've had it up to here with you and your bloody tongue!'' His hard-eyed glare raked the others, who cowered beneath it. ''God's bloody teeth, a fatter parcel of rubbish I've yet to hear! Witch? Utter nonsense, all of it!'' Yet the pieces of the puzzle were coming together—the stark little hut on the sand cliffs, the absence of visitors, the pain he'd seen in her eyes when she'd thought he wasn't looking. More than anything, Sam wanted to follow her and wrench the details out of her if it killed him. But to go chasing after her skirts would be viewed as a weakness, and weakness had no place in a pirate captain. In control once more, he leaned back against the gun and folded his arms across his chest. ''The *lady,*'' he said with cold finality, ''goes where I go and that's all there is to it. And if ye don't like it, put it to a vote and I'll take my leave of the damned lot of you right now.''

Young Johnnie stood up. ''Is she *really* a witch?''

An arm yanked the boy back before Sam's temper could burst its fragile seams. He took a deep, steady breath and then, with a deliberate cheerfulness that fooled no one, said, ''Well, now that you've enlightened our new crew, Stripes, why don't you call for a show of hands to see who still wants to sail with us, eh?''

"I tell ye, as long as *she's* aboard, yer safe," Stripes said importantly. ''And a better cap'n than Black Sam ye won't be findin'. But if ye put 'er off this ship, then I can't promise she won't do somethin' t' bring the cap'n back to 'er—''

"Enough of this bloody nonsense!" Sam thundered, slamming his fist to the rail. ''Now, who's staying, dammit?''

For a moment, there was silence. Someone chuckled, then someone else, and soon the whole group was laughing. Nat Paige raised his tankard high, heedless of the rum that sloshed down onto Silas's bandanna. ''I don't care if she's a witch or not! I'll drink to any wench as pretty as that one is!''

"Hell, after that dreg you had in Boston, I can see why," added Phil, looking up from his gleaming pistol.

"What are ye talking about? Don't ye think the cap'n's lady is the most exquisite creature ye've ever laid eyes on?''

"Aye, I do. But she's not for you.''

"She's not for *any* of you," Sam said, and there was a hardness in his eyes and a set to his jaw that showed he meant every word. He could already see that he was going to have his hands full with this lot. ''And if I catch any of you treating her with anything less than respect''—his flashing gaze swept them to be sure they understood—''I give you my sincerest promise that you'll wish you'd never met me. Do I make myself clear?'' And at their sheepish nods, he grinned to break the tension, strode to the rum barrel, and refilled his tankard.

"Now that such balderdash is behind us, perhaps we can get down to business. The first order of the day is, of course, to elect officers. On a pirate ship, this is done by popular vote, as all major decisions are made. The only exception to this is in battle, where the captain's word is law.'' Affable once more, he drank long and deeply of his rum. ''Now, let us choose our officers, lads.''

And so they did, taking up an afternoon to do so. There was no question over who would be captain, and the titles of quartermaster, sailing master, boatswain, and master gunner went to Silas West, Nat Paige, a young Irishman named Jake Gillespie, and Phil Stewart, respectively. At last only the position of surgeon remained unfilled.

As they sat pondering their dilemma, Stripes's voice broke the silence. "Hey, how 'bout Maria? I'll bet none of ye knew she 'ad 'er own little medical practice back on Cape Cod. Cured people with weeds an' stuff, or so they told me. In fact—"

"Stripes! That will be *enough!*" Sam barked.

"Heck, I'd give me right arm t' have 'er nurse me back t' health," Stripes added.

"Persist, and that can be arranged." Sam's tone was dry, his grin tight-lipped and not amused. "Besides, she'll not do it anyhow."

And so they left the position vacant, drew up Articles, and swore on Smuttynose's dusty old Bible to be true to the company. And it was only after the stars began to twinkle high overhead that Sam, bidding them good-night with orders to put out the lanterns at eight bells, turned to make his way below.

And as he descended the companionway the smile faded from his face, his eyes grew hard, and his hand closed around the tiny scraps of fabric that still lay in his pocket.

It was time that he and Maria had their talk.

Chapter 17

She whom I love is hard to catch and conquer,
Hard, but O the glory of the winning were she
won!

MEREDITH

The faint scents of tar, pitch, and damp wood. Deck supports and timbers, walling her in. A checkerboard of light from the hatch above, now fading with the day. For the hundredth time Maria, huddled miserably in the darkened hold between hogsheads of foodstuffs, water, and rum, cursed Captain Samuel Bellamy for the wicked monster he was.

To think she'd actually given herself to him last night! Oh God, not only had she *given* herself, she'd thrown herself at him. Disgust and shame filled her.

I hate you, Sam Bellamy!

The sounds of revelry drifted down from above; they were muffled, but she had no trouble hearing them. Someone—the kindly one named Nat Paige?—was belting out a rollicking tune in a voice thick with drink; now he was joined by too many others for her to count or recognize. She heard good-natured oaths that made her cheeks burn, the tinkle of breaking glass, and following it, bursts of drunken, raucous laughter.

And what was *he* doing? Leaning against the rail with the sea at his back, watching them all with the kind of amusement a proud parent might a mischievous child? Congratulating himself on his good fortune and, of course, his ability to take over a ship singlehandedly? Or tippling with the rest of them, enjoying himself, while behind those dark, impassive eyes his clever mind plotted some new and unlawful scheme?

She drew her legs up to her chest and dug her forehead into her kneecaps, trying to suppress her thoughts, her headache, and the stench of sour brine coming from a nearby pile of coiled hemp. Beneath her the deck gave a sudden lurch, and her outflung arm was all that saved her from toppling onto her side. The deck pitched again, and this time her elbow cracked against a barrel. Pain shot up her arm. And as she looked up, fighting tears, she saw that the last of the light from the grating had faded and she was sitting in total darkness.

"Maria?"

She went rigid, eyes staring into the gloom.

"Maria, lass? Are ye down here?"

A traitorous flutter of her heart, a thrill that tingled up her spine; she swallowed hard, her insides turning to syrup at the sound of that deep, resonant voice. Holding her breath, Maria flattened herself against a barrel. She would *not* let him see her tears, her agony. Let him look for her elsewhere. Let him waste his precious time searching the whole stinking ship for her.

"Maria, lass? I know you're down here somewhere. Please come out. I want to talk to you."

He was close; too close. Maria bit her lip and buried her face against her arm. In the heavy silence, even the whisper of her breath against her skin sounded like the howl of a gale wind. *Go away!* her mind screamed in silent agony. *I hate you. Hate you!*

"Princess, please," he said, and this time there was no mistaking that familiar, irritated edge to his voice. One hesitant football in the darkness, another; and then a thud, a crash, and sounds of something rolling across the deck. "God's teeth!" she heard him swear. "What kind of bloody idiot would put a cursed barrel in the middle of the god-damned . . .—*Maria?*"

Served him right for not bringing a lantern! Maria waited in the deafening silence, holding her breath, counting the frantic thud of her heartbeats. She was beginning to feel incredibly foolish, but pride won out and she didn't move. The moments dragged on until at last he muttered something she didn't catch and moved away, his footsteps receding into the darkness. Slowly, her breath came out in a mingled sigh of relief, and an absurd despair that he *hadn't* found her.

Frustration prevailed where triumph should have. Sooner of later Sam would find her, and when he did he was going to be downright furious. And suddenly Maria realized that the knife edge of her hatred had gone dull, for it was hard to hate someone who'd just managed to rob her of one of the reasons for doing so in the first place. Just as she'd been feeling sorry for herself that he hadn't come looking for her, he had. Oh . . . *damn him!* Why couldn't he have just left her alone with her anger? That, and hate, were her only weapons against him, and if she wanted to protect herself from further pain, she needed all the defenses she could muster.

But no. She still had *plenty* of things to hate him for. He'd made her an unwilling partner in his plans, hadn't he? And feeling somehow victorious, Maria smiled in the darkness and vowed to herself that she would keep *on* hating him.

Of course, it was unfortunate she didn't know what Sam was up to at that very moment—for if she had, she wouldn't be smiling.

* * *

"You summoned me, sir?"

Johnnie Taylor stared up in awe at the tall, formidable man who stood at the darkened stern windows with a tankard in one hand and a bottle of Smuttynose's prized Madeira in the other.

Sam's heavy sigh broke the stillness of the room. He was tired, he was annoyed, and as usual where Maria was concerned, he was nearing the end of his limited patience. Turning from the window, he eased himself into a chair. "Aye, I summoned you," he said, leaning back and setting both tankard and wine upon the table that was bolted to the bulkhead. "Sit down, please."

The boy hastily did so, staring with wide eyes as the pirate captain pushed aside the clutter of brass dividers, charts, quadrant, and telescope to make a place for his booted feet. These he propped on the tabletop, three inches away from an untouched bowl of lobscouse and a plate of biscuit and cheese. Too tired for pleasantries, Sam got right to the point. "I have a task for you, one that shouldn't prove too difficult." He carved a wedge of cheese, leaned back in his chair once more, and sat chewing the cheese, watching Johnnie with quietly assessing eyes. "How long have ye been at sea, lad?"

The boy quailed beneath that penetrating black gaze, but answered steadily, "Why, three years, sir."

Sam washed the cheese down with a generous amount of Madeira. "Hmm. You're rather young, aren't you?"

"I'm ten, sir. Not all *that* young." Not quite as unobtrusively as Sam was assessing him, the boy studied his new captain with reverent, admiring eyes. Pirate or not, he hadn't lost his temper with him, nor raised his hand to him as Smuttynose had been wont to do. Johnnie's bright gaze lingered on the hoop of gold in the captain's ear and the glossy waves of his thick, black hair, neatly queued at his nape with a strip of leather. A few locks had come loose to fall over his forehead and curl around his temples, giving him a slightly unscrupulous look that, coupled with his beard, made him appear devilish, almost sinister. But then, Johnnie thought,

Black Sam *was* a pirate captain—he was supposed to look that way.

Importantly, Johnnie's small unwhiskered chin came up. "Besides, I can set a sail and Stripes is going to show me how to fire a cannon. He said that you—"

"Never mind what Stripes told you. He's full of tales, and you'd be wise not to believe half the things he says."

"But did you *really* run out the guns during that thunderstorm, with the lightning flashing all around and the waves swamping the ship? Did you really fire them just to salute the gods and the thunder from above?"

Sam couldn't prevent a somewhat guilty smile. "Aye, I believe I *did* consider it."

"And did you really take over fifty prizes in less than a year?"

"Aye. I did that too, I guess."

"And did you really overthrow Ben Hornigold and take his captaincy, his crew, and his ship away from him? *The* Ben Hornigold, the one that—"

Sam sighed hopelessly and picked up his tankard. "Yes."

"Then how come you don't want me to believe what Stripes says? So far, everything he's told me about you is true! Besides, he's a nice man! He's gonna teach me how to fire the guns, and then *I'll* be able to run them out in a storm, just like you, and fight if we go into battle—"

Sam slammed his tankard down on the table. "I don't want you near the guns." His tone was final, adamant, and forbidding any argument.

The boy's face fell; crestfallen, he hung his head.

"At least, not until *I* can show you how to handle them properly myself."

Johnnie's head snapped up. *"You'll* show me?"

Sam grinned, silently cursing himself for tossing another log onto the boy's fire of hero worship. "Aye. Nothing to it. But first, you must do me a small favor."

"Yes, sir! Anything!" Excitement flared in the lad's eyes, and Sam wished with all his heart that Maria would hold him in such high esteem. But that, at the moment, was too much to hope for.

"Very well, then." Sam picked up his tankard. "I want

you to search this ship from stem to stern until you find the lady.''

Johnnie's eyes widened. "You mean the witch?"

"She is *not* a witch, and if I ever hear her referred to as such by anyone aboard this ship again I'll have him flogged!"

Chagrined, the boy's eyes filled with tears and Sam cursed himself for speaking so harshly. "See?" he said, more gently. "What did I tell you about Stripes? Another one of his damned stories. Pay it no heed. Just find Maria and bring her here, to me."

Johnnie jumped up, happy to be in his hero's good graces once again.

"And if she gives you any sass, tell her I've threatened ye with the lash if she doesn't follow." He grinned. "That'll bring her."

"Aye, sir!" Johnnie cried. "Right away!" And touching his fingers to his brow, he pounded from the cabin.

Alone again, Sam toyed with the handle of his tankard and stared in disbelief at the door. He smiled. He chuckled. And then he threw back his head in peals of helpless laughter until he was forced to put the tankard down before he spilled wine all over the fine linen shirt he'd found in one of Smuttynose's sea chests. By the gods, the lad had actually *saluted* him! He, a pirate captain! No one—not aboard *Lilith*, *Mary Anne*, nor even *Whydah*—had *ever* done so before.

He found the idea rather appealing.

Two bells of the mid-watch brought moonlight streaming through the salt-encrusted panes of *Dolphin's* stern windows and Maria Hallett, escorted by a sheepish but very proud Johnnie, into the great cabin.

Eyes blazing, hair askew, she marched across the room to where the cause of her anger was slumped over a yellowed chart, forehead cradled in one hand and quill pen held loosely in the other. He merely looked up as she sent the cabin door slamming back against the bulkhead, his handsome, swarthy face drawn and tired. The little laugh-lines at the corners of his eyes were more pronounced than usual and he offered her a hint of a smile, but he seemed anything but happy. Maria had no pity for him. "What is the meaning of this, you—"

"Thank you, Johnnie," Sam said impassively. "That will be all."

"Aye, sir." Humbly, Johnnie turned to go, casting one last awed glance at the dark, imposing man who, even slumped wearily over the desk, managed to inspire command and respect.

"And oh, Johnnie?"

The boy turned expectantly, eyes hopeful, a little wary.

"Mind that you report to me on the quarterdeck tomorrow following the morning watch."

"Sir?"

Sam grinned. "I believe we have a cannon to fire."

"Yes, *sir!*"

Saluting smartly, the boy raced from the cabin. Maria waited just long enough for the sound of his footsteps to fade. "Lash him, huh? You wouldn't raise a hand to that child if someone held a gun to your head! Already you have him eating out of your hand, just like you have everyone else doing aboard this ship!" She spat the last word with all the distaste she could muster. "You're the most vile, disgusting *parasite* I've ever met, do you know that? I hate you! I hate you with all of my heart!"

"Sit down, Maria."

"And to think I trusted you!" she cried, fists balled at her sides and eyes spitting fire as she glared up at him with the wrath of an angry lioness. "Oh, why did I believe you'd change? Go ahead, continue your robbing, your murdering, but do it without me, do you understand? I want no part of it. *And I want no part of you!*"

He listened to her tirade in calm silence, allowing her to vent her feelings while he leaned back in his chair, propped his booted feet upon the desk, and watched her with expressionless black eyes that told nothing about how deeply her words were cutting him.

And she was driving the knife deeper, searching for something vital. "You sicken me, do you know that? I should've left you there to die on that beach! In fact, if I'd known just what I was unleashing upon the world I *would* have! Now it's my fault that these men are going to follow you right into Hell, my fault that you're going to rob and kill innocent people who did nothing to deserve it, my fault that even a young boy is already polluted by the corruption in your cursed, blackened soul!''

Again he said nothing, only watching her in that strange way when he should've grown angry. The fact that he remained quiet began to unnerve her, and in the tension-filled silence her own rage backed off, leaving shame and guilt in its place. But oh, he'd provoked her! He deserved every word she'd flung at him! Well, almost. She really shouldn't have said anything about leaving him there to die, for that had been a terrible thing to say no matter *how* angry she was with him. It irked her, began to prickle her conscience like wool against bare skin, until finally she opened her mouth to apologize, but the words wouldn't come. Instead, she turned away so he wouldn't see the hole in her defenses, and in a sullen but decidedly less hostile voice demanded to know where they were going.

He sat idly tapping the quill against his thumb as though her hateful words hadn't affected him in the least. Finally, he tossed the pen onto the desk, stretched his well-muscled arms over his head, and sagged back against his chair. "Monhegan.''

"Monhegan? What, or where, pray tell, is that?''

Sam sighed heavily. "A small island off the coast of Maine. Wild, mostly uninhabited.''

"Oh. How nice,'' she said sarcastically. "Let me guess, more piratical activities, am I right?''

He gave her a benevolent smile that hinted not of mockery, but amusement. "Your astuteness amazes me, princess.''

"Damn you!'' she cried, whirling away from him. "Why would I even *dare* to hope otherwise? You care nothing about me, nor how I feel! All you've done is fill my head with lies, empty promises! First with your talk about making me a 'princess' of some stupid island, then your lies about wanting to marry me, and giving up piracy! Well, I've had it with your fairy tales, Sam! And I've had it with you! I hate you, do you understand? *Hate you!*''

He seemed content to let her blow out her rage like a sea squall, reefing his sails and lashing his guns against the onslaught of her wrath, but his casual, matter-of-fact manner only infuriated her all the more. Angry spots of color rode the hollows beneath each cheekbone, her eyes were unnaturally bright, and there was a whiteness around her mouth that he'd never seen before. Patiently, his eyes unreadable, Sam waited for her to finish, and then he calmly reached into his pocket, drew something out, and tossed it onto the table before her.

"Would you care to explain these, Maria?"

Her blustery wind fell short, her sails went slack, and she went so pale that Sam instinctively straightened up in his chair, ready to catch her if she should faint. "Stripes accused you of some rather serious things back there, princess. Namely, witchcraft. 'Tis hardly the sort of thing I'd expect a God-fearing lass like you to engage in." Watching her face intently, he leaned back in his chair and crossed his arms behind his dark head. "And what concerns me is that you didn't deny it."

Her gaze was nailed to the items on the table. She ignored his question and made a clawing motion at her throat. "H-how did you find these?"

"Oh, they just happened to be in the same trunk as my dagger. Nice and neatly folded, tucked away at the bottom. I thought you might enjoy telling me about them."

Maria stared at those fragile scraps of fabric through a thickening blur of tears. Charles's little gown. His blanket. *Oh, why was he doing this to her?* Memories came flooding back and with them heartache, overwhelming her, drowning her until nausea rose up in her stomach and wrenched the last bit of color from her cheeks. Never had she thought to see these precious little items again, and she was torn between a frantic impulse to throw her arms around Sam's neck in gratitude for bringing them to her and snatching them away before he put his vile, thieving hands upon them once more.

Casually, he plucked them out of her reach, regarding them thoughtfully as he turned them over and over in his big, searoughened hands. "Witchcraft," he mused, and his eyes flashed to hers. "Do you deny it now?"

She didn't answer.

"Do you?"

She stared at the little gown. A tear welled up, spilled, and trickled down her bloodless cheek. "Sam, please . . ."

"God's teeth, woman, I'm asking you a question!"

She found her voice. "And I'm choosing not to answer it!"

His rage, well-timed and calculated for once, had the desired effect of shocking her back to reality and now that he'd achieved it, Sam was not about to let up. "Oh yes you will. In fact, ye'll tell me every damned thing that went on while I was away if we both have to sit here all bloody night!"

"Why should I tell you? Why should I tell you *anything?*" she whispered, turning away to stare out the stern windows. Past the reflection of lantern light on the glass, she could see the ship's wake glittering and sparkling in the moonlight like a handful of fallen stars, broken dreams. One window was open, filling the cabin with the tangy scent of the sea. Crossing the room, she placed her hands against the sill and took a deep, steadying breath of that sea air, trying to draw strength from it. Her voice was flat and emotionless, and Sam, though he listened intently, had to strain his ears to hear it. "You don't care," she was saying. "You never have, never will. The only one you care about is yourself. You didn't go to Florida to bring up the treasure so we could get married. You did it for yourself, for the money. And when you didn't find it you turned to piracy instead. You didn't return to Eastham for me. In fact, you wouldn't even have ended up there at all if it wasn't for the storm." Her voice began to quiver, evidence of the hurt and bitterness that flooded the chambers of her heart. "You don't fool me, Sam." She turned from the window and regarded him steadily. "I know you for what you are."

"Do you, now?" he asked softly, crossing the room to her. He put a finger beneath her chin, tilting her head up and meeting her resolute gaze with an enigmatic one of his own. Despite herself, shivers coursed through her at his touch. "And what might that be, my dear? An uncaring beast? A heartless rascal? A self-centered barbarian?" She looked away, unable to bear this new tactic of his, and unbidden, her gaze went to the baby's things in his hand. "No, princess, I don't think you know me at all."

Nonchalantly, he let his hand fall away from her trembling chin, keenly aware of the alarm that leaped in her eyes as he casually studied the tiny garments he still held.

He had to hand it to her. She'd certainly made a gallant,

if unconscious, attempt to divert his attention away from the witchcraft matter. But really, she should've known better than to think she could sway him from a well-charted course. When he was hell-bent on something, nothing stood in his way—certainly not a young girl's inexperienced efforts to lead him from the truth. And at the moment, the truth was all that mattered.

He held up the little scraps of fabric, embroidery, and stitching. "You made these, didn't you?"

She looked as wary as a trapped rabbit. "Yes."

"And might I ask why?"

She turned away to look out the window once more. "It's none of your business."

"Ah, but I think it is very much my business, Maria." She could see his handsome reflection in the panes of glass, could see him running his thumb over the soft linen of the little gown. She whirled, terrified he was going to damage it, but instead he merely tossed the tiny items to her with careless indifference. Maria snatched them out of the air, and had he not known already, the possessive, protective manner in which she hugged them to her breast would've given her away. "You see, princess," he said mildly, pulling out his chair once more and studying her bent head, "while you've been down in the hold sulking and hiding from me all day, I've been doing some chatting with my former crew member, Stripes. The one who can't keep a silent tongue, the one who was at Higgins Tavern shortly after the *Whydah* wrecked."

Oh, God, did he know? Did he *know?*

"Sam, please . . ." she whispered, lifting her head and hugging the fragile little items to her breast. Her eyes implored him. "I—I don't want to talk about it. I beg of you, not now."

"Oh, but I do. And yes, I *do* know all about it," he said, reading her thoughts. "Do ye think you could hide such a thing from me forever? But I prefer to hear the story from you, rather than Stripes. He does tend to, shall I say, stretch the truth a bit sometimes." His voice grew soft, unbearably tender. "I hope he's done so where you are concerned, Maria."

Her lids sank over watery eyes, and she was unable to

speak for fear of losing control of the tears she so desperately
fought to keep back.

"You know, princess, you're only making it harder on
yourself."

He saw her throat working, her little hand shaking as she
came to the table and stood pitifully clutching the baby's gown
to her breast as though the tiny garment could contain the
grief within her heart. He felt like a beast for reducing her
to this, but now that he knew her secret he would not permit
her to keep it inside and bear the anguish alone. She hated
him, yes, and after this she'd probably hate him even more,
but he didn't care. Her happiness was all that mattered. With
that thought in mind, he said what he knew would unleash
the flood of tears she was trying so hard to hold back.

"Maria," he said gently, "I know about the baby."

She squeezed her eyes shut. His words hung in the silence,
echoing over and over in her brain: *I know about the baby
. . . the baby . . . the baby. . . .* She stared down at the table,
saw its outline grow fuzzy and blurred, and then her hands
came up to cover her eyes and she burst into tears.

It was what Sam had been waiting for. She heard the scrape
of his chair as he came to his feet, his footsteps as he came
to her. And then he was behind her, turning her, his hands
gentle and warm upon her shoulders.

"Ah, love. 'Tis all right, now. . . ."

She buried her face in his broad chest, sobbing pitifully.

"Oh, Sam. . . . Oh, God—"

"I know. 'Tis all right. . . . Easy, now. . . ."

"But it's true!" She looked up at him with eyes streaming,
chin trembling, cheeks awash. "God help me it is, every bit
of it!"

His arms enfolded her in their warmth. His chest was a
solid wall of comfort, his voice, barely stirring the air above
her head, soft, gentle, and questioning. "Tell me about it,
lass. Tell me what happened while I was gone."

And thus, he managed to get the tale from her own lips,
a tale that had been dreadful enough when he'd first heard it
from Stripes, a tale that made him sick with grief when he
got it from Maria's agonized soul. And when she'd finished,
trembling and red-eyed, the night was old, the ship was quiet,
and the hatred she'd felt for Sam had fled her heart. Snif-

fling, she drew back and gazed up at him. His jaw was set, his mouth was a hard line, but never had she seen such sheer, naked pain in his eyes, not even when he'd tortured himself about his dead crew members.

Moments passed, long moments where the only sounds were the rhythmic creaking of seasoned timbers, the gurgle of water against the rudder, the booming thunder of the mainsail above as the wind slacked, then bellied it out once more. At last, Sam's quiet voice broke the silence.

"What did you call him, Maria? Our . . . son?"

The tears started anew at the sound of the baby's name upon her lips. "Ch-Charles," she said brokenly. "After your middle name."

"Ah, sweeting," he crooned as she succumbed to choking, pitiful sobs once more. He drew her close, his arms enfolding her, his big hands cupping the back of her head. She felt the strength in those strapping arms, heard the thud of his heart beneath her cheek. But he was staring out the stern windows, seeing nothing but the tormented visions her words evoked.

"Oh, Sam, you don't know how much it hurt, how much it *still* hurts," she sobbed. His chest, slick with her tears, muffled her voice. "I loved him so much. . . . I thought I was over it, but I'm not. I thought I could forget him, but I can't. Every day I still see his little face, hear his cries—oh, when, *when*, will it ever stop hurting?"

Sam had never felt so frustratingly helpless in his life. He held her close, trying to soothe her with gentle hands upon her hair, her back. " 'Twill always hurt, Maria," he said quietly. "It only proves how much you loved him. You must stop blaming yourself for his death. 'Twasn't your fault."

"But it was! I should've known better than to take him into town!" She clawed at the closure of his shirt, burying her face within it and sending tears down the already-damp crease of his chest. "And when he"—it was hard to say it, even now—"when he d-died, my only consolation was that you'd come back for me some day. I lived for that, prayed for it, because I knew that when you did, you'd make everything all better and that everything would be all right again. You were the reason I built that hut on the beach, so I could watch the sea every day for your return. Oh Sam, you were all I had left, and now"—she raised her head, her eyes filled with anguish—"and now, I don't even have you!"

Her last words were drowned in a fresh wave of grief.

"Here, now. Of course you have me, princess."

"No, Sam," she cried, raising a hand to claw the tangled hair from her eyes. "Piracy has you now, and when it has finished with you the *hangman* will have you!"

With a helpless sigh he stood, gathered her up in his arms, and carried her to his desk, where he pulled out a chair, settled her onto his lap, and cradled her within the comforting circle of his arms. The bottle of Madeira sat within easy reach, and Sam had no reservations about pouring a healthy measure of it into his tankard. "Here," he said with firm gentleness, holding it up to her swollen lips. "Drink this. 'Twill make you feel better."

He hadn't known what else to do to calm her and fully expected her to refuse the wine, but she surprised him by taking the tankard in both trembling hands, lifting it to her tear-streaked face, and downing it like a seasoned tar. He said nothing, merely watching her until she finally set the empty vessel upon the desk.

"I think, princess, it's time we got a few things straight." He shifted his weight, settling her more comfortably in his lap and pulling her up against him so that her damp cheek lay against his chest, her thighs pressed intimately against his. One crimson droplet of wine clung to her swollen, softly bowed lip, and he reached down to tenderly brush it away with the tip of his finger. "First of all, I've never lied to you. True, I'd originally planned to salvage the Spanish treasure fleet for my own intents and purposes—but after I met you that all changed. Remember that day at your aunt's house when I asked for your hand?" Maria nodded. "And do you remember how she refused me? Well, I vowed then and there that I'd have you as my wife no matter what it took, and I left that house wracking my brain for a way to have you. 'Twas at that point that I realized the value of the treasure. Hell, I thought, if I came back to Eastham as a rich man your aunt would *never* refuse me." He paused, his hand stroking the heavy mass of her hair, lifting it off her neck, smoothing it. "'Twas only when I failed to raise the treasure that I turned to piracy.

"Secondly"—he reached behind her, poured another tankard of wine, and held it up to her lips while she sipped it— "I never set out to involve you in any of this business, nor to expose you to a crew of boozy tars who, I'm afraid, will be far more intent upon winning your favors than attending to the business of sailing this ship. As though I haven't enough headaches already. And thirdly, and most importantly, I had every intention of marrying you, and still do. As far as I'm concerned, nothing has changed between us." He paused, tipping her chin up until their eyes met. "You're all that I ever wanted, princess. And I tell you this, and tell you from the heart—I never, *ever* wanted to hurt you."

She wiped at her eyes with a knuckle and in a small, plaintive voice asked, "Then why did you take this ship, when you knew how I felt about it? Why can't you just give up piracy?"

"I had intended to, before the *Whydah* disaster," he explained. His voice grew sad. "But the wreck, of course, changed all that."

"Why?" she asked, exhaustion, and the wine, making her voice sound thick and sleepy.

"Why? Because two men survived that wreck, Maria, as well as the prize crew I put aboard the wine pink. They're my men, lass. They depended upon me for leadership and guidance, counted on me to lead them into battle and keep them safe. Now, they're in the most perilous battle they'll ever fight; now, they need me more than ever. I can't just desert them. How could I live with myself if I left them to their fates, without hope of ever being rescued?"

"But they don't *know* you're alive. They're no longer counting on you! You don't *have* to rescue them!"

"That's a coward's way out, and I'd be lower than a snake if I were to take it."

"Then why are we going to this . . . this island?"

"To rendezvous with the other two ships that were in my fleet that night. Before the storm struck we held council and agreed to meet there if we became separated. There's a chance—a slim one, but a chance, nevertheless—that they'll still be there, waiting for us; if so, we'll gather forces, then go about getting those poor lads out of the Boston gaol. . . ."

His voice was fading to a pleasant, soothing drone, and

the concentration it took to listen to and understand him was something that Maria was fast losing the ability to sustain. The wine flowed through her blood, dulling her senses and the reawakened pain over Charles's death. She took another sip of it, closed her eyes, and leaned her head back against the comforting hardness of Sam's shoulder. His voice drifted in and out of a pleasant, thickening haze.

"Don't worry, lass," he was saying, his warm breath stirring the hair at the top of her head. "I won't be at this game for long, I promise. After I get the men out, you have my word that I'll turn over command of this sloop to her quartermaster. I'll lower my flag, never sail under the Jolly Roger again. We *will* find some lovely, tropical island to settle on— hell, maybe I'll even grow sugarcane or something, anything to make you happy. We'll have a big, handsome house, where the trade winds sweep through and it never gets cold. We'll have grand parties, and maybe, just maybe, I'll even let you bring that confounded dog of yours down. . . . Maria?"

But she was fast asleep, her head lolling against his shoulder, one thick, yellow lock of hair tumbling across his arm. She hadn't heard a word he'd said.

He smiled, for his little Maria was obviously not accustomed to anything stronger than milk or water. But the wine had brought her peace, and though she might curse him come morning for it, he didn't regret giving it to her now. At least she was resting comfortably; he, unfortunately, would not be so lucky. He was so damned tired he could barely keep his eyes open, but how could he sleep, after what he'd learned tonight? Witchcraft, ostracism—and a baby. Oh God, a baby. His baby.

He stood up, tenderly cradling her limp form to his chest as he carried her to his bunk. She was a feather in his arms, nothing more than a scrap of soft skin and silken hair encased in a tumble of frilly petticoats and a dirt-smudged gown. As carefully as if she were made of porcelain, he set her on the bunk and drew the coverlet up over her shoulders.

For a long moment he stood gazing down at her, his dark eyes soft with love, his face troubled. And then he bent, dropped a kiss upon her brow, and made his way to the door. On the way out, he paused only long enough to retrieve the bottle of wine. It would not, of course, ease his troubled

mind any, but there was no harm in trying. And on second
thought, he reached for a second bottle, just in case, and
with a last look at the child-woman asleep in his bunk, quietly shut the door behind him.

Chapter 18

Change, as ye list, ye winds; my heart shall
be
The faithful compass that still points to thee.

GAY

An ear-splitting, thunderous roar brought Maria wide
awake and bolt upright in the bunk. She stared, momentarily confused, at the unfamiliar surroundings, and then
her heart settled back into her breast as the booming echoes
died away and a loud chorus of cheers drifted down to her
from above.

Of course. She was on a pirate ship, its crew was yelling
their heads off, and its captain was teaching a ten-year-old
how to fire a cannon.

The headache struck as she swung her legs off the bed,
driving a moan of pain from her lips and her fingertips to her
temples in a vain effort to contain it. He mouth was lined
with cotton, her stomach as sour as week-old milk, her unkempt hair falling in a tangled mess over her eyes. The creases
in her periwinkle skirts were mute testimony to the fact that
she'd fallen asleep fully clothed.

She gained her feet with a good deal of assistance from
the corner of the bunk and none at all from the sloop, rolling
pleasantly on the long ocean swells and taking a cruel delight
in framing a glaring, diamond-studded sea between its open
stern windows that made her feel as though someone had
taken the top of her head off and dumped hot coals behind

her eyes. Just how on earth was she going to survive aboard this ship? One night and she was already dying. And the food . . . she didn't want to even *think* about what the food would be like. . . .

A bowl and pitcher of cool water stood on the table, and Maria felt slightly better after washing her face. Easing the tangles from her hair, she plaited it, tossed the braid back over her shoulder, and sank down on the bunk to consider her situation.

She assumed that Sam had slept topside beneath the stars last night, a thought that made her feel empty and annoyed at the same time. But last night, with its turbulent then tender memories, was fresh in her mind. Mixed feelings pummeled her from all sides. She didn't know whether to be grateful to Sam for his tactical methods of making her reveal all, relieved that she'd finally done so, or angry for the fact that regardless of her desires, he'd still taken the sloop.

Oh, it had been heaven to be held so tenderly in his strong arms, to finally relinquish all the heartache of the past year to his very capable shoulders. But what were his feelings on the whole matter now? After all, he'd had a whole night to dwell on the things she'd told him—things that made her all the more vulnerable to him, things he could use against her if the need suited him.

She watched the pages of his open journal flutter in the salty breeze. Annoyance with her own loss of control, irritation with his persuasive ways, fear of the knowledge he now held—and the headache that was, after all, his fault—began to make her feel peevish. Another deafening crash from above and an answering boom of resounding thunder sent her temper spinning toward the edge. Irascibility won out; smoothing the creases from her skirts, she marched from the cabin.

Topside, water tossed and tumbled about the ship in every direction, rolling away to the north, the south, growing deep azure toward the west and so dazzlingly bright in the east that it hurt her eyes, and her head, to look at it. Yet she made a charming sight as she appeared on the sun-drenched open deck, her face still flushed with sleep, her hair shining like Egyptian gold. As usual, Maria was unaware of the effect she had on men, and that effect was no different upon this rough pack of sea dogs than it had been on the besotted lads back in Eastham. She mistook their good-natured elbow-bumping, roguish grins, and raised rum pots for mockery, not compliments. And if she'd been peevish when she left the cabin, now she was becoming downright angry.

No doubt they assumed that she and Sam had spent the night together—in bed. And for that matter, where *had* he slept? Her face flamed, and she avoided their eyes as she stumbled across the deck, nearly tripping over a pile of coiled rope and lurching drunkenly as the deck rolled steadily beneath her feet.

Oh, they probably thought she was a harlot all right, if not a witch, thanks to that meddlesome busybody . . . what was his name? Spot? Stripes? But then she looked up and saw that there was no condemnation at all coming from this rowdy group in seaman's kilts and leather vests. Several even raised their tankards to her in an odd gesture of respect as she passed.

But their seemingly good manners would not last for long. They'd only been pirates since yesterday. Give them a few more days of Sam, several prizes to get the blood-lust and gold-thirst running in their veins, and they'd never be the same.

As if to reprimand her for her bad thoughts about its captain, the ship crested a swell and tossed its bowsprit toward the sky. Thrown off balance, Maria stumbled and grabbed at a line, nearly snatching her hand back when she saw that it was stiff with a fresh coat of black tar. She clung there on the wind-raked, open deck as the ship plunged through foamy seas and flung spray back into her face, her stomach in knots while she tried to focus her attention on a gull wheeling just off the bow, now diving to pluck a piece of fish out of the air as the cook heaved the scraps of last night's meal overboard.

She was just starting to relax when her nerves were blown to bits by another calm-shattering detonation. A thick cloud of eye-stinging, yellow-black smoke drifted past, and as it cleared she saw a group of men gathered around a gun on the larboard side of the quarterdeck. In their midst, holding a smoldering match in his hand, was the boy, Johnnie. His hair was rumpled, his hands were black with powder, and he was listening with rapt attention to the patient words of his captain, who stood beside him.

"Now, try it again, lad. Sponge her out, ram the powder cartridge home. Now, the ball. That's it.'' Maria watched, horror-struck, as the boy gingerly followed Sam's instructions, then stabbed a long pick through the gun's touchhole to puncture the cartridge. Two burly men took up the cannon's side tackle and ran the gun forward. "Sight along the barrel—carefully, now! And keep that damned match to leeward, you don't want a spark to set her off before you're ready. Stand to the side, she's going to come back, *hard*. That's better. Now, wait 'til the ship begins to crest the next wave, and fire on the uproll—''

Maria clapped her hands to her ringing ears just in time. Belching smoke, the gun hurled itself back against the heavy breeching ropes. Deck planking shook beneath her feet. Bass reverberations rang through her head, her chest, and every part of her body. A half-mile beyond the gunwales, the ocean swallowed the ball and coughed up a plume of spray. As wind drove the thick smoke to leeward and off over the sea, Maria saw that Johnnie's audience was cheering and clapping him on the back. Gunner was there too, barking wildly. Someone thrust a tankard into the boy's hand, and Sam let him have a swallow or two before just as quickly passing it on to Stripes, who sat on an overturned barrel with bare feet swinging to and fro.

Sam. He stood there with a satisfied smile curving his lips, his flashing teeth appearing all the more white from the sheen of black powder that covered his face and made him look like some grinning devil straight from Hell itself. His eyes looked tired and red-rimmed, and the little creases at their corners— now white lines etched into the powder grime— were sharp with weariness. His hair was still tied in a queue, though it remained so rebelliously; it, like its owner, disliked constraint of any kind and now the strip of leather at his nape had all but abandoned its efforts at keeping the glossy black waves under control. As she stared at him, he happened to glance up and see her watching him.

"Maria, lass!'' he called, his eyes lighting up and suddenly not looking so tired anymore. "How nice of ye to join us! I was just showing Johnnie how to fire a gun.''

"So I've noticed.''

One black brow went up at her unexpected petulance. What

the devil had he done now? he thought. Deciding to make light of it—after all, maybe the Madeira had been too much for her—he came forward and took her hand. His smile was teasing, his dark eyes dancing as he reached out and tilted her face up to his. "What ails ye, princess? Too much wine last night?"

She jerked back as though his touch had burned her. "Too much wine? Yes, and no thanks to you! I suppose you think it's all a big joke!"

Instantly, the teasing light in his eye vanished. He was no longer grinning. "I can assure you, princess, 'tis no joke."

"Of course not, it wouldn't be. It's never a joke when a ten-year-old is corrupted by the evil of his elders, never a joke when someone is caught and hung for piracy!"

An unnatural hush fell over the ship at the brazen way in which she was addressing its captain; even the sloop seemed to listen, the creak of mast and spars ceasing for a long moment until only the sigh of wind through rigging could be heard. Behind her, Stripes pricked up his ears and watched this new development the way a starving man eyes a piece of bread, and several men hid amused coughs behind their hands and glanced quickly among themselves as they wondered how their captain would react to this tongue-lashing from a mere woman. Only Johnnie, who'd hoped to fire the cannon a few more times, looked dismayed.

Sam made one last attempt to be civil before he lost his temper. Obviously, the wine had not only made her irritable, but had dimmed her memory of all that he'd promised her as well. Back to the beginning, were they? Setting his jaw, he hefted a chunk of bar shot and bounced it in his hand several times. "Maria, lass, why don't you return to the cabin and go to sleep?" he advised, and although his voice was deceptively pleasant, there was a warning look in his eye. "Perhaps you'll feel better when you wake up."

Rolling up his shirtsleeves, he knelt down at a bucket of seawater, plunged his arms elbow-deep into it, and proceeded to scrub the grime from his face. Maria bit her lip. How could she be so irritated with him and yet admire him for the handsome man that he was? And as he stood up, vigorously rubbing his face with what looked to be a piece of sailcloth, she was unaware that the anger in her eyes had been replaced by a look that could only be described as wanting . . . like that of a child when a piece of candy is placed just out of reach, or a kitten eyeing a bowl of cream. Unconsciously, her gaze fastened upon the pleasant, oddly exciting sight of water streaming in rivulets down his arms and darkening the bunched fabric at his elbows, water trickling down the planes of his handsome face and losing itself in the soft hair of his beard, water racing between the hollows of his powerful chest muscles. One fat, glistening drop clung to a brush stroke of the black hair there, finally losing its tenuous hold and racing down his taut, flat belly and into the line of tapering dark hair that picked up where the droplet left off and now led her eyes down an enticing path to where it disappeared, almost unfairly, she thought, beneath the waistband of his breeches.

Sam wiped his brow with his kerchief and raising his head, caught her staring at him. He grinned slyly. "Keep looking at me like that, princess, and I'll personally escort you back to the cabin myself. And if that should happen, don't think that you'll be back on deck before nightfall." Instantly, Maria's face flamed anew, for she had no trouble understanding his meaning—and from the laughter of some of the men, neither did they. Humiliated and embarrassed, she tore her gaze from the handsome picture he made against the blue, blue backdrop of ocean and instead directed it toward the safety of the distant horizon.

Maria was uncomfortably aware that the crew had gathered around like spectators at a cockfight, whispering, laughing, elbowing each other, but she didn't see the coins being passed. Sam, however, was keenly aware of his men's actions. Typical tars who'd bet on anything, be it the roll of the dice or the outcome of a lovers' confrontation. Well, let them bet; the outcome of *this* match would not be a public one.

Selecting another cannonball, he hefted it in his hand and tossed it to his master gunner. "Here, Phil. Let the lad have another try or two at the cannon." Johnnie's face brightened like sunshine after a shower. "And make sure you leave it swabbed, loaded, and ready to fire when you're through. I don't want to be caught unprepared should Mr. Tozier sight a sail on the horizon." Leaving them, he went to where Maria stood with feet splayed and hands glued to the rail for balance. She went rigid as he took her arm and, jerking her free, led her out of earshot of Stripes. The decks were wet with spume and he had no wish to see her slip and fall just because of her damned, foolish pride. He had no wish to dive overboard to rescue her, either. He dragged her to the starboard rail, where, being the weather side, there was less spray to dampen her already sorry-looking skirts. The fact that the gown was still hanging loose at the nape did nothing to ease his irritation. Not only did it reveal a tempting display of creamy skin, it was an all too painful reminder of how badly he'd treated her.

He released her arm and leaned against a cannon, arms crossed at his chest and legs braced against the roll of the ship. "Now that we have some privacy, my dear, suppose you tell me just what the devil has gotten under your skin this morning."

"You," she snapped, flinging her braid over her shoulder. "You brought me aboard this ship against my will, plied me full of wine, and now you've made me look like a shameless hussy in front of all those men!"

"Well, you deserved it."

"But that's nothing! You want to know what's really bothering me?"

"What, pray tell?"

"The fact that you're teaching a ten-year-old how to fire a cannon!"

"Oh, does that offend you? Why, I'm dreadfully sorry. Would ye rather I instruct him in the use of a flintlock? How about a cutlass?"

"Oh why do you mock me so?" She spun away, making a helpless gesture of frustration. "You used to be so nice, but now you're insufferable!"

Sam crossed his arms, still glistening with water and treating her to an enticing display of bronzy skin and well-defined muscle. "Allow me to clarify something, my dear. First of all, if you're determined to treat me with the kind of disrespect you showed me a moment ago in front of my crew, then I can assure you that I shall reciprocate." He smiled, but it only emphasized, rather than masked, the hardness of his words. "I know of captains who would lash their men for less. And to be quite honest with you, your attacks on my chosen profession are beginning to wear on me. Keep it up, and I swear I'll lock you in that cabin 'til this whole business is over and done with. I told you last night I have a mission to accomplish, and like it or not, a pirate I am and a pirate I will remain until my men are out of that gaol and free once more!''

"And you are swinging right along with them!"

"Don't preach to me, Maria." Rubbing his chin, he gazed up at the fluttering pennant, then regarded her with black eyes that smacked of mockery. "Besides, what does the Good Book tell us? Something about . . . unchastity?"

Twin spots of color flamed in her cheeks. "How dare you accuse me of *unchastity* when 'twas you who raped me in the first place, you who promised to wed me and are now putting it off in favor of other things—riches, piracy, and rescuing a pack of wolves the world would be better off without!"

"Rape?" he said softly. "Do my ears fail me?" He arched one brow in that infuriating way of his and gave her a heated stare that set her heart to racing. "I hardly think that what transpired between us two nights past was 'rape.' Indeed—and please correct me if my memory serves me wrong—'twas *you*, my dear, who initiated it, not me."

Maria's mouth dropped open in indignation, but before she could respond a sudden gust of wind heeled the ship so far over that she found herself looking across a scant twenty feet of deck, a pitifully insignificant railing, and down into black, foam-flecked water rushing past the gunwales. A scream of pure terror rose in her throat, and then there was only the iron grip of Sam's hand as he nonchalantly reached out to steady her.

"Don't worry, princess," he said with an amused smile and infuriating calmness. His thumb slid over her wrist. "You'll get your sea legs soon enough."

"For your information, I do *not* intend to be on this vessel long enough to get sea legs, sea sickness, or sea anything else!" She wrenched her arm free as the ship righted itself, and gripped the rail so hard that her knuckles went white. And as she whirled to flee, his casual words stopped her.

"You know, Maria, should the ship heel over again—and it very well may—there's a good chance you'll lose your footing and slip overboard. I don't know if you can swim or not, but I can assure you that most of these tars cannot, and I, for one, have no desire to take another icy plunge in the North Atlantic so soon after my last one. Think upon it, my dear, before you so rashly go stomping off and away from me.''

She turned on him, her eyes flashing. ''If that is the only way off this ship and away from you, then I shall gladly take it!''

''Oh, come now. Surely you don't find my company all that bad.'' His lazy smile made her long to call him every foul name she'd ever heard, and those she'd recently learned. He reached up to graze her cheek with his knuckles, eliciting a murderous glare from her that could've soured milk. ''Besides,'' he continued in a thoughtful, infuriating way that would've put her instantly on guard had the cunning light that sprang to his eyes not done so already, 'I'll wager you're not mad at me at all. There's not much for a young lady to do on a pirate ship, is there? Nay, you're probably just bored, quite understandable, I would imagine, after running your little medical practice and providing Eastham with enough blankets to keep an elephant warm.''

''I am not *bored,*'' she ground out.

''And I must see to it that you do not become so,'' he declared, that spreading grin making her wonder what dark scheme he was up to now. Warning bells went off in her head. ''Oh, don't despair, my dear. 'Tis perfectly natural, boredom is. In fact, all tars suffer from it occasionally. Some of us relieve it by firing off a gun or two just to hear the noise, some by throwing dice, some drown it beneath a bit of grog. But we all work for the good of the company—after all, gun practice is always beneficial, dicing reminds us of the value of riches, and rum, of course, is an excellent way to gain the courage needed for battle. I cannot, however, see you doing any of these things. Therefore—''

''I have absolutely no intention of drinking, dicing, nor going near your precious cannon! And how many times must I tell you, *I am not bored!*''

''But you're still doing nothing for the good of the company,'' he explained nonchalantly, fully aware that he was fueling her wrath. But oh, how striking she was in such a fury, eyes flashing with spirit and spunk! 'Twas all he could do not to sweep her up into his arms and carry her below right now. Instead, he merely smiled and said, "You must make yourself useful, my dear, if you want to earn your keep aboard this ship."

Her eyes narrowed. "I do not intend to do *anything* to earn my keep aboard this ship, for I intend to be off of it the first chance I get!"

He acted like she hadn't spoken, though the fire that shot from her eyes could've burned him. "I want you to consider a suggestion made by one of my men and endorsed by all of them. 'Tis the small matter of ship's surgeon. Men do get sick and injured, you know. Stripes—damn his gossipy soul, but it *was* a beastly good idea—thought ye'd be the perfect candidate. I gave my consent, and the company, of course, agreed."

"I don't care what the damned company thinks! They're all going to Hell anyway, so why—"

"Uh, uh, uh, watch that language, princess. . . ."

"Damn you for an insufferable beast!" she cried, stamping her foot, stressing the "damn," and wishing she knew a hundred worse things to fling at him. "Don't think for one minute that I'd even *consider* playing doctor to a bunch of ill-mannered ruffians!"

"Oh? And were the people of Eastham any more deserving of your compassion, your evil but effective poultices, your foul-smelling concoctions of clamshells and bear's grease? They, who drove you out of town with rocks and stones and . . . everything else they did to you?"

It was an unfair way to attack. She turned away, teeth clenched, tears springing to her eyes. "I *knew* you would use what happened back at Eastham against me, and you'll do so whenever you want to hurt me, won't you?"

Instantly, his voice softened and his hands came up to brace her shoulders. He forced her to face him. "Maria, I never wished to cause you pain."

She refused to look at him, instead glaring up at the great boom of the mainsail above their heads. "Oh, but you have, and it seems there's no end to it. And here you are, taking pleasure in taunting me, knowing fully well that I'd never lift a finger to help this 'company' out, yet ordering me to do so anyway, just to pit me against my own beliefs. Why are you trying so hard to make me as lawless and unholy as you are? Why do you keep trying to change me?''

"My dear, I am not trying to change you, merely trying to get you to stop being so damned blind to everything but your own selfrighteousness. Besides, it's really the other way around. I love you perfectly well the way you are—'tis you who keeps trying to change me into what you want *me* to be. Someone respectable, someone you can take home to your aunt, someone who thinks and sees and breathes the same way you do.''

"Love? If you loved me, then you *would* change for me."

"And if you loved me, you'd stop asking me to."

"I don't love you. Not anymore."

"Ah, princess, your words belie the truth that is in your eyes, that ruddies your cheeks, that makes you stand here and fight me tooth and claw. Don't deny it. Ye love me, just as I do you. How easily you forget that when it is convenient to do so."

"I loved Sam Bellamy, not Black Sam, pirate captain, outlaw, and devil incarnate."

He tilted his head and regarded her thoughtfully. "Would you feel any different about me if I was still the man who sailed into Eastham so long ago? Would you love me any more if I was a fisherman, a merchant, a member of the clergy?"

"Yes. And if you were any of those I wouldn't be standing here arguing with you."

" 'Twould seem that arguing and love go hand in hand."

"Oh, what do you know about love?" With a helpless gesture, Maria turned to stare out over the sparkling sea. "The only thing you love is this ship, piracy, yourself. I'm just a convenience, nothing more. An amusement!"

"What do I know about love . . ." he echoed softly, bracing his forearms atop the rail and letting his hands hang limply as he gazed down at the frothy seas below. "Oh, I know a lot about it, Maria. I know that love means accepting a person for what he is, as I've accepted you. Do ye think that because I'm a pirate I don't love you? Christ, I lost the *Whydah*, my fortune, and nearly my life over you. Would I have done so for a mere 'amusement'? Even now, it's taking every bit of self-control I have to keep from sweeping you up, carrying you to my cabin, and having my way with you right now. Don't tell me I don't love you.''

"You're describing lust, *Captain,* not love. Another sin, I believe.''

He shoved away from the rail and threw up his hands in frustration. "To hell with sin! 'Tis not lust and ye damn well know it! What the hell does it take to make ye believe me? Do I have to lose *this* ship too? Do I have to stand on the highest yardarm and shout it out for the company to hear? My love for you transcends lust, Maria!'' And as if to prove it, he yanked her up against him, holding her struggling form against the solid wall of his chest while his mouth slammed down upon hers, forcing her backwards until she was bent over his arm and her head began to spin.

To no avail, she shoved at his still-damp chest with her palms. He was robbing her of her breath, her will, her very soul. She would not respond to his kiss, she *wouldn't!* No matter that her knees were growing weak, her head spinning, her heart thrumming like the lines and rigging so far above her head! She tried to escape that hard mouth, afraid that he'd see her weakening, but his hand caught in her hair and drew her head back, his tongue plunging into the softness of her mouth, scalding it with its heat and sending all sorts of heady sensations shooting through her body. Her struggles grew weak, and it was only when she began to return his kiss that he finally drew away.

Her eyes flew open. And there, a blatant reminder of how its owner had obtained it, was the Spanish coin, still hanging from his neck and now dangling against her knuckles.

It was the final, mocking insult. Maria's hand came up and her palm connected solidly with the side of his bearded cheek.

The blow stung her hand more than it did him, but the desire and love that had momentarily softened his features fled like the sun before storm clouds. His dark eyes narrowed dangerously.

"So, my dear, is that how ye return the affections of one who loves you? Perhaps it's time you and I had a little chat about showing the captain the respect he deserves.'' Maria winced as he grabbed her arm, his fingers biting into her flesh and dragging her forward until his eyes were just inches from her own. And then he flung her away, as though the sight of her sickened him. "Get back to the cabin, Maria. And if you're not there when I come down, I promise you're going to see a side of me you never knew existed!"

And with that, he stormed away without a backward glance, rapier slapping his hip, shoulders stiff with fury, features set in stone. Maria waited just long enough for him to descend the companionway before gathering her skirts and turning from the rail. Oh, she'd be there in his cabin waiting for him, all right! But it would be the *last* time, for she vowed to be off this ship and out of the jaws of the wolf before the sun set on another day.

Chapter 19

Love is a torment of the mind,
A tempest everlasting.

DANIEL

Leaving the ship was, of course, nothing more than wishful thinking on Maria's part. That very afternoon, the pirates held a drunken celebration to christen it, and Sam came down to the cabin to personally drag her back up on deck to participate in the ceremonies. Suggestions for a proper name were being flung from stem to stern like a volley of grapeshot, and as she emerged on deck, blinking in the sun and growing angrier by the minute, they all converged on her, demanding to know what *her* thoughts were on the matter. Nat Paige had shoved a bottle of Smuttynose's fine Madeira into her reluctant hand, and still smarting from Sam's chastisement, she'd taken the bottle, stood at the bow, and proclaimed that she couldn't put a name to such wickedness, that the sloop was nothing more than a training—and proving—ground for nefarious deeds that were too evil for this earth to suffer. This had been a mistake, of course, for Maria, who'd had no desire to partake in such a ridiculous ceremony in the first place, had unwittingly provided the most popular contribution yet. "Aye, *Nefarious!*" someone had shouted, and then, pushing his way through a deafening chorus of ayes and yeahs, Nat Paige had seized her wrist, brought her arm back, and forced her to toss the bottle. And while Sam had stood nearby, caught up in helpless laughter, the bottle had shattered upon the beakhead and the wine had run like blood before waves had come up to wash it away.

They reached Monhegan the following afternoon. At first glance it looked like a giant whale sunning itself on the horizon's bed, but as they drew closer, Maria put aside her bitterness to marvel at its stark, breathtaking beauty. Surf thundered and smashed at mighty walls of granite rising straight out of the ocean, spray glistened like diamonds on steep, austere rock faces as it trickled back into the sea. High above the cliff's cap of evergreens that were straighter, taller, and far more stately than Eastham's little scrub pines could ever hope to be, a bald eagle made a lazy circle, drifting in currents of warm air before finally floating out of sight behind the lofty spire of a spruce.

Monhegan. It was wild, it was desolate, and without Cape Cod's familiar sandy beaches, it was unlike anything Maria had ever seen.

It was also, as Sam had feared, deserted.

With sails loosely furled and the sea rolling beneath her keel, *Nefarious* had stood patiently at anchor while her captain and a few men took the launch and went ashore. By early evening they'd returned with several large logs, of all things, and the news that the snow, *Anne,* had indeed arrived at Monhegan to wait for its piratical consorts; but after relieving the locals of several vessels and causing so much trouble that the island's few occupants and those of the mainland port, Pemaquid, were too afraid to even venture out to fish, its troublesome crew had transferred to one of the prizes, left *Anne* behind, and finally stood off to sea, where they hadn't been seen or heard from since.

But one look at Sam's grim features told Maria all she needed to know as she stood at the forecastle rail and watched the launch nose its way back through the swells. Maybe he'd give up his reckless plan after all.

But her hopes were groundless. Sam was shouting orders before his bare feet even hit the deck, before the crew could cleat the still-dripping boat up to its davits. "Up anchor! All hands prepare to make sail! Jibs first, 'til we're clear of the island, then fores'l and tops'l. Put her on a broad reach, Mr. Flanagan, due north, if you please!"

Bare feet hammering across the deck. The squeal of winches, the excited cries of men racing each other aloft. The kelp-draped anchor cable went taut and trudged wearily out of the sea, a triad of canvas rose on *Nefarious*'s nose and climbed skyward, and then the deck tilted sharply as she heeled with a dancer's grace to leeward and leaped ahead like a racehorse.

Ignoring Sam, who stood with bare feet planted solidly on deck, hands clasped behind his back in the typical seaman's stance, and dark head tilted back to watch his adept topmen, Maria wandered the deck until she found Stripes. He was sprawled nearby with his back against the bulwark, a tankard in his loosely curled fingers and his hat pulled low over his eyes. To all appearances he was napping, but Maria knew him well enough by now to know that he was not, and her amusement at the lengths to which he'd go to catch a particularly juicy piece of information somewhat eased her anger with Sam. With a wry grin, she lurched awkwardly across the deck toward him, her balance still precarious, but improving by the day. "I know you're not sleeping," she said, gently poking him with her foot. "We both know you'd miss too much if you were."

He was enough of an actor to fake a yawn as he looked up, squinting and shading eyes that looked anything but sleepy with a nut-brown hand. "Why, there ain't nothin' t' miss, Maria."

"Oh?" she asked, one delicately arched brow standing higher than its twin. "You seem to have placed yourself conveniently close to where I was standing. Surely, close enough to hear what might've transpired between your captain and me."

He looked guiltier than a hound caught stealing the supper from his master's table. "Yer a sharp one, Maria," he said, and if she'd been angry with him—which she wasn't—his dancing brown eyes and mischievous grin would've quickly allayed it.

"Perhaps. But since you've said nothing more about my being a 'witch,' I can overlook your . . . curiosity."

"I'm real sorry fer tellin' the lads 'bout that," he explained. "But it was fer yer own good. If I 'adn't, they wouldn't 'ave let ye stay. A woman on board is bad luck, ye know. But they be rightly respectful of a witch."

"Is that so?" Maria crouched down so that he wouldn't have to stare up into the sunlight to see her. "Well then, if that was your intent, to make them fear or respect me, you have my gratitude. But if you did it just to call attention to yourself, then you have my sympathy, because some day your loose tongue will get you into more trouble than it will be able to get you out of. And fortunately for you"—she matched his grin with one of her own—"I've forgiven you for telling everyone I'm a 'witch.' Otherwise I might've turned you into a barnacle, where you could stick to the ship's hull and eavesdrop to your heart's content!"

He laughed then, appreciating her humor. Devil's blood, what was wrong with the cap'n? Goin' around cursing the day he met the sweet lass, rantin' and ravin' about that lovable mutt o' hers; didn't he know what a prize she was? Why, Maria was worth more than all the gold on the *Whydah*. He'd have to have a talk with Black Sam about treatin' her better.

"Well, if yer gonna turn me into anythin', don't make it a barnacle. Won't do me much good if I 'ear things but can't tell nobody!" He pulled himself upright, cast a quick, wary glance about to ensure that Black Sam wasn't within hearing distance, and lowred his voice to a conspiring whisper. "Cap'n's in a foul mood today, ain't 'e? Somethin' goin' on b'tween you two that ain't all sugar an' spice?"

"I'd say there's been much more spice of late than sugar," Maria said, sighing and not caring that he was pumping her for information. At least he was someone to talk to. "And maybe it *is* all my fault, but I just can't condone this life he's chosen, can't stand the thought of him attacking innocent people and robbing them of the things they worked so hard for. It just isn't right! And do you know what's even worse? Sooner or later the authorities will catch him, and . . . and . . ." She wrung her hands, unable to voice the thoughts that awful vision evoked. "Oh, Stripes—I don't want to see him die!"

" 'Ere, now," he said, reaching up to pat her hand. He caught the glimmer of tears in her eyes as she stared at a tern that suddenly made a knifing plunge into the sea off the larboard bow, then rose, wings spraying water droplets, with a glistening fish clamped securely in its orange beak. " 'Ave some faith in Black Sam! Nothin's gonna happen to 'im! Do ye think 'e got as far as 'e did by bein' careless? Nay, the cap'n's a crafty one, a rogue among rogues. An' this little sloop 'ere, why, she's as fast as the wind. There ain't nobody can catch 'er when she spreads 'er wings an' flies."

Maria thought of the king's ships she'd often seen from the Great Beach, ruthless, mighty men-of-war that showed no mercy toward their prey. "Even a swift sparrow can be brought down by a hawk."

"Aye, but the sparrow can 'ide in places where the hawk can't go."

"And then the fox will get him!"

Stripes merely laughed, but his confidence in his captain's piratical abilities did nothing to relieve her fears. "I think ye worry too much, Maria. Ain't healthy, ye know. Here." He held out the bottle of rum. "Maybe a swallow or two'll cool ye down a bit."

She shrank back. "Thank you, but I've learned that tipple only worsens problems that are bad enough to begin with. I don't want to taste another drop of it as long as I live."

He grinned. "Well, we can't have ye mopin' around like the world's gonna end. Which reminds me, the cap'n had somethin' 'e wanted me t' ask ye."

"His Majesty's wish is my every command," she said acidly.

" 'E wants t' know if ye'd like t' go ashore when we put in t'night. Said 'e thought ye'd like t' git some weeds." Stripes peered curiously at her. "Does that mean ye'll be the ship's doctor after all?"

Her good mood instantly evaporated. "It most certainly does not! I am a prisoner aboard this ship, not a participant!"

"Well, it ain't nothin' t' be gittin' all huffed up about. Cap'n's just tryin' t' be nice."

"Nice? He's doing his best to mock me, infuriate me, and

make me participate in something he knows I'm dead-set against! Piracy!" Sunlight flashed against metal as Johnnie passed with Gunner bounding at his side. "The day I lift a finger to further his wicked deeds is the day—"

She froze, jaw hanging slack as she realized just what that metallic flash had been. Stripes saw the look on her face, and instantly raised a hand. "Now don't ye be blamin' the cap'n fer that," he said. "Young Johnnie went an' begged Gillespie t' pierce 'is ear fer 'im 'cause 'e wanted it t' be jus' like Black Sam's, an' let me tell ye, the cap'n went int' one of 'is tempers when 'e found out! Said the lad weren't old enough t' be wearin' gold in 'is ear, an' that if we ever did get caught, they'd hang 'im sure as they'd string up the rest of us!"

"Is that so? Well, regardless of whether or not Sam condoned the earring, if it wasn't for him Johnnie wouldn't be wearing it, nor serving upon a pirate vessel! And furthermore, 'tis beyond me why he's upset about a mere piece of jewelry yet doesn't think a thing about teaching that same child how to fire a cannon!"

"Oh, well ye have t' understand," Stripes informed her, vaulting atop a weathered barrel and swinging his tar-blackened feet back and forth. "The cap'n jus' wanted t' let the boy 'ave some fun, that's all. Black Sam's got a heart o' gold, try as 'e might t' hide it. Ain't nothin' wrong with what 'e did, no more than a mama lettin' 'er little girl play at servin' tea to 'er friends. Makes the boy feel grown-up an' important-like." His eyes were serious for once. "Besides, if we was ever t' go into battle the cap'n wouldn't let him near the guns. I'd bet me last cob on that. Oh! Speakin' o' guns, what d'ye think o' the cap'n's latest scheme? Pretty clever, ain't 'e?"

"Scheme? *What* scheme?" Maria asked warily.

"Oh, ye mean 'e didn't tell ye 'bout the quakers?"

"What, may I ask"—she gave him a level look—"is a *quaker?*"

Stripes pointed to the heap of logs that lay amidships. "See that timber over there? Those're guns."

"Guns, huh? You and your captain have both drowned in your tipple if you can't make a distinction between a piece of firewood and a cannon."

"But those who see the logs from the decks of another ship will not make that distinction," came a deep, clipped voice from behind her.

Whirling, Maria met Sam's amused gaze. "And just how long have *you* been listening?" she snapped. "You're as bad as Stripes! And if you honestly expect me to believe you're going to pass off a bunch of logs as guns—"

"Told ye he was pretty clever, didn't I?" Stripes commented.

"Clever? A person would have to be blind as well as stupid to make the mistake of believing such a ruse!"

"Ah, but 'twill be an easy mistake to make, princess. Those logs yonder will look very *much* like cannon after we've put the adze to them, blackened them with tar, and run them out of the new gun ports. From a distance, they shall look quite intimidating. And intimidation, my dear"—again, that infuriating, lazy smile—"is the name of the game."

"You already *have* enough guns!" she spat, thinking that even one cannon, when used for such wicked purposes, was too many.

"Enough?" The creases cornering Sam's eyes deepened and his teeth flashed against the swarthiness of his skin, his beard, his hair. "Pirates never have enough guns, do they, Stripes?" She stiffened as he wrapped his arm around her waist. "If our decks are bristling with cannon, our bulwarks teeming with men, don't you think a prize will be more likely to strike her colors without resistance at such a show of force? Of course it will," he said, answering his question when she would not. "But if the pirate ship appears to be an equal, if not lesser, match, the prize might be inclined to fight. And while I am no coward, neither am I a fool. Fighting may bring death and destruction to his decks, but it will also bring them to mine, and I have every intention of keeping my men— *and* my woman—all in one piece."

"I am *not* your woman," she bit out, trying to escape, but the forearm he'd clamped beneath her ribs prevented it. Her irritation with him—and herself, for the feel of that arm just beneath her breasts was doing strange things to her pulse— increased. "You put an end to that when you took this ship. And your arrogance amazes me. Do you actually think that by playing the bully no one'll stand up to you?"

"Precisely." He released her, leaned back against the bulwark, and studied the waves that danced and frolicked around them for as far as the eye could see. "Right now we have a most pitiful armament, certainly not formidable enough to strike fear into anyone. But, I intend to change all that. You see, I don't like resistance." He turned to her. "Not from *any* prize."

Maria gave him a sidelong glance. "Perhaps some *prizes* are better left to sail their own courses."

"Ah, but then the best ones would get away. And we can't have that, now, can we?" He came forward, curved his arm behind her back, and drew her away from Stripes, whose eyes had gone brighter than Sirius on a winter's night.

"Didn't I make it clear that I'd prefer you to keep your hands to yourself?" She tore herself from his grip.

"You made it perfectly clear, my dear." Leaning close, his eyes mere inches from hers, he hefted her thick braid, deliberately letting his knuckles brush against her nape, her shoulders, her back, until she shivered uncontrollably. " 'Tis just that I'm choosing to ignore your wishes."

"As you've done from the start!"

"Aye, and 'twas a good thing, too. One of us has to take the initiative."

He was now at work at the end of her braid, deftly loosening it until the ends hung in S-shaped fringes. His hands were gentle, but she knew he wasn't about to release her. Not wanting to have her hair pulled out, Maria stood and suffered his touch. And the worst part of it was, she wasn't suffering; the gentle tug of her hair against her scalp was pleasant, the feel of his fingers loosening the plait, sensual. . . .

Nay! She would not let him defuse her anger, nor coax her forgiveness for his actions! "I told you to get your hands off"—she reached up and tore what was left of the braid from his fingers—"my hair!"

"But I like your hair," he said smoothly, "especially when it's free of that damnable braid and hanging loose and full down your back. Why don't you wear it like that more often, princess? Just for me?"

"Because I don't *want* to! Why don't you get rid of that hideous beard? 'Just for me?' "

"Does it really bother you so?" he asked, grinning.

"Everything about you bothers me. I wish I'd never met you!"

"A feeling that others will soon be echoing, I should think."

She twisted around to face him. "And what sort of schemes are you cooking up now?"

He regarded her with the mischievous innocence of a child, one brow raised, his smile deceivingly guileless. "Schemes, princess? My, my, for one who makes it plain she'd rather be anywhere but here you're terribly interested in my plans, aren't you?"

"As I am to be an unwilling part of them, I have a right to know what my fate is to be!"

"Your fate?" He stood back to admire her hair, now whipping in the wind and framing the exquisite loveliness of her face. "Why, didn't I make myself clear, princess? You're going to be my wife. I thought we settled that."

"*You* settled that, not *we*. I've never had anything to say about it. And what kind of marriage would it be, anyhow? Surely, not one based on trust. Already you keep secrets from me!"

"What secrets, lass?" The deck rolled steeply atop a large comber, and Sam reached out to steady her, his touch searing her skin even through the soft cotton of her sleeve. "My plans are no secret. First, we'll find a deserted cove and turn this pretty little bird into a warhawk. We'll chop away her deckhouses, her railing, cut more gun ports and mount the quakers." His eyes grew thoughtful, and she could see the visions in his mind's eye as if they were her own. "And then we'll go hunting. The seas are rich with prizes, Maria. Hate me for it if you will, but I intend to take those prizes, recruit new men, and build up a fleet so damned powerful 'twill make the one I lost at Eastham seem like a covey of pleasure yachts. Only this time, my flagship won't be a big square rigger, but a nimble, swift little sloop." Leaning both elbows on the rail, he presented his profile to her as he stared out over the sea, dreams in his eye, a wistful, determined smile curving his lips. "Inevitably, we'll meet up with Paul Williams, and maybe even Louis Lebous, one of my old consorts. Hell, with any luck we'll even find Ned Teach. I hear he has his own ship now. With such worthies at my side nothing can stop me. And when I have such a formidable squadron, what do you think I'll do, Maria?''

She looked down at her hands. ''Attack Boston, and free your men from the gaol,'' she said bleakly.

''Aye. And when I've accomplished that, *then* what do you think I shall do?''

''Hang,'' she said, even more bleakly.

But at that he simply laughed, for hanging was definitely not part of his plans. ''Nay, lass. After my men are free to sail the seas again, I'll turn over command of *Nefarious* to my quartermaster. No more pirating, I promise. Just this one mission, this one vow I've made to myself, and then it'll be over. By the gods, lass, I swear it on my mother's grave—''

''Sam, spare me.''

''Honestly, Maria, I'll give it up, I promise. I *will* be the kind of husband you've always wanted. We can be happy together.'' He took her face between his roughened palms, smoothed the hair back from her cheeks, and searched the depths of her eyes. ''Can't we?''

She looked up at him, his hair free of its queue now and falling in thick, handsome waves to his shoulders, his eyes like velvet and full of undeniable love. His hands burned against her chin, her cheeks, but in a single movement she reached up and flung them away. ''Yes, Sam,'' she said hollowly. ''We can. But only if you give up piracy. It's just that somehow, I don't think you ever will.''

His sharp words halted her as she turned to leave. ''What d' ye mean? Didn't I just finish telling you that I would? For God's sake, lass, don't my words mean anything to you?''

''They mean everything, Sam. And I believe you fully intend to give it up.'' Her chin came up, and his image blurred behind a sheen of tears. ''It's just that I don't think you'll live long enough to keep that promise.''

With that she turned, swallowed the dry lump in her burning throat, and left him standing in confusion by the rail.

Chapter 20

The sweets of love are mixed with tears.

HERRICK

"That one mission" was one that Sam drove himself toward with relentless obsession. The false cannon weren't the only measures he took to turn *Nefarious* into the pirate ship he wanted her to be: he taught the crew how to make stinkpots—nauseating bombs of saltpeter, limestone, rotten fish, and resin packed into empty wine bottles that, when set afire and hurled onto an enemy's deck, would quell even the most stubborn resistance; he had them making shot—grape, chain, and bar—until even young Johnnie grew weary of hauling it below. He held eagerly awaited contests between the gun crews to sharpen their speed and accuracy, promised Moses' law to anyone who didn't keep his cannon loaded and ready to fire at all times, and conducted unannounced, random inspections of those sturdy black monsters while the sweat ran from every man's pores, for no one wanted to be the one to displease him. But in general he was happy with their performance, and if he drove them a little bit too hard, it was only because such skills might someday save their lives.

As pirates, they were their own little world, with every man equal to his peers. As pirates, they were their own masters, free to do as they wished and no longer having to bow to the whims of those who happened, by birth, wealth, or circumstance, to be on a higher rung of society's ladder. As pirates, they enjoyed the self-respect and dignity that had been denied them in the "civilized" but unfair world of class and order. Personal freedom was what it all boiled down to, Sam told them. And as the days passed, Maria began to understand why his men called him "the free prince of the seas."

Sometimes, his views almost made sense to her.

Almost . . . but not quite.

And it was the *almost* that frightened her.

On a quiet night while the sun was setting and the crew was at supper topside, Maria stood in Sam's cabin. He had yet to spend a night in it, for they'd been avoiding each other like the plague. Beyond the cannon mounted at the stern windows, the dying sun stained the sea, threw checkers of red light across the floor planking, and shone upon the brass dividers on Sam's desk. And as it sank into the scarlet ocean, a last searching ray crept higher and higher until it finally found and bloodied the cutlass that hung on the wall. The sight of it tugged at Maria's heart and she looked away, growing more melancholy by the minute.

An agent of death, that cutlass. Just like the cannon, sleeping quietly in its carriage and leashed to the bulkhead like a fearsome beast, but all too eager to bite if provoked. And there, a flintlock lying on the desk, a length of silk wound around its grip, the grotesque face on its buttcap laughing at her, mocking her. All of them, thirsty for blood. Innocent blood.

Gunner joined her at the stern windows, nuzzling her hand and licking her fingers until she absently reached down to rub his head. She thought of what she'd overhead this afternoon as she'd passed beneath a deck grating where Stripes, just above, had been sitting in idle conversation with Nat Paige.

"Did ye hear the latest?"

She'd paused, listening.

"What latest?" Nat had asked, echoing her thoughts.

"Why, Black Sam's thinkin' o' startin' a pirate kingdom up in the Maine wilderness. Kinda like our own New Providence."

"A pirate kingdom?"

"Aye!" And then, "I'm tellin' ye, if ye think the lass is riled now, wait 'til she hears o' this."

Riled? Downright *furious* was more like it.

Perhaps this final indignation was what had finally pushed her over the edge, strengthening her resolve to leave him. But it wasn't just her anger or her helplessness against Sam's wicked intentions that made Maria long to escape him; it was her attraction to him. The hours spent topside, trying to avoid the sight of his handsome figure strolling the quarterdeck, were sheer torture. And if the days were bad the nights were even worse, for they were spent tossing and turning in the bunk while her flesh ached for the feel of his strong arms and craved the memory of his hard male body. He was the Forbidden Fruit. No, he was the Serpent—deadly, sinister, irresistible—and torn between yielding to him and clinging to her own deep-rooted values, Maria felt as though she was being torn in two; head versus heart, body versus soul. And the worst part of it was, there could never be a winner.

The sun was gone now, leaving the cabin a colorless tone of gray. Soon it would be dark and she'd have to light a lantern. Already, the lights of a coastal settlement winked on the horizon. Stripes had casually mentioned that some of the more restless men were planning to take the boat after the watch ended and go see what trouble they could stir up there. In proper disguise, she could sneak off with them. No one would recognize her—and no one would notice that one less crew member would be returning to *Nefarious*'s wicked decks come morning.

Leave him . . . tonight, while you have the chance. . . .

She listened to the water gurgling around the rudder, the wash of the sea as it pressed against the hull not several feet from where she sat. The ship was settling down for the night, and with it came raucous laughter from above, the sound of breaking glass as some tar tossed his wine bottle against a gun. Curses that no longer made her face burn, a random pistol shot, more laughter. They were familiar sounds now, and Maria accepted them as being as much a part of the ship as the sails, the rigging, the deck planking beneath her feet.

What she hadn't been able to accept had been the ragged cheers, the huzzahs, and the thunderous salute of *Nefarious*'s guns that had accompanied the first hoisting of the Jolly Roger.

Leave him. . . .

She crossed the room to Sam's cluttered desk, where the only neatness to be found was in his bold handwriting, sprawled across the vellum of the open log. A quill pen and inkwell sat nearby, and several pieces of bar shot at its corners prevented an open chart from curling back into a scroll shape. She frowned. Couldn't he find something better to use as a paperweight than *bar shot?* But as she looked down at the chart, her anger flared to life once again, bolstering her courage to initiate her escape attempt. Her braid fell down to brush the yellowed paper, and impatiently she flung it back over her shoulder. Maine. A pirate kingdom, huh? With her to be enthroned as its queen? Not if she could help it. She traced the ragged New England coastline with her fingertip. Pemaquid. Portsmouth. Newbury. Boston. Plymouth . . . Cape Cod.

Cape Cod. The salt spray rose would be blooming there now and perfuming the moors with heady fragrance, the bearberry softening the severe face of the dunes with tiny flowers. Aunt Helen would be on her hands and knees in the vegetable garden, and beyond her weathered house, beyond the green lawn where that same robin was probably tugging at one last worm before retiring for the night, and beneath the apple tree at the edge of the pastures, there would be a tiny headstone marking a little grave. . . .

A single, stinging tear trickled from Maria's eye, followed the gentle curve of her cheek, and dropped silently upon her breast. Childhood memories, Aunt Helen, little Charles—they were all there in Eastham, but she could never go back, nor would she, without Sam. Those cliffs she used to walk in the hopes of sighting his returning ship? Never again. The days she used to count until he returned for her? Never again.

She knelt down, bending her head and using Gunner's soft ears to blot her tears. She'd miss her dog, but at least he'd be loved and well cared for under Johnnie's watchful eye. But Sam? Could she leave *him?* Would the resulting loneliness be any worse than the bitter ache that filled her heart now, the utter sense of loss over what her handsome sea captain had become, the empty bed she faced every night while he slept topside with his crew?

Someone had hung a lantern at the stern, and now its reflection, broken by waves and the swirling wake, reached across the dark ocean before melting into the night. Maria stared for a long time at that reflection. Like the path of her life, God only knew where it led.

Finally, she raised her chin. Resolve. Sam had taught her about that, and taught her well. She would leave tonight, while she had the opportunity, and the absence of a moon would work in her favor. Blinking back the tears, she turned and walked quietly across the cabin, pulled out a chair, and reached for the pen and ink at his desk.

The lights on *Nefarious* shone brightly—one at her nose, the other at her stern—their golden glow casting eerie shadows over her decks and making the bewhiskered faces of the men sitting around the mast look like those of a legion of unkempt, grinning demons.

Their captain had pushed them especially hard today, ordering the decks painted red to mask the blood of possible battles, moving cannon into his cabin to serve as stern chasers, and chopping down the deckhouses to lessen the chance of flying splinters in battle. That wood had been donated to the galley fire, where the cook had managed to turn out a fish chowder that was actually edible; now, the crew sat slurping it noisily and enjoying their nightly ritual—story-telling.

Each wild tale was more exaggerated, more fantastic, than the one preceding it. But out of respect for Maria, who seemed awfully quiet tonight as she sat stroking Gunner's velvety ears, the men did their best to water down the natural harshness of their language. Perhaps she was ashamed of the shirt and breeches she'd finally had to beg from Johnnie not an hour past, clothes that she'd accepted with a brave little smile and her chin held high. But that gown of hers, ragged and unsuited for the decks of a pirate ship, had certainly seen better days. . . .

Maria laughed at their tales, but it was a hollow sound to her own ears and she was thankful for the darkness that cloaked the misery that must've been written all over her face. Her hand moved rhythmically over Gunner's sleek neck, his soft ears, but there was no comfort to be found even there. She looked up, and her pain only intensified as her gaze fell upon the shadowed features of the man leaning against a cannon some distance away.

Sam.

The night breeze tousled his hair and rippled his sleeves. A bottle dangled from his fingers, and tongues of lantern light flickered against the Spanish coin nestled within the shadows of his chest. And while he chuckled at the wild stories, a person would have to be blind—or as drunk as his crew—to think that his mind was here among his raucous, pipe-smoking group of young rowdies. Was he thinking of the two ships he'd hoped to find at Monhegan? Maria wondered. Was he planning a way to recruit enough pirates to rescue his men from the Boston gaol? Or was he reliving the tragedy of the *Whydah* all over again?

Don't think about him.

Her hand tightened on Gunner's collar.

Don't think about him! Don't even look at him! She shut her eyes and trembled. *Don't, don't, DON'T. You're leaving him . . . tonight.*

She tried to immerse herself in the story-telling. Stripes had the stand now, describing the mermaid he'd once seen off the coast of Saba for what must be the twentieth time this week. Ludicrous to begin with, the tale got better with each telling. Except now, the mermaid seemed to have changed a bit; she no longer had hair as black as jet, but long, golden tresses, and eyes mirroring the Caribbean that had been her playground.

From the shadows, she heard Sam swear beneath his breath.

Her courage for the upcoming escape attempt flagged. Trying to bolster it, to fool herself, at least, Maria laughed openly at Stripes's tale when she should've been blushing, and even accepted a mug of wine from Nat Paige with shaky hands.

"Aw, Stripes, *really*," little Johnnie was protesting, with a glance at his captain for approval, "you don't really expect me to *believe* that story, do you?"

"What d' ye mean? She really *did* 'ave golden hair and a necklace o' seaweed, ivory skin an' breasts as bare as a newborn's bottom—"

At the rail, Sam straightened up.

"Cap'n, where ye goin'? I was just gittin' t' the part when I was gonna dive off the railin' t' go after 'er!"

Several men guffawed, and Sam added a few chuckles of his own to mask his heavy heart. He raised his bottle, emptied it, and tossed it over the rail. "Sorry, lad, but I've some notes to make in the log. Do carry on with your tale." And as Stripes stared at him in surprise, he added dryly, "Just be sure ye tell them how she left you there to drown and we had to toss a grapple over the side to fish you out."

A burst of laughter followed this remark as he turned his back on his raucous crew. As he disappeared aft and was swallowed up by the shadows, he didn't know that a pair of haunted turquoise eyes followed him.

Maria stared at the darkness where he'd disappeared, suddenly feeling uncertain and apprehensive and overcome by a terrible feeling of deceit. She stroked Gunner one last time and stood up. Now that his captain had retired for the night, Johnnie was making short work of his rum, gulping it down as fast as he could fill his mug from the nearby hogshead. Maria frowned, caught his eye, and took a meaningful sip of her own watered-down wine. Looking chastised, Johnnie set down his cup and got up to escort her below.

Stripes was disappointed at losing the most precious member of his audience. "Where ye goin', Maria? Didn't ye like my mermaid story?"

"Liked it, yes. Believed it? . . . No." Maria smiled, a soft, haunted smile that brought several sighs and groans from those sitting close enough to see it. "But I suppose we all must believe in . . . fairy tales. Good night, everyone."

Their voices rose in drunken chorus.

"G'night, Maria!"

"See ye in the mornin'!"

"Take care, Johnnie, that she doesn't slip and fall on those decks! The captain'll have yer hide!"

"Damn the captain, *I'll* have his hide!"

She would miss them, this rough-talking, hard-drinking band of sea tars. And Sam? Oh God, she couldn't think about him until it was all over, for to do so now would rob her of the courage she'd fought so hard to maintain. With a heavy heart, Maria took Johnnie's hand and allowed him to lead her aft.

He left her at the door to the cabin, and without knocking, Maria quietly pushed it open.

She'd thought to find Sam at work, but in the faint starlight she saw that the leather-bound log book was closed, the inkwell tightly capped, the chair pushed up flush to the desk. It was obvious that he'd never had any intention of making notations, nor studying charts. In fact, it seemed as though he'd had no intention of doing work of any kind, for the cabin was dark and shadowed. Her gaze wandered the gloom and there, a tall silhouette standing by the open stern windows, she saw him.

He was still and unmoving, his hands clasped behind his back, his gaze far out over the darkened sea. No spirit animated his tall form, and the dejection and sadness emanating from him was so strong it was palpable. Maria swallowed the lump that rose in her throat, for it was hard enough to contemplate leaving him when he was being a brute; it was far harder when he was so plainly miserable.

She took a deep breath, steeling herself for what she was about to do. "Sam?"

He started, turned, saw her as nothing more than a shadow in the doorway. "Maria, lass. Forgive me, I didn't hear you come in."

There was no anger, no bitterness, no mockery in his voice. Nothing but emptiness, and that lack of emotion pulled at Maria's heart.

She closed the door quietly behind her, and when he still didn't move from the window, took a hesitant step forward. *Don't do it,* her mind screamed, *not like this.* But she forced that little voice back. She *had* to do it like this, had to leave him with the truth—that she loved him. And while it might tear him apart when morning came and he awoke to find her gone, some day the pain would fade and he'd realize it had been her final act of love.

Her conscience, though, thought otherwise. *Deceitful hussy,* it accused, and faltering, Maria almost turned around to leave him to his musings. But from somewhere deep inside she found the strength to continue. She stepped forward, her hand closing around a full bottle of Smuttynose's Madeira. "I'm sorry about your men," she said, when he remained staring out over the sea. "You must feel badly that they weren't at Monhegan."

"I didn't really expect them to be." She saw the shrug of his powerful shoulders in the darkness, but even the gloom couldn't mask their uncharacteristic slump and the weariness

that made it seem as though he carried the weight of the
world's problems upon them. "After all, the *Whydah* went
down weeks ago. No pirate in his right mind would remain
in one place for long. 'Twas just a faint hope, I guess."

Maria leaned against the back of the door, biting her lip.
If only he was angry with her, as he'd been earlier. If only
he'd vent his temper, make an unkind remark, anything. But
no, he was just standing there, looking almost . . . *vulnerable*. It was making things all the more difficult for her.

"Why did you follow me down here, Maria?" he asked wearily. "I should think you've had enough of me for one day."

She couldn't tell him that she'd come to say good-bye. She
couldn't tell him that this was the last time they'd be together.
But she couldn't lie to him either, so she told him a half-truth.

"I came to apologize."

"Apologize? For what?"

"For all the mean things I've said to you lately. For treating you so disrespectfully in front of your crew. For making
a nuisance of myself, and acting like the witch I was once
accused of being. You're right, of course. I've been . . . such
a shrew. You can blame the fact that we've not . . . lain
together since boarding this ship on me. 'Tis all my fault,
and I know it." Slowly, she crossed the room, her soft footsteps coaxing faint creaks from the deck planking.

"Don't apologize. After all, you have every right to hate
me. If you weren't angry, I'd have cause to doubt your integ-
rity."

"But I'm no longer angry, Sam." She swallowed tightly,
hating herself for what she was about to do. "And I . . . I
even have something to prove it." Finding his hand in the
darkness, she pressed the bottle of wine into his palm and
curled his fingers around it. "I thought we might have a glass
or two together, just you and me."

His voice was stern. "Maria, just because I gave you wine
once does not mean you have to indulge in it all the time."

"Come now, Sam. I'm a grown woman, not a child. Besides, I'm offering it as . . . a truce. And after we drink it"—
she sidled up to him suggestively—"I'll prove to you that I'm
really *not* angry anymore."

Darkness hid the puzzlement in his eyes, the confusion that
drew his brows together. Why had she suddenly forgiven him

after vowing that she'd never accept him for what he was—a pirate? And now she was not only welcoming him into her bed but inviting him into it—and this after she'd made it painfully clear she'd wanted no part of him? It didn't make a damned bit of sense. But at the moment, Sam had no wish to question her, he just wanted to take the truce she was offering and let it go at that.

"Well then, let me light a lantern," he said, somewhat more cheerfully as he searched in the darkness for a flint. Presently the scent of burning tallow mingled with that of salt air, and a dull glow illuminated the cabin and threw long, eerie shadows across the bulkhead. He settled her into a chair, eased himself into another, and poured the wine into two pewter mugs. With a faint grin, he pushed one of them across the table to her.

"I'm sorry, too." He touched his mug to hers before wearily lifting it to his lips and downing it in several practiced gulps. "I've been a real bastard lately. I had no right to treat you like that."

"But as you said of me, you had your reasons." She reached across the table and laid her hand over his. "Let's just forget it, Sam, and think instead of tonight."

The lantern light picked out the handsome planes of his face, threw the curve of his cheekbones into shadow, and emphasized the strength of his jaw, his chin, the stout line of his shoulders. Maria saw hope in his eyes, and something very like relief. He met her gaze and smiled. Warmth flooded her heart and suddenly it was easy to forget that he was a notorious pirate captain who was supposedly dead. In fact, at the moment he looked very much like the eager young adventurer she'd fallen in love with so long ago.

She put her glass down and reached up to touch his cheek. His bearded jaw was wiry but soft, and she stroked it with the pads of her fingers, wanting to sear the feel of him in her memory where she could always take it out and treasure it. His eyes closed, and she saw his chest rise in a deep sigh. He caught her hand, brought her fingers to his mouth, and pressed them lovingly to his lips. Their softness, coupled with the tickle of his mustache and beard against her knuckles, sent ripples of sensation washing through her. Again, she almost abandoned her decision to leave him. "Ah, Maria, my sweet princess," he whispered hoarsely. Dark eyes opened and bared a troubled soul. "I don't think I could've stood too many days like these past ones."

His breath was a warm flutter against her fingers. The resonance of his voice turned her bones to custard. "Nor I," she said, "but please, Sam, let's just put it behind us. I don't want to think about it anymore." She pulled her hand away from his lips and picked up the bottle. "Here, have some more wine."

The amount she poured into his mug was generous, but he drank it down quickly. And then he took her hand once more, rubbing her soft palm against his bristly cheek and gripping her fingers as though he'd never let her go.

"You don't know how much this means to me, lass."

Suddenly, Maria realized that for the first time, Sam was baring his heart to her. He was allowing her to see the unguarded love in his eyes, and it suddenly struck her like a clout across the chest that that same love might prove to be his undoing.

Good Lord . . . why hadn't she realized it before? *Her very presence* aboard *Nefarious* was a danger to him, for he would need all of his wits about him to survive, to keep the ship beyond the reach of the men-of-war that prowled the coast. What he *didn't* need was her around to worry about. . . .

It was a wonderful excuse to ease her feelings of guilt and deceit. Maybe, just maybe, her decision to leave him might end up saving his life some day.

"We'll have to do something about getting you some proper clothes," he was saying, studying her in that thoughtful way and rubbing his chin between thumb and forefinger. "Those breeches aren't fit for a lady. They're indecent."

"Oh?" She threw him a sly look. "Since when have you cared a whit about decency?"

"Since I've seen you take up bad language, drinking, and dicing all in the space of a week." He smiled. "I can't allow you to become totally corrupted."

She got up and came around the table to sit intimately on his lap. His thighs were stout and hard beneath her, his body wonderfully strong. It was sheer bliss to lay her cheek against the solid wall of his chest, heaven to nuzzle the fine, silky hairs there with her lips. He tasted of salt spray, wind, and the freedom of the open sea. "Why Sam, I do believe that *you* were the one to corrupt me in the first place." Her hand came up, fingers gently tracing the firm outline of his sensual lips, the shape of his jaw beneath the thick, neatly cropped hairs of his beard; they whispered over the curve of his shoulder, across the taut bands of his upper arm, around his elbow, and finally to his strong, warm hand, which she grasped and tucked beneath the closure of that same shirt he found so indecent. Kittenlike, she rubbed her cheek against his chest as his fingers began caressing her breast.

"Maria?"

"Oh Sam, I've missed you so. . . ."

"Christ, lass. I've missed you too, but—" He caught his breath as her feathery touch travelled back up his arm and began to trace lazy circles through the wedge of dark hair on his chest. "God's blood, what the devil's gotten into ye?"

"Nothing that hasn't been there for over a year," she purred. "Here, Captain, have some more wine." She looked up at him with feline eyes, her palm hot against his belly, his ribs, teasing the waistband of his breeches. " 'Twill heighten the pleasure, don't you think?"

"Maria, I'm exhausted. Any more tipple will only put me to sleep."

That was precisely her intent, but discerning as he was, Sam didn't guess that it was all part of an escape plan he would never have thought her devious enough to create nor courageous enough to carry out. And even if he had known, the way her hand was now fumbling with the buttons of his breeches would've chased such nonsensical notions from his head. Her lips were achingly sweet against his chest, her voice soft and husky with invitation. "Put you to sleep, Sam? Do you find me that . . . boring?"

"Jesus," he muttered, then gasped as her hand found his already throbbing manhood. His head fell back against the top rung of the chair, and he squeezed his eyes shut in blissful agony. He was hard and rigid in her gentle grasp, and still holding him, teasing him with her soft fingers, she slid her other hand beneath his neck, pulled his head up, and cradling his weight within the curve of her arm, fastened her lips to his.

If he was tired, there was no trace of it as he returned the
kiss with fierce hunger, taking her lips like a drowning man
and skillfully managing to unbutton her shirt at the same
time. He slid the soft linen over her creamy shoulders to
better access her breasts, his callused hands sending exquisite
sensations of pleasure tingling through her skin, simmering
through her flesh, boiling through her blood. With gentle
fingers, he caressed her aching nipples, rubbing their taut
peaks until they bloomed and budded beneath his touch. Liquid heat pulsed through her veins, filling her senses with him
and nothing but him, pushing her reasons for doing this into
a far, forgotten corner of her mind.

She drew back only long enough to loosen her gleaming
braid. Mesmerized, he watched as she ran her fingers through
the thick silken tresses until her glorious mane tumbled in a
riot of curls down her back.

"Oh, God, princess," he moaned, and then his strong
arms were beneath the backs of her knees and under her
shoulders. Effortlessly, he swept her up and carried her to
the bunk. She lay back against his arm, feeling weightless
and giddy, her eyes clouded with passion, her slightly parted
lips open in invitation. He set her down as gently as if she
were made of glass, one rock-hard arm supporting her back,
and she felt the bed dip as he joined her there, bracing a hand
on each side of her shoulders and bending his head to kiss
her once more.

A witch, they'd called her, and he was as helplessly caught
in her spell as a fly in a spider's web. Clothes were shed, lips
grazed bare flesh. Passions heightened, damp skin already
glowing with gentle tones of lantern light. Sam trembled, and
Maria felt his heartbeat quicken beneath the pads of her fingertips. She closed her eyes lest he see the truth in them and
turned her face into the silken spread of her hair that fanned
the pillow. This would be the last time she'd ever clasp him
to her, taste his fervent kisses, take him within herself. She
buried her lips against his forearm, kissing him, moving her
lips against the soft hairs there, the taste of him mingling
with the saltiness of her tears.

She opened her eyes, saw the top of his dark head through
a blurry sheen as his lips grazed her neck, her shoulders, the
pulse that beat frantically in the hollow of her throat. He

caught a mass of her golden curls in one hand, crushing them, dragging kisses across the base of her neck, her collarbone, the rise of her shoulders. She shivered uncontrollably, her breathing ragged and sharp.

Maria . . . Oh, Maria . . . His thoughts tumbled over each other. She was the sweetest flower, the softest silk, Stripes's mermaid come to life. Her hands inflamed him, soft and yet bold, innocent yet skillful, and he knew he wouldn't be able to stand this sort of torment for long. Hungrily, he took each swelling breast into his mouth, tracing their nipples with his tongue, sucking on their tender buds until she arched beneath him and begged him to take her.

But first, he claimed her lips once more, driving his tongue deep within the recesses of her mouth until she writhed beneath him in exquisite torment. She was all softness, satiny skin and silken hair, gentle curves and long legs that came up to twine themselves around his back and clasp him to her. He buried his face in her fragrant curls, losing himself in the thick piles of silk; he nuzzled her ear, her bare shoulder, gently traced the fragile curve of her jaw and let his finger drift down the cords of her pale throat. His hand encompassed one aching breast, his callused thumb flicking over the rosy nipple; slowly, his warm palm travelled the valley between the soft globes, swept across the flat expanse of her stomach, and finally lost itself in the silky curls that framed her femininity.

"Ah, Maria. . . . If I were to die tomorrow, I would go to my grave a happy man. God, I love you."

She shuddered and pulled him down upon her, clutching him with a fierce desperateness that he misinterpreted as urgency. But he was in no hurry. He wanted her, craved her. But he wanted to bring her to the loftiest heights, wanted her to realize the full extent of his love for her. He took his time. He left no inch of her unexplored, and his big warm hands were everywhere, relearning the soft curves of her breasts, the gentle ridge of her ribs, the hollows where torso met hips, the slick heat at the junction of her velvety thighs. His mouth was hot upon hers, needful, wanting, demanding every response she could give—and give it she did, for she wanted this night to remain forever in her memory, as well as his.

Her fingers caught in the damp hair at his nape, pressing

against his skull as if seeking to hold him forever against her lips. She felt the thick muscles at the back of his neck, the fine, downy hairs that grew there, the silken spill of his dark locks falling over her hand, her knuckles. He was the free prince of the sea, born of the ocean. The taste of it dewed his skin . . . its pull was echoed in his hands, his lips, the sheer power of his body as he drew her like a riptide into deep water, swirling currents, fathomless depths . . . and then she was drowning, his movements as he entered her timeless, rhythmic, as surging and beautiful as the sea itself.

"Sam . . . oh, Sam, forgive me," she sobbed, but only she knew what she was asking his forgiveness for. Their hot breaths mingled, became one. Storm tides crashed over her senses. Her fingers slid down the back of his damp neck, dug against his straining, powerful shoulders where muscle moved like knotted cording beneath the skin.

Faster and faster he took her until she cried out with the lurching spasms of fulfillment that swept through her in agonizing, merciless sweetness. He made a last, driving plunge into her and went rigid, her name tumbling from his lips into the damp curls that lay on the pillow beside her ear.

For a long time they simply held each other, forgetting everything in the world but themselves. He eased himself down atop her, his forearms supporting his weight while he nestled his head within the curve of her creamy shoulder, his fingers absently toying with a curl that gleamed like gold against the pillow. He didn't see the tears that dampened her cheeks, didn't see the agony in her eyes as he gently kissed her ear and told her over and over again how much he loved her.

He was lean and warm and strong, his weight comforting and secure. Maria held him close, clasping him to her, her slender arms locked around his back even as he grew drowsy and more and more time elapsed between each gentle kiss, each softly spoken word. Slowly he relaxed, his weight growing heavy atop her, his limbs twitching once or twice; yet still she held him, her lips pressed against his shoulder, her hands stroking his hair, unwilling to let him go and dreading the moment when the forecastle bell tolled out the end of the watch and she would have to. And when at last he was nothing but dead weight upon her, his heart thumping steadily against her own, his deep, steady breathing stirring the air at her ear, she carefully wriggled out from beneath him.

There were tears in her eyes as she dragged on her shirt and breeches and stared down at him, forever imprinting his handsome face and powerful body in her memory; the hair, so black against the pillow, the lips, parted and sensual, the lines of exhaustion and weariness—and maybe sorrow, too—that slumber was already smoothing away. She reached up to wipe a tear away with her knuckle, then drew the coverlet up over his scarred back, his brawny shoulders, and the big, seaman's arms she loved so well.

Exhaustion, fine spirits, love, and forgiveness. She'd been right. It hadn't taken much. One of her tears fell upon his dark cheek, trickled into the glossy, stiff hairs of his beard. She didn't wipe it away. Instead, she bent down, pressed her lips to his brow, and turned away.

"I love you, Sam. No matter what, I'll always love you."

She put out the lantern. She pulled out her letter, its ink stained with her tears, and placed it on his desk beneath the bar shot. And then, with a heavy, aching heart, she quietly left the cabin.

Chapter 21

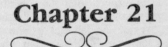

The rocks do not so cruelly
Repulse the waves continually,
As she my suit and affection.

WYATT

In the forecastle, the bell was tolling as Maria, huddled in a frayed greatcoat that was several sizes too large for her, came up on the shadowy moonless deck.

She paused, gazing up into the heavens as though seeking divine reassurance for what she had done, what she was about to do. The Milky Way was a band of white fog stretching across the zenith. Vega twinkled and sparkled like a diamond on black velvet. A thousand billion stars sprinkled their reflections upon the vast surface of the ocean, but no divine voice came from their infinite depths to guide and reassure her.

Her nervous gaze swept the darkened decks. She'd gotten here just in time. By the glow of a lantern, several men were already hoisting the boat from its cradle abaft the mast. They were talking, laughing, sharing a joke or two. Maria hesitated before approaching them. What if they recognized her? But no. They were too busy, and much too drunk, to pay any attention to one more seaman.

And in her coarse cotton breeches and oversized greatcoat of well-worn black frieze, her long hair stuffed up beneath a wide-brimmed felt hat, she *was* just one more seaman; more slight of form, more delicate of face, but that was all.

Nervously, Maria glanced aft, expecting, and—*yes, admit it,* she thought—hoping to see Sam come charging up on deck to stop her. But the shadows from whence she'd come were painfully dark and empty. She thought of him as she'd left him, deeply asleep, dead to the world and ignorant of her plans. Did he know about the shore party? Probably. Sam was keenly aware of everything that went on aboard his sloop.

Everything, that is, except what she was about to do.

Fidgeting, Maria plucked at the salt-encrusted nap of the old coat's sleeve. Again, she felt sick as she thought of how she was betraying Sam's love, his trust. It would be the first good night's sleep he'd gotten in weeks, yet how would he feel when he woke up in the morning and found her gone? Her treachery burned like acid in her throat, and she choked it down, trying not to cry as she stared across the water to where the lights of the settlement winked like fireflies in the darkness.

But no. She mustn't think about it. She *had* to leave. It was for the best. Best for her, best for Sam. And now, she could deliberate on it no longer; already, the men were lining up to go down the ladder, passing a bottle of Madeira around, making ribald jokes and laughing as they went over the side like monkeys.

Taking a deep, steadying breath, Maria crept out of the

shadows and as unobtrusively as possible slunk to the rail. The boat bobbed in the gentle swells far below, thumping against *Nefarious*'s sleek sides. The last tar's head disappeared over the gunwale, and with a sinking feeling, she realized that she was the only one left. They were all waiting for her.

But at the top of the gunwale, she froze. Below her, far, far below her, Silas West held up the lantern, a tiny spot of light in a vast sea of darkness. Its feeble glow shone upon the upturned faces of the men and reflected upon the waves— waves that would swallow her up without mercy if she lost her footing and fell.

"C'mon, ye bloke!" someone yelled. "What's takin' ye so damned long, anyway?"

"The lad's afeard, that's what! Whaddye expect? Looks barely old enough to be outta his swaddlin' clothes, I tell ye!"

"Well, if he ain't old enough, he ain't got no business goin' ashore. This is man's work!" "C'mon, laddie. We ain't got all night!"

Swallowing, Maria took a shaky breath and closed her eyes. She clutched the top of the damp gunwale for dear life, then gingerly put one leg over the side, trembling as her groping foot met empty space and, finally, the first rung of the swaying rope ladder. Stiff with fear, she began to inch down it.

"Sakes alive, matey, what's taking ye so damned long?"

She bit her lip to keep from screaming at them to leave her alone and let her go at her own pace. One step, two. The top of the gunwale was at eye level now, and terrified of relinquishing that last hold on the ship, she clung to it with hands that were white in the darkness. *What on earth was she doing?* Fear paralyzed her. Cold sweat slicked her palms. She felt sick, dizzy, faint. *Oh God,* she thought, *please, help me,* and took another uncertain step downwards.

And then a hand closed over her wrist.

"Going somewhere, princess?"

Her head jerked up, her breath caught in her throat, and the blood drained from her face. "Sam!"

Silhouetted against the serenity of the night sky, he looked like some angry, avenging god. A sword belt girded his lean waist; the scabbard hung at his hip. He was clad in nothing but canvas breeches, and these, he must've hastily pulled on upon finding her gone. Although his voice was deceptively mild, his face was thunderous, his grip on the fragile bones of her wrist almost cruel. Maria panicked, grew faint, and would've fallen into the black waves so far below if it wasn't for that viselike grip. "Have you forgotten what a light sleeper I am, Maria? Obviously. Otherwise you might've taken more drastic measures to make sure I *stayed* asleep!"

"Sam, I—"

"Belay it, princess. You'll have all night to explain." He looked past her and down into the boat, where the men stared up at them in curiosity. "Carry on, lads," he called with a casual wave of his free hand, dispelling any doubts she might've had that he was unaware of their little excursion. "Just be back by first light or we leave without you."

"Are ye keeping the laddie with you then, sir?"

"Laddie?" Sam laughed then, a cold, chilling sound that was completely without humor. "Aye, I'm keeping the *lad* with me. And you can thank your bloody stars that I caught him before he quit this ship, for so help me God, every damned one of ye'd be paying the price in Hell if I hadn't!"

It was not an idle threat and Maria knew it. *Oh, God*, she thought, biting down on her trembling lip and trying not to cry. The pounding of her heart deafened her. Cold sweat broke from every pore. The rope ladder was scratchy and damp against her cheek and inches from her nose, the glistening black wall of the sloop's hull filled her vision. And though she dared not look down, she could hear the boat crew's hushed whispers.

"What's he so mad about?"

"Mad? Hell, man, what's he *talkin'* about?"

"The lass."

"What lass?"

" 'T'ain't no lad he's got there, ye numbskull, 'tis the wench!"

"The wench?"

Hushed, shocked silence, then laughter, yelling, and much back-slapping. Maria looked down. Far below, Phil Steward raised his mug to her, and she heard the splash of oars, fading as the boat moved away from the sloop.

But looking down had been a terrible mistake, for now there was nothing beneath her moccasins but empty space, darkness, and the black, black sea.

She panicked. Fear clawed at her heart, moisture trickled between her shoulderblades and down the curve of her spine—and then her neck snapped back as Sam, cursing all the while, yanked her up and off the rope rung, held her suspended in space, and heaved the ladder to the deck. He lowered her, the rigid muscles of his arm standing out, and with feet dangling, kicking, against the sloop's wet hull, Maria screamed in sheer terror. Her hat fell off and tumbled over and over again before losing itself in the darkness.

"Sam, please!" Desperately, she clawed for something to hold on to. But he only lowered her farther until his arm was fully extended and she could feel the cold moisture that slicked the hull seeping through her clothing and dampening her chest, her stomach, the front of her legs.

" 'Sam, please' what?" he asked harshly. " 'Sam, please let me go so that I can swim to shore'? 'Sam, please forgive me for deceiving you'? Or, is it 'Sam, please, take me back to the cabin and do with me what you will'?" Never had she seen his eyes so terribly black, so cold—like the deep waters of a lake beneath a foot of winter's ice—and she began to cry piteously, terror robbing her of any dignity she might've sought to maintain. "Oh, don't worry, Maria, I plan to take ye back to that cabin, God help me!"

"Sam, no! Please, let me explain—"

He ignored her sobs. "I trusted you," he ground out. "Trusted you, believed you, thought our differences were all straightened out. But now it seems they're just beginning." Eyes glittering with fury, he glared at her down the length of his arm. "Or shall I say that *your* difficulties are just beginning, Maria?"

"Sam, please, don't let go. Oh God, please Sam, *please*, don't let go!"

"And why the hell not, princess? 'Twould seem that you were most eager to leave me a moment ago. Changed your mind already? Fickle, fickle woman!"

"Sam, *pleeeeeeeeease!*"

His grip on her wrist slipped the barest fraction of an inch. Screaming loudly enough to wake the dead, Maria clawed desperately with her free hand, mindlessly trying to clutch his arm but leaving long, bloody rake marks from her nails instead. Darkness speckled her vision, her head began to spin, and through the deafening roar that started up in her ears, she heard his voice.

"Don't 'Sam please' me," he was snarling. "You deserve no quarter! You're more cold-blooded than the worst of this lot. Even the pirates ye so despise are more loyal than you are! Aye, I think I'll let ye go, right here and now, and have done with ye! Let ye swim back to Eastham!"

At that moment the sloop rolled gracefully atop an errant swell, the mast traced a dizzy circle against the stars—and Maria's world went black.

Sam felt her go limp. Frowning, he looked down in momentary surprise at the fingers that, a second ago, had been curled into claws. But his bewilderment turned quickly to anger, at her and with himself. Cursing, he hauled her up and over the side in a single fluid movement. Her head fell back, sending the long fall of her hair tumbling down to brush his bare toes. Effortlessly, he scooped her into his arms and stared down into her beautiful, innocent features, agonizing over how such deceit could lie beneath the face of an angel.

He'd had absolutely no intention of dropping her, of course. He'd just wanted to frighten her, teach her a lesson she wouldn't forget. He didn't think she'd actually *faint!* Now he really felt like a wretch. But what about what she had been about to do to him?

Tenderly, he cleared a finely spun strand of gold from her pale cheek. The silken curl was damp with tears, her skin moist against his fingertip. "Why, princess?" he asked in a strangled, tortured whisper. He cradled her against his bare chest, his heart breaking as he buried his face within the fragrant silk of her hair. "Why this way? Do ye hate me so much you'll risk your very life to escape me?"

He didn't know the answer. But he soon would, he vowed, his wrath springing to life once more. Cursing, he swung around and collided with a pack of bodies thicker than soldiers on a battlefield. Stripes, curious, concerned, and craning his neck to peer at Maria's still visage. Nat Paige, his features taut with worry. Even little Johnnie, now hiding behind Billy Flanagan, and Jake Gillespie, whose hand was wrapped securely around the collar of a growling Gunner.

"What the bloody hell are you all gawking at?" Sam snarled, protectively cradling Maria against his chest to shield her from their eyes. "Go back to sleep, damn the lot of ye!"

"But Cap'n, we was just worried 'bout the lass," Stripes offered, somewhat meekly. "She was screamin' fit t' wake the dead. . . ."

"The only dead to be woken will be you, unless ye get the hell out of the way and let me pass!" Angry and embarrassed that they'd seen his display of tenderness and heard his anguished words, he stormed past them, his stride long and purposeful, his scabbard slapping his thigh. Behind him they exchanged nervous glances, then meekly followed him to the cabin.

"Captain, I think—"

With a vicious kick, he slammed the door in their startled faces and stormed straight to the bunk, where he tossed Maria atop the blue-and-white coverlet without a backward glance. Damned, meddling busybodies! Troublesome, treacherous female! God's bloody *teeth!* He went straight for a bottle of wine and severed its neck with a single, practiced swipe of his cutlass. And it was to this sight, of Sam with tankard in hand, stiff-backed and glowering as he stared out the stern windows, that Maria awakened.

He hadn't let go of her, after all. She was alive.

Slowly, the fog drifted from her head and she watched in silence as he brought the tankard to his lips again and again with the kind of mechanical precision his men exhibited when they loaded their guns. The glow of the lantern picked out the familiar crisscross of scars that a long-ago lash had etched into his back, emphasized the taut bands of muscle working beneath them. He turned then and saw that she was awake, his black eyes finding and holding hers.

He slammed the tankard down with a bang. "Consider yourself fortunate, princess, that I chose to spare your treacherous hide." His voice was flat, cold, and devoid of all emotion. " 'Tis not my style to go easy on those who betray me."

From outside came voices, Gunner's angry barking, and then a wary knock upon the heavy, solid door that became an incessant pounding when Sam ignored it. "Captain? Is she all right?"

"Answer them," he commanded, his black gaze boring into hers. "They think I've murdered you, as well I might if I don't get some goddamned answers!"

Maria glanced from Sam to the door, then back again. "I'm fine," she managed. "Just a bit shaken. Please, don't worry about me."

"Are ye sure, Miz Hallett?"

"Yes. I'm . . . quite sure."

Sam stalked over from the windows and sat at the foot of the bunk. His dark eyes were upon her, angry, hurt, confused, and if she wasn't so afraid of him at the moment, she would've succumbed to the urge to comfort him, to reach up and touch the thick black hair that swept from his wide brow and temples and curled upon his shoulders. But nothing about him invited closeness; she might as well try to comfort an injured wolf. "Satisfied, lads?" he drawled, his back to the door. "God's blood, I'd think if ye were as worried about your own hides as you are about hers, ye'd find something better to do than hover at that door like a pack of sharks dangling after fish bait!"

"Aye, Cap'n. We be leavin' now. Jus' wanted t' be sure the lady came t' no harm."

More growls, and the sound of Gunner's claws digging into the deck as they forcibly hauled him away. Muffled conversation. The heavy tread of retreating footsteps.

And then she was alone to face the devil's wrath.

He stared down at her, waiting. His jaw was set, his mustache fairly bristling with fury; but in his eyes, Maria saw the pain of betrayal, and something that was not unlike the look of a lost, abandoned child. She started to speak, not knowing what to say, how to explain her actions. Oh, why had she chosen to escape him in the manner she had? Open defiance of him would've been better—what she'd done was terrible. Even a pirate deserved more.

Wearily, he rose, as though he could no longer stand the sight of her. His step was lifeless as he crossed the room and went to his desk, where he stood gripping its edge, his back toward her, his head bowed. He stood that way for a long time. "What the bloody hell am I going to do with you?" he inally asked in a strangely quiet voice. "How long must I beat my head against the wall? I'm the biggest of fools, aren't ? Well, no more. If you want to leave, then fine. But at least lo it safely." He raised his head, eyes staring sightlessly at he bulkhead before him. "Tomorrow, I'll make port at Provincetown and put you off the ship there. You shouldn't have any trouble finding your way home."

Maria swallowed tightly. "But Sam—"

"No 'buts,' Maria. I'm tired of fighting you. I've made my decision, and like it or not, tomorrow we part company." He filled his tankard, downed its contents in one single, quick motion, and began to pace.

"But Sam . . . now I don't want to leave."

"You don't want—" And then, seized by a sudden impulse, he crossed the room and flung the door open.

Stripes fell stumbling into the cabin. "Oh! Cap'n! I was just comin' back t' see if ye needed anythin'!"

"Right." Sam's voice was tight with barely controlled fury. "And I suppose pigs fly, too."

"Honestly! I swear on a stack of Bibles that—"

"Damn your eyes, man!" he exploded, his deep voice shaking the very timbers of the cabin. "You and your bloody eavesdropping! Can't ye put it to better use than spying on my private affairs? Where the hell were ye when she was plotting to escape? Didn't you know the danger she'd be in? And don't just stand there like a gaping fish, answer me, damn you!"

"I—"

Sam slammed his tankard down on the desk. Wine sprayed up like blood, spattering the papers and charts, the navigational instruments, and Maria's letter, unnoticed and unread beneath the bar shot. He whirled on her. "I want some answers, woman, and I want them now. And you can start by telling me where the bloody hell ye got those clothes!"

"I found them."

He stormed across the cabin, ripped the coverlet off her, and hauled her up by her shirt. "Don't lie to me, Maria! You didn't just find them, and ye damn well know it! Don't make me ask you again, or your backside's going to be so damned sore you won't want to cover it with anything, be it breeches or skirts!"

"I told you. I found them!"

"Where . . . the . . . bloody . . . hell—" he yanked her forward until her frightened eyes were inches from his own— *"did you find them?"*

"Uh, Cap'n, I b'lieve I saw 'er askin' young Johnnie t' hunt up somethin' warmer than just that ol' shirt," Stripes offered.

Sam smiled, a cold, chilling grin. He shoved Maria away from him and back to the bunk, where she lay fighting tears. "Why, thank you, Stripes. I'm glad that someone in this room can understand English. Your talents may yet prove themselves of worth. Now, suppose you tell me what else you . . . noticed?"

Stripes, who knew Black Sam well, was not fooled by his captain's suddenly calm tone. Desperately, he wished he was anywhere but here. "Well, I, uh, think she's been askin' Nat Paige just what our fixin's are on that there map ye got spread out on yer desk."

"You *think?*"

"Well, I know, sir."

"Yes, I'm not surprised that you do." Once more he turned to Maria. "Is that so, *princess?* Have you been consulting the sailing master on how to read a chart? And tell me, did you learn anything you'd care to share?"

"Yes! And so what if I did? It's not as if I have a lot of friends aboard this boat that I can talk to!"

"Ship," he corrected her. "And it would seem, dear lady, that you have too many *friends* aboard it!" He raked his hand through the gleaming waves of his hair. "Know something? I *should've* let ye go with those men tonight, just to teach ye a damned good lesson!"

She stared at him in confusion.

"Didn't know, did ye? Why, I'll bet ye thought they're just venturing ashore for some mild entertainment, eh?"

"I—"

"Well, do you?"

"That's what Stripes said!"

"Ah, what did I tell you? Naive, gullible, foolish child! There's a fishing boat lying at anchor close inshore, poorly guarded and ripe for the plucking. Figure it out for yourself, princess, what they intend to do with it!"

As if to confirm his words, the distant report of a pistol cleaved the sudden silence.

"You arrogant bastard, you!"

"Stripes, please go."

"But Cap'n, perhaps—"

"Damn your eyes, man, I said leave us!"

"Aye, Cap'n. Anythin' ye say." Stripes hurried out.

Sam waited just long enough to be sure that he'd really gone before turning on her once again, grabbing her wrists and yanking her up against his chest. His eyes were mere inches from her own. "Now, suppose you tell me just what the hell ye were trying to prove, Maria!"

"I wasn't trying to *prove* anything!" she cried, attempting to jerk free. "I was trying to leave you!"

"To leave me." He thrust her away. "Is that all? Hell, why didn't you just *ask,* then? D'ye think I would've refused?"

"Do I *think?* I'd bet my life on it you would have!"

Whirling, he slammed his fist into a cringing bulkhead. "Damn you, just what kind of monster do you take me for? And just what is it about me that's so repugnant you can't stand my company another night?"

" 'Twasn't your company, Sam!"

"Then what the hell was it?"

"Lots of things!" she cried, bursting into tears. "I was afraid for you! I thought you'd be able to concentrate better without me here! I couldn't stand to be a part of such wickedness! And I don't like feeling so *helpless!*" She swiped at the tears streaming down her cheeks, dug the heels of her hands into her eyes, and hung her head. The thick curtain of her hair muffled her voice. "Do you think I want to sit idly by and watch you hang? Do you think I want to watch you dig your own grave, as well as those of twoscore of innocent others, too? Do you think it makes me happy, knowing this road you've chosen is going to lead to one place, and one place only—the next cell over from your men in the gaol?" She raised her head to beseech him with red-rimmed, streaming eyes. "Oh, Sam. Never think I don't love you! I love you with every fiber of my heart, my soul. But I can't just sit here and watch you die!"

"I can assure you that I am far from dead, Maria!"

"But you will be, if you persist in this!"

"I will persist until my men are safely out of the gaol!"

"And you are hanged in their place!"

Aargh! He slammed his fist against the desk, uttered a string of curses, and once more began to pace. "Just what does it take, woman? Damn it, do ye think me a child who has to be minded? Do ye think I can't take care of myself, my men, my ship? I'm sick and tired of your foolish, womanish worrying over me!"

"I worry about you because I love you! 'Tis you who doesn't understand!"

"If ye loved me as much as you claim to ye'd never have resorted to such—*wiles*—as you did tonight. And if you loved me you wouldn't sit there and lie through your pretty little teeth!"

"But I'm *not* lying!" she pleaded, eyes desperate, candle-light gleaming against her wet cheeks. "You must believe me, Sam, I'm not!" Sobbing, she tossed the coverlet aside, came to her feet, and tried to stop him as he passed.

He flung her hand away in cold rejection, his angry pacing not slowing in the least. "And how am I to know that? Do you expect me to believe you after your little performance tonight? Hah! Once, I thought you a splendid actress, Maria. 'Twould seem I was not so mistaken after all!"

"Damn you, I told you I'm not lying!"

"No matter. I told *you* I don't believe you. Now, if you don't mind, I'd like to go to bed." His eyes glittered, grew cunning, and a slow, devil's smile parted the blackness of his beard. "But before I do, I'd like a very convincing performance of this . . . so-called *love.*"

She stared at him, horrified. Did he think he could command such a thing? He was a flame, burning too hot for her to approach. He was snow, with the coldness of an Eastham winter glinting in his eyes. And he was angry, downright furious.

He was asking the impossible.

"And you can go to Hell, Captain Bellamy."

"A fate long since decided, and not by you. Now, get over here, princess. Need I remind you I'm not a patient man?"

"There are a lot of things you needn't remind me of, and your lack of patience is the least of them!"

"I said, come here."

She remained rooted to the floor, her own eyes growing angry behind the sparkle of tears.

"Now."

She took a deep breath and matched him glare for glare. "I will *not* be commanded to pleasure you like some painted, purchased whore! When we come together, 'tis for love. To do so now would be vile!"

"To do so now would make me very happy, and I can assure you that you will find me even more vile if you do not. Now, get over here before I lose my temper, dammit!"

"Go ahead, then, lose it!" she cried, her gaze locking with his. "Throw things, break things, yell at the top of your lungs for all I care! It's your cabin! If you want to destroy it, then go ahead and do so. I'm not stopping you!"

She stood glaring at him, arms akimbo, hair spilling down her back, color high and eyes flashing sea fire. His gaze roved over her appreciatively, finally settling upon the creamy rise of her breasts and the enticing shadow of the valley between them. His voice lost its harshness and grew husky. Black eyes lifted, pinning her to the bulkhead. "Do I have to come over there and get you, Maria?"

"Why not? You will anyway!"

"Yes . . . I will. How well you know me, princess." He took a step toward her. Another. "Would you like to know me in another way, as well?"

"Damn you!" she cried, springing away from him. But before she could lunge for the door she was jerked backward and yanked up against his hard chest. His laughter tickled the downy hair around her ear, his fingertips blistered the side of her neck. "What must I do to tame such a she-cat?" he murmured. "Take her—"

He was cut off by the impact of her hand, coming up with enough force to rock his head back upon his neck. "She-cat? I thought you liked cats, you arrogant, barbaric—"

His mouth slammed down hard upon hers, forcing her lips apart and driving the breath from her lungs in a frantic moan that did nothing whatsoever to make him stop this ruthless attack upon her heightened senses. His tongue burned against hers, his hand was harsh, then gentle, as his fingers threaded, caught, buried themselves in the soft hair at her temple. Sensation flooded through her, settled between her thighs. And just when she thought she'd swoon for want of air, he drew back, scooped her up in his thewy arms, and carried her, spitting and scratching, across the cabin, where he dumped her unceremoniously upon the bunk. Ignoring her insults, he unbuckled his sword belt, tossed it aside, and was just reaching for the waistband of his breeches when a knock sounded on the door.

"Uh, Cap'n?"

The set of his jaw went from granite to glacier rock. *"What*, Stripes?"

"Uh, young Johnnie's up in the crosstrees. Says there's some lights out t' sta'b'd of us a bit. Thought ye might like t'know about 'em, sir."

"Christ." He braced an arm against the bulwark, leaned his face into the crease of his elbow. "How far to starboard, Stripes?"

" 'Bout half a league, mebbe."

"Fine. Touch off one of the bow chasers to signal the boat to return at once; we may have to make a run for it. The men can go ashore some other night."

"They ain't gonna be too happy, sir."

"I will not be too happy if I'm forced to leave them here, and the company won't be happy if we're nailed by a navy hound or end up forfeiting a fine prize just so a few miserable blokes can practice a bit of piracy on a worthless fishing boat! Signal them, if you please. *Now."*

"Aye, sir."

He turned to Maria. "Get dressed."

"But—"

"I said get dressed. And while you're at it, pack your things. You'll find a ditty bag in my sea chest in which to put them."

"P-pack my things?"

His was the resolute stride of a general going into what he knows to be his last battle. At the door, he turned. "Aye, your things. Remember? Ye wanted to leave. Take a good look around the ship, Maria, for 'twill be your last. We'll make Provincetown by six bells of the morning watch."

"But *Sam!"*

"You heard me." And with that he slammed the door and was gone.

For a long time Maria stared at that door. *Leave?* But . . . but now she didn't *want* to leave. Here was her chance to go and suddenly it was the last thing on earth she wanted to do. She got up, went to the darkened stern windows. She picked up his tankard, wrinkled her nose, put it down again. *Leave?* Oh God, she didn't know *what* she wanted!

She didn't go to the sea chest to find his ditty bag. She didn't shed her boyish clothes for the gown she'd made from material gleaned from a Spanish merchantman captured two days past. Instead, she crossed the room on numb feet, left the cabin, and blindly made her way topside.

Chapter 22

And the lion there lay dying.

TENNYSON

"**D**amned overeager brat," Sam was muttering as he stalked back to his cabin. But no, he liked the boy. Too bad the whole damned crew wasn't so bloody sharp-eyed. Aye, 'twould be another prize, he'd assured them. No, not 'til morning. Why? Because there was something about taking a prize under cover of night that bothered him, that's why. Something sneaky, something ungallant. Aye, he was a pirate, just shut up and leave him alone. The prize would wait 'til morning!

Morning. Dread struck him in the chest like a stallion's kick. Once, in the heat of battle, a ball had snapped a line and the block had nearly taken his head off, but instead, had caught him across the ribs, putting him out of action for the rest of the fight. That's how he felt now—like he'd been kicked in the ribs, had them staved in by forces he couldn't predict, couldn't control. Morning. Several more hours and he'd have to put Maria ashore. *Christ,* he thought. *Why the bloody hell did I say that? I don't want her to go. But she hates me. I have to. I can't hold her here against her will, her principles, her beliefs.*

He was not surprised to find his cabin empty. He thought about searching every inch of the sloop until he found her, but what good would that do? She'd hate him no less. No, better to let her go, give her her freedom. Let her go back to Eastham and be a damned Puritan. Let her marry some farmer, some fisherman. He collapsed into a chair and leaned his brow into his hand. Let her live her life without him.

At least he had his tipple. Nature took its course. He grabbed a bottle and let the wine slide down his throat. Too bad it couldn't drive the pain from his heart, dull the knife edges of his anguish. He lifted the bottle again and again, dragged his log book toward him through the clutter, uncapped his ink, found a pen, and began to write. "Wind east." *Two more hours.* "Seas easy, high clouds to the north." *Two more hours and she'll be gone.* "Prize sighted half-league to windward. Pursuit in morning." *Christ, can I do it? Can I really let her go?*

He never saw the widening bar of light that appeared between door and bulkhead. He never heard the scratching of a paw, the snuffling of a wet nose, and never saw the dog, stalking across the cabin toward him with deadly, menacing intent.

With a savage snarl, Gunner was upon him.

Christ! Seventy pounds of solid, flying muscle caught him in the chest, knocking him out of the chair and slamming him into the bulkhead so hard his jaws smashed together and bloodied his tongue. The bottle flew from his hand, exploding against the wall. He went down hard in a litter of glass and wine, cursing roundly at the feel of hot breath and snapping teeth against his neck, and the loss of a good bottle of wine.

"Damned bloody whelp, so help me God, 'tis the last time ye'll ever back me into a corner again!"

For Sam Bellamy had been born a fighter, had lived a

fighter, and if he was going to succumb to the jaws of this canine shark, then he'd damn well die a fighter, too. Bellowing, he lunged to his feet and threw his full weight at the dog. Gunner's eyes registered astonishment, confusion, and fear in the single moment it took Sam to wrestle him to the floor and lock a brawny arm around his soft, white neck.

"Not so high and mighty now, are ye?" Gunner began to struggle, his dark eyes now ringed in white, telltale circles of proper terror. Sam tightened his grip around the dog's neck, his hand closing around the velvety flews that draped that unfriendly muzzle. "Damned, snivelling whelp. I ought to carve out your liver and feed it to the sharks. I ought to string ye up by the collar and let ye swing from the yardarm. I ought"—he tightened his throat-hold as the dog began to struggle once more, wildly this time, wriggling backwards until the base of his brown-and-white tail edged up against the bulkhead and stopped his retreat—"to hack every one of those teeth from your blasted head and make a goddamned necklace out of them!"

And then Sam felt a tremor, then another, until the whole inside of his inner arm seemed to vibrate with a will of its own. He looked down, and if he hadn't seen it with his own eyes, felt it against his own skin, he'd never have believed it.

By the gods, the beast was trembling.

And as Sam cautiously let his arm fall away, Gunner got up, slunk across the room, and flattened himself against the door.

With a triumphant guffaw, Sam got to his feet, brushing bits of glass from his torn shirt and smearing it with puddles of wine that looked like blood. "Not so damned impudent now, are ye? Damned snivelling coward. Knew all along ye were made of nothing but milk and water."

As though understanding the words, Gunner sank to the floor and looked up at him in proper humiliation.

"Aye, go ahead, grovel. I know your ilk."

Gunner tucked his tail, slowly rolled over, and presented his soft underbelly and wiggling paws in a classic gesture of canine submission. For a moment, Sam could only stare at this creature that had managed to terrify him when the might of the Royal Navy, the wrath of a murderous northeaster, and the crazy cure-alls of a purported witch had not. And with a mixture of bewilderment and amusement he finally turned away, for grovelling, no matter if it came from man or beast, was something he didn't care to see.

He went to his desk and plunked himself down atop its surface, cluttered with navigational instruments, ammunition, scattered papers, and wine bottles in various stages of emptiness. Something pushed against his thigh. Looking down, he saw that it was his pistol. With careless indifference, he shoved it away across the tangle of paperwork, and as he did so he caught sight of an unfamiliar slip of paper, generously covered with the delicate script of a woman's hand. Frowning, he groped blindly behind him for a forgotten bottle of wine, and raising the tipple to his lips, unfolded the parchment and began to read.

He did so once quickly, twice, more thoroughly. He set it down and stared absently out the window, then picked it up and read it a third time just to make sure his eyes hadn't lied to him. What the hell was all this balderdash about his life being in danger if she stayed on the ship? Why on earth did she think he was going to die? And whatever gave her the numbskulled idea that he wasn't at his sharpest if she was aboard? *Christ.* He leaned his brow into his big, callused palm and wearily kneaded his eyes, his temples. The wine bottle hung forgotten from his hand, and it was only when he felt a persistent but gentle nudge against the back of his knuckles that he was shaken from his reverie. He looked down. Gunner was there, nose wet against the inside of his wrist, eyes hopeful if not pleading, white fur and whiskered muzzle soft against his hand.

"What the hell do you want?"

Again, the dog nuzzled him, harder this time.

"Go on, leave me be."

And this time Gunner made a carefully timed flip of his muzzle that jostled Sam's hand hard enough to send a stream of crimson liquid leaping from the bottle. Like blood, it dribbled down the back of his knuckles, darkened his breeches, raced down his bare calves, and dripped to the floor.

"God's teeth, now look what ye've done! Go on, get the hell out of here, ye cursed pack of fish bait. The last thing I need is—"

His mouth sagged open. And as Gunner greedily began

lapping up the ruby puddle of spilt wine, an incredulous grin tugged at Sam's austere features, and in that moment his friendship with his old nemesis was forever sealed.

"Well, I'll be damned. . . ."

Gunner looked up, licking pink-and-white chops. Seized by a sudden impulse, Sam found a pewter plate and unselfishly splashed a generous quantity of the wine into it. With his bare toes he pushed it toward the dog, and what had been merely a wry grin became a guffaw of hearty amusement.

"God's teeth!" he exclaimed, still laughing. "Maybe there's a spit of worth in ye after all, lad!" And not to be outdone by a mere whelp, he downed the rest of the bottle with vehemence.

But the wine, though it mellowed his agony over Maria's rejection, did not deaden it. And for once in his life, he cursed his body for the strong, impenetrable thing that it was, for no matter how much wine he consumed, he could not lose himself in the foggy oblivion the tipple should've brought.

With legs swinging idly, he sat amidst the clutter on his desk, picked up the parchment once more, and finally tossed it aside in despair. "Hell, I can't figure her out. One minute she says she loves me, the next she hates me. She moves out onto a goddamned cliff to watch and wait for me, and now that we're finally together she can't wait to leave me. Women! Why the Christ must they be so damned difficult? By God I'll never understand them!"

Gunner scoured the floor with his tongue, raised his head, and eyed the bottle once more.

"I'm telling ye, the last thing I expected her to do was pull a stunt like that one." He dropped his forehead into his hand once more and stared at his bare, bronzy feet. "I just cringe when I think of her going over the side like that. What if she'd lost her footing? What if she'd swooned *before* I had hold of her? Jesus, what if she *had* managed to make shore?" He groaned, tormented by vivid images of knife-wielding Indians, hungry wolves, and dark forests.

He dumped more wine in his tankard. "Here she is, professing to love me, yet ever since she boarded this ship she's done nothing but demonstrate her hatred." He let the bottle drop from his fingers to thunk upon the floor, uncaring that a stain puddled out over the planking, unseeing, even, for his head had dropped to the heels of his hands and thick waves of sable hair spilled down over his eyes. "What have I *done?* I've treated her all right, haven't I? Granted, my language is a bit rough, but damn, I'm working on it. I even promised to give up piracy! Jesus, lad, what the hell more does she *want?*"

He slid off the desk, staggered, and crumpled to the floor. During his soliloquy, his legs had fallen asleep. But Gunner was too noble—or perhaps too busy with the wine—to acknowledge Sam's humiliation as he hauled himself up by the edge of the desk and waited for the pins and needles to fade from his calves. He looked down, grimacing. With his shirt in ribbons and wine darkening what was left of it, let alone the better part of one side of his breeches, he looked as if he'd just come through a war. And of course, it was at precisely that moment that the door crashed open and an astonished Stripes stood regarding him in openmouthed horror.

"Mother o' God, Cap'n! What *happened* t' ye?"

Sam's gaze went from the dog, now crawling atop the bunk as though he owned it, to the broken wine bottles on the floor, and finally, back to his lieutenant. "Never mind, 'tis a long story."

"Oh?"

"I *said*, it's a long story. And you can stop making fish eyes at me." He raked a tired hand through his hair, dishevelling the sable waves and sending them tumbling back from his broad forehead. "What brings you down here in the dead of night, anyhow?"

"Dead o' night? Why, 'tis almost mornin', Cap'n. I just wanted ye t' know that sail off the sta'b'd quarter looks like a brig. She's bearin' away from us, prob'ly reco'nizes us fer pirates."

"Sail?" Sam shook his head, trying to clear it of the cobwebs that were making a tangled mess of his weary brain.

"Aye, don't ye remember? The one Johnnie spotted durin'—"

"Yes, yes of course. I'll be up shortly. In the meantime, prepare the ship for battle. When we get within range we'll hail her and hope she gives us an easy time of it."

"Aye. But ye oughta see the boy, Cap'n! All excited 'e is,

seein's how 'e'll get first pick o' the booty. Says 'e wants a cutlass just like yers, with emeralds all decoratin' the hilt, but how 'e intends t' lift the damned thing I'll never know. Kid's as scrawny as a splinter, 'e is." His eyes narrowed. "Say, ye sure yer all right, Cap'n? Ye don't look so good."

"I'm fine. Stop pressing for details, would ye? Christ, where the hell is my bloody pistol? 'Twas just here a minute ago." He pawed through the clutter on the desk, found it, and knotted it into a length of crimson silk with cool, businesslike efficiency.

Stripes eyed him as if he'd lost his senses. "Are ye goin' up on deck lookin' like *that*, Cap'n?"

"Why the hell not? Am I a pirate or some bloody aristocrat? Now come on, let's go. I've wasted enough time daddling here in this damned cabin."

"But Cap'n. . . ."

"Are you coming or not?"

Sam watched impatiently as Stripes shrugged, then settled his hat atop his chocolate-brown hair. He'd forgotten about the prize. 'Twas just what he needed to get his mind off Maria and back where it belonged; above his shoulders and not grovelling at his feet. Dawn was gilding the horizon now, but he would not think about what it meant, what this day would bring. *He would not.* Snatching up his boarding axe and a dagger as long as his forearm, he strode from the cabin, a handsome specter in torn shirt and red-stained breeches.

Behind him, the dog picked himself up with infinite weariness to trot faithfully at his bare heels. But Sam never saw him.

Maria had spent a lonely, sleepless night staring off across the darkened waves. But loneliness can be the devil's advocate, and introspection its handmaiden. And in the long hours since her escape attempt, she'd had more than enough time to think about what she'd done, first with a feeling of justified, haughty righteousness, then with a nagging uncertainty, and now, with nothing short of heartfelt regret.

Topside, the men were preparing the ship for battle, and the thick, restless tension was not unlike the charged air heralding a thunderstorm. Johnnie hurried past, lugging buckets of sloshing water. Feet pounded above her head, wheels rumbled across the deck as the cannon were run out, and above it all came Sam's voice, deep, resonant, and commanding. As always, she admired his ability to conceal his emotions from his crew and even Stripes, who knew him well. But how he must be suffering inside after what she'd done to him.

She entered his cabin, shocked at the sight of the crimson puddles on the floor, the broken bottles, the obvious signs of a struggle. Gunner had been trailing in his wake when he'd gone topside to take command; that he and Sam had finally had it out was apparent, but just who the winner had been she had yet to find out. There'd been an awful lot of red stains on Sam's shirt that could only have been blood. Trying not to think about it, she side-stepped a pile of broken glass and made her way to the desk. And there, lying upon its cluttered surface, was her note.

She picked it up. Sam had read it; she had no doubt. The parchment was wrinkled and dog-eared, and stained by a large fingerprint of what looked to be more blood. Maria crumpled it in her fist and sank into a chair. *Oh, God.* It was all she could do not to fling herself down on the bunk and cry her eyes out for the sheer frustration and futility of her situation. And now, she heard his voice drifting down from above to torment her with its belovedness. That deep, accented voice of her wonderfully handsome sea captain. Not only did it send little shivers up and down *her* spine; the ship, faithful lady that she was, also thrilled to it and came to life at its command, the decks tilting sharply as she heeled over on a fresh tack.

Yes, the ship leaped to obey him, little Johnnie worshipped the ground he walked on, and even this ragged band of sea dogs had nothing but respect and admiration for him. And now, Gunner. What, then, was wrong with *her?*

Everything.

She was a fool. And it came to her with sudden clarity that his insouciance and casual, mocking words to her had been nothing more than a mask to hide the anguish in his heart. How carefully he protected himself behind the stout walls of impassiveness, wickedness, and bluster. But those walls were just that, cold, deceiving slabs of falseness that guarded the soul of a man who was neither impassive, wicked, nor full of bluster.

The soul of the man she loved more than anyone or anything on this earth.

Not only was she a fool, but a coward, leaving a heartless note for him to find and wasting the night sulking in the forecastle when she could've been proving just how much she *did* love him.

So what if he was a pirate.

There. She'd said it, at last. It could never change the fact that she loved him; nay, if anything, it only proved how *much* she loved him, for no matter what he was, her heartbeat still quickened at the sound of his voice, her will still went to butter at his touch, and her every waking moment was spent thinking of him and naught but him. He could be the worst criminal on earth and *still* she would love him—it was as simple a truth as that.

A resounding rumble filled the cabin as a cannon was dragged into position on the deck above, but Maria paid it no heed. She felt like a spectator looking into herself, saw herself as others must see her. A spoiled brat, yes. A witch, a hypocrite, a selfish, distempered little shrew.

And still, Sam loved her.

And how had she repaid that love? He'd never done a blessed thing to warrant her treatment of him, had never deliberately set out to hurt her, mistreat her. Oh, there'd been times he'd made her cry, but in retrospect Maria knew, with a fresh pang of guilt, that she'd gotten no less than she'd deserved. When he'd hurt *her,* it had been because she'd driven him—sometimes intentionally—over the edge of his explosive temper. And afterward, he'd been contrite, anguished. Maybe she could stand to learn something about values, about human dignity, from him; someone who was, ironically, a *pirate.*

Nay, all he'd done was set out with a single, noble purpose in mind—to rescue the men he felt such an obligation toward. He hadn't returned to piracy to anger or alienate her, hadn't deliberately wanted to hurt her. But she? She *had* intentionally hurt him, and hadn't even said she was sorry.

It was uncalled for.

Tears stung her eyes, clumped in the back of her dry throat.

No more sulking. No more hating him. And oh, *no more judging him*. That was the Lord's job, not hers. Instead of condemning him, she would do what she should've been doing all along; pray gently for his soul and plead with God to forgive him for his sins against mankind, against society, against Him. And she'd pray for her own soul as well. Sam had been right about trying to change a loved one. He'd accepted her for what she was; now, it was her turn to accept *him*. And given the fact that she loved him so deeply she could feel it radiating out of her heart and flooding every cell in her body, it shouldn't be very hard.

Her chin came up, and in the morning light, her eyes shone with determination. A pirate he was, and a pirate he might always be. She thought of Tim's long-ago words, and Justice Doane's: *He's a wild one, that Sam Bellamy*. Well, perhaps that was true, perhaps her Sam *was* a wild one. But he was also gentle and patient and kind, taking the time to teach a young orphaned boy how to fire a cannon, or holding her in his big, thickly muscled seaman's arms while she'd sobbed out her agony over the loss of her baby. He was patient and understanding. He was strong, and he was brave. And he did not deserve her contempt.

Her chin came up another inch. *Nefarious* was preparing for battle, and her captain should look the part. Bloody, shredded shirt? Nay! Stained breeches and shoeless feet? Never! He was the free prince of the seas—let the whole world know it!

Maria marched to that same sea chest containing the ditty bag he'd ordered her to pack. The seas would go dry before she'd do it! She tossed back the heavy lid, rummaging about until she found what she was looking for. There, the coat of ocean-blue broadcloth she'd made for him back in Eastham, lavishly embroidered with gold thread and fit attire for an aristocrat, a nobleman, a haughty pirate captain! From its peg in the bulkhead she took down his gold-braided hat, quickly turning up the floppy brim and securing its three sides with silver pins. She found his boots wedged beneath the carriage of the stern chaser, took his cutlass down from the wall. And thus armed, she made her way topside with head high and eyes shining with pride.

The scene that greeted her almost shook her haughty demeanor. Someone had spread sand upon the red decks, and Johnnie was running everywhere, fetching ball and shot for the guns, setting buckets of water beside each one. Resolutely, she marched across the deck like Joan of Arc. Johnnie saw her and froze. Men, hiding beneath the bulwarks out of sight of the unsuspecting brig, speculating on what its cargo might be as they nervously fingered their knives and pistols, went slack-jawed at sight of her. Even the Union Jack streaming proudly from the mast snapped to attention as she passed beneath its shadow.

The heavy coat draped her arm, the boots pressed against her breast, the sword dangled from her wrist. Across those sandy decks she marched. Past the guns, the swivels, the weapons chest. Past the slack-jawed pirates. Past a man who stared at her numbly, a forgotten grenade in his hand. Up the steps to the quarterdeck, past a four-pounder and its astonished gun crew, and boldly up to where Sam, oblivious to her presence, held *Nefarious* on a close-hauled course. The ship was fighting her tight reins and bucking with annoyance, and in that moment Maria vowed that in the future it would be the sloop, not her, that fought him.

"I brought you something," she announced.

He started, turned, stared. "Maria! Good God lass, you shouldn't be up here!"

"And neither should you, dressed in those rags. Here." She held her well-laden arms out to him. Their eyes met, and in hers he saw a depth of apology that words could never have conveyed. "I think a pirate captain should look the part, don't you?" She swallowed tightly. "At least, when he's going into battle."

Bewildered, he could only stare at her. Had she lost her mind or was this another one of her tricks? His eyes narrowed, and hesitantly, he took the clean, sail-white shirt she offered. "Why, thank you . . . lass." He pulled off the wine-stained wreckage of the one he wore, tossed it over the rail, and drew the fresh one over his head, eyeing her distrustfully all the while. Then, he reached out, took the boots, and pulled them on over his bare feet. It was so quiet he could've heard a fish jump. Out of the corner of his eye he saw his men watching him in frozen silence. Beside him, Silas West nervously cleared his throat. And Maria? He stared at her, unwilling to believe his eyes, but she was grinning, looking at him as if she was actually *proud* of him, not ashamed. Her eyes were as soft as a doe's in her sweet, beautiful face, and shone with tears that could never have been ones of deceit.

His heart began to hammer as he took the coat, thrust his arms into the sleeves, and straightened its pleated skirts over his hips to cover the wine-stained breeches. And as she handed him his cutlass, he heard a hoarse, ragged sound come up from beneath the shadow of the bulwarks.

His men were cheering.

And a single tear was following the curve of Maria's petal-soft cheek.

Stripes appeared at his elbow, a grin splitting his face from ear to ear. ''Well now, would ye look at this. 'Bout time you two made up yer diff'rences. I tell ye, the lads were a bit nervous, with ye at odds with the witch. Never know what might 'appen to us with 'er riled so.''

Sam turned on Stripes, ready to rebuke him for his words, but couldn't summon his anger. Maria had forgiven him! By the Gods, she'd actually *forgiven* him! And now, when he needed her most—and expected it least—she'd made it clear that she loved him, had proudly proclaimed it for the whole world to see. His shy, gentle Maria wasn't quailing beneath his crew's roguish stares, was no longer blushing at the comments that were enough to make a lesser maid turn scarlet. No, his Maria had marched right up on deck, had turned a deaf ear to his crew's whispers, and was now offering her full support and love. In light of such a monumental event, how could he be angry with Stripes?

He clapped his garrulous young lieutenant on the back. ''Know something, lad? You're the only bloke on this damned ship I won't put the lash to for uttering such balderdash!'' Grinning broadly, he took the smart three-cornered hat that Maria offered him and set it on his head at a jaunty, cocky angle. ''And if you want to retain that status, then ye'd best take her below and get her safely settled in the cabin. For if ye don't, and she comes to harm here on deck, the consequences ye suffer will be far worse than if she and I were merely at odds with each other!''

''Now, don't ye worry, Cap'n,'' Stripes assured him as he took Maria's elbow. ''She be in safe hands.''

But Maria had other ideas. Her shining gaze drank in the handsome picture Sam made, standing tall and proud with the broad, blue sea at his back. Go belowdecks? Oh, no. She'd spent too many lonely, miserable hours there as it was. She wanted to be where she could see him, hear him—and above all, appreciate him. And no threat of battle would take that away from her. She touched his wrist, her fingers lying lightly upon the silky dark hairs there. "Sam, please, let me stay." Her eyes were clear, bright, guileless. "I won't be any trouble."

"That's right. You *won't* be any trouble." Grinning, he hefted the cutlass and slashed the air to loosen his tight muscles. "That's why you'll remain in the cabin, Maria. Now off with ye, before ye have the lads forgetting just what we're about!"

"Is that the only reason? So I won't distract the men?"

An overpowering surge of love flooded his heart. "The men? Bah! Get belowdecks, woman, so ye don't distract *me!*"

Lower lip trembling and heedless of their intent audience, Maria flung her arms around his neck and buried her face in his sea-damp, silky hair. His arms went around her, and lifting her high, he swung her in a joyous circle, clasping her to his chest with force enough to crack her ribs. He set her down, and then she was gone, running lightly across the deck and leaving him reeling and uncertain about just what had happened.

"Well, well, I'd take that as a sure sign o' good luck, Cap'n," Stripes said, shaking his head and making a great show of examining the chipped glass of his wine bottle.

"Aye, the blessings of the Sea Witch," Silas West mused. His captain's hands seemed to have gone numb, and now the stoic quartermaster took the wheel before *Nefarious* could get into mischief. "What better luck can we ask for?"

But Black Sam was staring at the companionway down which Maria had gone. A faint smile lingered on his lips, and in his eyes was the sightless stare of a dazed man. He looked up, took the wheel once more. "Indeed, Mr. West, we cannot ask for anything better." His manner became brisk and businesslike, and full of himself once more, he turned, cupped his hands over his mouth, and shouted an order for all to hear.

"Run up the colors, lads! By the gods, we've a prize to take!"

Chapter 23

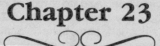

Rich the treasure,
Sweet the pleasure,
Sweet is pleasure after pain.

                                        DRYDEN

"**Y**our glass please, Mr. Paige."

They were ten leagues off the New York coast and heading south. Several days had passed since Maria's escape attempt, and abrupt—and to all concerned, welcome—change of thought regarding Black Sam's activities. Peaceful days they'd been, too. Maybe a bit too peaceful, Nat Paige thought.

It had rained softly during the night, and now Nat tore his eyes from the water-swollen halyards, the still-dripping ratlines, the steam that the morning sun pulled from the moist decks. Black Sam stood at the rail beside him, bareheaded and barefoot, his dark hair swept back in a loose queue threaded with a fiery slash of crimson silk and hanging pigtail-like between his broad shoulders. One bronzed hand shaded his eyes as he squinted into the sun hovering above the distant horizon.

"A sail, sir?" Nat asked, handing him the glass.

"Aye, perhaps." Sam extended it and lifted it to his eye. In its circular field, waves, still excited from the showers of the night before, danced away toward the horizon, where a few last clouds still lingered stubbornly. He swept the glass to the left. There it was, the distant speck that had caught his eye. But in the glass, topsails just visible above the horizon, it was much more than just a speck. He hadn't been mistaken after all.

"Aah . . ." A faint smile crept across his handsome, sun-toasted features. "A brigantine, I think. Hull-down and wearing French colors." He lowered the glass, tapped it smartly across his palm, and handed it back to Nat. "You lads are going to have to do better than this, you know. What sort of pirates let their captain sight a prize first, eh?"

At that moment an excited cry was heard from high above their heads. "Sail ho! Fine off the larboard bows!"

Sam threw his sailing master a sidelong glance. "What'd I tell you, eh?"

"Er, maybe he was sleeping, sir?"

"Sleeping? More likely chasing his coffee down with a tot of rum." He watched his crew come swarming up on deck, some rubbing the sleep from their eyes, others cramming the last bites of their breakfasts into their mouths and swiping crumbs from their lips as they ran to the rail for a first look at the distant ship. Silas West ambled over, pulling a beat-up hat over his scalp to protect it from the strengthening sunlight.

"Don't tell me it's our mysterious hanger-on," he said, squinting toward the horizon.

Propping his elbows upon the rail, Sam rubbed his chin and studied the distant pyramid of sails. "Nay, 'tis not. We must've lost him during the night, whoever he is. Damned cowardly bloke, I wish he'd bloody show himself. I hate surprises."

"So do I," West mumbled, echoing the sentiments of the small group at the rail. For two days, the sails of an unknown sloop had poked above the horizon, never coming close enough to actually make a threat, but trailing them all the same. And while it might have made some of them a bit uneasy, for the most part the lads of *Nefarious* had grown more and more cocky with every passing day.

"Well, if he bothers to show his slinking face before noon," Sam said, "we'll come about and show *him* how it feels to be followed. Keep an eye on that brigantine, will ye, Mr. West? I'm going below to get some breakfast." He straightened up, tossed what was left of his morning beverage—an empty wine bottle—into the sea, and made his way aft.

He found Maria in his cabin, sitting up in bed wth a pile of posy-patterned fabric in her lap, a threaded needle in her graceful hand, and a half-finished gown spread over her knees. His stomach was growling, but the sight of her, all morning fresh with the sun backlighting her hair and those same rippling locks spreading out over the pillow and tumbling over the edge of the bed, drove thoughts of breakfast from his mind. She looked up and gave him her sweetest smile. "Hungry?"

He tossed his pistol to the desk and crossed the cabin in two strides. "Insatiable," he said, not referring to his stomach at all.

She saw the heat in his black eyes. "I told Johnnie to bring your breakfast by at seven o'clock. I mean . . . six bells." She put the gown she was making aside.

"Ah, you're learning, princess." He sat down beside her and pulled her into his arms.

"We're having buttered eggs . . ."

"I don't want buttered eggs," he murmured, his teeth nipping her nape, his breath warm against her neck, her ear, her throat.

She shivered in delight. "And cornbread with jam . . ."

"I don't want that either." His warm lips found her ear and nuzzled it until Maria giggled in delight. "Breakfast be damned. Ah, lass, ye feel so good. . . ."

She melted blissfully back into the thick pile of pillows and linens, still warm with the scents of morning and sunshine. Her eyes drifted shut and she moaned softly, absorbing the wonderful sensations of his lips roving over the sensitive skin behind her ear, down the hollows of her throat, across the gentle rise of her shoulders. Big, callused hands smoothed the sunny tumble of hair from her forehead, cleared gossamer strands from her lashes, her cheeks. His thumbs lifted her jaw and he kissed her hungrily, deeply, with all the ardor of a starving man attacking the heaping plate that Johnnie, pausing just outside the doorway, held.

"Uh-ahem," the boy said, shuffling his feet and looking down at the steaming plate of buttered eggs, fried bacon, and cornbread. Maria flushed, Sam chuckled, and with good hunor dancing in his eyes, left her to relieve Johnnie of his burden.

"Mmmm." He took the plate in one hand and the jug of cider tucked in the crook of Johnnie's skinny elbow in the other. "Looks like the cook's outdone himself today, eh? God's teeth, if they keep feeding me like this I'll never want to return to land."

"You'll never want to return regardless of what they feed you," Maria remarked, but her voice held no rancor. She waited for Johnnie to leave, which he did quite hastily, then crawled out of bed and began to don the hated breeches.

"And just what do you think you're doing?" Sam asked, quirking a brow. He set the platter on the table, took the breeches, and tossed them over his shoulder, where they landed in an undignified heap upon the bunk. His gaze roved appreciatively over her slim figure. "Can't I even enjoy the sight of my future wife's lovely body while I eat my breakfast?"

"Sam, 'tisn't proper. . . . "

"To hell with *proper*. Sit down and eat your eggs."

She blushed and shyly pulled out the chair beside him. Glancing at him through her downswept lashes, she picked up her fork, dug into her food, and began to nibble delicately.

"For God's sake, lass, you can stop watching the door. No one's going to come barging in. I locked it, remember?"

Nevertheless, she reached for one of his fine linen shirts and, pulling it over her head, yanked it down over her peach-pale hips. Self-consciously, she crossed her legs. It was awfully hard to eat with the weight of his admiring stare on her, and even more so when his hand reached beneath the table and began a slow, tantalizing exploration of her calves and thighs. She glanced up to find him regarding her with a lazy smile in his dark eyes.

"Thanks, lass."

She gave him a curious look, then swallowed hard, his touch making her heart race, making it impossible to think straight. "Thanks? For what?"

"For not hating me anymore."

"I never hated you. I was angry, but I never hated you."

His hand dragged up with infinite slowness to tease the soft curls that framed her womanhood. Maria sucked in her breath. "Ye know," he said, grinning wickedly, "I think I know the *real* reason ye tried to leave me."

She caught his hand, her fingers pressing against the hair that sprinkled the back of it. "I told you why."

"No, I mean the *real* reason. It hasn't anything to do with being angry with me, being worried about me, or taking revenge on me. I think . . ." his fingers, tracing a slow circle against the inside of her thighs, made her shiver ". . . that it has more to do with this."

"Pleasures of the flesh," she breathed, her eyes slipping shut.

"Eh?"

"Oh, just the subject that started dominating old Reverend Treat's sermons after *you* sailed into Eastham. You wouldn't know, of course; after all, you never did set foot inside that church."

"And I wouldn't have been welcome even if I had."

"Not by the pastor, at least." She opened her eyes and gave him a sly grin. "Though the ladies would've loved it."

"Ah, the ladies. . . ." He quirked a smile at her and teased the curve of her kneecap until she shivered once more.

"That tickles!" Giggling, she slapped his hand away. "Shouldn't you be topside keeping an eye on things and plotting the capture of that brigantine?" She laughed as he stroked the underside of her knee. " 'Twould be terrible if your men deposed you. I wouldn't want to see you become another Ben Hornigold."

" 'Twill never happen, my dear," he said, grinning and pushing his plate away. Stretching his burly arms over his head, he watched her clear the table. "But tell me, what made you so suddenly forgive me?"

She shrugged, smiling. "Some things you said that I took the time to think about. But mostly"—she padded across the cabin in her bare feet, her hair swinging gently around her buttocks, and traced the curve of his lip beneath his black mustache—"the realization of how much I love you."

"Enough to overlook some aspects of my character that didn't sit so well at first?"

"And still don't. But if truth be told, those are the very things that made me fall in love with you in the first place. Your recalcitrance. Your . . . nobleness. Your—"

"Me, noble?" There, the quirk of one dark brow again.

"Yes, noble! And brave, and compassionate—"

That quirk in his brow was now affecting a corner of his mouth.

"If you laugh at me I'm going to stomp on your toe!"

He did laugh then, yanking his foot away as her bare heel thumped down to the deck.

"And arrogant," she finished.

"Arrogant?"

She smiled sweetly. "You think you're invincible, that you can conquer the world, don't you? Stripes told me what you once said to some poor captain whose ship you'd taken shortly before the *Whydah* wrecked—"

"Oh, *please.*" He buried his forehead in the heel of his hand.

"You don't want to remember, do you? Well then, let me refresh your memory. He told me that you said, 'I am a free prince, and I have as much authority to make war on the whole world—' "

" '—as he who has a hundred sail of ships at sea and a hundred thousand men in field,' " he finished, giving a little half-smile as he idly tapped his fork against the table's edge. "Aye, I did say that. And so what, lass? I *do* have the authority. To make war on Boston, to make war on George's bloody England if I so desire. Name one person who might stop me."

"The entire Royal Navy, for one. That sloop that's been following us, for another."

"What, that little pestilence? I hardly think so."

"She hasn't drawn close enough for you to determine if she's so little."

"Oh for God's sake, Maria, will you *please* stop worrying?"

"All right," she said, a bit too cheerfully.

He gave her a wary stare. "What?"

"Well, you *are* captain," she said sweetly, "and I wouldn't *think* of defying you. Therefore, I'll stop worrying, but only"—she came forward to loop her arms around his neck and gaze up into his dark eyes—"if you go back up on deck. I would feel much better knowing that *you* are in command up there."

He stared hungrily at the swell of her breasts. ''I'll go, in a bit.''

''I really do think you should go now, Sam.''

She pressed against him, teasing him, and rubbing her sleek, satiny leg against his knee and up the length of his thigh until she felt his arousal spring to life.

Heat simmered in his black eyes. ''You look quite fetching in that shirt of mine,'' he murmured, plying the softness of her cheek, her throat, with a roughened finger.

''Is that all? Fetching?''

''All right, tempting.''

''You don't look very tempted, Sam,'' she teased. ''If this is your reaction to temptation, then I fear I must try harder.''

Hoarsely, he said, ''What d' ye want, princess? For me to command the ship or tear the shirt off your body and make wild, passionate love to you?''

Maria looked up at him from beneath the thick fringe of her lashes and smiled. ''Why, to tear off the shirt and make wild, passionate love to me, of course.''

The little crinkle lines she loves so much danced out from the corners of his handsome dark eyes. A wicked smile lifted the edges of his mouth and framed it in deep, parallel creases of good humor that only emphasized the strength of his chin and roguishness of his smile. ''You would, eh?'' he asked, clasping his hands behind his back and beginning to walk a thoughtful, cursory circle around her. The play of muscle beneath his snug breeches left little to her imagination. ''And what else would ye like, my dear little witch?''

''I'd like you to stop your pacing, carry me to your bed, and love me until the sun sets in the east!''

''I am not pacing.''

''You are.''

He stopped, crossed his arms over his chest, and studied her with a lazy, appreciative expression that made her feel as if she stood garbed in nothing but the sheer veil of her hair.

''You see, princess? I am not pacing. And as for your second request . . . why, I do believe 'tis one I can easily grant.''

Without warning, he scooped her up in his arms, holding her close against the solidity of his chest and gazed down into her beautiful eyes as he carried her with determination and purpose to the bunk. Her arms came up to twine about his neck, her hands slid beneath his queued hair. The soft brush of the flamboyant silk he'd so rakishly threaded through it tickled her fingers, and moaning softly, she pulled his head down to hers.

Warm, sensuous lips moving against hers with fierce gentleness. That queer but familiar fluttering in her secret, womanly regions, and the moist heat that accompanied it. The feel of his chest crushing one aching breast, the crisp, black hairs pressing into her skin, the solid, unfailing strength of his arms beneath her shoulders, the backs of her knees. She melted against him like butter left in the August sun. Everything ceased to matter; the ship, the planned raid on Boston, piracy—everything. There was nothing but his wondrous, overwhelming presence and a heady, floating sensation as he took the last few steps to the bed. Her head fell back against his chest, and she gazed dreamily up at him through the brush of her lashes. Her cheeks were flushed the color of peaches, her lips already swollen and parted in invitation. She smiled then, and when she spoke, her voice was the soft, throaty purr of a kitten, nay, a *cat*.

"And my third request?"

"Ah, princess . . . you're a greedy, impatient wench, aren't ye?"

"Set me down, my bold pirate, and I'll show you just *how* greedy."

He did so, letting her slide gently, sensuously down the muscled length of his forearms until her feet touched the floor. Her hands palmed the slightly rough skin at the sides of his neck, heating the sinews and muscles that stood taut beneath her fingers. She felt his pulse beating beneath her thumb, heard the quick, indrawn gasp of his breath. Slowly, she dragged her hands lower and slid them beneath the loose lacing of his shirt.

"Princess. . . ." he murmured huskily, shuddering as she dragged the shirt over his head and lightly grazed the curve of his spine, the ridges of his scarred back, with her nails. "God, ye make me unable to think straight."

"There's no need to think, my love," she breathed. "Just *feel*." She reached up, touched his lips, then trailed her finger over the bearded ridge of his hard jaw, the shadowed, stubbled skin of his throat, the rise of his collarbone, the indent of his sternum. His heart pulsed beneath her palms, moisture sheened his skin. The Spanish coin he always wore warmed her hand, and slowly she dragged her palms over his hard, curving muscles, threaded her fingers through the pelt of hair on his chest, and gently rubbed his tiny nipples with her thumbs. His eyelids turned heavy and dropped over obsidian eyes in silent torture. His breathing grew harsh and ragged. His waist was as lean and strong as a ship's mast, his ribs well defined and framed by flat muscle, his chest and shoulders a study in masculine grace, perfection, and beauty. He was power, he was magnificence. He was everything that a woman might dream about, and more. And as her eyes followed the dark path of hair that trailed down his taut belly and plunged beneath the waistband of his breeches, her eyes confirmed what her hands had already told her—that he was desperate with need for her.

The keen dark eyes opened to regard her through the hazy fog of passion. "Must ye torture me so, woman? Such soft hands, such sweet flesh. Christ. . . ."

"Torture? I have not even begun to show you *torture.*" Down over the muscles sheathing his ribs Maria's hands went until she found his sword belt. She unbuckled it, let it and its cruel-looking weapon fall to the floor with a dull, metallic clatter. She pressed her lips to his chest, nosing downwards through the crisp dark hair there even as her hands slipped beneath the waistband of his breeches, slid around his narrow, lean hips, and found the buttons that fastened the cloth. She was nimble, yet agonizingly slow; she was sure of herself, yet not so confident that she lost that last bit of simple innocence that had never failed to endear her to him. Her hands teased the throbbing, rigid length of him until he thought he'd go mad with longing; her thumb slowly pushed buttons through buttonholes, first one—and as she dragged her soft cheek and sweet lips down his chest, his abdomen— then the other. And then he was freed to her, his manhood hot and hard in her soft little hands, his breeches sliding down his strong legs to lie about his ankles.

And for Maria, it was suddenly the most natural thing in the world to lay the velvet-shrouded length of him against her cheek, to explore him with her lips, to feel the rapid ham-

ering of his pulse echoed in this wonderful, totally mas-
line part of him. He shuddered and groaned deeply, head
rown back in sweet agony as he dug his fingers into her
oulders and broke the stillness of the room with the hoarse
arpness of his breathing. He let the torture go on until he
uld take it no longer, and finally pulled her up, drove his
outh against hers, and forced her over his arm and down
on the bunk. Her wrists locked around his back as he lowed himself on thick, brawny arms so as not to crush her.
is hand burned the silken flesh of her ankle, her calf, and
ally the recesses of her damp thighs until she squirmed
d arched upwards as he stroked her to the peak of passion.

Cool sea air swept in from the stern windows and kissed
r heated flesh. She turned her head, her cheek pressing
ainst the tumble of her own golden curls fanned across the
llow. Her breasts were burning, and when his hands, then
s mouth, found them, she cried out with her own sweet
rture.

"Oh God, Sam—love me, now! *Please*. . . ."

And with a deep, driving plunge that ripped through that
veet ache and scattered it to the stars above, he granted her
ird request.

An hour later they were interrupted again.

"Er, Cap'n?"

Sam lay in the bunk, Maria drowsing against him with her
tle hand warming his chest. She opened a sleepy eye at the
und of Stripes's voice. Cursing the interruption, Sam drew
e blankets up over the creamy rise of her shoulders. "What
it, man? Christ, can't a body have any peace or privacy
ound here?"

Smirking, Stripes lifted his wine bottle. His brown eyes
eamed mischievously. "Just thought ye oughta come top-
de, Cap'n. That brigantine's within hailin' range and is run-
n' like a dog with her tail tucked b'tween 'er legs."

"Christ."

"Does that mean ye don't wanna take 'er, then?" Stripes
ked, hiding his grin behind his bottle.

"It most certainly does not! Prepare the ship for action

and keep your glass trained on her. I'll be up . . . momen
tarily.''

''Aye, Cap'n.'' Wiping his mouth, Stripes winked at Ma
ria and exited the cabin.

Scowling, Sam rose from the bed and yanked his breeche
on. Maria hid her smile. Piracy, it seemed, had come secon
in his preferences; *she* had come first. Wordlessly, sh
watched from the bunk as he donned his coat, kicked hi
boots out of the way, snatched up his hat, and gathered hi
pistols. Taking his cutlass down from the wall, he turned an
faced her. ''I'll be back,'' he said, his gaze lingering on th
tempting swell of her breasts. ''And I'd like you to stay be
low. Things might get a bit hot up there if it comes down t
a fight, and I'd never forgive myself if anything happened t
you.''

She got up and went to him, smiling sweetly and pressin
her breasts against his shirt. Groaning, he folded her in hi
arms, torn between desire and duty. His hands drove into he
tangled tresses, then his hard, thewy arms locked behind he
back.

''Go, Sam,'' she said softly, tilting her head back to loo
up at him. Their gazes met. ''I'll still be here when you g
back.''

Reluctantly, he set her away from him. He stared at he
creamy breasts, her graceful collarbone. Then he reached ov
and caught a lock of her hair, crushing the silken curl in hi
hand and rubbing it against his lips. ''Promise?''

''Promise.''

He smiled, wistfully. And then he abruptly dropped th
curl, straightened his shoulders, and swept from the cabin.

Maria's invitation was enough to restore Sam's good hu
mor. By the time he emerged on the sun-baked deck, he wa
full of high spirits, the devil, and himself. The sun sparkle
off an endless sea; the brigantine was a mere league off thei
bow. Sam's bare feet and jaunty stride carried him straigh
to the quarterdeck, where Silas West was agitatedly runnin
a hand over his blistered pate.

''Well, what are we waiting for, lad?'' He turned to Bill
Flanagan, who hummed a bawdy tune beneath his breath a

he lazily kept the sloop on a pursuing course. "Mr. Flanagan, kindly alter course two points to windward. We'll stand out to sea, come about, then swoop down on them like a falcon after a rabbit." He grinned boyishly. "She's fast and able, lads. Time to see what our own little ship can do with a *real* prize!"

"And this crew," grumbled Stripes, who'd come up to join him. "Times like this I sure wish I 'ad ol' Simon Van Vorst b'side me, or Paul Williams, or even—"

Sam cut him off with a sharp glare. "You have Mr. West, who is a capable officer, you have Phil Stewart, who even now is casting the lashings from the starboard battery, and you have me. Now stop complaining and get this ship ready for action. I'll not have a show of apprehension on your part, Stripes!"

Such enthusiasm was infectious, and Stripes hastily ambled off to rally up the crew. Thank God the cap'n and 'is woman had finally put their differences aside; it was about time Black Sam got down to business and netted 'em a fine prize, just as he'd done so many, many times in the good ol' days aboard the *Whydah*, and before that the *Mary Anne*, now under the command of Paul Williams.

And just like the good ol' days, there he was pacin' the deck as cool as ye please, wearin' that damnable grin while he oversaw his crew's activities with a satisfied gleam in those devilish black eyes o' his.

But whether Black Sam shared his doubts over the competency of this young, unseasoned crew Stripes was not to know, for his captain concealed such things well. Even now his voice was brisk and authoritative as it rang out over the sun-drenched decks.

"Topmen aloft to loose the tops'l, and prepare to come about! Fetch her up on the starboard tack, then swing her across the wind and come up on the brigantine's stern! 'Twill give us the wind gauge and keep us out of range of her guns." He swept the decks with an assessing black gaze. "Stripes! For God's sake, tell Johnnie to keep his head down, will ye? He's bloody likely to get it shot off!"

Closer and closer they came to the brigantine.

Men crouched beneath the bulwarks. Gunners held smoldering matches. Topmen waited with muskets and stinkpots in the rigging. All eyes were on their captain, every will awaited his command. The tension built, thickened, until it charged through the ship, hummed in Sam's blood, tingled in his fingertips. He counted the seconds. Ten. . . . Fifteen. . . . *Far enough.* "Put up the helm lad, now!"

Heeling sharply, *Nefarious* skidded into the oncoming waves, flinging curtains of spray high over her decks in great, shimmering arcs of crystal. Sails shaking, she faltered, confused, as the pirates threw their weight upon her sheets. Her great boom swung, her sails began to draw once more. Slowly, gracefully, her bowsprit swung away from the wind, coming around farther and farther still, tracing a full half-circle before finally aligning with a marksman's accuracy on her unwary prey.

"Run up the colors, lads!"

Clean, hungry wind filled the huge mainsail, billowed the topsail, bellied jibs and straining foresail. Gathering speed, *Nefarious* charged the French ship, her death-flag vaulting to the top of her mast, her gun ports chunking open to reveal her bristling array of four-pounders. Spray leaped and hissed from her bow, her sails thundered and boomed, and in no time, she was abeam of the brigantine.

Sam's fingers tightened around the wire-wrapped grip of his cutlass. Above his head the Jolly Roger streamed boldly, blotting out the sun and throwing a dancing shadow across the deck. Damn them for a pack of fools, why hadn't they struck? Hell, if it was a fight they wanted, 'twas a fight they'd damn well get! He folded his arms across his chest and inclined his head toward his quartermaster. "Would ye look at that, Mr. West. She's still running. Why, I'd almost think she doesn't know we're here!"

" 'Bout time she realizes it, don't you think?"

"My sentiments exactly." Sam turned and bellowed a command to his master gunner. "Mr. Stewart, lay a shot across her bow! If she doesn't heave to by the time the smoke clears, load up with chain shot and take out her rigging!"

He smiled craftily, eyes gleaming as he tugged at his beard. Out of the corner of his eye he saw Johnnie watching him with blatant admiration. He saw his men leap up from beneath the bulwarks, screaming, yelling, and howling. And he saw Stewart's faint smile as he crouched, sighted along the gun's long muzzle, and lowered his match to the touchhole.

The awesome explosion deafened him and thundered through his head, the deck quaked beneath his bare feet, and a thick cloud of smoke billowed back to sting his eyes and choke him. But as it cleared, he saw the French colors come tumbling down from the mast.

"She's struck, lads!" He raised his cutlass and took the companionway stairs in a single bound. "Ready with grapples!"

Great claws of iron sang across the rapidly decreasing distance between sloop and hapless brigantine. Muscles strained beneath bare backs as the pirates threw their weight on the grappling ropes and snugged the ships together, hull to hull. Some leaped the distance between them before the ropes were even pulled taut, overwhelming the terrified French crew before thoughts of resistance could enter their minds. Pistol in one hand and cutlass raised high in the other, Sam vaulted atop a cannon's breech, leaped into space, and landed lightly upon the brigantine's holystoned deck.

Commotion and chaos reigned all about him. Everything was flashes of color as his men raced through the swirling smoke, some whooping at the top of their lungs, others rounding up the French crew with swinging cutlasses that needed no translator to make their meaning known. There was a roar of sound, the screams of frightened men, random pistol shots, blasphemous oaths, and pirates pounding past in every direction.

Sam strode through the melee like a victorious general, a half-smile flitting across his swarthy face. That smile widened as his slow, purposeful strides carried him to the brigantine's quarterdeck, where the French commander, a trickle of sweaty grime racing down his temple, stood quaking in his silver-buckled shoes. The man's hand was shaking as he offered his sword in surrender.

"*Bonjour, Capitaine!*" Sam declared, taking the sword, sweeping off his hat and bowing gallantly. "*Nous sommes de la mer!*"

The French captain went the color of oatmeal and took an involuntary step backwards. Sam's smile became a grin of genuine amusement. "*Oui, pirates,*" he affirmed, with a glance at Silas West, who was already hacking away at a hatch cover with powerful swings of his axe. Pirates surged into the hold before the last splinters could even be torn away. "Now, if you're easy, *mon capitaine,*" Sam continued, "we'll get this nasty business over and done with in no time, and ye can get on your way with minimal inconvenience. But if you're not . . ." Deliberately leaving his words hanging, he turned and shouted, "Mr. West! Line up these lads and ask them if their captain has been a good master, and then see if any are inclined to join us. If so, take them back to the sloop and show them the Articles!"

"Aye, Captain!"

Ignoring the confusion and commotion surrounding them, Sam turned back to the Frenchman. *"Parlez-vous anglais?"* he demanded.

"Non—"

Slamming his cutlass down on the rail, he snarled, "Damn ye for a liar! Ye think I didn't see ye go pale when I ordered my quartermaster to question your men about your treatment of them?"

"I—I am . . . sorry, *Capitaine* Lebous."

"Lebous? I'm not Lebous, ye blithering idiot, 'though I know him well. And save your apologies for your men, 'tis they who'll decide your fate, not I!" He jabbed his cutlass toward the horizon, where his discerning eye picked out the smudge that broke that line between sea and sky. "Ye know anything about that ship?"

"Wh-what ship, *Capitaine?"*

"Don't play the idiot with me," Sam warned. *"That* one."

"I know only zat he has been chazing me zince sunrise," the Frenchman said, shrugging. *"Mais, Capitaine,* if you are not zee pirate Lebous, zen who are you?"

" 'Tis of no matter who I am. You may call me Captain . . . *Black."*

Something like recognition came over the Frenchman's face. Sam's eyes narrowed. "What, have ye heard of me, then?"

"Word of your exploits, *Capitaine,* precede you." Hopelessly, the Frenchman turned to watch the pirate quartermaster moving up and down the line of his men, relieving them of their pistols, swords, and finer pieces of jewelry.

Sam's curiosity was aroused. "Oh? And what is it they say about me, eh?"

"Zat you are a bloodthirsty killer. Zat your ship has wings and disappears into zee mist at will. Zat you are expert with sword, pistol, and wits, neither of which I should care to test. But *Capitaine,* I would give you a word of warning."

Sam's gaze had fastened on a group of men who were axing the brigantine's cargo crates to splinters. "And that is?"

"Zat there ees a man who has sworn to kill you. He says zat you murdered hees cousin some months past. . . ."

"*What?*"

"Yes, it ees true. As we speak he and zee governor fit out a ship in Boston. If you are wise, *Capitaine,* you'd do well to avoid zeese waters."

"And if *they* are wise they'll realize 'tis I who rule them." He smiled, tipped back his hat, and slanted a thoughtful glance at the Frenchman. "And pray tell, lad, who might this imbecile be?"

"Heez name," the Frenchman said quietly, "ees Ingols."

Chapter 24

And alone dwell for ever
The kings of the sea.

ARNOLD

"Ye know, Maria, I've been thinkin' bout this Ingols bloke," Stripes said the morning after the brigantine had been taken, plundered, and sent on its way, due to its rotten, leaking bottom. They were sitting together beneath the shadow of the gently swinging boom, listening to the dawn breezes sigh through the rigging and watching a gull wheel lazily overhead. "An' what I still can't figure out is how 'e knows our cap'n's the Black Bellamy. Doesn't everyone think 'e died on the *Whydah?*''

"Apparently not," Maria said, gazing forward where the bowsprit plunged and rose above the sudsy, oncoming rollers. The wind breathed life into her hair, making it float about her face like a cloud of dawn sunlight. "But what troubles me is that this man has the audacity to call Sam a murderer. Wasn't his cousin the one who purposely let the storm drive the *Whydah* off course and into the breakers in the first place?''

"Aye, but that don't change the fact that 'e was still on the ship," Stripes pointed out, "and if 'e *wasn't,* I s'pose 'e'd still be alive." He looked over at her, sitting there with her back against the mast and her hair all awash in the breeze, thinking that Black Sam was the luckiest man in the world to have such a prize as Maria Hallett. "All's I wanna know is how this cousin o' his knows it's our Sam who masters *Nefarious.*''

"I'm sure that was even easier to figure out."

"Whaddya mean?''

"Well, how many pirate captains go around delivering speeches on personal freedom to their prisoners?''

Stripes chuckled and picked at a frayed edge of his sleeve. "Ye know, we're prob'ly gettin' all worked up over nothin'. Ye heard the cap'n. Said 'e's laughed himself silly over worse things than some bloke and 'is petty thirst fer vengeance.''

"Like the storm that nearly killed him?''

"Aye, I do believe 'e found it rather amusin', at least 'til we heard them breakers. . . .''

"I'm not surprised. Sounds just like him. But somehow, I don't think he finds that sloop back there amusing at all.''

"Prob'ly not. And if *you* wasn't aboard, 'e'd turn around an' give 'er a good thrashin' with our guns. Never used t' play it so safe back in the ol' days. . . .''

A morning mist still hung upon the sea to the west, the glittering waves danced away to a silver horizon, and there, the sails of the mysterious ship were just materializing.

"Now don't ye go worryin' none," Stripes advised. "Cap'n said 'imself she ain't from the Royal Navy.''

"Well, who do you think she is then? And why does she

hang back like that? Why doesn't she just hail us and let us know her intent?''

"Heck if I know. Think I'm a mind reader? Yer supposed t' be the witch, not me. Who d'*you* think she is?''

"I don't know either. But if I *was* a witch I'd wave my magic wand and make her disappear.''

"Oh, she'll disappear fast enough. Cap'n's tired o' playin' cat an' mouse with 'er. He'll lose her among them there islands off in the distance t'night, mark me words.'' Stripes followed Maria's gaze to the bowsprit, where Sam stood far out on the jib-boom, a glass to his eye and a hand curled nonchalantly around a stay. Now, he thrust the glass into his sash, turned, and strode purposefully down the pitching length of the spar, heedless of the sea that glittered and danced so far beneath his bare feet. "If not before . . .'' Stripes added.

"Up with ye, lads! 'Tis time we show our heels to our little friend, eh?'' Sam said, seizing a line and swinging himself onto the forecastle. "Now, let's look lively about it!''

But after celebrating the brigantine's capture into the wee hours of the morning, the crew lay sprawled across the deck in a state that could only be called comatose. No one moved, not even Johnnie, who lay curled up in the launch with his head pillowed, childlike, on his hand and a skinny arm thrown over Gunner's ribs. Only the dog looked up, and this he did rather lazily before letting his head drop back against the curve of the boat's hull.

Arms akimbo, Sam stood glaring at the lot of them. "I said up with ye, ye lazy pack of drunken curs!''

Nothing.

Very calmly, he reached down, drew his pistols, and fired them harmlessly toward the clouds.

A gull screamed, Gunner lunged to his feet, and the deck came alive as though a broadside had hit it.

"Holy mother of God, what the hell was *that?*''

"We're being attacked! To quarters I say, to quarters!''

Wild eyes. Frantic scrambling for cutlasses, knives, pistols. And then, they caught sight of their captain, standing imperiously atop the barrel of a cannon, arms crossed at his chest and two smoking pistols in his hands. He was grinning widely.

"Good morning, lads."

For a moment, no one moved. And then Nat groaned and rubbed the dark circles beneath his eyes with a grimy fist. "Good God, the captain's lost his mind."

"Lost my mind? Perhaps. I must've to burden myself with such a lazy pack of good-for-nothing whelps!" Still standing on the cannon, Sam jabbed his pistol toward the eastern horizon. "See those sails yonder? Well, I'm *sick* of seeing them. What d'ye say we stop playing games and show her what our little sloop can do, eh? Get the mainsail up, Mr. Paige, and while you're at it, the fore and tops'l, too. In fact, lay on every stitch of canvas she'll hold."

Maria felt Stripes's elbow in her ribs. "I think 'e knows somethin' we don't. 'E's grinnin' like the devil 'imself!"

"That doesn't mean he'll tell us. And knowing Sam he'd be grinning whether it was the Royal Navy, this Ingols character, or a mere fishing boat out there." She frowned as Stripes lurched to his feet. "Wait, where are you going?"

"Why, t' see if I can find out jus' *what* 'e knows that 'e ain't sharin' with the rest o' us!"

Sam was all business. "Lay her on a larboard tack, Mr. Flanagan, then prepare to come about. Stripes! Stop feigning sleep and get this ship ready for action!" He glared disgustedly at the littered decks, the luffing foresail, the sluggish, hampered movements of his crew. "Shake out tops'l and jib and look lively about it, damn you! This is a fighting ship, not a bloody alehouse!"

It didn't take long for *Nefarious* to show her heels to her pursuer like the thoroughbred that she was. By noon, when the sun stood pasted in the sky and melting a hole in that wide expanse of blue, the horizon was empty for the first time in days. Her captain's order brought her due west, toward a ragged coastline of coves, islands, and hidden sandbars—pirate's country—where they could hide for days, weeks even. And as *Nefarious* nosed into the shallows, Sam sent a leadsman forward to take soundings, took the helm, and with a skill born of years of seamanship, brought her over the treacherous, shifting bars under nothing but the jib at her needle-sharp nose. And there, screened by a narrow peninsula and a wall of tall pines, she finally dropped her anchor.

* * *

They lay quietly together, oblivious to the crew's revelry coming from the beach a quarter-mile away. A balmy breeze whispered through the trees and cooled their naked flesh. The night air was heavy with the scents of roast venison, pine, and the sea, and through the trees, *Nefarious*'s lights glittered upon the dark and peaceful water.

But Maria wasn't interested in the sloop. She didn't care about the celebration down on the beach. There was only one person in the world who had her attention, and that was the dark, wonderful pirate captain stretched out beside her in the sand.

Forgotten clothes lay scattered nearby, colorless shapes in the darkness. A sword was thrust into the sand, carving shadows from moonlight and throwing them over the brace of pistols beside it. And the pirate himself lay comfortably on his back, arms crossed beneath his head, thick, glossy hair falling away from his face and curling in dark contrast upon his silvered forearms.

He was looking up at her with a lazy smile and eyes that gleamed with love, contentment, and a devilish sort of charm that never failed to set her blood afire.

"Witch," he said so softly that his voice barely stirred the air about them.

"As I would have to be, to lie with the devil himself."

"Ah, princess. We make quite a pair, do we not?"

She gave a soft laugh, her finger wandering to the corner of his mouth. Sam lay quietly, enjoying the sensations of her kitteny touch, only his eyes moving as he looked at the back of her hand, then up into her beautiful, moonlit face.

And as Maria dragged her fingers over the soft curve of his lower lip, feeling his hard, strong teeth beneath, he gently nipped the pad of her forefinger and held her gaze, his eyes smoldering like embers. His hand closed around her wrist, his big fingers spanning her fragile bones and capturing them in a gentle but viselike grip of iron.

"Are you never sated, my little princess?" he asked softly.

"Me? Sated?" Her laughter was as gentle as the lap of water against the distant beach. "Never, you rogue. Not when it comes to you." She palmed the rise of his chest, her graceful fingers fanning the muscles as she sought his heartbeat. And then a smile—slightly triumphant, Sam thought—brightened her eyes, and he knew she'd found what she was looking for.

Found it? Only now? Christ, it was hammering against his ribs and slamming the blood through his head so fast the sound it made was like torrential rains beating an empty deck. Through it he managed to find his voice. "You are, you know."

"I am? What?"

"A *witch*," he murmured. "A sorceress, a siren. God, Maria, look what you're doing to me. . . ."

She gave him a smile of feline satisfaction, her gaze roving hungrily down the handsome, honed length of him. The caress of her gaze did as much to fan his desires as if she'd actually trailed her finger down that splendid chest, that flat belly, that rigid shaft of masculinity. Unable to take it anymore, he hooked an arm around her neck and pulled her down until she lay dwarfed upon his big, broad chest, her chin propped on her wrists, her unbound hair melting with his like cream and black coffee. She gazed into his smoldering eyes, just inches from her own. "Know something?" she said, tickling the hollow above his collarbone. Her voice was soft, sultry, and anything but innocent.

"Mmmm. . . . What's that, princess?"

She edged forward, her breasts pressing into his chest. He was clay in her hands and she knew it. She was driving him crazy, and she knew that too. She *was* a witch, and he was as much under her spell as he'd been that long-ago day when he'd first met her. He couldn't get enough of her. He'd *never* get enough. He could take her lovely body over and over again, could lose himself in her sweet, throbbing warmth, and it would never ease his craving for her, a craving that went beyond mere pleasures of the flesh and lodged itself within the deepest regions of his heart.

"God, I love you," he said.

And now she was rubbing against him, driving him on until his hands came up to sweep the velvety curves of her back, the firmness of her buttocks with mounting urgency. She teased him with her petal-soft lips, the tickle of her hair on his cheeks. His eyes closed. He swallowed thickly. And then he heard her voice, the barest of whispers, filmy silk floating over every taut, throbbing nerve. "And I love you too, Sam."

He couldn't take it anymore. With a savage growl, he rolled over, spilling her onto the sand that still bore the warmth of the sun and the imprint of his big body. Her heart took wings, her eyes filled with happy tears as the night sky was blotted out by his powerful shoulders, his darkly handsome face. His lips came down hard upon hers, his tongue seeking the hot, honeyed recesses of her mouth. Black, unqueued hair tickled her throat, her neck, and that intriguing scent that was his alone—fresh wind and sea salt—filled her reeling senses.

"Oh Sam," she whispered, for he'd drawn back, aware in the deeper regions of his mind that he might be hurting her with his urgency. "Please, don't stop. Take me, be my savage pirate captain. Show me no quarter."

His smile flashed in the moonlight. "Do ye strike your colors then, wench?"

"I . . . strike."

He rubbed one hard, aching nipple between thumb and forefinger, passed his callused palm over the sleekness of each breast, swept it down the curves of her hips, in and around her sleek thighs, and finally between them, where his fingers found and fanned the center of her desire. She gasped out loud, arching against his hand. "See what ye do to me, princess? No quarter, you ask? By God, ye'll get none!"

She giggled helplessly, and then he became delightfully savage once more, demanding as ardent a response from her as she had built in him. The sand crunched beneath his elbow as his weight came down on one arm, his hand, his fingers, his mouth plundering her helpless flesh where her desires flared the •hottest. She heard his ragged breath, felt the scorching heat of his lips as they roved upward, now brushing her forehead, her eyelids, her cheeks, and finally her parted mouth. She took him greedily, winding her arms around his neck and pulling his head down to hers. The glossy waves of his hair were silk beneath her fingers. His flesh was a hot blanket over her own. And her own blood was running so hot she felt delirious as though with fever.

He was a bold, handsome pirate captain. He was the free prince of the seas . . . and he was hers.

She could wait no longer, and neither could he. His arousal stabbed against her soft thighs and her innermost regions were a swirling mass of wet, writhing heat. She opened herself to him, drawing him into that hot, aching flesh, wrapping her legs about the lean trunk of his waist and pushing herself upward in her fierce need to get closer to him. His breath heated the damp curls near her ear, and he began to move within her, slowly at first, then savagely, every thrust of his powerful hips driving her buttocks deeper and deeper into the soft, warm sand.

Her nails dug into the scarred flesh of his shoulders. She cried out his name. Higher and higher he took them until with one last, mighty plunge he drove into her and sent them both spinning out over the edge of sensual oblivion.

Tears of rapture streamed down her flushed cheeks. She clasped his shuddering body fiercely to hers as the tremors of aftershock rocked her, going on and on like ripples in a pond, slowly fading until once more she became aware of the pounding of his heart against her tingling breasts, the feel of his damp hair against her neck, the peaceful sounds of the night, and the not-so-peaceful revelry down on the beach.

Suddenly a mighty thunderclap shattered the night.

A chorus of frightened, confused yelling came up from the beach along with the sharp reports of a pistol and Gunner's insane barking. Maria grabbed for her clothes.

"Captain! Captain, come quick! We're being attacked!"

But Sam was already on his feet, donning his breeches and snatching up his pistols, cutlass, and sword belt. There was no need to tell Maria to dress, and dress quickly she did, for no sooner had she found her breeches and yanked her own shirt over her head than Billy Flanagan came crashing out of the trees, howling at the top of his lungs.

He was too distraught to notice what his captain had been doing. "Oh sir, hurry! There's a ship coming over the bars and firing her guns—"

"I know, Mr. Flanagan. Do you think me deaf?" He saw the terrified look in his helmsman's eyes. "Now calm down, please. She didn't fire into the sloop, did she?"

"No, in fact, I'd think it a salute if she wasn't coming in so fast! Sir, only a madman would venture across those bars at night in a ship as big as this one!"

"Hmm. A madman, eh?" Sam stroked his beard between thumb and forefinger, a preoccupied, thoughtful look in his eye. He had no doubt that thunderclap had been just that—a salute. "Must be our little friend then. Sounds like he's decided not to be bashful anymore, eh?"

"Oh, it's him all right! Oh sir, please *hurry!*"

Flanagan tore off through the trees like a bolting deer. Sam found his knife, calmly wiped the flat of the blade against his breeches, and tucked the weapon into his belt. And then he smiled, took Maria's hand, and with unnerving indifference, led her through the woods to the beach where *Nefarious* lay unprotected at her anchorage.

It was chaos: men screaming, dousing the fire, cursing, and digging frantically in the sand for weapons they'd carelessly tossed aside. Gunner raced the beach, his frenzied barks filling the air, and for a moment Maria couldn't move as Sam melted into the crowd. Then terror slammed into her and spurred her to action. *Good Lord,* she thought, *don't just stand there!* And then *she* was on her hands and knees, flinging her hair out of her eyes and searching frantically for a pistol, a knife, anything! And it was only as her fingers closed around the hilt of a half-buried dagger that her head snapped up and her frightened gaze darted past the beach, over the water, and toward the sea.

Her breath caught in her throat. Her heart stopped. And in her veins, the blood went cold.

For out on those bars was a great ship, lights blazing through its open ports like hideous, hellish eyes, huge sails obliterating the stars, and an eerie, horrible noise coming from its decks that seemed to rise from the very depths of Hell itself.

And shoving off from that ship was a boat, and in its bow, hair afire and casting a flickering, orange glow over his smoke-wreathed face and the straining backs of his evil rowers, stood Satan in all his horror.

The world darkened and Maria clutched at her throat to keep from fainting. The screams, the shots, Gunner's frantic barking, all melted and meshed and faded to a deafening, roaring din. She stumbled backwards, unable to tear her gaze from the dreadful apparition. And then Johnnie's shriek pierced the night, ringing through her brain and jolting her back to awareness.

For there was Sam at the water's edge, feet slightly apart, head high, and arms crossed imperiously over his bare chest—not trying to protect them, not trying to protect himself, not doing *anything* but simply watching that hideous specter as it came closer and closer.

With a sharp cry Maria lunged forward, only to be jerked back by Stripes's restraining hand. "Let me go! Sam! Don't just *stand* there, run!" Frenzied, she kicked out at Stripes's foot and struggled wildly. *"Sa-a-a-a-m!"*

"Be still, Maria!" Stripes urged, tightening his grip.

Sam stood unmoving. And closer and closer that awful boat with its terrible passenger came. So close that she could smell the pungent smoke of the embers glowing in its matted hair. So close she could hear the steady dip and splash of oars, the evil laughter of its demon crew. So close she could see into the depths of its soulless black eyes, the flame points reflected in those unholy orbs. . . .

And then it turned its awful face toward her beloved Sam.

Maria's scream bubbled up in her throat. Sobbing, she turned her face into Stripes's chest, but it was too late to block what she'd already seen.

A black, mangy, horse's tail of a beard that began somewhere beneath gaunt cheekbones and ended beneath the curve of a massive chest, a horrible, evil growth that spouted hair in every direction of the compass and writhed like snakes in the breeze. No less than six pistols were strapped to the thick leather bandoliers that crisscrossed that awesome chest, two more dangled from around that terrible neck, another was held in that awful, hair-covered fist. A skirt of knives paid homage to the cutlass at its belt, and from the crown of its broad hat to the tops of its knee boots, it was dressed entirely in the stygian color of the grave—black.

Maria risked another look. Now those death-cold eyes were flickering over her, the cowering crew of *Nefarious,* and Sam, whose broad, bared shoulders showed no trace of fear, whose proud stance offered no such respect to this demon as his men's did. He didn't move as the apparition's mouth split in a terrible grin, didn't flinch as the boat met the beach with an ominous crunch, didn't say a word as the terrible creature

eaped into the surf, drew that wicked length of steel, and
waded slowly out of the water towards him.

All was silent. The creature came forward. One step. Two.
Still Sam didn't move, and some of his men began to whim-
per as they awaited the ruthless slaughter of their captain.
Three steps. Four. Five. Its eyes were black marble, colder
than the crypt—and then, raising its cutlass high in both
hands, it lurched to a stop in front of Sam.

As one, *Nefarious*'s men caught their breath, Johnnie hid
his face behind his hands, and Maria's guttural scream broke
the heavy silence.

No-o-o-o-o-o!

And as her cry died into the night, she heard the deep
boom of Sam's laughter.

"Teach," he said, raising his own cutlass in mutual salute.
"Taking it a bit to the extreme, aren't you?"

Her mouth snapped shut. Confusion glazed her senses. He
knew this awful apparition, this unholy, terrible demon?

The creature's voice rumbled up from the depths of its
pistol-crossed chest. It was not the voice of one who spoke
in normal, conversational tones. It was nothing short of a
bellow, as though accustomed to commanding the very le-
gions of Hell itself.

"Bellamy, ye old rascal! Damn and thunderation, the rumors be true then! Would ye take a look at this, m' boys!
Tis me old shipmate Bellamy, straight from a stint with Satan himself!"

Shipmate? thought Maria rather dazedly, as did every crew
member of *Nefarious* save Stripes, who just now relinquished
his grip on her.

Sam's smile was a wry one, but the pleased gleam in his
eye was unmistakable. "And I might say the same of you,
old friend." He turned to his men. "Relax, lads. This is Ned
Teach from Bristol, an old friend of mine. We served together
in Hornigold's sloop—"

"Until ye stole it right out from under him, ye conniving
young fox!" Teach clapped Sam across the back with a force
that nearly knocked him down. "And old Hornigold ain't
forgiven ye for it yet! He was madder 'n hell with ye, Bellamy! Swore by Lucifer and all his saints that if ye ever

showed yer colors in New Providence again he'd blow ye clean out of the water whether ye was Brethren or not!''

Sam merely threw back his head and laughed. ''Never could stand to be bested, could he?''

''And neither could you, m' boy! 'Twas no wonder ye wrestled his ship and crew right out from under him. Me, I bided me time 'til he gave me a ship. Said I earned it, and was the best damned pupil he ever had. Hell, I didn't *steal* it from him like you did! Why, I do believe they call that . . . piratin'!'' Pleased with his own joke, Teach slapped his thigh and roared with laughter.

But Stripes was the only one of *Nefarious*'s wary crew who seemed pleased—if not relieved—to have this fearsome visitor. ''Ye knew, Cap'n!'' he exclaimed, looking from Teach and then back to Sam. ''Ye knew who was tailin' us all along, didn't ye?''

''Aye, lad, I knew.''

''But how?''

''Same way I knew 'twas Black Sam who mastered that pretty little sloop yonder!'' Teach roared, answering the question for him. ''Old Hornigold taught us ways of sailing a ship that are just plain unmistakable, right m' boy? But ah, Bellamy, ye still led me a merry chase. Knew ye'd be waitin' here in our old rendezvous spot!''

Maria watched this exchange with a mixture of awe, relief, and a growing urge to knock that smug grin from Sam's face for allowing them all to believe the worst. And to think that he hadn't been fleeing, but merely playing games and contesting his old shipmate's sailing skills! And now he was slowly shaking his head and grinning as though he found this whole thing unbearably amusing—which indeed, he did.

He looked his old friend up and down. ''I must say, Ned, devil or not, you certainly look the part. What's this, match cords you've stuck beneath your hat and set afire? The effect is most dreadful. And odorous, I might add. Almost had me fooled, even. Almost''—he reached out and flicked one of those burning lengths of hemp—''but not quite.'' He grinned. ''Must have your victims screaming in terror before ye ever hoist your colors, eh? How the hell did you arrive at this . . . image? Oh, never mind. You can tell me over a pot of rum.

Come, join me, and see if you can still outdrink me, old friend!''

"Rum? Hell, I ain't never been one to refuse a drink with an old mate, and one back from the dead at that! A pox on ye, Bellamy! Ye still haven't told me how ye did it!''

He started to follow Sam, but his cunning eyes found—and fastened on—Maria.

"Ho, there! What say, Bellamy? What are ye, daft, hiding this sugary little treat in a pair of breeches and shirt?'' He stretched a massive paw toward Maria, who shrank back in terror. "Come here, lassie! Ol' Ned Teach from Bristol ain't never been one to harm a lady!''

"Shear off, Ned.'' Sam took Maria's elbow and drew her to his side. "She's my future wife—Maria Hallett.''

"Ho, the celebrated Witch of Eastham herself!'' Maria went stiff as he grasped her hand with surprising gentleness and bowed gallantly, a motion that seemed strangely out of place coming from one so ferocious, so barbaric. "The pleasure is mine, mistress! Tales of yer exploits are told from New Hampshire to New Providence. And damn me eyes if they ain't all true! Why, yer prettier than pirate's gold!''

"Mind yourself, Teach,'' Sam warned, touching the hilt of his cutlass. "I've called men out for less.''

Teach's gaunt face looked thunderstruck. "Why, I'll be damned fer a monkey's arse! Black Sam is *jealous!*'' His guffaws shaking the air, he turned to a seaman and bellowed, "Fetch me a drink there, Hands! I gotta have something to toast me friend's upcoming nuptials!'' His glittering eyes raked Maria from head to toe. "Ye ain't really a witch now, are ye?''

Maria got the distinct impression that nothing would please Teach more than if she actually was. Sam's arm stiffened beneath her fingers, and his mouth went hard. "A pox on ye, Bellamy! I'm just riling ye. Don't ye go gettin' all hot and hellfire 'bout it. Besides, I'm just getting an eyeful of 'er, 'tis all. Have ye no heart, m' boy?''

"Maria's no more a witch than you are Satan. I'll not have her name besmirched with such rot, old friend.''

"Hell, it ain't like I'm condemning her to the gallows! Haul in yer guns, fer God's sake! And where the hell did me rum go? Hands! I'm thirsty, damn you!''

And as he ambled off in search of his rum, Maria heard bits of conversation from the men clustered around the fire.

"I don't care what they say, she ain't no witch but an angel! Why, I think I've died and met me maker!"

And Stripes, "Yer maker don't entertain angels, t' be sure."

"But Teach has his eye on her, and he always gets what he wants. If I know my captain, he'll have the wench before dawn!"

"And if I know *mine,* Teach'll be dead by sunup if he so much as tries it!"

Maria's face flamed. She looked up at Sam, who, judging by the way his lips were twitching, must've heard the conversation as well. He grinned down at her. "Don't let them get to you, princess. Men will be men, and pirates will be pirates. Lots of bluster and swagger, but down deep they're like any other. Pay them no heed."

" 'Tis not the men that worry me, but their captain."

"Who, Teach? Why, he's the biggest windbag of them all. Now let's see a smile. We wouldn't want him to think you're a timid little doe now, would we?"

"And what little doe wouldn't be timid when surrounded by such a hungry pack of wolves?"

Sam drew a gnarled old log close to the fire, pulled her into his lap, and steadied her with an arm about her shoulders. "The one who belongs to the leader of that pack, my dear, that's who."

"But you heard them. They said he means to have me!"

"Over my dead body."

"But what if—oh, good heavens, here he comes."

"With enough tipple to keep a king's ship in ration for a twelve-month. I'm afraid this is going to be a long night, my dear."

But Teach had paused beside a group of his men, who were betting on a pair of grimy, yellowed dice carved from the bones of a long-dead whale. As he squatted down and reached for the dice, they fell silent.

"What're ye playing there, mates?" he boomed. The men looked ill at ease, but Teach merely shook the dice and tossed them to a piece of planking that had been set on the sand as a playing surface. From his thunderous look it was obvious the roll hadn't pleased him. Cursing the dice for being weighted, he snatched up a nearby bottle and hurled it savagely against the planking. It shattered, spraying those unfortunates nearest it with glass, wine, and bits of wood. One of them jumped up and, screaming, clapped a hand over his face.

"Oh, mercy, sir, I think ye blinded me!" he wailed. "Ye hit me in the eye, fer God's sake!"

But Teach only roared with laughter and retrieved the mugs—all six of them—that he'd set in the sand. "Don't let it trouble ye, Henderson! Ye still have the other one!"

Outraged, Maria leaped to her feet. "That poor man!"

"Sit down, princess."

"But he has glass in his eye!"

"I said *sit down.*" Sam grabbed for her, swore, and let his arm fall back to his side as Maria marched indignantly past a grinning Teach and went to the man's aid.

Sam's curses brought a cannon blast of laughter from Teach. "Let her be, Bellamy. I daresay, the wench can take care of herself!" He shoved a mug into Sam's hand. "Here, have some tipple. To our health, I say!"

"Aye, to our health," Sam muttered, lifting the tankard to his lips. Yet his dark gaze remained on Maria as she bent over the injured man and pried his hand from his eye. Cursing, he tossed down the tipple quickly—too quickly—and came up coughing and sputtering.

"Good stuff, ain't it?" Teach roared, already reaching for his second tankard. "Told the boys to make sure they put plenty of gunpowder in it! Tears the very breath from yer lungs, eh?"

"Aye," Sam croaked, wiping a hand across a tearing eye. "You have an unusual sense of humor, my friend."

"So I've been told, tho' I daresay not all share yer opinion!" Teach was laughing so hard he nearly choked on his rum. "So tell me, m'boy, what's this I hear about yer men being up in the Boston gaol?"

"You heard correctly," Sam said, steeling himself for another gulp of the burning liquid.

"Hell and damnation, don't ye know Boston ain't never been one to show mercy toward the Brethren? What say ye we cook up a way to get 'em out, eh?"

"What do you think I've *been* doing for the past two months? Taking a sightseeing cruise up and down the bloody coast?"

"Well, what *have* ye been doing? Tumbling that green-eyed witch?"

Refusing to be baited, Sam quaffed his rum and choked down an involuntary gasp of shock. "Waiting for that damned Paul Williams to show up. *Christ,* I'd give my right arm to know where *he* is right now!"

Teach eyed him in confusion.

"Well, I can hardly bust them out alone, can I?"

" 'Sdeath, what do ye need him for? He's been sailin' with Lebous. Nah, do yerself a favor and ferget Williams. Besides"—his eyes gleamed over the rim of his tankard—"ye got *me* now."

"You? And just what do *you* have to gain from such antics, my friend? They were Paul's and my men, not yours."

"Why, a reputation, for one! Think of what it'll do fer me image, blasting into Boston with every gun a-roaring, the rogues all hot and ready. Ah, what a sight we'll be, Black Sam and Blackbeard."

Sam raised a dark brow and set down his rum. *"Black-beard?"*

"Like it?" Teach stroked the long, greasy length of hair that streamed from his cheeks, his jaw, his chin. "Ye should see it when it's all braided up. Scares the living daylights out of the prizes. I tie the tails off with little ribbons, stick some of these"—he yanked one of the smoldering match cords from beneath his hat—"into it, and I'm telling ye, ye've never seen colors come down so damned fast! Mark me, m' boy, I'm going to be the greatest rascal that ever lived!"

Sam merely shook his head.

"Ye don't mind now if I help out, do ye? I wouldn't want to be stealin' yer glory!"

"Mind? Hell, I need all the help I can get." His gaze strayed to Maria, still bent over the injured man and tenderly examining his eye.

"Well then, what are we waiting for?"

Sam grinned, feeling as though a sudden weight had been lifted from his shoulders. With Teach, there was no need to ry and find Paul. With Teach, there was no longer a need to build up a fleet. With Teach, he had all the help he needed.

And with Teach, he could finally put the last ghosts of the *Whydah* to rest, haul down his flag, and—his heart leaped with joy—marry his sweet Maria.

"Nothing," he said. "Nothing at all. In fact, let's start the thing in motion on the morrow. I'll take a little jaunt up to Boston to assess the situation, and we'll rendezvous on Sunday off the Isles of Shoals."

"A damned good plan! Just mind yerself in Boston, m' boy. Though the world might think yer dead, there's one bloke who don't and he'll be giving ye a damned hot reception if he finds ye're visiting yer lads right under his nose."

"Ah yes, my friend Ingols." Sam dismissed the unknown enemy with a wave of his hand. "Don't worry, I've heard all about him. Ah, here comes Maria. Don't say anything about him to her, eh? She worries too much as it is."

"Mistress Hallett!" Teach boomed. "I see ye've worked yer potions on me crewman and restored him to health! Here, sit down and join us. I was just about to propose a toast!"

"A toast?" She eyed him warily.

"Aye, a toast! To the wickedest pair o' rogues to sail the seas—Black Sam and Blackbeard!"

The crews gathered around. Rum pots were thrust toward the pale moon.

"Aye!"

"To the Brethren!"

"To licking Boston with the fires o' Hell!"

Wild cheering drowned out the reports of gleefully fired pistols. Uncertainly, Maria looked up at Sam, and felt his excitement. For once, she could read his mind, and knew that Teach, for the good or bad of it, would be joining them in the rescue attempt.

But Teach was quick to spot the soft look she bestowed upon his former shipmate. "And what does the Sea Witch have to say about it, eh?" he roared, grabbing a piece of venison from a crewman's plate.

Maria raised her chin and met Teach's glittering, demonic gaze. She thought of *Nefarious* anchored a short distance away, of Teach's madness in bringing that devil's ship of his over the bar.

"Well?"

Sam's determination, his reckless bravado. Teach's brute
strength and hellish temperament. . . .

"God help Boston," she said quietly.

Chapter 25

*Then issues forth the storm with sudden burst,
And hurls the whole precipitated air
Down in a torrent.*

THOMSON

"Captain Ingols, I do hope you are aware of the mag-
nitude of your request."

Samuel Shute, Esquire, the recently appointed governor of
Massachusetts Bay and New Hampshire, leaned back in his
chair, hooked his fingers over the brocaded waistcoat that
covered the slight paunch of his belly, and regarded the man
across the table from him with mild impatience.

"But Your Excellency, I am well aware of it." James Ingols picked up his glass and absently swirled his port. He
smiled, a cold smile lacking in feeling and humor, a smile
that the benevolent governor did not like at all. "As you
should be well aware of the rewards that the success of such
a venture will bring you."

"Rewards? How many times have we had this discussion,
Ingols? And how many times must we have it before you
finally abandon your silly attempts to persuade me that Bellamy is alive and well?" He crumpled his napkin, plunked
it down beside his plate, and began to rise. "Now if you'll
excuse me, I have other matters to attend to. Chasing dead
pirates is not very high on my list of priorities."

"Your Excellency, I beg of you, please hear me out!

understand your reluctance to pursue the matter, but I can assure you that the pirate Bellamy is not dead!''

"I have Southack's confirmation that he is, and that is all I need.''

"But you heard Captain Beer—''

"Just because Beer spent a couple of hours aboard the *Whydah* as Bellamy's prisoner does not make him an authority on the man. Just because Bellamy forced him to endure a tedious speech extolling his far-flung ideas on piracy does not mean he can say with certainty that he still lives. Just because he happened to see this captain of—what was she called? yes, the *Nefarious*—doesn't mean he can state he's one and the same as Bellamy. Let's face it, Ingols, all pirates look alike. Devilish, dark-skinned, and impossibly arrogant. 'Twould be a simple matter to mistake one for another. And furthermore, any man who spent a few hours in the company of a crew such as Bellamy's can hardly be entrusted to remember every detail of what the man looked like. Beer was probably terrified out of his senses. Who can blame him for mistaking every pirate he sees for the one who frightens him so?''

"All right. Assuming that Bellamy is dead—your assumption, not mine—can you deny that this Black character isn't a thorn in your side? Give him time and he'll be worse than Bellamy ever was. Clearing the coast of such a pestilence can only be to your benefit. Why, think of what a favorable impression it would make upon the king.''

With a heavy sigh, the governor pulled out his chair and thoughtfully drummed his fingers upon the table. "Indeed, that it would,'' he mused. He fixed his guest with a pensive gaze. If he allowed Ingols to take his ship and go in pursuit of the pirate, he could be rid of Ingols's nagging and free to concentrate on other, more frustrating, problems: his trouble with the Indians, for one; his acceptance by his peers, for another. And regardless of whose body Ingols brought back, he didn't believe for a moment that Bellamy had survived that cursed shipwreck that had become such a headache for him and the agent, Southack, he'd sent to Eastham to salvage it. He could just picture Bellamy's ghost laughing at him, laughing at *all* of them, no doubt, from his throne in Hell. And he must've laughed himself right off that throne when

back in Eastham, thanks to wind, waves, stubborn Cape Codders, and a certain pirate named Paul Williams, Southack had
been unable to salvage anything but a few worthless pieces
of that damned ship.

Williams. That's who he really ought to be worrying about,
not this other rapscallion, Black. Perhaps he should send Ingols out against *him*, just as Governor Cranston of Rhode
Island had tried unsuccessfully to do several months ago. But
he'd have more luck than the hapless Cranston in catching
Williams. And if he came up with Black, *and* this new devil,
Teach, at the same time, it certainly *would* make an impression upon his king, wouldn't it? He smiled. Ingols was right
on *that* account.

He steepled his forefingers and tapped them against his
chin. "Captain Ingols, I understand your desire to avenge
your cousin's death, but I do believe the man who caused it
is far too dead to pay the price. Instead, perhaps you might
consider directing your attention to his old consort, Paul Williams. Not as satisfying a revenge, but the two of them *were*,
after all, partners. Or, how about this new rogue, Teach, who
goes by the name of, uh . . . Blackbeard? Now *there's* a
problem. He's going to be more of a nuisance than Bellamy
ever was, I fear." Shute paused, allowing Ingols to absorb
his plan. The man's russet eyes were beginning to gleam.
Satisfied, he pressed on. "That would please me greatly, you
know—if you netted me Williams *and* Teach. And you might
start by looking around the Isles of Shoals for him. They've
become one of Teach's favorite haunts, I'm told. He has those
poor islanders frightened out of their senses."

Ingols sat back, twirling the stem of his wineglass between
his fingers. "Your Excellency, that is a splendid idea," he
said at length. "If not revenge upon Bellamy, then upon Williams, who was, I suppose, also responsible for my cousin's
death in his own small way. Of course, there's always the
chance that Black will be found in company with Williams
and Teach."

"Yes, a very good chance, I should think. Very well then."
He leaned back, calling for a servant to bring him paper and
pen. "As captain of the king's ship *Majestic* you shall sail in
company with Captain Thorndike of the sloop *Porpoise* for
the Isles of Shoals. There, you shall await Teach's arrival.

He's about due for a visit there, I should think. You know Thorndike, don't you? A likable enough sort, though a bit overzealous at times. No matter. I'm sure you'll get on well together.'' He reached for the pen, scrawled something on the paper, and pushed it across the table to Ingols. ''Here, your personal orders. Are you satisfied now, Ingols?''

Ingols took the paper. ''Thank you, Your Excellency. I promise that you shan't be disappointed.''

''After all this bother, I should hope not. Be prepared to depart on the morning tide. I will advise Captain Thorndike of the mission, and the two of you can work out whatever strategy you deem fit.'' The governor yawned and got to his feet. ''Now, if you'll excuse me, Captain, I fear I must bid you good-night. It has been a long, trying day for me.''

''Yes, of course, Your Excellency. Thank you for a most enjoyable dinner, and of course''—he held up the paper—''my new orders. I promise, you shall not find cause to regret them.''

With a triumphant smile, Ingols took his leave.

Hooves clip-clopped against cobblestone. Carriages and carts rolled through the streets, squeaking tiredly. Laughter, voices raised in heated bargaining, the shouts of a merchant as a child stole an orange and bolted through the milling crowd; Boston was a lively town, and Maria had never seen its like.

She clung to Stripes's arm as they picked their way around crates of produce, cages of squawking chickens, and the occasional pile of steaming horse dung that littered the marketplace bordering Boston Harbor.

''I can feel ye shakin', Maria,'' the pirate said in a low tone. ''Now, quit yer worryin', fer God's sake. How many times do I have t' tell ye? The cap'n can take care of 'imself.''

Maria lifted the hem of the posy-patterned gown she'd finally finished making and stepped gingerly over a pile of rotten vegetables. She was every inch the lady, even if the man who escorted her was unmistakably a seaman. Her hair, braided, coiled, and pinned atop her head, was covered by a

delicate lace cap. A few soft curls fell about her face, an
now she reached up to tuck one back beneath the cap.

"I know he can," she sighed, gazing wide-eyed at th
hustle and bustle surrounding them. Sailors ran to and fro
merchants hawked their wares, smartly dressed businessme
pawed through cargoes as they were brought from the ship
and set upon the pier. Between the docks and one of the man
islands that dotted Boston Harbor, *Nefarious,* her nam
slightly changed to spell *Nebulous* instead, stood patientl
atop her shimmering reflection. The sight of her gave Mari
a small measure of comfort, and even from this distance sh
could see someone—Johnnie, maybe?—sitting astride th
great jib-boom, legs swinging back and forth, a book in hi
hand. Yes, it had to be Johnnie.

But her thoughts were on Sam. "What if someone recog
nizes him? What if they get suspicious about his wanting t
see the pirates in the gaol?" She stood on tiptoe, scannin
the crowds for him. "Oh, Stripes! He should've been bac
by now!"

"Nonsense," the pirate assured her. "Besides, Black Sar
'as a good reason fer wantin' t' see the poor lads. Would y
begrudge a prisoner the right t' talk to 'is own brother? An
the brother bein' a fancy lawyer at that?"

She raised a hand to shade her eyes, swept the crowd
final time, and threw him a sidelong glance. "Is that how h
planned on getting in to see them? By saying he was one c
their *brothers?*"

"Aye, Tom Baker's. Oops, watch out there." He yanke
her aside before her dainty new shoes of brocaded silk—pai
of the booty from the French ship—could squish into a pud
dle of mud that looked anything but innocent. "Why, look
All yer worryin' was fer nothin', see? 'Ere comes the cap'
now."

Maria's head jerked up. It took her a moment to spot him
for she instinctively sought the dashing insurgent who com
manded the pirate ship *Nefarious.* But a full-bottomed wi
hid that magnificent mane of black hair, the strong jaw wa
beardless, and he looked anything but disreputable in a roya
blue coat sporting yards of gold braid. A brocaded waistcoa
had been carelessly left open to show off a fine shirt of snow
white lawn, and a neatly tied Steinkirk accentuated the dark

ness of his skin and almost, but not quite, hid the Spanish coin within its frothy folds; a subtle clue that Mr. Seth Baker, Esquire, was not all that he appeared to be.

And unlike the pirate, who would've had a boarding axe or dagger, or both, tucked in his belt, this gentleman wore a thin rapier peeping from between the coat's pleated skirts. Only his companions knew that he wore that fine sword not for dress, as the gentleman would have, but for their defense and protection if the need arose.

Yes, it had taken her a moment to recognize him, but beneath that white peruke the slash of brows were just as black and wicked, the eyes as bold as ever, and now glittering with something else, too—outrage.

Stripes took one look and muttered that long-standing forecast of doom. "Uh-oh."

Maria laid a calming hand on Sam's velvet-clad arm, feeling the tenseness of his hard muscles just beneath his sleeve. "Was it that bad?"

"Aye. Horrible. Chained like dogs and treated worse." He started to rake his hands through his hair, remembered the peruke, and instead rubbed his eyes as though to wipe away the memory of his men—dirty, wretched, devoid of hope, and stripped of spirit—that had plagued him since leaving the gaol. "Stripes, I want to act as soon as possible. Now, of course, is not the time or place to talk about it. Meet me back on the sloop in three hours so we can go over our plans."

"Aye, Cap'n. And where will ye be, then?"

"In town, of course," he said. "I'm going to find a place to take some supper and force it down the lass's throat if it kills her. She's too damned thin. And make sure the ship's ready to weigh by the time I return. I've no wish to spend any more time in this bloody hellhole than I have to."

"Aye, sir," Stripes tipped his hat to Maria, bid them goodbye, and melted into the crowd.

Sam took a deep, steadying sigh, wishing he could expel his bitterness and anger along with it. The sight of his men in the gaol had brought all of the guilt, all the nightmares, all the memories of that awful stormy night flooding back. So many, many had died, and it was all his fault. And it was his fault that those who hadn't were rotting in that dirty, stinking cell and looking forward to their executions to ease their torment. How tempting it was to assuage that guilt by falling back into despair and self-hatred, but Sam was a wiser man than he'd been several months ago. Those same feelings had nearly destroyed the precious love he shared with Maria; he'd be damned if he'd let them do so again. Instead, he took her elbow and led her away from the dock.

"Perhaps m'lady would care for some supper?" he asked, making a heroic attempt at cheerfulness. Yet as he smiled down at her, he found that her beauty and gentleness of manner were already doing much to take the sharpness out of his temper. God love her. He caressed her elbow through the fine spill of lace, wishing he was alone with her and not in the midst of this damned crowd. Their gazes met, and he reached up to caress her cheek with the back of his hand. "You must be heartily sick of salt beef and ship's biscuit."

She pressed his knuckles against the side of her face. "Sick of it? I'd kill for a piece of fresh pork, a slice of pie, a piece of cheese that I don't have to scrape the mold from. Believe me, Sam, you will not have to *force* them down my throat."

"Ah, then you shall have them, princess!" He guided her past the corn and fish markets and swept his arm to indicate a weathered structure at the head of the town dock. "The Whale's Tail Inn. Generous with their tipple, and even more so with their food." He lifted her off her feet when she would have stepped in a puddle of muddy water, and they both abandoned their stuffy roles of lawyer and his lady for the moment and erupted in peals of laughter.

The loud racket—drunken singing, catcalls, clinking of glasses and plates—emanating from the inn made Maria wonder if the weary old dwelling was going to shake itself loose and tumble right into the harbor. She had misgivings about entering the noisy, smoke-filled room. But inside, well-dressed merchants bumped elbows with roughened tars who would've been right at home alongside *Nefarious*'s crew, and for a moment Maria thought they might actually find a table without attracting attention. She shrank behind the safety of Sam's arm. But heads were turning, the noise dying. A serving maid strutted past and raked Sam with bold, hungry eyes. Men regarded him with caution and awe, not knowing who he was but mindful of his aura of command. And then tall ceased altogether as the eyes of sea tars and fancy gentlemen, of whores and jealous serving maids alike, settled upon her, and Maria never guessed that it was her beauty, and not the fact that she'd entered the tavern in the first place, that caused those many tongues to still. She edged closer to the tall, handsome man at her side.

"Something wrong, my love?" he asked, bending down so that his deep voice was close to her ear, his breath stirring the soft curls there and sending little shivers down her spine.

"No." Maria looked up into his concerned eyes to avoid meeting the curious stares. "I just feel uncomfortable, 'tis all."

"Uncomfortable? Why, you've mingled with a worse sort."

"Perhaps, but your crew wouldn't hang you if they learned you were someone other than who you're pretending to be."

"You're right, they wouldn't. They'd draw and quarter me, then they'd hang me. Or is it the other way around? No matter. Ah, there's the innkeeper. Shall we?"

An elegant fall of lace spilled from Sam's wrist as he raised his hand with all the hauteur befitting a fine gentleman—or perhaps a pirate captain, Maria thought—to gain the man's attention. The innkeeper, a short, balding man with nervous brown eyes and a fleeting smile, hurried over, anxious to please such a handsome and obviously affluent young couple.

"What can I get for you, sir?" he twittered, his darting gaze taking in the fine cut of Sam's coat, the snowy lace at his throat and wrists, the powdered, costly peruke that contrasted so sharply with the swarthiness of his face and the blackness of his brows and eyes.

"A quiet table so that we may take our supper. Preferably, overlooking the water." He winked. "The view, you know."

"Of course," the innkeeper said, nervously wringing his hands. "Right this way, if you please." He hastened to a far corner of the room and with a wave of his pudgy arm indicated a scarred, empty table overlooking the harbor. Already the shadows were lengthening and the sunlight waning, no longer bright and pale but now a deep, rusty orange sheeting the harbor and glinting from the stern windows of anchored ships.

Sam seated Maria, letting his fingers trail against the back

of her neck, her creamy shoulders. Then he strode around
the table to take his own chair and gazed out the grimy window. To a casual observer, he might've been absently watching the little fishing boats returning from sea, or admiring
the graceful, imposing profiles of the two warships whose
masts and spars towered over those of the other craft in the
harbor; but Maria was well aware of the keen, calculating
perusal he gave those two ships as he silently took in their
armament, their sea-readiness, and their strength, mulling
them over in his mind and committing the details to memory.
His gaze flickered back toward *Nefarious*, as innocent as a
sleeping wolf, and a satisfied smile eased the hard line of his
mouth.

"View, huh?" Maria teased, touching his arm. "You just
wanted to sit near the window so you could keep an eye on
the ship."

"Aye. Wouldn't want that skittish pack to take flight and
leave us here in this godforsaken town."

The innkeeper returned, tray in hand. With a flourish, he
set an ale quart of spiced, sweetened cider in front of Sam
and a cup of milk before Maria. This was followed by two
steaming plates piled high with food. Handing the man a
coin, Sam ignored his incredulous stare. It was more than
enough to pay for their supper.

"Why, th-thank you, sir," he said, beaming. And then
hastily, "Can I get you anything else?"

" 'Twill be all for now." Sam was already reaching for a
piece of thick, crusty bread slathered with fresh butter, his
gaze straying back to the window as the little man bustled
away. All was dark aboard the warships, which pleased, but
didn't surprise, him; their crews had no reason to become
suspicious about *Nefarious*. On the sloop, someone had hung
a lantern in the shrouds, its glow stretching rippling fingers
across the water toward him. He stared at that light, feeling
oddly at peace; after all these months, his plans would finally
come to pass. By tomorrow night the lads would be free. By
tomorrow night, the *Whydah*'s ghosts would be forever laid
to rest.

He glanced over at Maria. A candle spluttered in a pewter
base between them, and in its glow her face was exotically
beautiful, a study of fine planes and enchanting hollows. She

wasn't eating, merely pushing her food around with her fork. He eyed her the way a father might a child for not eating its vegetables. "Aren't ye hungry, lass?"

She looked up with an apologetic smile. "Yes, but my stomach's in knots." And as Sam frowned and began to set down his fork, she added hastily, "But it always gets like that when I'm nervous."

"Will you *please* stop your bloody worrying?" he asked, stabbing a potato with more fervor than was necessary. And then, at her crestfallen look, his tone became more gentle. He set down the fork, potato and all, and reached across the table to touch her cheek. "I'm sorry, princess. I guess I'm a bit on edge, too. But please, eat. You're far too thin, and I don't know when you'll get the chance to enjoy a decent meal again." He gave her his most ill-boding smile as she merely stared down at her plate. "And I wasn't joking, you know, when I said I'd force it down your throat if I had to."

He would, too. She picked up her spoon, trying to muster enough appetite to eat her Indian pudding. Had she not been so nervous, she would've found it delicious; now, it tasted like damp sawdust in her mouth. "I thought you said there's nothing to worry about."

"There isn't," he assured her, picking up his fork once more and attacking another potato. " 'Tis the thought of my men that's getting to me. Christ, I've been wracking my brain trying to figure out a way to get them out if Teach doesn't show up at our rendezvous point tomorrow." Agitatedly, he began to tap his fork against his plate, the ring of pewter against pewter mingling with the noise around them. Finally he threw the fork down. It hit the plate with a metallic clatter. "Oh, Maria. You should've seen them. Poor Baker, he used to be so damned arrogant I wanted to strangle him; now he just sits there staring at the floor. And Simon Van Vorst? He used to be a big bear of a man. Now, I can count every bone in his body. And if ye think that's bad, the poor lads have to sit there and listen to that insufferable Cotton Mather praying for their souls. God's teeth, if that isn't enough to do them in, nothing is. 'Twould've been better if they *had* died that night and gone to their maker than be forced to listen to his tirades!"

To Maria, there were worse things in the world than lis-

tening to a preacher, especially one as revered as Cotton
Mather. "I just hope no one recognized you," she said, pick
ing up her knife. "How about your men? Did they?" Sh
sawed halfheartedly at a piece of hot beef and put it in he
mouth. It, at least, woke up her appetite; she took anothe
bite.

"I don't think so. If they did, they didn't believe thei
eyes. To them, I'm as dead as your old neighbors believe m
to be. Nay, they've given up hope, Maria. All of them."

"So what will happen now?"

"We leave Boston tonight, on the outgoing tide. Tomorrow
we sail north and meet Teach off the Isles of Shoals. Hope
fully, he'll keep his word and show up. If not"—he sighed
then stabbed the last slice of beef with his fork—"then I d
this without him."

"Oh, Sam."

"Hush, Maria, and eat your potatoes. They're gettin
cold."

The wind had shifted by the time they finished their mea
and left the tavern. Wonderful sailing weather, but not ver
helpful for getting out of the harbor. Sam cursed and eye
the sloop in frustration.

"Now what?" Maria asked, her hand tucked within hi
elbow as they stood on the quay and listened to the wate
lapping against its thick posts.

Sam tugged thoughtfully at his clean but shadowed chin
The gesture seemed rather empty without the beard, and Ma
ria realized she missed the darkly handsome, slightly unscru
pulous look it had given him. But no "fancy lawyer"
would've sported such an atrocity, and such a thick, blac
one at that.

"I guess we spend the night in town," he muttered hope
lessly, "unless, of course, ye'd prefer to go back to th
sloop."

But Maria had grown rather fond of having solid groun
beneath her feet, even if it did reek of offal and other name
less scents. "Actually, I wouldn't mind staying here," sh
said, smoothing a wrinkle from his velvety sleeve. "But wha
about Teach? Don't you have to meet him tomorrow?"

"Aye, but we can sail first thing in the morning. The Isles are not that far away."

"And the sloop? Your men will be waiting for you."

"Good God, Maria, leave the worrying to me, will ye? I'll merely advise them that we'll weigh tomorrow instead. The lads'll be happy—'twill give them a chance for some shore leave."

A seaman was sitting on the quay, his pipe a tiny pinpoint of light in the thick, cloying darkness. Maria waited while Sam handed him a silver coin and a message to deliver to the trim little sloop sitting out in the harbor.

They found another inn, slightly more scrupulous than the first, and secured a room upstairs for the night. Sam closed the door, tore the peruke from his hair, and gave her a lazy smile of bold promise as he sat on the bed and tugged off his boots. No longer the stuffy, proper lawyer but the lawless rogue who'd won her heart, he went to her, swept her up in his arms as though she were a feather, and carried her to the big, sturdy bed that awaited them. And there they made love, passionately, giving all that they had to each other and receiving back tenfold.

The same wind that had kept *Nefarious* in the harbor the night before now drove her swiftly northward, filling her great sails and making them harden on booms and yards. On her decks her crew lounged, most of them, after a hard night of drinking and wenching, in the same sorry state that their captain had been following his tippling match with Teach.

But this morning Black Sam had a spring in his stride as he paced the quarterdeck, hands clasped behind his back, bare feet leaving wet prints on the crimson planking. With a fine, billowing shirt open to the waist, black breeches buckled at the knee, and a wicked-looking cutlass hanging from his belt, he was an impressive, charismatic figure, and there was not a man among them who had any misgivings about this venture with such a capable leader as Black Sam in command.

The crew was eager to reach their rendezvous point, but not so much in a hurry that they could pass up a small ketch off the coast of Marblehead. Finding her bottom full of rot, they sent the little vessel to the bottom, gave her fishy cargo to Cook to prepare for supper, and set her unhappy crew, who declined the offer to join them, adrift in a boat.

Of course, none of them—not the crew, nor Black Sam, who'd been against sinking the ketch but whose single opposing vote counted little when everyone else was for it, nor the woman watching from the quarterdeck—could've known that the ketch would be their undoing. But when James Ingols and the H.M.S. *Majestic* came upon the tiny, drifting craft two hours later, its occupants' testimonies were all they needed to condemn *Nefarious* as a pirate ship.

Majestic spread her great sails to the wind, and her master set a course that would take her north, where Captain Thorndike's *Porpoise* was already lying in wait for Teach at the Isle of Shoals, and where *Nefarious* had no doubt gone.

In the haze-enshrouded distance, they appeared first as tiny spots of land atop the blue ocean. Appledore, Malaga, and White Islands, and of course, Teach's favorite haunt, Star Island, whose township of Gosport was renowned as far away as Europe for its special fish-curing technique. Lonely outposts that had long been a haven for pirates, the isles were really nothing more than barren lumps of rock holding their breath above the collar of high tide.

Maria, standing at the forecastle rail absently rubbing Gunner's soft ears, prayed silently that the fearsome Teach would keep his word and be there waiting for them. *Please, God,* she thought, knowing that if he wasn't, Sam would turn the ship around and storm back to Boston to free the men on his own. *Please let him be there.* And although she strained her eyes to see into the distance, the islands were still too far away to pick out any details, let alone the raking masts of even a great ship.

Restlessly, she left the rail and made her way past the surplus spars stored in the ship's waist, the four-pounders waiting quietly in their carriages, and up the stairs to the quarterdeck. Silas West was there, sitting in the sun and patiently making notes in the book that he used to keep track of every man's share of booty. Phil Stewart leaned against one of his guns, explaining to young Johnnie some of the finer techniques of markmanship during heavy seas; and Sam sat in his precarious place upon the taffrail, a knife in one hand and an odd-shaped piece of wood in the other.

His hair was queued, hanging between his powerful shoulders and jauntily threaded with a fiery length of silk. As usual, a few dark locks had worked themselves loose, and the wind tumbled them over his brow, now furrowed in concentration. His earring, his cutlass, the dagger he wielded so carefully all glinted in the hot sunlight, and so intent was he on his work that he didn't notice her approach.

"What are you doing, Sam?"

He started, winced, and let out a curse before shoving his thumb into his mouth. "Damn it, lass, must ye be so quiet?" he asked, trying to hide the piece of wood he'd been working on behind his back.

"I'm sorry." Maria reached behind him and pulled his arm forward. His fist was curled over the wood, hiding it. One by one, she pried each finger away. First his thumb, and beneath it she saw what looked like a fin; then his fore, middle, and ring fingers, and finally his little one. Smooth sides, a gracefully leaping form. He looked up, a relenting smile brightening his dark face. In his palm leaped a playful, sleek dolphin.

He held it out to her. "For you, princess. It was to be a surprise, but . . ."

"Oh, Sam . . . 'tis beautiful!" With girlish excitement, she studied it briefly before hugging it to her breast. Then she flung her arms around his neck, nearly knocking him off the rail and into the sea below, pulled his head down, and buried her face against his shoulder. "I didn't know you could carve!"

"I can't," he said, grinning and holding up a thumb which bore, along with the slash he'd just given himself, a fine checkerboard of lines that still oozed blood.

"Deck there! Sloop in the lee o' Star Island!"

Instantly alert, Sam jumped down from his precarious perch and strode smartly to the weather rail. "That'll be Teach and the *Revenge*," he said, pulling out his glass.

They were now close enough to see the one lone mast poking up beyond the sun-washed granite. Grinning, Sam leaned his elbows against the rail and trained his glass on it.

Canvas was dropping from its topsail yard. His smile faded to a frown. Something wasn't right.

"Bring her in a little closer, Flanagan," he called, never moving the glass.

Nefarious responded, heeling slightly and sending thousands of bubbles dancing in her gurgling wake. Maria clutched the little dolphin, as tense as the others as they crowded the rail beside their intent captain. Suddenly he tore the glass from his eye, shoved it into Maria's hand, and was pounding across the deck before the lookout could even report that another sail had appeared off their starboard quarter.

"Damn your eyes, Gillespie!" he roared, as the hidden ship detached itself from behind the island for all to see. "That's not Teach! *It's a bloody naval sloop!*"

Chapter 26

> *Ye shallow Censures! sometimes, see ye not,*
> *In greatest perils some men pleasant be?*
> *Where Fame by death is only to be got,*
> *They resolute! So stands the case with me.*

> DRAYTON

With a naval sloop rounding the headland toward them, another ship—a big one, judging by the amount of sail filling the sky—closing rapidly astern, the mainland in their lee, and a stiff breeze whipping out of the east, Sam wasted no time in making a decision. He vaulted the companionway and raced forward, his voice ringing out from forecastle to poop. "All hands make sail! If it's a chase they want, then damn it, 'tis a chase they'll get! No bloody hounds are going to catch this fox!"

Maria had been biting her lip so hard it was numb. Clutching the rail with white-knuckled hands, she glanced behind them. Wind blew her hair straight out toward the purple-green line of the mainland. Her heart plummeted to her toes and bounced back to her breast in a way that left her feeling sick with apprehension. Not three miles astern of them was the great, towering pyramid of sails that the lookout had sighted, and it was coming on with alarming speed.

"Hands to the sheets! Alter course, Mr. Flanagan, north-northeast! Let's get her out to sea before those bastards are close enough to bring their guns to bear!"

The naval sloop would lose valuable time in coming about if she wanted to catch them. The pirate crew sprang to action. Men leaped into shrouds, swarmed up the ratlines, raced out along the topyards. Maria squeezed her eyes shut as the on-coming bow of the other sloop bore down on them directly off their larboard beam. A puff of smoke burst from her chaser at the same moment a reverberating boom of cannon fire rolled across the water. The shot hissed into the ocean a hundred feet off their starboard bow.

"Heave to, in the name of the king!"

Brandishing his cutlass, Sam leaped atop the gunwale and clung there with bare toes. "By the bloody Christ I will! Damn your king and you along with him! Larboard gallery, load up with grape and fire as she bears . . . now!"

One by one *Nefarious*'s guns belted out a deafening broadside. Flanagan swung the tiller, the sloop heeled sharply, and the enemy's bow swept past their larboard quarter. Sam held his breath, waiting, but they had not anticipated his dash toward the open sea, and the return broadside, when it came, plunged harmlessly into *Nefarious*'s swirling wake. A wild cheer went up from the pirate crew.

"Ye fooled 'im, Cap'n!" Stripes shouted, hopping up and down and waving his cutlass at the enemy's stern, now just a hazy image through the cloud of choking, acrid smoke. But her decks were alive, her shrouds crawling with dark figures as her crew tried frantically to wear ship and catch the fleeing *Nefarious*. Sam was anything but confident.

"I've bought precious little time, Stripes," he said calmly, raising his glass to study the distant frigate. Their broadside hadn't done much damage to the naval sloop—a few tattered holes in her jibs, some splintered railing, and that was about all. He swore under his breath. "Let's just hope we can outsail her. That frigate yonder, I'm not concerned with. 'Tis not a square-rigger's wind. But the sloop. . . ."

"D' ye think we might've 'ad a better chance of losin' 'em closer t' shore?" Stripes asked. "We could hide among the coves where they can't reach us."

Sam's reply was meant for both Stripes and the circle of men who gathered around to glean assurance from their calm, cool-as-ice captain. "It is precisely those coves that I have no wish to be cornered into. There are two of them, one of us. If they trap us between the mainland and these islands— let alone themselves—they'll blast us to kindling wood."

Realizing the wisdom of his captain's words, Stripes glanced among his peers, echoing the question that stood in their eyes. "So what're we gonna do, then?"

Sam turned and gave them all a lazy grin that made them feel as though the answer should've been quite obvious. It was a simple gesture, really, but it went far to bolster the men's confidence. "Why, go to Maine of course, lad. And once we get there, *then* we'll lose them among the isles and coves." He turned to his quartermaster. "Bring out the rum, Mr. West. I want some good, stiff fire running in the lads' veins should it come down to a fight."

Once more, Sam raised his glass and studied the bulging sails of the pursuing frigate. *Nefarious*'s sudden maneuver had forced the big ship to change tack. Sam hoped to lose her quickly; a square-rigger, unlike a sloop, was not at her best sailing close-hauled, and if the frigate had any prayer of catching them she'd have to do just that. If he could only put enough distance between *Nefarious* and the frigate, they'd be able to slip among the hundreds of islands that peppered the waters off the Maine coast by nightfall.

But nightfall was still a good eight hours away.

He uttered a silent curse. It had been a trap, of that he was sure. But how had his plans become known? Had someone recognized him in Boston? Had one of his men downed too much tipple and spilled his guts to the wrong listener? Or had the two ships set a trap to capture Teach? And speaking of Teach, where the bloody hell *was* he?

The ship plunged and rose beneath the toes he'd curled over the gunwale, but his balance was faultless, his mind oblivious to the sea that churned blue and green and white far beneath him. He studied his pursuers. The sloop had finished wearing, had swung her jib-boom toward them, and was now gaining speed. *Damn!* He resisted the urge to hurl the glass to the deck; such a show of temper and loss of control wouldn't do. But *how?* his mind screamed. *How the bloody hell had his intentions become known?*

Christ, did it matter? They had two of the king's ships on their tail and his only concern at the moment must be to outsail, outwit, and, if it came down to it, outfight them. He desperately hoped it wouldn't. *Nefarious* could handle the naval sloop well enough, but beneath the guns of a fifth-rate warship she'd be blown to bits.

He sensed a presence beneath and behind him. Distractedly, without lowering the glass, he snapped, "What is it?"

"Sam?"

The glass came down in an instant. "What the bloody hell are you doing up here? God's teeth, I *knew* I should've put you ashore at Provincetown! Get below, Maria, *now.*"

But her eyes were huge, her face chalky, her voice little more than a whisper. She made no move to obey him. "Will they catch us, do you think?"

He sighed. He might as well give orders to Gunner for all the good it did him. "Of course not," he replied offhandedly, hoping his casual tone would allay her fears. "What do ye think this is, a rowboat? Christ, let them damn well try!" But inside, he felt anything but confident. They were losing the frigate, but it was no trick of the eye that the sloop was gaining on them. And Maria? He had enough things to worry about without her presence topside adding to them.

Not wanting to have her forcibly removed from the quarterdeck, he tried another tack. "Why don't you go below and tidy up the sick bay? 'Twill keep you out of trouble for a bit."

"Sam," she said quietly, hooking a hand around his bare ankle and tilting her head back to look up at him. She felt the tendons and muscles of his foot jumping as he held his precarious balance. His toes were wet with spray, his skin cold to the touch. "You don't fool me a bit. I'm not blind, you know, nor am I deaf. I heard Stripes talking to West. The sloop is gaining, isn't she? And you want me to prepare the sick bay for the wounded . . . in case we have to fight."

He opened his mouth to reply, but at that moment Johnnie, breathless, pounded up in time to hear her last words. "Fight? Do you really think we'll get to trade broadsides with 'em, Cap'n?"

"I should hope not, lad, and so should you. But if it comes down to it, we ought to be ready, eh? You can start by bringing shot up from the locker and making sure there are at least two buckets of seawater beside each gun." His steady gaze remained on the two pursuing ships. "And when you've finished, I want you to report to Mr. Stewart. His gun captains will need powder, shot, sponges, and rammers at the ready." For once there was no fatherly tone in his voice; he was addressing the boy as a crew member and expected him to behave as one.

Johnnie touched his fingers to his temple. "Aye, sir!" And then he was off and running, Gunner barking at his heels.

Maria looked up at Sam, at the crimson silk fluttering from his braided queue, at the glossy black locks blowing against his brow and the vastness of the cerulean sky. Suddenly he stiffened, and she felt the muscles of his foot go rigid. Her gaze swept to the sloop. She wasn't imagining it—it *was* gaining. And as she stared, the pennant licking from its masthead changed direction. The wind was shifting.

"Oh, bloody *hell!*" Sam leaped down from the gunwale, aware that every face was turned toward him—some with fear, some with apprehension, some with excitement—for now a battle looked inevitable. With the wind dead astern, they could very well flee out to sea, but it was a prime wind for the frigate, and with her superior amount of sail she'd run them down in no time. And the sloop was so damned close he could read her name: *Porpoise.*

Resolutely, briskly, he strode to the mast, scabbard slapping his black-clad thigh. The men were already gathering. Some had snatched up cutlasses, pistols, and boarding axes. Phil Stewart was silently caressing the stock of his blunderbuss, a preoccupied, eager half-smile splitting his dark face. Flanagan peered at them from his place at the helm, his lion's mane whipping madly in the wind. Silas West had removed the scarf from his balding head, folded it with a sort of meticulous care that bordered on the absurd, and was now tying t around his ears to protect them from the gunfire that would soon shatter the peaceful stillness of the early afternoon.

They whispered among themselves, wondering how Black Sam was going to get them out of this one. Some shuffled their feet nervously. Some tried to steal courage from their grog. But all fidgeted with their sword hilts and axe handles, and every gaze was fastened upon their captain. He would not let them down. He was Black Sam, the free prince of the seas, and in his defiant, dark eyes, there was not the barest trace of fear.

"Well, lads, looks like we might get our feathers singed, eh?" Whispers ceased and instantly it was quiet. Only the sigh of wind through the rigging and the splash of water at the bow could be heard. Hands clasped behind his back, Sam began to walk a slow circle around them. Sunlight glinted off the gold at his ear, the coin at his chest, the emerald on his finger. He glanced beyond them to the enemy, silently noting that the frigate was already overtaking *Porpoise* in her haste to catch them. *Not good,* he thought. *Not good at all.* Skillfully, he masked his apprehension behind a carefree smile, a self-assured stride.

"Turn around, lads, and have a good, long look at them." He pointed his cutlass toward the bulging, sun-dappled sails that doggedly pursued them. "His Majesty's ships. Pretty damned frightening, aren't they? All those guns, the marines in their tops, even their figurehead fashioned as a snarling lion to induce fear. Why, I'd say it's supposed to symbolize the might of bloody England, eh? No, don't look at me, lads, look at *them.* At their guns, their sails, their officers. Look long, and look *hard.* And now, I want you to picture the men upon those decks, beneath those sails, and at those guns. Think of how their backs've been laid open with the cat, as many of yours have been; think of keelhauling and shortened rations, of punishments, abuse, mutinies, and desertions. Nasty treatment. Certainly doesn't make for a loyal, tight company now, does it?" He chuckled cunningly, black eyes flashing in his swarthy face. "Ah, yes, those ships make a glorious sight, don't they? But remember, lads, a ship is only as fine as the men who sail her!"

A thrill tore through Maria at his stirring words. Pride threatened to burst her heart. Memories flashed to mind. . . .

Of a long-ago visitor to Eastham, of persuasive speeches and talk of Spanish gold. . . . Of a pirate, his body weak and battered but his charisma intact enough to unite a crew of young malcontents and turn them into a wolf pack. Always, Sam had been able to lead men, to persuade them to do his bidding. And today would be the ultimate test of that skill, for if they could not, did not, follow him, death would be waiting. At the bottom of the sea, at the end of a noose, it didn't matter where, but it would be there.

"Aye . . . mutineers, press-gangs, would-be deserters," he was saying, eyes gleaming as he pulled the ornate pistols that Paul Williams had given him from the bright gold sash about his waist. Someone tossed him a fine length of silk, and calmly, not taking his eyes from their frightened faces as he strode with princely hauteur among them, he tied a pistol in each end and slung it around his neck so the dangling weapons could be easily reached. "A surly pack of dogs who've not been treated fairly. *That* is the nature of your enemy! Think about it, lads—think of those men and then think of *your* shipmates." He foled his arms across his chest and raked the lot of them with challenging eyes. "I want each and every one of you to take a good look around you. Look at the man who will stand beside you today. Touch your rum cup to his, shake his hand. You will depend upon each other, but you will be depending upon the very best there is. Mutineers, deserters, murderers, aye! Criminals and outlaws, aye, the finest the world has to offer! Let's show 'em what we're made of, lads!" His cutlass slashed down to chop into the rail. "Damn them, *let's show them we're not to be trifled with!*"

The decks came alive. "Three cheers for Black Sam!"

"Long live the Free Prince of the Seas!"

"Huzzah! Huzzah!"

Sam let them whoop and holler and throw their hats into the air for a moment, realizing they needed an outlet for their nervous energy. "Consider this *practice* for our raid on Boston," he declared, leaping to the gunwales once more. "And now, let's see how fast we can get this little lady ready for battle! Sand the decks. Drape the powder kegs with wet canvas, make sure the galley fire is out." Barefoot and balanced atop the narrow gunwale, he began to pace, his words coming

aster in his enthusiasm. ''I want the best marksmen above
vith muskets and grenades; take out the officers first, if ye can.
Those of ye who aren't handling sail will man the guns. That
ncludes the swivels, too.'' He indicated the deadly, minia-
ure cannon mounted at the bulwarks in iron stirrups. ''Hoist
he boat and tow it; we don't need excess splinters of wood
lying about deck once they start firing. And I want chains
igged from the yards to replace the hemp. 'Twouldn't do to
ave spars crashing down on deck and taking out our own
company, now, would it?''

Whooping, shouting, yelling, they spread out in all directions. Sam watched them for a moment, and then he heard a
stiff, crackling noise from high above. He glanced skyward
and smiled. Someone had hoisted the Jolly Roger. Win or
lose, *Nefarious* would be defiant until the end.

''I don't *want* to go below,'' Maria said firmly, chin raised
and eyes spitting defiance as she met Sam's dark, impatient
gaze. ''I am not a child, to be ordered about!''

''You are a woman, and as such your place is not on deck
during a fight! *Stripes!*'' The lieutenant came running, his
curiosity giving way to a knowing smirk as he realized that
Black Sam was, as usual, having problems with his most
difficult crew member. ''Take Maria below, please, and lock
her in my cabin.'' He glanced over the top of her sunny head,
at the taut, oncoming sails of the frigate. *''Now.''*

''But Sam, *please!* I want to stay here with you!'' She
looked up, eyes desperate, fingers like claws around his bare
ankle. ''I won't be in the way, I promise! You can even give
me a flintlock—I know how to shoot one. Please, Sam! I
want to be by your side!''

''What, and run the risk of having ye shot? 'Tis out of the
question, lass.'' Her pale hand was squeezing and clutching
the little dolphin as though to draw comfort from it, and
immediately Sam softened his harsh tone, but he did not re-
lent. Jumping down to the deck, he bent his head to hers. He
longed to sweep her into his arms and crush her to him, but
for the sake of his crew he did not. Instead, he placed both
brown, callused hands beneath her pale jaw, stroked her soft
cheeks with his thumbs, and raising her head so that her

pleading eyes met his, kissed her long and hard. Her eyes closed over a sheen of tears. It took every ounce of his will power to break the kiss and gently set her away from him. "Now get below, Maria," he said quietly. "Battle is not a pretty sight."

With a cry, she threw herself into his arms, hugging him shamelessly, pressing herself against him to imprint the feel of his hard, masculine body against her soft, pliant one forever. His arms closed fiercely around her; she felt the press of his scabbard against her thigh. He held her for a long moment. Then gently, he set her away, turned, and stared resolutely out to sea once more, steeling himself against her pleas. Maria's throat constricted and tears scalded her eyes and nose as she allowed Stripes to take her elbow. *Oh, Sam,* she thought. The world was crumbling to pieces around her. She took one last, searching look at him, committing the sight of him forever to memory: resplendent and commanding, proud and fearless, cutlass at one hip, dagger at the other, and bare feet planted firmly to the blood-red, sanded decks.

"I love you," she whispered, lips trembling. "Oh God, I love you." He turned then, and she saw her own heart reflected in the mirror of his black eyes. And then Stripes was pulling on her arm and guiding her below, just as the first shots from the frigate's bow chasers came screaming overhead.

Her anxious, worried face haunted him, her pleading eyes could not be forgotten. He could still taste her sweet kiss and feel the press of her body against his own. More than anything in the world he longed to go below and comfort her, to take her in his arms and assure her that things would be all right. But he couldn't. So instead, he sat atop the taffrail where he had an unhampered view of his ship, his men, and the vessel that was sweeping in off their quarter.

Porpoise. He'd heard of her and her captain, but that didn't faze him. They would've heard of him too—if not under his real name, then that of Captain Black. Were they afraid of him? Did they feel the same nervous excitement his men did? And did their captain have a woman who was dearer to him

...an life itself? He forced the image of Maria from his mind. *Don't think of her,* he thought. *Not now.*

His finger tightened around the hilt of his cutlass. Slowly, ...e raised his arm. *Porpoise* was almost within range. Phil ...tewart strode among his gun captains, checking each iron ...onster and awaiting Sam's signal to fire.

Another moment. . . . *Porpoise's* gun ports were opening ...ow, cannon rumbling across angled decks as they were run ...ut. "Get ready, lads!" he called. "The wind gauge is ours, ...t's use it to our advantage!"

The wind strengthened. *Nefarious* heeled sharply, guns ...ointing toward the sea; but that same wind also brought a ...ealthy strip of *Porpoise's* vulnerable, tallowed belly free of ...he waves.

"Stand by on the starboard guns!" Sam raised the heavy ...utlass still higher. "A little closer, lads. I don't want to ...ripple her, I want to *sink* her! Enough holes below the wa...erline and it can be done!"

His arm swept down. Thunder split the air, deafening him ...nd rocking *Nefarious* like a child's toy in a tin tub. With ...ecks shuddering and trembling, she righted herself as the ...wesome echo rolled across the water and smoke billowed ...ownwind, cloaking *Porpoise* in a thick, choking blackness ...nd the acrid stink of gunpowder. The enemy's guns an...wered. Tongues of flame stabbed through that dense cloud, ...nd a murderous hail of iron went shrieking overhead to slam ...nto sails, rigging, and spars.

Screams, cries, and in hideous slow motion, a mangled ...orpse tumbled from the topsail yard, catching upon a back...tay, hanging for a moment, and then plunging downward to ...it the deck with a horrible, sickening thud. Debris rained ...own: pieces of sail, chain, and deadly wooden blocks trail...ng pieces of singed hemp. Calmly shielding his face and ...ead, Sam looked up to survey the damage. Ragged holes ...otted the clewed-up canvas and the topmast was dangling ...recariously. They'd taken a bad hit.

"Hold tight, lass," he said softly, and Silas West, standing ...utifully beside him, wondered if Black Sam's words of en...ouragement were for the beauty in his cabin or for the lovely, ...ancing sloop herself. "Just hold tight, a bit longer. . . ."

Suddenly the pirates began cheering. The smoke was

clearing and Sam saw, as she sheared off, that *Porpoise* wa
wounded. Great jagged holes and ragged planking marke
the spots where *Nefarious*'s broadside had found its mark
some at the waterline, a few above it, and most, thank God
below it.

"Nice work, lads! She's taking on water! Now, sponge ou
and let's see ye do it again!"

Porpoise wore away from the wind, with her vulnerabl
stern swinging toward them. Sam counted the seconds a
Flanagan brought *Nefarious* in position to deliver anothe
deadly broadside. This one had to be lethal. He had to crippl
her enough to put her out of action, and then use every re
source he had to escape the frigate, now a deadly, threatenin
menace closing in off their stern. He paced the quarterdeck
checking the aim of each gun; he heard the pop of musketfir
high above, tasted the thick pungency of gunpowder. A par
of his mind—the necessary part—worked swiftly to plot thei
next move, to ponder the best strategy to get them out of thi
alive; but another part was on Maria. If only the legend
about her were true. He'd sell his soul for a witch's help righ
about now.

By the gods, princess, I'll not let ye down!

Leaping over fallen debris, he reached the larboard bul
warks and peered out over the gunwale between two smokin
guns. Stewart's men awaited his signal; *Porpoise* loomed un
protected and in range. He raised his arm, the muscles stand
ing out in relief, the cutlass catching beams of sunlight on it
tip and spilling them in a dazzling display; then his arm cam
down, and thunder rocked the elements as *Nefarious* loosee
her deadly broadside. A chorus of agonized, horrible scream
rose from the enemy sloop.

The smoke cleared. Out of control, *Porpoise*, her rudde
blown to splinters, fell away with the thick black smoke tha
cloaked her. Sam let out a whoop of triumph. One down
one to go. The pirate crew went wild.

"Hot work, lads!" he cried, black eyes dancing with tri
umph. "Damned hot work! Mr. Stewart! Load up again
Pepper them with a broadside as we pass and then hole he
with the chasers as a final good-bye!"

Still grinning, he ripped his gaze from the sloop and turnee

bilant eyes toward his own decks. And saw the frigate just
f their starboard beam.

With *Porpoise* licking her wounds and out of the fight, and
open but unattainable sea just beyond the towering sails
the frigate, Sam had no choice but to run *Nefarious* close
the wild, rocky shore where their only hope of survival
w lay among the shallow coves and inlets.

Her little four-pounders were all but useless against the
ight of the frigate's big guns. She was taking a beating. Her
pmast hung by its stays, the pennant drooping sadly against
e remains of her once-proud topsail. Bodies lay sprawled
on decks that were no longer colored with paint but with
e gore and blood that washed across them with every pitch
d roll of the sloop.

Sam's face was grim, his mouth hard. There were no little
ugh lines crinkling the corners of his dark eyes now. He
atched the frigate coming about, preparing to dump her
urderous broadside into them once again. If only he had
om to maneuver, a place to hide. He peered up at the torn,
ot-blackened sails. Canvas had been reduced to jib and a
ewed-up foresail for easy handling of the ship, and these
d been watered down in the hopes of preventing fire. But
en if they'd had every sail set, even if their topmast wasn't
nging uselessly by threads, they'd be doomed—for the wind
d betrayed them, become their worst enemy.

Now, he watched the shore easing closer and closer off
eir larboard beam. Wild, rocky coast, where only dense
ands of fir and pine could grow, where gulls stood on sea-
orn granite and watched the battle with indifference. The
ater would be shallow there; too shallow for the frigate's
ep draft, but not for *Nefarious*.

He had to act now, before *Majestic* completed her stately
rn and slammed another volley of iron into *Nefarious*'s hull,
r rigging, her tattered sails. He had to bring her in close
shore, as close as he possibly could, closer, maybe, than
dared. Beneath the keel, colors sparkled . . . indigo . . .
ep blue . . . dark green. . . .

He looked up. The frigate was bearing down on them now,
e beakhead growing larger and larger. Sam could see the

bared and snarling teeth of the figurehead, with its golde
paws poised on a shield of the royal arms.

The lion, rushing in for the kill.

"Here she comes, lads!" The foam at her stern creste
Her great sails stamped out the sun. Her black shadow fe
across *Nefarious*'s decks like an executioner's axe. "Read
on the starboard battery! Give it all ye got, lads! *Now!*"

And they did. Loaded with scrap iron, broken wine bo
tles, and every possible projectile they could find, the gur
thundered inboard and shook the very decks beneath Sam
bare feet. An unholy scream of flying metal rent the air lik
a legion of demons straight from Hell. Smoke clogged hi
vision. He brushed at his stinging eyes, peered through th
haze. Holes peppered the frigate's spritsail, and what was le
of that arrogant figurehead—symbol of the might of Er
gland—was exploding out over the water in beautiful, slo
motion. Stays snapped, rigging was blasted away, and th
foremast was shaking wildly, but did not topple. *Christ, h
thought, *it didn't topple!*

Undaunted, enraged, the frigate came on.

"Starboard your helm, Flanagan!" he barked.

Frantically, the helmsman obeyed. *Nefarious* heele
sharply, making for the safety of the shore. The frigate heele
too, almost dragging the tips of her yards in the waves. Sh
righted, running parallel to them now, every one of thos
terrible, black cannon mouths yawning at them from fore
castle to poop.

"Run her close to shore, Flanagan! As close as you dare
For God's sake, man, *now!*"

A thunderous explosion rent the air as the frigate belche
her broadside. Guns toppled, falling on screaming men an
silencing them beneath thousands of pounds of red-hot iror
Limbs were severed, and the scuppers frothed with seawate
and blood. *Nefarious* wept with each ball that slammed int
her sleek hull, shuddered as her yards came crashing to he
bloodstained decks, but never faltered in her desperate ru
toward shore.

"Flanagan!" Sam leaped atop the gunwale, wildly wavin
his cutlass. "Not that close, damn you!"

But it was too late. With a hollow, sickening boom, th
keel crashed against submerged granite, rocking the mas

snapping stays, throwing men off their feet and sending them toppling over the side. The impact flung Sam from the gunwale, and he saw stars as his shoulder crashed hard against the carriage of a gun. He fell heavily to the deck, the sound of splintering wood ringing in his ears as the mainsail's huge gaff broke free, dragging the sail and a writhing network of lines down with it. And still *Nefarious*'s great speed carried her forward, at last gaining her open water once more. But her spine had been broken. She staggered, limping, her beautiful mainsail and gaff trailing in her dying wake like a broken wing.

Dazed, Sam picked himself up. "Damn you, Flanagan! What the hell . . ."

The reprimand died on his lips; Flanagan lay slumped over the tiller, his jaw and most of his neck blown away by the frigate's last broadside.

They were doomed. *Christ,* he thought numbly. *Oh God, Maria!* He hit the deck at a dead run, barely breaking stride to yank a whimpering, sobbing Johnnie to his feet and hurl him over the gunwales to safety. He sent a protesting Stripes the way of the boy, sent his crew diving over the side with urgent threats of his cutlass. And as he tripped over a cowering white body and almost went sprawling, he gathered the dog in his arms and flung him to safety, too.

A ball whizzed past his ear, so close that its wind stirred his hair, but he never stopped in his mad rush toward the cabin. Another shot rang out. White-hot pain lanced up his leg. He stumbled, fell. And then, with a savage curse, he picked himself up, raised his cutlass, and turned to face the enemy as the first grappling hooks came snaking across the bulwarks and a swarm of British seamen leaped onto *Nefarious*'s bloodstained decks.

Chapter 27

Yet I strode on austere;
No hope could have no fear.

THOMSON

"Sam! Sam, let me out!" Maria beat her fists against the door until they were raw and numb. "For the love of God, someone, *please* let me out!"

It was futile. No one was coming for her. She clutched the little dolphin to her chest in an unconscious, desperate attempt to draw its maker's strength from it and slid, sobbing, the length of the door. The floor planking was hard beneath her knees; prayerlike, her head fell forward over her clasped hands. Tears raced between her knotted fingers and trickled down her arms. Thick, golden hair spilled over her eyes, and 'twas fortunate for her she'd left it unbound, for it was the only thing that saved her face a moment later when thunder rent the air, the stern windows imploded on a blast of a dragon's breath, and giltwork, burning wood chips, and needles of glass shot through the cabin, settling to the floor in a tinkling storm.

Screaming, Maria sprang to her feet, gaining three steps before the floor rocked violently beneath her and flung her to her knees. From somewhere in the depths of the ship came a horrible, ripping crash, and then the sickening roar of wood giving way.

Gasping for breath, she lurched to her feet, squeezing the little dolphin so hard its fins bit into her palm. A thick, blinding cloud of smoke pushed through the yawning hole where the windows had been. *Sam!* Wild-eyed, she beat against the door with renewed vigor, screaming at the top of her lungs. Why didn't he come for her? Why had the defiant report of

Nefarious's guns ceased? And why didn't she hear his voice anymore, rallying his men, spurring them on?

Realization hit her hard between the shoulders, kicking the breath from her lungs and leaving her reeling and gasping for air. He hadn't come for her because . . . because he was . . .

She couldn't say it.

Dead.

She tore across the cabin, wood chips and glass flying from her hair and skirts. Like the hand of some angry deity the blast had swept the desk clean; a still-quivering pair of dividers was impaled in the bulkhead, and charts, dripping ink, and navigational instruments were strewn the length of the room. *Dead. . . . Dead. . . . Dead. . . . No!!!* She ripped open the desk drawer, sobbing, her hands shaking so badly she could barely get her fingers around the emerald-studded hilt of Sam's favorite dagger.

She'd never know what dreadful premonition made her freeze and whip her head around to stare, trancelike, beyond that gaping hole where the windows had been. The sloop was drifting helplessly, the scene before her eyes changing; huge boulders of granite loomed into view, then slid out of sight. A dark, terrible shadow fell across the water, and a second later the frigate's elaborate, shattered beakhead, glistening planking, and a long, terrible row of guns filed past her view, one by one, extinguishing the sunlight and filling up every inch of space beyond that ragged hole.

Sobbing in raw terror, she turned and clawed her way back through eye-burning smoke to the door. Coughing, choking, crying, she found the crack that separated it from the bulkhead, shoved the dagger into it, and sawed desperately at the leather hinges.

The cabin grew darker.

Above, a last swivel barked. "Open up, damn you!" she screamed, her arm moving furiously now, hair whipping her face. The knife plunged through the last tongue of leather. With a cry of terrified hope Maria raised her foot, kicked the door open, and with the dagger in one fist, the little dolphin in the other, pounded from the cabin without a backwards glance.

* * *

She came to an abrupt stop, blinking in the sunlight and staring numbly at the carnage that surrounded her. The deck looked like it had been smashed by the fist of an angry god. Corpses lay everywhere, some crushed beneath overturned cannon, others so torn and mutilated they were beyond recognition. One man dangled by his foot from the shrouds, blood dripping from his lifeless fingers and spattering upon the still-smoking barrel of an upended four-pounder. Blood. Rivers of it raced across cluttered, listing planking, frothed with seawater in the scuppers, poured like rivers into the ocean. The iron-sweet stench of it mingled with gunpowder, so thick and cloying that even the fresh sea air couldn't remove it. Maria clutched her throat, swallowing hard to quell the nausea. She looked up. The foresail yard hung by a single chain, swinging perilously amid a cloud of shot-up, fluttering sail that was blackened with soot. And beneath her feet came the deadly whooshing roar of water pouring into the hull.

A trembling started in her heart. It radiated in all directions, flooding to her toes, wrapping chilly fingers around her throat, and dumping ice water down her spine.

The decks were silent. Maria pressed the little dolphin to her heart, too numbed, too dazed, to feel the pain of its wooden flukes. She saw the titan hull of the frigate snugged up against *Nefarious*, saw its towering masts climbing through the smoke that drifted lazily in the wind.

And then she heard the clang of steel against steel.

She knew it was him before her feet were even in motion. Leaping piles of debris, she raced past fallen guns, vaulted the steps to the quarterdeck, and burst through the ring of British seamen. And it *was* him, fighting for his life with a desperate intensity that was beautiful, yet terrible to watch.

He moved with the fluid grace of a dancer, fought with the brutal strength of a seaman. Chopping, hacking, lashing out here, punching there, and wielding the heavy cutlass with savage purpose. This was no gentleman's art; this was survival. Sam's brow was beaded with sweat; the muscles stood out on his arms. Parry, thrust, slash. His bare foot flashed out, caught a seaman in the gut who rushed in from behind. The man went sprawling and another moved in to take his place. Sam's cutlass thwacked against the tar's ribs, sent him screaming to the deck in a spray of blood. Powerful chest heaving, Sam raised the weapon for the final blow.

A lieutenant jerked up his pistol.

"Don't shoot him!" barked the frigate's captain. "I want him taken alive! Plead quarter, pirate! Damn you, plead quarter!"

Sam's eyes were glittering, proudly defiant. "Never! I'll taste the fires of Hell before I strike to you, tyrant!" And then his cutlass flashed down in a vicious arc.

The pistol went off, the cutlass missed the seaman's rolling form by a hairsbreadth, and the ball plowed a groove in the railing three feet behind Sam's shoulder. Maria's enraged scream rent the air. This time they noticed her—and so did he.

The briefest flicker of despair in those intrepid eyes, a split second of hesitation, and then the cutlass was singing with renewed, savage fervor as he fought not only for his life, but hers. Screaming, Maria lunged toward him.

"Jump, Sam! For God's sake, *jump!*"

Her body slammed into his hard, unyielding one in a desperate attempt to knock him off his feet and send him toppling over the rail to the only chance they had. He staggered under the impact, one arm flashing out to regain his balance, but like a stalwart oak in a gentle breeze, didn't go down. The seamen rushed in; steel glinted above her head and blood spilled from Sam's forearm. And then rough hands were around her wrists, hauling her to her feet and dragging her, kicking, fighting, and screaming, away from him.

The dagger. Blindly, she swung it with all of her strength. Soft resistance as it entered flesh. A man's howl of pain ringing through her head, warm wetness flooding over her fingers. And then a hand cracked hard against her jaw, rocking her vision and hurling her to her knees.

Stunned, she saw only a flash of black and white and crimson, a glint of gold and steel as Sam, bellowing in rage, broke loose from those who restrained him and lunged at her captor with cutlass raised. Something cold and hard jabbed against her temple, and from above her head she heard a voice, calm and controlled with subdued triumph.

Sam stopped short, chest heaving, eyes wild, the cutlass,   ·

by a supreme effort of control and skill on his part, slamming up against empty air.

"Go ahead," the voice taunted. "Do it and she's a dead woman."

A hundred emotions flickered in those black eyes before defeat finally brought to them an agony that physical pain could never have achieved. Maria saw his chest rise and fall in a deep, steadying breath as he waged an inner battle for control. And then, slowly, his big, seaman's arm lowered in defeat.

Maria's throat worked, and bitter tears seared her nose, her eyes, her soul. She tried to speak but her voice stuck in her throat like sand. She struggled against her captor's grasp, tears spilling down her cheeks. "Sam—" she got out. "Oh, Sam."

His black gaze caressed her face as though memorizing its every detail. "Ah, princess. . . . I love ye," he said softly. He took a step forward; then another. Someone made a grab for him, moving too fast, and with no warning and lightning speed, Sam's elbow came back to slam brutally into ribs.

"Stop him!"

Amid frantic shouts, her own screams rang through her head. Maria saw it all in slow motion. . . . The blur of movement, the flash of sunlight against a pistol's brass buttcap as the lieutenant's arm came up, bold challenge in Sam's eyes as he spun around—too late. The butt of the pistol slammed down on the back of Sam's head with a terrible, thunking sound like that of an axe splitting wood, wiping away pride, wiping away consciousness even, as those dark eyes rolled up and his legs folded beneath him. The cutlass slid from his limp fingers, clattering to the deck an instant before his big body fell sprawling atop it.

For a moment Maria could only stare in dumbstruck horror; then she was screaming, clawing, beating at flesh in a frenzied, desperate attempt to free herself. Breaking loose, she stumbled toward him, falling to her knees and sobbing as she cradled his still body in her arms. She pressed her cheek to his pale one, buried her face in his glossy black hair. The red silk of his queue fluttered weakly against her lips. His arm was limp as seaweed, the heavy muscles lying flaccid, and where that arm pressed against her ribs she felt his lifeblood flowing warmly. Silently.

She looked up, her eyes cold, chilling, and glittering with malice as they fastened upon the lieutenant. The dagger was still in her hand. Slowly, she rose, and the Sea Witch's smile was one that no man aboard the *Majestic* would ever forget as she drew back her arm for the lethal throw.

An iron hand closed about her wrist. Her head snapped up. And then that mild, controlled voice came once more. "You must be Maria Hallett," the man said pleasantly. "Allow me to introduce myself." The fingers tightened, biting cruelly into her wrist as he bowed over it. "Captain James Ingols, of His Majesty's ship *Majestic*. At your service."

Captain James Ingols leaned forward in his chair, made a tent of his hands, and rested his haughty chin upon them. His gaze, as he studied his silent companion, was amused. "Eat your supper, Miss Hallett," he said, his taunting voice grating on her nerves. "It won't taste very good if you allow it to go cold."

Her golden head was bent, her eyes downcast and staring at the rich roast of venison on her plate without the slightest bit of interest. How could she eat? How could she, when Sam was locked in the cellar of some gloating town official, while this *monster* forced her to eat a meal fit for . . .

A princess.

"I said *eat!*" he thundered, losing patience with her.

Slowly, Maria raised her head. Her eyes were colder than winter starlight, glittering with sparks of blue-green flame. She spoke slowly, directly. "You go to Hell."

Wordlessly, he reached out and slapped her, rocking her head back and leaving the print of his hand on her cheek.

Just as wordlessly Maria picked up her plate and flung it in his face.

Screaming, he crashed out of the chair like an enraged bull, one hand clawing at his face, the other groping blindly for a napkin. "You little bitch, you'll pay for this!" he shrieked. "Nay, your *lover* will pay for it!"

He caught her before she could reach the door, yanking her around until her breasts slammed up against his satin-covered chest. She kicked. She screamed. She raked at his face with vicious claws but was no match for him. Savagely he caught her wrist and twisted her arm behind her back.

"Bastard! Bloody son of a whoremonger! Slimy sea-sucking scum!" The toe of her shoe caught his shin, and he yelped in pain but didn't release her. Like a tigress she fought him, writhing, struggling, long hair whipping about her beautiful, flushed face and eyes wild with fury.

"Damn you for a hellcat!" he cried, savagely thrusting her away from him when her nails caught the side of his cheek. Her slight body hit the wall, but undeterred, she was up again and running, her hand flashing out to grab the knife that still rested beside her fork and goblet of untouched wine.

Cursing, Ingols lunged forward, tore it from her grasp, and, yanking her against him, pinned her to his chest with an arm locked around her pale, slender throat. Maria struggled, the feel of his loins pressing against her buttocks making her nauseous.

"By all accounts," he ground out, his harsh breath stirring the hair at the top of her head, "you used to be quite a sweet young maid. I see you must've learned a few things aboard that pirate ship. Namely, how to curse, and defend yourself like a seaman. I'm sure your . . . *teacher* would be pleased. Too bad he won't be around long enough to see the fruit of his efforts."

Maria went wild. The pressure on her throat tightened. Specks blurred her vision, and she clawed frantically at his arm, his hands. He loosened his grip just enough to let her cough.

"Tell me, mistress, what *else* has he taught you?"

Her elbow slammed back against his ribs. This time he only laughed, carelessly shoving her away as though tired of her games. "Ah, Miss Hallett. Such a fiery temper you have. No doubt you got that from the . . . what was it they called him? Ah, yes. The *free prince.*" His cold laugh sent needles up her spine. "Such a pity, though. Your temper, I mean. All that energy could be used in other, more . . . pleasurable pursuits."

"I demand to know what you've done with him!"

"My dear lady. Why concern yourself with the likes of

m? By week's end he'll be gull's food. That is, if we allow
m to live that long.''

"He must have a trial! No man can be condemned and
ecuted without a trial!''

He laughed again, a high, awful sound that sent apprehen-
on crawling beneath her skin and leaving it cold and
ammy. "Ah, but there you stand to be corrected, Miss Hal-
tt. The Royal Navy can—and will—do as it pleases when it
mes to pirates. After all, they *are* the worst of criminals;
urderers, thieves, and godless wretches all wrapped up in
e dirty, stinking package. Wastes of humanity, parasites
on mankind. If they get a trial, it's a courtesy on our part.
e can do with them whatever we like. In fact, if I'd wanted
, I could've hung your dear captain from my mainyard—we
metimes do that with the ones who are particularly . . .
farious.''

The color drained from Maria's lips. "Oh, don't worry,
iss Hallett. I wouldn't *dream* of doing that. 'Twould be a
tiful waste, you know. No, I have a better idea. Making a
ectacle of his execution, on land, would be far more effec-
ve, don't you think? A warning, if you will, to the scum
'll leave behind. Men like Williams, Teach, Lebous.'' He
cked up his goblet, studied the dusky liquid, and sipped it
ith slow, obvious relish. "You see, Miss Hallett, we'll leave
e body up long after it rots, and every damned pirate who
ils past those gallows will see that grim reminder—''

She clapped her hands over her ears. "Stop it!''

His russet eyes were as cold and unfriendly as a serpent's.
What, do you find that thought distressing, Miss Hallett?
hy, just think, you can go and visit him as often as you
ke, then!'' He burst into renewed laughter at the stricken,
ckened horror in her eyes.

She turned away, her gaze moving about the room, her
ind trying desperately to block the terrible visions his words
ught to breed.

"Don't get any ideas, Miss Hallett. There's absolutely
othing you can do to save his worthless skin, I can assure
ou. Besides, I won't let you out of my sight. Except, maybe,
n hanging day.'' Again, that wicked, evil smile. "But then,
might be nice to personally escort you to that gala
vent. . . .''

"What?"

"Why, you simply *must* go. We wouldn't want your lov to depart this earth without a last look at his lady love, woul we? Especially since *I'll* be escorting her. You'll be doin him a favor, actually. Just think how much more he'll we come death when he realizes that your favors—and your a tentions—now lie with me."

"Never!" she cried, whirling to snatch up her fork. "I' never do your bidding, do you understand? *Never!* May yo rot in Hell, Ingols! I'll have no part of you, and Sam won go to his grave thinking I betrayed his love!"

The fork plunged downward and Ingols twisted, the stal bing, lethal tines missing him by an inch. He caught her fi as it flashed by his face, cruelly twisting her arm until sh cried out in outrage and pain.

"Now, you listen to me, you little viper," he ground out "Like it or not—"

A knock sounded on the door, interrupting them.

"Enter, damn it!"

A servant peeped inside. "Captain Ingols?"

Ingols didn't care that he was a guest, not master, of thi house, and his tone of voice toward a servant that wasn't hi own reflected it. "What is it?"

"There's a gentleman here to see you, sir. A representativ sent by His Excellency, the governor. Shall I show him in?"

"By all means," he snapped. The servant fled the roon without waiting to be dismissed. Ingols shoved Maria away his contemptuous gaze raking her dishevelled hair and wrin kled gown, still blotched and spattered with the pirate cap tain's blood. The condemning, rust-colored patches looke strangely out of place on the delicate posy-sprigged fabric "Get out of those rags and into something presentable," h snapped, disgusted. " 'Twould be an insult for the man t see you in clothing soiled by the blood of that thieving, mur dering blackguard."

"Oh, would it?" Enraged, she glared up at him, eyes afir with contempt and hate. "Hypocrite! *You're* the one wit blood on your hands, *Captain,* and some day you'll pay fo it. You blame Sam for your cousin's death, do you? Well, le me tell you, 'twas your cousin who sent *Whydah* to her grave not Sam. Don't believe me, do you? Well, I speak the truth

nd you have the audacity to call Sam a murderer? Hah!
would seem that murder's a crime that runs strong in *your*
mily! First your cousin and his disgusting attempt at being
hero, and now you. *You're* the real murderers! 'Twas his
ult so many died on the *Whydah,* and yours that *Nefarious's*
en were cut down fighting your damned frigate! You con-
mn them for pirates, do you? Well, let me tell you, they
ere good men! They were my friends! And may their blood
 upon your soul, Ingols!''

He lifted his wineglass with elegant hauteur. "I was merely
ing my duty as a good subject of the king.''

Fresh rage boiled up inside her. "Duty? You call murder
ty?''

"Oh, for God's sake, stop calling it murder. They were
st pirates, nothing more.''

Enraged, she lunged to her feet as a knock sounded on the
or.

"Enter," Ingols commanded, then lowered his voice to an
gry hiss. "Damn it, what's he going to think when he sees
ur gown?''

"No less than he'll think when he sees my wrists!" Maria
torted, thrusting her purple, bruised arms in front of him.
Oh, don't worry, Ingols, I'll have plenty to tell him about.''

The door swung open. Maria's breath came out in a de-
airing whoosh and she all but collapsed into her chair. The
ll, authoritative figure she'd expected and hoped for was
nything but. His head was bare of any fine, expensive pe-
ke, and his brown hair, threaded with gray at the temples,
as closely shorn and neat. He was a young man, perhaps
 his fourth decade, but he walked with a limp and his
ooped shoulders lent him another score of years he probably
idn't deserve. He clutched a walking stick, and his fingers,
is hand, his very arm trembled upon it as he lurched in his
roken gait toward them.

Maria felt sick. There was nothing remarkable or author-
ative about him at all, let alone sympathetic, and she de-
paired of finding any help from this quarter. She looked at
is well-tailored coat of mud-colored broadcloth, the fine lace
 his throat and wrists, and felt her heart sink into her toes.

Leaning so hard upon his walking stick she wondered why
 didn't snap, the man managed a shaky bow. "Are you . . .

Captain Ingols?'' he asked, his voice as cracked and britt as his body was.

Sneering, Ingols made no attempt to keep the derision o of his eyes, nor his voice, at the sight of this unfortuna wreckage of a man. ''At your service . . . sir.''

Wheezing, the stranger struggled to pull out a chair, the settled himself into it gratefully. ''I am Captain Barrymor on behalf of His Excellency, Governor Shute.'' He reache for the half-empty bottle of Madeira that reposed on th snowy lace tablecloth. ''And who, pray tell, is this . . . f male?''

Squint-eyed and decrepit he might be, but his stare wa keen, and had settled upon Maria's bloodstained gown. Sh bristled at the expression in his eyes.

''Oh, don't mind her,'' Ingols declared with a wave of h lace-framed hand. ''Miss Hallett, why don't you leave us fo a while? Captain Barrymore and I have important busines to discuss.''

The visitor held up an unsteady hand. ''No, I wish her t stay.'' His gaze was angry now, as though he found her d shevelled appearance insulting. His next words confirmed i ''Although I *do* find it rather distressing to be sharing com pany with a woman who garbs herself in a bloodstained gow Have you no other attire, madam?''

Maria's temper began to boil. Just who did he think h was, anyway? She'd hoped to plead with him to give Sam fair trial, to do whatever was in his power to save him. B there was nothing but distaste and anger in his eyes as the fixed upon her soiled gown and tangled hair. No, he'd be o no help. None at all.

''I *have* no others, sir,'' she said cooly. ''Your Excellen cy's most precious servant sank the vessel that carried m belongings almost out from under my feet.''

''The pirate ship,'' Ingols offered, sneering.

''Ah, yes,'' rasped Captain Barrymore. ''Then you mus be the infamous Maria Hallett, Sea Witch of Eastham and uh, companion of the prisoner. My apologies, madam. I r alize now why you have no other clothes. But please, see t it that you make an attempt to clean the ones you have. I fin them most . . . offensive.''

"And you'd find them even more so if you knew *whose* ood darkens them," Ingols quipped.

"I am fully aware of whose blood it is, thank you," Barmore rasped with a disdain that easily surpassed Ingols's. The blood of a pirate runs blacker than most, don't you ree?" He turned to Maria, his hand now shaking so badly he lifted his goblet that she feared, and hoped, he'd spill ne all down the front of his immaculate clothes. "Now ease, before I send you away, Miss Hallett, I'd like a word th you concerning the activities of Captain Black."

Maria's eyes went sullen.

"Good luck," Ingols said acidly. "She'd trade her life for if she could, foolish little waif. You'll get nothing out of r."

Barrymore fixed Ingols with a cold stare of impatience. Perhaps if you gave us some privacy, Captain, she might eak to me. 'Tis obvious she's not overly fond of you."

The idea didn't please Ingols. "I can't let her out of my ght. I've got the idiots of this town believing she's dead— d them all she escaped me and ran off into the woods, ere the Indians got her. Until the trial I'd like to keep ngs that way. 'Tis for her own protection, you know. These ople have put up with pirates for long enough, and they'd clamoring for her blood too, if they knew she was alive." sat back in his chair and twirled the stem of his wineglass his fingers, a habit that Maria already hated as much as erything else about him. "Besides, it would be a pity to e her chained up alongside that dog, let alone have her hang side him. I realize she doesn't look like much now, but lieve me, clean her up a bit and she's a pretty little thing. r too pretty to waste on such vermin."

"I'd rather die with Sam than be forced to sit here with u!" Maria cried, leaping to her feet.

"Sit down, dear," Captain Barrymore wheezed, putting t a tremulous hand to touch her arm. "See, Captain? You're setting her. Please, allow us a moment or two to speak in vate. You've my promise she'll be safe with me."

Ingols hesitated a moment, his eyes distrustful. At last, he t up and strode to the door. "Fine," he said, favoring rrymore with a falsely pleasant smile. "Have your little

chat. I'll be back in ten minutes. But I warn you not to tu
your back on her. Her reputation as a witch is well founded.

The door slammed behind him. Sullenly, Maria toyed wi
her napkin, mutely vowing that Barrymore could question h
until he shrivelled up and died of old age. He'd get nothi
from her. *Nothing*.

A moment passed. The silence grew heavy, oppressiv
uncomfortable as she sat staring down at her hands, but s
refused to look up, to even speak to him.

And then she felt his hand upon her arm, and this time h
fingers weren't trembling. She heard the rustle of fabric
he rose to his feet, saw that the shadow he threw across t
white tablecloth was anything but crooked and bent. Her he
jerked up in surprise, and she saw that he was tall and prou
strong and well muscled. The stoop, the trembling, the ag
were gone.

And when he spoke, his voice was no longer cracked a
rasping; it was a vibrant voice, deep and reassuring.

It was a voice that she remembered well.

"That damned pirate of ours sure keeps us hoppin
doesn't he? Well, don't you worry, sweeting." He squeez
her hand reassuringly, then reached up to tenderly brush t
hot tears from her cheek. "You just leave everything to m
because *I* have a plan. . . ."

It was the peruke, of course. She hadn't recognized hi
without it. She burst into choking sobs and went into his op
arms like a terrified child.

Paul Williams.

She had never been so happy to see anyone in her life.

Chapter 28

Freedom alone is the salt and the spirit that gives
Life, and without her is nothing that verily lives.

SWINBURNE

eally, Phoebe, why do you keep trying to feed him?
He's not a dog, you know, that you can just throw
ne to. I tell you, he's *not* going to eat it.''

he two women stared at the pirate captain chained in
ebe Beckfield's dark cellar, unable to believe he was the
e one the king's men had brought in last week. His fine
shirt was soiled and caked with his own blood, and if
ebe hadn't crept in and dressed the terrible gash on his
he'd probably be dead of infection by now. His skin,
so healthy and tanned, was now the color of suet, and
eath the sinewy muscles that sheathed his lean torso they
d count every rib. And it was no wonder. He had de-
ed everything from the salt fish to the apple tarts that
ebe had sneaked down to him, instead passing his time
ng vacantly into space, his eyes devoid of life.

was a pity. He'd been such a bold, defiant one at first,
those black eyes flashing like the devil's own, his hand-
e body mast-straight and proud, his very manner so com-
ding that Satan himself must've done his bidding. Phoebe
d still remember him staggering to his feet after he'd
ined consciousness, demanding to know the fate of his
ng lover in a voice she had no trouble imagining carrying
length of a dark and stormy quarterdeck.

he should never have told him.

low, the spark had fizzled out of those obsidian eyes, the

broad shoulders were slumped in defeat, and the corners
that fine, sensual mouth drooped with a sadness that w
beyond grief.

It was the young woman's death, of course. How
must've loved her to mourn her so. Hour after hour he
upon his pitiful bed of straw on the cold dirt, his head in
hands, his dark hair falling over his knuckles as he sile
grieved. He was no longer a dangerous criminal, just an
guished, heartbroken man who welcomed his impend
death with open, greedy arms. The news of his lover's de
had destroyed him, broken that defiant spirit, and now Pho
wished with all her heart that she could take back her wo
No matter who he was, what he'd done, it just wasn't ri
that his last hours should be spent in such anguished suff
ing.

But now there was nothing she could do for him exc
try to make him comfortable. Sighing, she approached hi
a hot, steaming bowl of baked Indian pudding in her han

"Phoebe, he'll get you!" Joan shrieked in needless ter

"Fiddlesticks," Phoebe returned. "We're good frien
aren't we, Captain?"

He didn't answer her. He didn't even raise his head. Sitt
there with his back against the mildewy wall, his knees dra
up to his chest, and his chin, now covered with a rough
of thick, black whiskers, propped lifelessly upon his wrist
he stared at the floor, he looked to be asleep. But she s
him blink his eyes, and knew that he was not.

"I brought you something to eat," she said softly, digg
her spoon into the pudding. "See? 'Tis still hot. I even
lots of molasses in it. You like molasses, don't you?"

No answer.

She knelt down beside him, hoping to tempt him with
delicious smell of the food she held out before him. His thr
constricted and he shut his eyes so they wouldn't see
tears.

"Here you go, Captain."

The spoon pressed against his lips. He turned his f
away.

"See, I told you he's not going to eat!" Joan sang.

Sighing hopelessly, Phoebe placed the bowl at his b
feet, stood up, and left him to his private agony. She kn

at when she returned the bowl would still be sitting there, e untouched pudding cold and congealed. But at the foot f the stairs she paused, wishing that a spark of interest would nimate those handsome, dark eyes, that he would eat what ould turn out to be his last meal.

For tomorrow morning he would die.

But he didn't move, didn't look up, didn't even acknowl-dge her presence. And if she'd been able to see him clearly rough the choking gloom of the dank cellar, she would've oticed those broad shoulders quaking with quiet sobs of eartrending grief.

Softly, the women trudged up the stairs, and as they shut e door behind them, the last of the feeble light was snuffed ut.

Sam sat unmoving in the darkness. Outside, rain had egun to fall. He could hear it pattering softly against the ouse's stout frame and seeping into the ground. He could ear water, running swiftly, trickling away into the thread of ternity—like sand in a glass—like the remaining hours of his fe.

The first flicker of something; interest, maybe, or just a orbid sort of eagerness, stirred in his heart. He smiled to imself.

Several more hours, and it would be dawn. Several more ours, and he'd be choking his life out on the end of a rope. everal more hours—and he would be with his beloved Ma-a.

Dawn broke through cheerless clouds still pregnant with ain. The earth smelled freshly scrubbed, the air pungent vith the scent of pine, summer grasses, and wildflowers. A entle breeze swept in from the sea and sent the tall pines nd spruces to whispering quietly, their hushed voices min-ling with the lonely, soul-stirring cries of the gulls that rheeled above them. Birds began to twitter in the thick for-st, and an eagle, floating high above the steep cliff face, cast graceful shadow over the crude, hastily built gallows that tood atop it.

In the parlor of their host, a prosperous merchant named 'enwick who, with his passel of children and shrewish wife, had departed nearly an hour ago to get a prime spot to view the hanging, Captain James Ingols of His Majesty's Royal Navy stood in front of a looking glass. He was smiling, anticipating the event he was taking such pains to prepare his appearance for, dreaming of the rewards that the governor— if not the king—would surely bestow upon him for ridding the harassed coast of its most dreaded enemy.

He raised his chin to better fuss over the tie of his snow-white, lacy necktie. "Such a pity that Barrymore was called away to Boston," he said airily. "I'm sure he would've liked to see the execution, aren't you?"

Maria stood looking out the window. Dawn's pink streaks shot like arrows through the fluffy clouds hanging over the sea. "Go to Hell," she said flatly.

"Still angry, my little spitfire?" He laughed as her slender back went rigid and her small, graceful hands clenched in unladylike fists at her side. "I thought I could appease you with that new gown. Maybe you're having difficulties buttoning it up the back? Here, let me assist you."

Her voice was chilling, vibrant with hate. "I repeat, Captain Ingols—*go . . . to . . . Hell."*

Each word had been meticulously, slowly pronounced through clenched teeth. He laughed, admiring her in the mirror; now that she was out of that bloodstained rag and cleaned up a bit, she was truly a work of art. A vision. Plush folds of coral-colored velvet, yards of lace at the sleeves, her full, proud bosom swelling above the scalloped decolletage; and that hair.

God, that hair.

Pressure tightened his loins, nudged against his breeches. Ingols didn't take his eyes off her as she turned back to the window.

Yes, she was a sight to make the devil weep, let alone Black Sam. Ah, wouldn't *he* be in for a surprise when he saw her. How his black heart would break at sight of his lady love, standing with him, Captain James Ingols, moments before the executioner snuffed out his worthless life.

Ah, but revenge was sweet, wasn't it?

Ingols was well aware that the pirate captain was already living in his own private hell. Black Sam refused food, refused to respond to their interrogations, and refused to say

nything in his own defense. Why, if Ingols hadn't seen him
a action on the decks of that damned sloop of his, he would
ever have believed that the lifeless, wretched prisoner rot-
ng in the Beckfields' cellar was the same man.

He grinned in genuine pleasure. Certainly, the thought of
is own impending death would not have brought about such
ehavior; Black Sam had made it obvious by his actions that
e didn't give a damn about his own well-being. But Maria
allett? Ah, now *she* was another story; *she* was where the
ue weapons of revenge, of torture, lay. Bribing his host into
lence, Ingols had hidden her here without allowing her out
f the house and had personally spread the story of her
'death'' in the hope that the tale would get back to Black
am; to his immense satisfaction, it had. And the townsfolk?
tupid colonials. If they'd filed past Penwick's home, it was
erely to get a glimpse of himself, the heroic naval com-
ander who'd brought down the pirate.

Of course, he'd have to explain Maria's presence at the
anging, but it would be an easy matter to say she'd found
er way, miraculously unharmed, back to this little town of
rown's Point. Such an ingenious plan. He really was bril-
ant, wasn't he? But he couldn't care less what the towns-
eople thought. Breaking the pirate captain's spirit was all
at really mattered, and from what he'd seen and heard, he'd
ucceeded in doing just that.

Yes, life was grand.

Ah, Robert. He thought of his cousin, dead these many
onths now after the wreck of the *Whydah. If revenge could
nly bring you back. . . .*

"Do hurry, my dear. We wouldn't want to be late." Push-
g Robert from his mind, he made a last primp in the mirror,
rushed a speck of dust from the sleeve of his uniform, and
rned. For a long moment he gazed at her stiff spine and
himmering gold curls, loose and lovely and spilling all the
ay to her tiny, enchanting waist.

And felt again the lust snaking in his loins.

Revenge. Yes, the *ultimate* revenge. And it would only
ke a moment.

"Are you certain I can't help you with those buttons?"

"I do not need—or desire—your help."

She didn't see his slow smile as he poured himself a glass

of port. And he could not know, of course, that beneath he
frigid exterior, Maria's heart was bouncing off the walls o
her chest like a butterfly trapped in an airless jar. Every nerv
in her body was strung bow tight; she'd lost count of hov
many times she'd wiped her moist hands on her skirts, and i
felt like someone had thrown a handful of living, jumpin;
bullfrogs into her stomach. But she couldn't let Ingols se
her nervousness, couldn't give him any reason to becom
suspicious.

For Maria had no intention of buttoning up his hated gown
She'd be out of it soon enough, anyway.

Shock them, Maria! Paul Williams had urged, and by God
she would.

"But it's getting late, dear. We wouldn't want you to arriv
half-dressed now, would we? What would your lover think'
Don't you want to look nice for him? And for me? Don'
forget, you're in *my* company today."

"A fact that causes me undue embarrassment," she sai
sullenly, with a quick glance from beneath lowered lashes t
the sand glass on the mantel.

"Yes, *do* look at the time, Miss Hallett. Not much left, i
there? Count the precious moments that remain in Blacl
Sam's life!" Laughing, he turned his back and with a flour
ish, picked up his goblet.

Now.

Biting her lip Maria padded across the room toward him
her footfalls masked by the satin slippers he'd given her. Tha
hated back. That hated uniform. That hated *man*, hummin;
now as he set the glass back down on the table. . . .

Two years ago she would not have been able to do it. Tw
years ago she would not have even considered it.

But two years ago she had not known Sam Bellamy.

Trembling, she started to reach into the pocket of her skir
for the long, bejewelled dagger that Paul had given her, anc
hesitated.

At that moment Ingols turned and Maria saw the thick
ugly lust in his eyes, in his smile, in his—

She screamed, dropped the dagger, and bolted for the door

He caught her as her hand hit the latch, bringing her dow
so savagely that her shoulder struck the table and sent it skit
tering across the floor. Crying, kicking, clawing, she fough

m madly, viciously, feeling his hands groping beneath
er skirts, his knee driving between her thighs—

Screaming, she tried to shove him away. And then, her
ngers found—and closed upon—the dagger.

Crying, she shut her eyes and brought it down with all her
rength into the curve of his back. Blood sprayed up, raining
on the bodice, the skirts, the sleeves of the beautiful, hated
own as she lunged out from beneath him.

He crashed to his feet with a chilling, ungodly scream.
Bitch!'' Blood gurgled from his mouth and darkened his
istine white neckcloth. He stumbled over a chair. ''God-
mned whore, devil's daughter, witch! You'll die for this,
help me!''

He lunged for her, the dagger still protruding from his
ck, his eyes wild with blood-lust. Retreating backwards,
aria came up against the table's edge and grabbed the first
ing her hand fell upon, the heavy silver candlestick that had
aced their table the night before. She swung it with all of
er strength. A tremor jolted her arms as the weighty instru-
ent struck his skull, the dull, heavy thud of metal against
one reverberating up through her fingers. He groaned once,
en slid quietly to the floor.

Dazed, Maria stood looking down at him for a moment.
nd then she pulled the dagger from his back and with a
ethodical calmness that belied her wildly shaking hands,
iped the blade upon the fine silk of his coat.

''That,'' she said tremulously, ''was for Sam.''

She drove her hand into her pocket. Then she opened
embling fingers and gazed with teary eyes at the object that
ood upon her moist palm. The little dolphin. Hurling the
ndlestick at Ingols's feet, she turned and raced for the door.

There was no time to lose.

Brown's Point stretched its limits to a great, U-shaped wall
f granite that rose a hundred feet out of the indigo sea
rashing against its base. Ringed by dense stands of spruce
d pine, the little cove was a deep, natural harbor for any
ho dared to venture within the half-circle of ominous,
nposing rock. Today, there were more boats and canoes

moored there than even old Reverend Harrison could remember.

The rain grudgingly held off, but storm clouds wer
gathering once more, their dirty, woolen undersides almo
scraping the tops of the highest spruces. The sunlight shi
ered, then faded out, defeated.

Despite the ominous weather a throng had gathered ato
the cliff's rocky summit, shuffling their feet and casting ne
vous glances at the sky and the restless sea, now a thicl
brooding gray-green with the retreat of the sunlight. Som
uttered silent prayers, others sidled closer to their spouse:
'Twas an omen, they thought, as the wind picked up; a ba
omen. The devil was not happy. One of his own was bein
put to death today.

Brown's Point had never hosted such a gala event, an
people had come for miles, dressed for the occasion. The
wore their finest homespuns, brightest calicos, most colorf
ribbons. Children tugged impatiently at their mothers' skirt:
Dogs barked, sensing the rising tension. And the men, ot
of earshot of the ladies, speculated upon the terrible atrociti
the pirate must've committed upon the women passengers o
the many ships he'd plundered, the innocent men he'd n
doubt murdered to get to them. But suddenly all of the hushe
whispering, the sounds of crying children and barking dog:
ceased. Out of the woods the procession was coming.

The people were eager and excited for their first glimp:
of the devil's progeny, for unlike the way they did things i
places like distant Boston, this pirate had not been parade
through the streets, had not been dragged to the meetin;
house to be made the subject of one of Reverend Harrison
fervent sermons. And he had not even been given a trial. Th
nervous young lieutenant leading the procession who ke]
glancing over his shoulder (where was Captain Ingols? son
wondered) carried a simple dress sword instead of the silv
oar that symbolized the Admiralty Court's authority. The ga
lows had not been erected within "flux and reflux" of th
sea, or, more specifically, high and low tide, because Brown
Point, built high upon the rock cliffs, *had* no such tid
boundaries.

But one aspect of the whole affair remained true to custon
and it was the reason that the absent Ingols, knowing th

other sea wolves such as Teach were wont to frequent these Maine waters, had chosen this granite promontory to carry out the execution. The body would be left to hang in chains as a gruesome reminder to Teach and others like him that piracy did indeed have its just rewards. And from the lonely height of these sheer cliffs, such a ghastly, blatant reminder would be easily visible from the sea that the pirates infested.

But the crowd was not thinking of standards, nor other hangings they'd heard about but never seen. Their excited voices rose once more as their somber-faced pastor filed past. Necks craned, children were hoisted to shoulders, and the murmurs died to silence as they all stood on tiptoe to catch first glimpse of the pirate captain himself.

He sat straight-backed and proud in a cart flanked by Majestic's lieutenants, all dressed in their best uniforms for the occasion. The cart was drawn by a lathering black horse that was—either from the tension of the approaching storm or the very presence of the devil behind him, or perhaps a disturbing combination of both—prancing skittishly and threatening to bolt. The pirate's big, sun-darkened hands were tied securely behind his back, and angry red welts marked his wrists where the rope had burned and chafed his skin. At sight of it the whispers and murmurs started once more; 'twas said that the rope had been taken from the dreaded pirate sloop itself before the king's good men had sunk it.

The procession moved closer, and the crowd reluctantly stepped back to let it pass, craning their necks for a better look at the prisoner. This was the man they'd come to see; yet children hid behind their mother's skirts and the men glanced nervously about them. The fear they had expected to see in the pirate captain's gaze was in their own, for the ominous clouds were thickening by the minute, a far-off echo of thunder rolled across the sea, and there was an intrepid challenge in those gleaming black eyes that made their blood run cold. And even as they yanked him out of the cart and led him toward his death, he seemed unafraid, his head held high, his handsome features aristocratic, his black eyes raking them with contempt. Everything about him—his bearing, his regal air, the absolute resolve he seemed to have for his fate—hinted at a nobleness his sort shouldn't have, and he held himself with all the dignity of a prince.

From off in the eerie, gray-black distance over the sea, the thunder came again.

The women,-unlike their families, were not fearful. They stared at the pirate in awe, amazed and somewhat rueful that such handsomeness was wasted on a man who'd soon be dead. He was not what they'd thought he'd be. Thick sable waves framed his arresting countenance in glory and streamed down his back. His eyes were dark and smoldering. He was no dirty scoundrel but a strong and virile man. . . .

Like an animal being led to slaughter, Sam's senses were acute. He could almost smell the apprehension of the crowd. Their whispers thundered in his ears. And by the nervous glances they cast at the sky and darkening ocean he knew they feared something other than just rain.

He heard the thunder too. Ahead, the gallows loomed like a disjointed skeleton against the leaden skies, but still he was not afraid. Death was not a closed door; it was an open one and on the other side of it, Maria waited. And soon now very soon, he'd be with her.

He wore a contented smile as the wind began to gust, for with it came the heady, tangy scent of the ocean, the sea that he loved second only to her. When he mounted the gallows he'd be able to look out over its wide, beloved expanse. He would die with it spread out before him, reflected forever in his eyes. It was all he might've hoped for. It was all he desired.

"All right ye filthy rogue, time to meet your maker," came the gruff voice of the first lieutenant. A sword pricked his back, but Sam needed no urging. There was no fear, no resistance in his body as they approached the great, forbidding structure of the waiting gallows, where the hangman—and somehow, somewhere, Maria herself—waited. With the same dauntless courage that had marked his career as a pirate, Sam strode forward. Cool grass folded under his bare feet. Overhead, a sea gull cried.

The first drop of rain fell upon his brow.

As they mounted the last hill and stood at the cliff's edge, the ocean came into view just as Sam had known it would, glorious, untamed, majestic, and *free*.

As he would soon be.

He raised his head, a strange sort of peace spreading

through him as he mounted those creaking steps. The sun had fallen off and the wind blew chilly and damp. Another drop of rain fell, this time upon his cheek. Another step. Higher. Higher. There, the executioner, black hood in place, waited silently. When Sam reached the top step, the hooded man's skeletal claws grasped Sam's torn sleeve, still dark with old, dried blood, and yanked him to the center of the platform.

For the first time since that terrible sea battle, there was life in Sam's dark eyes. The old defiant spark, that astute, intelligent gleam. *Fools,* he thought to himself. Don't they know they were doing him a favor? He smiled, a profound, knowing smile as he let his eyes sweep the gaping faces below him. At the front of the crowd stood the first lieutenant, nervous and uncertain and still looking over his boyish young shoulder. Beyond him, Sam saw poor Phoebe Beckfield. Her eyes were red and swollen and a handkerchief was pressed to her nose. A good woman, Phoebe. Next stood the Reverend Harrison, the pages of his huge, leather-bound Bible jumping nervously in the wind. The pastor found his place, held the pages down with a long finger, and, clearing his throat importantly, recited a prayer for Sam's black, unholy soul.

The words rolled past Sam's unhearing ears. His gaze, his very thoughts, were directed far above and beyond their waiting faces and out over the blackening sea. Lightning flickered there. The thunder rumbled again, louder, more incessant this time. Nervously, the pastor hurried his words, said a quick amen, and closed the Holy Book with a snap.

"Does the prisoner have anything to say to the people before he enters the Hell from whence he came?"

The crowd went deathly silent.

Sam's level, knowing eyes met the pastor's. He was an orator and the man knew it; he could've said something, could've made a stirring speech as he'd done so often upon the decks of his pirate ships to prisoners, to his own crews.

He could've defended his expression of personal freedom, that which the world labelled *piracy.* He could've left his words, his thoughts, his justification for what he'd done ringing in their ears. He could've left them with a memory of him they'd never forget. He could've—but he didn't. They were just frightened, ordinary people.

And they would never understand.

He fixed his gaze on a point somewhere over and beyond their heads, past the lofty spruces that framed his view of the angry, majestic sea. "Nay," he said clearly, heedless of the disappointment that flitted over the pastor's face. "None at all." Head high, he turned and faced the hooded executioner. "Be done with it, lad, if ye please."

Ah, Maria, my love. . . . Soon now. . . .

"Do you desire a blindfold, sir?" The executioner's voice was muffled through the black hood.

A blindfold? No, he wanted to depart this world with a clear view of what lay before him. He wanted to look upon the sea's wild freedom as he took his final, choking breath, wanted to die with the sight of it stamped forever in his eyes. He shook his head. "Nay," he said once again, his gaze returning to the flickering horizon.

Wordlessly, the executioner placed the heavy loop of hemp—once part of *Nefarious*'s running rigging—over Sam's head. He settled it around his neck, adjusting the knot to rest beneath Sam's left ear. The rope was stiff with sea salt and its fibers prickled against his skin.

Another drop of rain splashed down upon his nose.

His stoic, unwavering gaze never left the sea, nor the tall spruces that beckoned his eye out and over that swiftly darkening water.

And suddenly, Sam Bellamy, pirate captain, smiled.

One of those treetops was moving.

Except it wasn't a treetop at all, but the proud, sweeping mast of a great ship.

"Let us proceed," the lieutenant said.

The mast was gliding around the headland now, but only Sam, facing the ocean, saw it.

Damn you, Teach! Can't I even die *in peace?*

He saw the black flag vault to that mast as she came about and into the harbor, saw her gun ports sliding open. . . .

"Well then, if no one has any objections," the lieutenant was saying, "please carry on—"

"*I do!*"

A single pistol shot rang out. Someone screamed. The black horse bolted. The executioner paused, his hand on the rope, and as one, the crowd whirled in the direction from whence the shot had come.

Sam stared, blinked, and then closed his eyes against the ~~ting~~ of sudden tears.

For there, surrounded by Paul Williams's men and sitting ~~brazenly~~ astride a magnificent chestnut stallion, was a ~~woman~~; a woman with long, golden tresses whipping in the ~~wind~~, a woman brilliantly silhouetted in the first flickers of ~~lightning~~ behind her. She was clad in a billowing lawn shirt, ~~her~~ long, lovely legs clasped by breeches cut shockingly off ~~at~~ mid-thigh. Her sea-colored eyes blazed with savage tri~~umph~~, and in her hand she held a smoking pistol.

The Sea Witch of Eastham.

"Damn my eyes," Sam swore softly, and then all hell ~~broke~~ loose.

For at precisely that moment, the skies opened up and the *Revenge*, trailed by the smaller fleet *Mary Anne* swept fully ~~into~~ view.

And as she came storming down upon them, every sail ~~bulging~~, water plowing up at her bow, Sam saw the fiendish, ~~hellish~~ figure of Ned Teach—Blackbeard—standing upon the ~~deck~~.

The devil himself, some would say later, come to claim ~~his~~ own.

Thunder exploded from the great ship's guns, and was ech~~oed~~ by *Mary Anne*'s and then by the storm clouds themselves. ~~The~~ very ground beneath their feet trembled as a screaming ~~hail~~ of solid iron slammed into the rock face. Chunks of ~~granite~~ exploded heavenward, falling away in slow motion ~~into~~ the sea.

And flying proudly from the mastheads of both ships was ~~the~~ black, terrible promise of the Jolly Roger.

The crowd was screaming, panicking, stampeding like a ~~herd~~ of cattle. Horses whinnied in terror. The wind's fervor ~~increased~~, howling in fury now, hardening the *Revenge*'s gray ~~sails~~ as it drove her relentlessly toward the rock face.

And still Teach sent her forward, straight for the cliff, all ~~guns~~ ablaze, the very air reverberating with terrible, endless ~~thunder~~.

"Bloody madman!" cried the executioner. He whirled, his ~~hand~~ on the rope that would end Sam's life.

But Maria was charging forward, her golden hair stream~~ing~~ out behind her, her horse's hooves making a thunder of their own. Shrieking in pure fury, she yanked a pistol from the sash around her tiny waist, training it dead-center on the hangman's chest as the horse thundered toward the gallows with all of the madness with which *Revenge* was storming toward the cliff. The executioner dropped the rope, fleeing for his life. And then she was there, leaping from the horse to the gallows in one graceful, fluid movement. Her breath fluttered against his cheek. Tendrils of golden hair stung his eyes as she whipped out a dagger and sawed madly at the ropes that bound his hands. The hemp fell away. He was free, *free!* Tearing the noose up and over his head, she grasped his hand—warm and strong and full of life—and as one, they hit the ground.

They ran through the frightened crowd. Through the acrid smoke from the pirate ships' guns. Through the slashing rain and right up to the cliff's edge, where they never paused in their flight. As one, their hands clasped tightly together, they leaped as far out as their racing legs could take them, sailed through a hundred feet of empty space, and plunged into the comforting arms of the sea below.

Epilogue

It was a typical day in the Caribbean: sparkling seas of brilliant turquoise, green islands wearing necklaces of pearly foam to mark vivid coral reefs, a cloudless sky, and sea turtles basking in the sun just off the larboard beam. Dolphins crested the bow wake, and gentle trade winds filled the sails above.

On the quarterdeck of the sea-weathered *Mary Anne,* Paul Williams stood listening to the rhythmic hiss of spray as he waited patiently. His satisfied gaze took in his assembled crew, who stood before him arrayed in their finest, gaudiest clothes, with all the pride a father might bestow on his beloved children.

"Shall I go get 'em, Cap'n?" came the voice of that troublesome busybody, Stripes, from the shrouds above his head.

"Nay, let them be," Paul said. Idly, he tapped his thumb against the smooth leather cover of the Bible in his hand. They'll be up shortly."

The crew waited. Unlike himself, they weren't quite so patient. Some, like Stripes, clung to the shrouds for a better view. Others sat on the sunny decks, where they could stay close to the hogsheads of rum that had been hauled topside for the occasion. To a man, they were all there: the good crew of *Mary Anne;* the survivors from *Nefarious;* even that dastardly dog who, for some strange reason, had developed a dislike for Paul that went beyond vicious. . . .'Twas a good thing someone had tethered it to the mast.

Yes, everyone was present. Silas West, who seemed relieved to relinquish the duties of quartermaster to someone else; young Johnnie, whose enthusiasm for the trade—and reverence for his old captain—grew stronger by the day; Phil Stewart, Nat Paige, and a handful of others who, thanks to Black Sam, stood here today to witness the happiest event of his life.

Seeing movement out of the corner of his eye, Paul turned. Sam, with Maria beside him, had come up on deck. Paul's ruddy features broke into a smile as he gazed at his best friend, who now stood, as he had for much of the voyage south, at the fo'c'sle rail with his arm locked possessively around Maria Hallett's trim little waist. There was no separating those two. Paul shook his head. It had been close, too close. Thank God he'd known where to find Teach, thank God things had worked out the way they had. And the harassed coastline would thank God too, for now there'd be one less pirate to contend with.

Sam, true to his promise to Maria, was finally giving it up.

And the men in the Boston gaol? Paul didn't want to think about them just yet, for they were *his* problem now—his and Teach's. But they had, after all, been his men too.

His smile grew sad. Hard to believe, wasn't it? Sam, who'd been such an enthusiastic supporter of the Brethren's life; Sam, who'd embraced the calling with such reckless fervor; Sam, giving it all up for the love of a woman. But it was just

as well, wasn't it? Oh, he'd miss his friend, but there wer
other ventures he could take the rollicking crew of *Mary Ann*
on, other seas to sail. The North American coast; the Ca
ribbean; hell, there was even Madagascar, the East Indies . .
why, the possibilities that awaited a good pirate were endless

From behind him came a telltale gurgle and the splash c
liquid hitting a cup as the rum began to flow. Still fingerin
the Bible, Paul gazed at the expectant faces around him an
shrugged.

They were in no hurry. . . .

On the spray-washed forecastle deck Maria, laughing
threw back her head and let the balmy tropical breeze threa
its fingers through her hair. Sea spray cooled her bare feet
kissed her ankles, flecked her cheeks. Just off the starboar
bow a group of islands were approaching, emerald-green cap
on a sea of turquoise. Drawing the sea's heady fragranc
deeply into her lungs, she closed her eyes and let the sunligh
dance against her lids with joyous abandon.

"Oh, Sam! You were right! 'Tis so beautiful here—lik
paradise!" Never had he seen such excitement, such joy i
her eyes. She was dancing up and down like a ten-year-old
"Look at the color of the water! I can see our shadow on th
sea floor, and it must be a hundred feet down! And thos
birds! Why, there's another one!" She grasped his arm
pointing to a great, sack-billed creature winging its way ove
Mary Anne's masthead. "Look at its throat!"

" 'Tis a pelican, lass." Smiling at her childish exuber
ance, he drew her close, loving the feel of her soft, curv
body against his. And then he chuckled to himself as hi
favorite memory of her flashed through his mind; Maria
charging through the crowd to his rescue. Why, she'd been
veritable pirate princess that day.

He sighed, then smiled. "Ah, such a pity," he said, an
the corners of his eyes crinkled with those little laugh line
she loved so much.

"What?" she asked, lovingly tracing the line of his ja
with a soft, teasing finger.

"Oh, I was just thinking. You missed your calling, I be
lieve." She looked at him, confused, until he smiled onc
more and went on. "God, Maria, if only you could've see
yourself that day. You proved yourself to be a true pirate, an

t as I'm finally striking my colors! That's the pity, don't
think? We would've made a fine team.''

"We *still* make a fine team,'' she assured him. Her eyes,
e mirrors reflecting the brilliant ocean that surrounded
m, grew dreamy and distant. ''Oh, what next, Sam? Now
t you're starting a new life?''

"What next?'' he mused, gazing fondly down at her ex-
site face, with its eyes he could gladly drown in. Thank
d he'd finally let Paul convince him that it was *his* turn to
and get the men out of the Boston gaol; with Teach in
sort, Sam had no qualms about relinquishing the respon-
ility to his two capable friends. He looked down at Maria,
dark eyes soft with love. ''Why, first, I'm going to marry
. Here. Today. With a pirate captain to perform the cer-
ony, and a ship full of thieving rascals as our honored
sts.''

"And then what, my Captain?'' She was smiling up at
, now, her golden hair floating around her face, her eyes
rkling like sunlight on the morning sea.

"Then, we'll put in at a safe port, for good. What do you
k of Barbados? Or, how about Antiqua?'' But she knew
hing of those Caribbean islands; any of them would suit
just fine. ''I suppose it doesn't matter. I can grow sugar-
e, and trade with my *contacts*''—he flashed a quick grin
ard Paul, still standing patiently on the distant quarter-
k—''on any of them.''

Her eyes were dancing.

"And you,'' he said, tipping her chin up so that he could
e down into her sweet, upturned face, ''will be at my
.'' He took her hand, so small and delicate, in his own,
lifted it to his lips. ''Long ago, Maria, I promised to
ke you a princess of a West Indies isle. Now, I intend to
ke good that promise.''

"A princess!'' She threw her arms around the broad col-
n of his neck, thinking that fairy tales did, after all, come
e.

He lifted her up, swung her high. ''Aye, a princess!''

"And *then* what, Sam?''

"And then,'' he said huskily, his head bending to hers in
nizing slowness, ''I plan on spending my time plundering
greatest prize, my *real* treasure.'' His lips were sweet

and gentle as they found hers, and then his arms were arou
her, crushing her hungrily to his chest.

They kissed long and hard, heedless of the elbow-jostli
and whistles that rose from the quarterdeck.

At last, Sam reluctantly pulled away. Everyone was wai
ing, but for a long moment he held her gaze with his ow
loving her with every fiber of his being. That was the way
was, and that was the way it would always be. No one cou
ever take that away from them. Sighing, he trailed a fing
through a shining lock of her golden hair.

"And when do you plan to begin . . . plundering this tre
sure, my free prince?"

He smiled then, and his black gaze smoldered with hea
that old familiar fire. Lazily, he looked down at her, admirin
her impish, striking eyes, her seashell-pink mouth, the mo
ten gold of her hair that was richer than any pirate's treasu
could ever be. And he knew he couldn't wait any longer.

"Now," he whispered hoarsely. "But first, we must sett
a certain thing between us."

"And what is that, Captain?"

"We have a wedding to attend." And taking her hand, I
led her aft, to where the captain and crew of the *Mary Anr*
waited.

Author's Note

T he wind never stops blowing at the lonely cliffs of Ca
Cod's great outer beach. Sometimes it subsides a litt
and the thunder of booming surf becomes deafening; at oth
times it howls so fiercely that one is hard-pressed to hear t
roar of the ocean beneath it. But if you listen closely, t
wind has a story to tell, things to say and memories to shar

The legend of Maria Hallett and the Black Bellamy is
intrinsic to Cape Cod as sand, salt grass, and wildflower
and when the storms roar in off the ocean and the nights gro

black, legend persists . . . of a pirate ghost who still wanders that midnight stretch of the lonely outer beach, waiting for the skeletal hands of his dead crewmen to toss him an old silver coin or two from the waves . . . and "Goodie Hallett," who hung lanterns on the flukes of her pet whale and lured innocent seamen to their deaths on dark, foggy nights for many years following the *Whydah* disaster.

I have drawn Sam Bellamy using contemporary newspaper accounts, surviving depositions from members of his crew, native folklore, a hefty dose of fictional license, and my own findings during my work as a research associate for Maritime Explorations, Inc. We will probably never know whether or not he survived the wreck of the ship that was carrying him back to his young lover that cold, stormy night of April 26, 1717. Of the 144 men purported to be aboard the *Whydah*, only two are known to have made it through the violent surf and to the safety of the beach: Thomas Davis, the ship's carpenter, and John Julian, the young Indian that Sam hired to help pilot his flagship through the dangerous shoal waters surrounding Cape Cod. A total of 102 bodies were recovered from the waves and buried by Captain Cyprian Southack during the weeks following the disaster; what became of the rest of the crew is a secret that the sea has kept to herself for nearly three centuries.

The fate of other players in the *Whydah* story is well documented and leaves little for speculation. Paul Williams later teamed up with the French pirate Louis Lebous and spent the summer of 1717 harassing the New England coast before finally setting sail for Madagascar and distant seas, where he was quite successful in his trade. Blackbeard was killed off the coast of North Carolina in 1718 during a bloody battle with a young naval lieutenant. Julian was thought to have died in jail, but 1732 and 1733 issues of *The Boston News-Letter* tend to make one reexamine that theory. In them can be found the account of an Indian by the same name who stabbed a man with a jackknife and was later tried and executed for murder.

The fate of the prize crew that Sam Bellamy put aboard the leaky wine ship is most certain, thanks to contemporary accounts and depositions made by the pirates themselves. Along with the hapless Thomas Davis, these men spent the

long summer of 1717 incarcerated in the Boston gaol, where
they no doubt *did* entertain hope of rescue by one of the
Brethren while they endured the well-meaning but tedious
ministrations of none other than the famous Cotton Mather
himself. But despite Mather's attempts to save their souls—
and some light talk on Blackbeard's part about saving their
lives—the pirates went on trial in October of 1717, facing
charges of "Piracy, Robbery and Felony committed on the
high seas." The court of admiralty, presided over by Governor Samuel Shute, judged two of them, Thomas Davis and
Thomas South, to be "forced men" and acquitted them. The
others—Thomas Baker, Peter Cornelius Hoof, Simon Van
Vorst, John Brown, Hendrick Quintor, and John Shuan—were
all found guilty of the crimes they were charged with and
sentenced to "hang by the neck until dead."

On November 15, 1717, the six pirates of the *Whydah*,
escorted by a solemn Cotton Mather, were led through the
streets of Boston and down to the cold, gray harbor, where
they were rowed out to the gallows that awaited them on
Charlestown Ferry. There, within "flux and reflux" of the
sea, their tormented souls finally joined those of their shipmates.

Today, the *Whydah* is very much alive on Cape Cod, thanks
to the dedicated work of Barry Clifford, who, in 1984, discovered her remains in just thirty feet of water a quarter-mile
off Wellfleet's Marconi Beach, where she had slept undisturbed for 267 years. To date, *Whydah* remains the only authenticated pirate ship ever found. With a museum to display
them in Provincetown, Massachusetts, Maritime Explorations, Inc., and Whydah Joint Venture, Inc., continue to recover, preserve, and study thousands of artifacts: pistols,
swords, and other weaponry; jewelry, eating utensils, musket
balls, and navigational instruments; rapier hilts, their blades
long since rusted into the centuries; cannon, coming up from
the murky depths still loaded; clothing, bones, parts of the
fabled ship herself; and yes, that fabulous hoard of pirate's
treasure, gold bars and gold doubloons, Spanish reales and
pieces of eight, all part of the princess's ransom stored between the ship's decks when she went down within sight of
the great sand cliffs that awful, stormy night.

After nearly three centuries, the *Whydah* is finally at rest.

Yet the tales still persist, of ghosts who walk the outer beach after dark when the fog rolls in over the waves and the skies grow black with storm. One night three years ago, I took my courage in tow and drove out there during a spring thunderstorm to see if there was any truth to the old legends.

People often ask me—did I *see* anything?

To which I merely give a little smile.

I'll never tell.

Danelle Harmon
Cape Cod, Massachusetts
February 1991

Avon Romances—
the best in exceptional authors and unforgettable novels!

America Loves Lindsey!

The Timeless Romances
of #1 Bestselling Author

Johanna Lindsey

PRISONER OF MY DESIRE 75627-7/$5.99 US/$6.99 Can
Spirited Rowena Belleme *must* produce an heir, and the magnificent Warrick deChaville is the perfect choice to sire her child—though it means imprisoning the handsome knight.

ONCE A PRINCESS 75625-0/$5.95 US/$6.95 Can
From a far off land, a bold and brazen prince came to America to claim his promised bride. But the spirited vixen spurned his affections while inflaming his royal blood with passion's fire.

GENTLE ROGUE 75302-2/$4.95 US/$5.95 Can
On the high seas, the irrepressible rake Captain James Malory is bested by a high-spirited beauty whose love of freedom and adventure rivaled his own.

WARRIOR'S WOMAN 75301-4/$4.95 US/$5.95 Can
In the year 2139, Tedra De Arr, a fearless beautiful Amazon unwittingly flies into the arms of the one man she can never hope to vanquish: the bronzed barbarian Challen Ly-San-Ter

SAVAGE THUNDER 75300-6/$4.95 US/$5.95 Can
Feisty, flame-haired aristocrat Jocelyn Fleming's world collides with that of Colt Thunder, an impossibly handsome rebel of the American West. Together they ignite an unstoppable firestorm of frontier passion.

If you enjoyed this book, take advantage of this special offer. Subscribe now and get a

FREE
Historical
Romance

No Obligation (a $4.50 value)

Each month the editors of True Value select the four *very best* novels from America's leading publishers of romantic fiction. Preview them in your home *Free* for 10 days. With the first four books you receive, we'll send you a FREE book as our introductory gift. No Obligation!

If for any reason you decide not to keep them, just return them and owe nothing. If you like them as much as we think you will, you'll pay just $4.00 each and save at *least* $.50 each off the cover price. (Your savings are *guaranteed* to be at least $2.00 each month.) There is NO postage and handling – or other hidden charges. There are no minimum number of books to buy and you may cancel at any time.

Send in the Coupon Below

To get your FREE historical romance fill out the coupon below and mail it today. As soon as we receive it we'll send you your FREE Book along with your first month's selections.